Jenny Holmes lives in a beautiful part of Yorkshire and sets her sagas in the industrial heartland nearby. She enjoys horse riding, gardening and walking her dog in the dales. She also writes children's books as Jenny Oldfield.

Find her on Facebook at:
Facebook.com/JennyHolmesAuthor

www.penguin.co.uk

Also by Jenny Holmes

The Mill Girls of Albion Lane
The Shop Girls of Chapel Street
The Midwives of Raglan Road
The Telephone Girls

The Land Girls
The Land Girls at Christmas
Wedding Bells for Land Girls
A Christmas Wish for the Land Girls

The Spitfire Girls
The Spitfire Girls
The Spitfire Girls Fly for Victory
Christmas with the Spitfire Girls

The Air Raid Girls
The Air Raid Girls
The Air Raid Girls at Christmas
The Air Raid Girls: Wartime Brides

THE *Ballroom*
GIRLS

JENNY HOLMES

PENGUIN BOOKS

TRANSWORLD PUBLISHERS
Penguin Random House, One Embassy Gardens,
8 Viaduct Gardens, London SW11 7BW
www.penguin.co.uk

Transworld is part of the Penguin Random House group of companies
whose addresses can be found at global.penguinrandomhouse.com

Penguin
Random House
UK

First published in Great Britain in 2023 by Bantam
an imprint of Transworld Publishers
Penguin paperback edition published 2023

Copyright © Jenny Oldfield 2023

Jenny Oldfield has asserted her right under the Copyright,
Designs and Patents Act 1988 to be identified as the author of this work.

This book is a work of fiction and, except in the case of historical fact, any
resemblance to actual persons, living or dead, is purely coincidental.

Lyrics on p. 173 from 'Tangerine' written by Johnny Mercer.
Lyrics on p. 229 from 'Don't Sit Under The Apple Tree (With Anyone
Else But Me)' written by Lew Brown and Charles Tobias.
Lyrics on p. 231 from 'Leaning On A Lamp-post' written by Noel Gay.
Lyrics on p. 251 and p. 309 from 'Let's Face The Music And Dance'
written by Irving Berlin.
Reference to lyrics on p. 326 from 'Get Happy' written by Ted Koehler.
Lyrics on p. 347 from 'Pennies From Heaven' written by Johnny Burke.

Every effort has been made to obtain the necessary permissions with
reference to copyright material, both illustrative and quoted. We apologize
for any omissions in this respect and will be pleased to make the
appropriate acknowledgements in any future edition.

A CIP catalogue record for this book
is available from the British Library.

ISBN
9781529176537

Typeset in New Baskerville Std by Jouve (UK), Milton Keynes.
Printed and bound in Great Britain by Clays Ltd, Elcograf S.p.A.

The authorized representative in the EEA is Penguin Random House Ireland,
Morrison Chambers, 32 Nassau Street, Dublin D02 YH68.

Penguin Random House is committed to a sustainable future
for our business, our readers and our planet. This book is made
from Forest Stewardship Council® certified paper.

MIX
Paper from
responsible sources
FSC® C018179

Remembering Jane Winearls,
my inspirational dance teacher.

CHAPTER ONE

June 1942

'Would you like to go on the waltzers or the Ferris wheel?' Pearl Scott offered her little sister the choice.

Eight-year-old Elsie made a beeline for the teacup-shaped waltzers. She scampered ahead in her bright-yellow summer dress and white ankle socks, ignoring screeches from riders on Blackpool's Big Dipper and weaving through the long queue for the ghost train, dashing up the wide wooden steps to her favourite ride.

'The waltzers it is.' Pearl smiled to herself. Today was Elsie's birthday and with present money burning a hole in her pocket, the world was her oyster.

Pearl joined her at the entrance to the ride. Music blared through the loudspeakers, along with the familiar cry: 'Scream if you want to go faster!'

Bernie Greene worked the ride as girls screamed blue murder. He grabbed the backs of each waltzer in turn and spun them mightily. More screams, more glee, as dizziness descended.

Bernie winked at Pearl and Elsie waiting on the platform as the carriages whizzed by. 'What's up?' he yelled over the racket.

1

'Today is her birthday!' Pearl mouthed. She and Bernie had grown up together. They'd played in the back streets of the town – the narrow ones that backed on to the Tower, squeezed in between the famous seafront attraction and a bustling open-air market – where Pearl had been regarded as one of the lads: a tomboy who could hit a cricket ball for six with the best of them. Bernie was like a brother to her – a quick-witted charmer who could talk himself out of any hole he found himself in.

'When is it our turn?' Elsie fidgeted at the edge of the ride, tilting her freckled face up at Pearl and clutching the three-penny bit that would pay for her treat.

'Faster?' blared the tinny voice over the Tannoy.

'Yes!' Strangled cries hovered on the cusp between delight and terror.

Bernie spun the teacups and grinned at Pearl as he sped by again. Round and round, with heads and shoulders pushed back against the seats by centrifugal force, riders gripped the safety bar until their knuckles turned white.

'When?' Elsie demanded.

'Soon,' Pearl promised.

And lo; the Tannoy fell silent and the roundabout slowed. The music faded. Bernie helped windswept, groggy customers back on to terra firma then extended his hand to Elsie. 'Happy Birthday, littl'un,' he told her as he settled her and Pearl into their waltzer and they strapped themselves in. 'Hold on to your hats,' he warned.

'We're not wearing hats,' literal-minded Elsie protested.

Pearl grinned. She was glad she'd squeezed in this trip to the Pleasure Beach after finishing her afternoon stint at her mother's fish and chip stall and before joining a gaggle of girlfriends for a jolly night of ballroom dancing at the Tower. True, it meant she wouldn't have many minutes to get dolled up back home in Empire Street – a quick change from casual slacks into skirt and frilly blouse before running a comb through her dark hair (mercifully short and easy to manage); then a slick of lipstick and a pat of rouge. Tonight, Pearl and her gang would enjoy the lavish surroundings of the Tower Ballroom; no common-or-garden, back-street palais for them, ta very much.

'Ready?' Pearl asked the birthday girl. 'Sit back and hold tight.'

Elsie's eyes gleamed with excitement. A hurdy-gurdy tune struck up and the ride eased into action.

Bernie wove between the teacups, setting them spinning, flirting with the girls, bending over to tell a quick joke to one of his fairground pals. He looked relaxed in his open-necked white shirt and dark-blue trousers. As the ride gathered speed, he approached Elsie and Pearl's waltzer. 'Now then, birthday girl.'

'Will you spin us really, really fast?' Elsie pleaded.

'Fast as you like,' he agreed with an exaggerated wink.

'You want to watch out,' Pearl warned him. 'Your face will get stuck in that position.'

'Yeah, yeah.' Bernie set them off spinning. 'What are you doing later?' He threw a casual question at Pearl.

'I'm going dancing at the Tower. What about you?

Do you fancy jitterbugging me around the floor for an hour or two?' Pearl knew it would be useful to have a partner on hand for the evening, what with the current shortage of local men. *Blame conscription for that*, she thought. Almost three years into the war against Germany, and with no end in sight, life for everyone had changed utterly.

'Count me out,' Bernie shot back. 'No offence, but I've got better things to do on a Saturday night than trip the light fantastic with you.'

'Suit yourself. They're holding a competition – there's money to be won.'

Bernie spun them faster. Coloured lights above their heads began to blur. The music reached a crescendo. 'Is there now? How much?'

'Ten bob for the best couple. I'll see you there?'

Bernie underwent a sudden change of heart. 'You're on,' he agreed.

Round and round under a whirl of electric lights. 'Scream if you want to go faster!'

'If Bernie and you dance together, will he be your boyfriend?' Elsie piped above the din, her face alive with excitement.

'Give over!' Pearl laughed. 'The only thing Bernie is interested in is going home with that ten-bob note in his pocket.'

Elsie kept at it like a dog at a bone. 'So no kissing?'

'Definitely not – no kissing!' Pearl swore, hand on heart. The very thought of her and Bernie walking out together as a couple was absurd. *Single and fancy-free, that's me.*

'Faster?'

Pressed back, spinning like tops, stomachs churning, deafened, screeching and laughing, Pearl and Elsie revelled in the fun of the fair.

Sylvia Ellis stared intently into her dressing-table mirror. It had taken her the usual age to get ready; there mustn't be a blonde hair out of place and her eyebrows must be perfectly, symmetrically pencilled in. Was it her imagination, or were her cheeks a little bit plumper? Oh God, was she putting on weight? Jumping to her feet, Sylvia pinched at the flesh on her waistline then turned sideways to study her reflection, tightening her stomach muscles as she did so. Not too bad after all.

Relieved, she sat down again to remove her curlers then style her hair. This was what took the longest: smoothing and arranging each lock so that they cascaded around her shoulders in an apparently effortless golden waterfall. The frock she'd chosen to wear for an evening at the Tower Ballroom hung from a hook on the door – a three-quarter-length, sky-blue affair that was nipped in at the waist, with off-the-shoulder straps and a bodice that was carefully sculpted to show off her slim torso. She would wear it with a light, wrap-around stole made of silvery tulle.

But first, the make-up. Blue eyeshadow to match the colour of her eyes, a flick of dark mascara, with a touch of coral-pink lipstick; nothing too brash. When Sylvia was satisfied with the overall effect, she removed her gauzy negligee and stepped into the dress then made her way into the lounge for help with the zip.

At first Sylvia's mother, Lorna, didn't look up from her copy of the *Dancing Times*. She sat on a green sofa

5

with her feet resting on a plump leather pouffe and with the wireless playing softly in the background in a room lined with silver-framed photographs signed by stars of the professional dance world. Victor Silvester beamed down at Lorna from pride of place on the chimney breast, with Phyllis Haylor and Joanne Bradley to either side. Lorna was a big Silvester fan – she ranked him above Frank and Peggy Spencer and she listened avidly to his BBC *Dancing Club* programme on the wireless. The half-hour broadcasts provided her with a template for the lessons that she taught in the studio beneath their stylish living quarters. She and Sylvia were both proud of the fact that the Lorna Ellis Dance Academy was situated in the best part of Blackpool – on broad and fashionable King Alfred Road, alongside smart shops and offices, with the Majestic Hotel at the end of the street and on a main tramline route down to the promenade.

'Mother,' Sylvia prompted.

'Yes, dear?' Lorna glanced up with a weary sigh. Three beginners dance classes on the trot had left her feeling thoroughly wrung out. 'You're going out, I see?'

'Yes, I told you so earlier.' Preparing herself for her mother's version of the Spanish Inquisition, Sylvia hovered by the door.

'Did you? I don't remember. I thought you might stay in and keep me company for a change.'

'No; I did tell you.'

'And where are you gadding off to?'

'To the Tower.'

'Who with?'

'With Eddie.'

'Edward. I do wish you'd call him Edward.'

'He prefers Eddie.' Sylvia regretted her choice of dress. She should have stuck to one that she was able to fasten herself. 'Can you do this zip for me, please?'

'How will you get there?' Lorna pushed herself up from the sofa then turned her daughter round to face the door before easing up the zip.

'Eddie will call here for me.'

'Good. And how will you get back?'

'Eddie will bring me.'

'Because I won't permit you to walk the streets alone late at night – you know that perfectly well.'

'That's why I've asked him to walk me home,' Sylvia said petulantly. 'Honestly, Mother, I'm twenty-one years old; you mustn't fret over me as if I were still a schoolgirl.'

'If I don't, who will?' Lorna smoothed the satin fabric and adjusted Sylvia's sequinned waistband. Gone were the days when Lorna herself graced the professional dance floor as a Ginger Rogers lookalike. People had insisted that the resemblance was remarkable – the same dainty features and swan-like neck, the grace of movement as if she floated on air. Lorna had sparkled in the world of sequins and gauzy net petticoats until an unlooked-for pregnancy had put paid to her hopes of international fame.

Now, at the age of forty-two (whisper it under your breath), all of Lorna's hopes were pinned on Sylvia making the grade in the world of dance while she, Lorna, gave lessons and served on the committee of the ISTD – the Imperial Society of Teachers of Dancing. Her method was exclusively English: a standardized style that avoided the wild excesses of

7

the Charleston and swing. No 'freak dancing' for the Lorna Ellis Dance Academy, she proclaimed.

Sadly for Lorna, on the personal front, Sylvia had become a handful of late – moody in the extreme, dismissive of her mother's opinions and all too willing to play on her exceptional looks to get what she wanted. Beauty was skin deep, Lorna often made a point of reminding her. Above all, a young woman needed to develop a skill and the ability to earn her own money to secure a decent, long-term future. 'Look at me,' was Lorna's mantra; 'when I was expecting you and your father wanted nothing to do with us, I was able to set up my academy to support us.'

With the zip securely fastened, Sylvia broke free from her mother's fussing and exited the room, grabbing the stole and a silver clutch bag from her bedroom before rushing down to answer the door to Eddie Winter's knock.

'Be back by eleven,' Lorna called from the head of the stairs. 'Don't be late.'

Eddie stepped into the narrow hallway. 'Don't worry, Mrs Ellis; I'll make sure Sylvia's home on time.'

Handsome Edward in his linen jacket and crimson bow tie; clean cut and clean shaven, with those startling pale-grey eyes staring up at her. Such a nice young man, Lorna thought, and he clearly adored Sylvia, if only her increasingly self-centred daughter would realize it. 'Thank you, dear,' she told him.

Eddie offered Sylvia his arm and they were gone, out into the evening sunlight and sea air. A strikingly handsome couple, they drew admiring glances from the holidaymakers with buckets and spades and striped canvas windbreaks streaming up King Alfred

8

Road on their way to their cramped boarding houses set back from the seafront. Desultory drinkers drifted into the Queen's Arms and dozens of RAF men in their smart uniforms disembarked from the buses that had ferried them into town from their base at Squires Gate, bound for the Tower Ballroom to see what off-duty fun was to be had.

'Boo!' Tommy Rossi, one of the whiteface clowns at the Tower Circus, made Joy Hebden jump. He popped out from his dressing room in full regalia – a spangled, Pierrot-style costume with padded shoulders and pantaloons, topped with a white dunce's hat.

Joy gasped before defending herself against Tommy's advances with her mop. 'Menace – stop doing that, or else!' she protested.

'Give over, Cinders – you love me really,' Tommy taunted as he snatched Joy's mop then ran down the steps and danced away with it across the empty circus ring.

'Don't call me Cinders.' Honestly, Tommy Rossi was the limit; the way he would seek Joy out and torment her at the end of each cleaning shift. 'It's not funny. Give me my mop ... Tommy, I'm warning you!' She chased after him, around the ring then back up the steps into a Moroccan-style, tiled corridor lined with posters advertising past animal acts at the Tower Circus. '12 Devils of the Forest', '20 Wonder Horses', '15 Maltese Dogs'.

'Catch me if you can!' he challenged. 'See; you can't – I'm too quick for you.' He whirled on the spot, sequins glittering, his white face creased into a broad grin.

'Tommy, for heaven's sake; you'll get me the sack – the audience will start arriving any minute now.' Joy lunged and snatched back her mop. 'Thanks for nothing!' She marched along the curving corridor towards the broom cupboard at the far end. The sooner she made herself scarce the better.

Tommy trotted after her. 'Why not stop and watch the show?' he cajoled as he watched Joy lift her coat from the hook. Less boisterous now, he grew more thoughtful. 'You know what they say about all work and no play.'

'I can't stay. I'm paid to clean, not to be part of the audience.' Once Joy was finished here, she would head straight home, where with luck she would evade Mrs Grigg, her dragon of a landlady, and get herself an early night.

'It's Saturday. Stop and watch the performance, then afterwards I'll take you dancing.' How come someone as pretty as Joy had ended up in this dead-end job? Tommy wondered. The question hung unspoken between them but it lay behind the bout of energetic teasing and flirting that he'd embarked on over the past week or two. More than pretty – Joy was one of those rare, delicate creatures whose brown eyes flashed at him from beneath dark lashes and whose manner reminded him of a shy forest fawn glimpsed in dappled sunlight in the heart of the woods. Beneath the thick layer of greasepaint, Tommy's Italian background gave him a romantic bent that allowed him to compare attractive women to characters from Walt Disney cartoons.

'I don't dance,' Joy stated flatly. 'Sorry, Tommy – I have to go.'

She swept out without a backwards glance as the audience began to filter in; away from the spectacle of elephants standing on their hind legs and waving their trunks at the crowd, away from snarling lions and tigers in cages with their leotard-clad tamer cracking his whip, far away from the noise and razzle-dazzle of clowns, acrobats and jugglers.

'Goodnight, Gerald,' she said to the man on duty at the entrance to the subterranean aquarium. 'Goodnight, Irena,' to the Polish acrobat rushing along the corridor to change into her costume.

Faint strains of music from the famous Wurlitzer organ drifted from the ballroom on to the broad street below as Joy made her hasty exit. Goodbye to that fun-filled world and hello to her poky attic room on Silver Street. Not that Joy was complaining; at least she'd avoided the bombing raid on Manchester that had killed her parents and older sister at the start of the war. The disaster had happened just five short weeks after Joy had been evacuated to Blackpool as a fifteen-year-old schoolgirl. She was seventeen now and making her own quiet way in life.

A heedless Pearl Scott in glamorous dancing gear brushed past Joy outside the main entrance to the ballroom. 'Get a move on, you lot!' she cried to her three girlfriends, Ida, Doris and Thora. It was still daylight and the nearby Central Pier, as well as similar piers to the north and south, thronged with holiday-makers enjoying the balmy evening air. A green-and-cream tram rattled to a halt outside the ballroom then disgorged its passengers. 'At this rate you'll miss

11

your chance of grabbing a decent partner. I'm all right, Jack – I collared Bernie Greene for the night.'

A queue snaked across the vast, carpeted entrance hall. At its head were Sylvia Ellis and Eddie Winter.

'Two tickets, please.' No question about it – Eddie would pay for Sylvia's as well as his own. Sylvia patted her curls and smiled graciously.

Pearl and her gang craned their necks to catch sight of Blackpool's premier pair of ballroom dancers. 'Crikey, look at that dress!' Pearl whispered under her breath. *Blue as the sky on a bright summer's day.* 'How does Sylvia do it on clothing coupons?'

'I bet it belonged to her mother once upon a time,' Ida whispered back. 'From twenty years ago, when Lorna Ellis was big in the dance world. Sylvia has probably brought it up to date by adding a bow or two.'

Pearl watched Eddie lead Sylvia up the wide stairs to the ballroom. Eventually she reached the desk and slid her money under the glass barrier. 'One ticket, please.' She'd paid and was halfway up the stairs when she turned to her chums with an impatient cry. 'Come on, girls; chop-chop!'

Outside on the promenade, Joy kept her head down as she passed stalls selling Blackpool rock, candy floss and fish and chips. 'Palmistry – Past, Present and Future.' She glanced at the familiar sign outside Madam Rosie's small booth. A large poster in the window showed the Line of the Heart, Line of the Head, Line of Life, and Line of Marriage.

Joy walked on, a solitary figure, as far as Silver Street, where she turned. Behind her lay the seafront and a mile of golden sand. Water, earth, fire and air; one of these days she would gather the courage to pay her sixpence and enter the fortune teller's booth to discover which category she belonged to. She fancied being air or water. Taking her door key from her pocket, Joy paused to study her palm – her Line of Life was clear and unbroken, but the Line of Marriage was hard to make out. *No surprise there*, she said to herself as she turned her key in the lock.

CHAPTER TWO

There was no peace for the wicked. After dancing her feet off at the Tower on Saturday night, Pearl found herself at the kitchen sink next morning, looking out into the scruffy backyard where her father, Henry Scott, was putting the finishing touches to a new sign for his amusement arcade. He was convinced that a recently acquired set of one-armed bandits was his latest sure-fire way to make a fortune. His arcade had a prime location close to the Central Pier; all it needed was a bright new sign above the entrance.

'Fill 'Em Up, Little Mickey, Playball, Lucky Star and What's My Line – that's the name of the game these days,' he'd declared over the breakfast table that morning. 'Top-of-the-range Allwin machines, the lot of them; all with automatic payout mechanisms.'

Pearl's mother, Maria, had been unimpressed. 'How much did they set you back? More to the point, which lorry did they fall off the back of?'

This had led to a heated argument – money down the drain, mind your own business, and so on – during which the younger Scotts, Ernie, Wilf and Elsie, had wisely made themselves scarce. Pearl had simply cleared the table and started the washing-up.

14

'Call yourself Mr Blackpool!' Maria had scoffed at her husband. 'Swaggering around town, reckoning to have a finger in every pie. But where's the profits from those pies? That's what I'd like to know.'

'Shut your mouth, woman.' Henry hadn't bothered to raise his voice – why waste the energy? 'I know what I'm doing. Slot machines are the business these days. I'll stick young Ernie on the door and charge sixpence to get in – and Bob's your uncle.'

Pearl's mother, who had worked for years to make ends meet, took this with a large pinch of salt. At the tender age of nineteen she'd married handsome Henry and they'd had Pearl soon afterwards, then there'd been a long gap before Ernie, Wilf and Elsie had been born in reasonably quick succession. Maria was forty-four now – still eye-catching and vivacious; a popular figure along the seafront, where she served behind the counter of her fish and chip stall in floral dresses and heeled shoes, her glossy dark hair pinned high on her head and finished off with a bright silk scarf.

'What's the betting we don't see a penny of those profits if there ever are any?' she'd grumbled as, paintbrush in hand, Henry had retreated to a yard cluttered with dustbins, rusty signs from previous failed business ventures, old bikes and odd bits of fairground machinery. 'The bookies will see most of it and what's left will disappear down your father's gullet at the Black Horse.'

Now Pearl smiled to herself at the sight of him dabbing away with his paintbrush. She imagined the satisfying thud of the trigger against a metal ball that would fly round its circular track with a tinny rattle before plopping into a small steel cup: winner or loser? Yes, she could see the appeal of slot machines and the arcade was definitely located at the very heart of the Golden Mile – so maybe her mother would be proved wrong for once. There again, it was true that her father's boastfulness rarely paid off in terms of pounds, shillings and pence.

Pearl watched him put the lid on his small pot of red enamel paint then carefully swill his brush in a jar of methylated spirits. These days there was a touch of grey in her father's thick dark hair and his waistline had expanded, but he was still a broad-shouldered, good-looking man with the gift of the gab. Maybe this time . . .?

Finishing the dishes, Pearl dried her hands then slipped out on to the street for a breath of air. Here she found Bernie lolling against a lamp-post, arms crossed and staring glumly at a group of boys, including her ten-year-old brother Wilf, who were squatting on their haunches and playing marbles outside the weed-choked entrance to Mason's disused stable yard.

Bernie glanced in her direction and scowled. 'So much for your bloody dance competition,' he mumbled. 'We never stood a chance against Sylvia flippin' Ellis and Eddie What's-'is-name.'

'Eddie Winter,' Pearl reminded him. 'If we'd been allowed to jitterbug like I was expecting, it would've been different; but no, it turned out to be the Viennese waltz.'

'Too right – and it turns out I don't know my reverse turn from my turkey trot, so we were snookered from the off.'

'Now, if it had been anything more modern,' Pearl

continued her train of thought, 'we'd have high-kicked and shaken our hips with the best of them.'

'Dance madness' it was called by snooty old-school observers – but all that wild swinging out and coming back together in gay abandon was definitely more her and Bernie's style.

Suddenly launching himself from the lamp-post, Bernie seized Pearl by the waist and swung her into the middle of the road. 'Like this, you mean?' He pulled her close then rocked her from side to side, attracting the attention of the grubby marble players.

'Woo!' they called, as Pearl's skirt swung out to reveal her petticoat.

'Watch out, our Pearl; we can see your knickers!' Wilf cackled.

Pearl broke free and tugged at her skirt. 'Fibber!' she challenged.

Bernie laughed and went on shaking his hips and shoulders. 'Look; I've got rhythm!'

'Yes, but none of the right moves, you idiot!'

Stopping as suddenly as he'd begun, Bernie pulled a half-smoked cigarette from his shirt pocket and lit it. 'It's not right, though: Sylvia and Eddie have been taking dance lessons since they were tiddlers. What chance did the rest of us have of walking away with the prize money? It's not even as if they need it. Eddie Winter must earn a tidy packet working for the Inland Revenue and Sylvia brings in a few bob on her own account, helping her ma with the youngsters at their academy.'

'I hear Eddie's moved to the Vickers Armstrong factory out at Squires Gate.' Pearl put Bernie right on the facts. 'He works in the office, ordering parts for Wellington bombers.'

'Same difference. Anyway, why isn't he out in Egypt, doing his bit for king and country?'

Pearl shrugged. 'No idea. Why aren't you?'

'Because I help build hangars for the RAF, as if you didn't know.' Bernie puffed away at his cigarette. 'Essential war work, they call it. And in my spare time I help out at the Pleasure Beach, providing a fun time to our war-weary masses.'

'Excuses, excuses.' A glance at her watch told Pearl that it was eleven o'clock. 'Shouldn't you be there now?' she reminded him.

'Oh Lord, yes – I'll get skinned alive!' Bernie flung down his cigarette and shot to the end of the street, leaving the boys to grub about in the gutter for the butt.

'Wilf!' Pearl bellowed a warning as Bernie disappeared from view. 'If you pick up that fag end I'll make sure you get a good hiding off Mam.'

A pity Bernie has his hands full with work, she thought. For he definitely did have rhythm and a dance lesson or two at the Lorna Ellis Dance Academy – or maybe even at Cliff Seymour's new place on North View Parade – wouldn't go amiss. 'One of these days I might save up for a few lessons myself,' she muttered, glancing up at the iron tower – a massive landmark construction of criss-crossing girders stretching skywards that dominated their street and all those nearby – as she collared her youngest brother and dragged him inside the house.

At the crack of dawn next day, Joy prepared to leave for work. Cleaning had to be done when workplace buildings were empty, before the day got properly underway. This suited early bird Joy, especially during the summer months when the sun rose soon after five and suffused the sky with a soft pink glow. However, today, Monday, proved to be a disappointment, as Joy found when she opened the front door to heavy grey clouds and light drizzle. She was buttoning up her sensible, navy-blue coat when Iris Grigg emerged from the kitchen.

'You're late with your rent.' The landlady barked the accusation at Joy, who whirled round to see her advancing in full sail, dressed in faded candlewick dressing-gown, hair curlers and woollen slippers – the type of seaside gorgon who appeared on Donald McGill postcards up and down the land. 'I expect my money to be paid on the dot, five o'clock Sunday teatime.'

'I'm sorry, Mrs Grigg; I had to work late yesterday. Your light was already off when I got back.' A flustered Joy dipped into her purse to find the money that she owed.

Iris took the coins with a disgruntled frown and counted them. 'Don't let it happen again,' she warned.

'I won't, I promise.' Joy escaped into the fresh air. *If only I could afford better lodgings*, she mused as she hurried towards South Shore Terrace. Her attic room was cramped, lit only by a skylight stained with bird droppings. It had an uncomfortable bed tucked under the eaves and scarcely room for a washstand and small chest of drawers, let alone a proper wardrobe. Joy's dresses hung on a hook behind the door and her few possessions – including a brush and comb, a small make-up purse and a precious black-and-white snapshot of her family taken in the summer of 1935 – were arranged along the narrow mantelpiece above a fireplace that was never lit.

'Chimney's blocked,' Iris had informed her as they'd agreed rental terms the previous September. 'Damned crows build their nests in it. Can't get rid of 'em.'

Nicer lodgings would cost too much, Joy knew. Even with the extra cleaning work she'd recently secured at the circus plus a string of jobs she did for private individuals – the Ward family near the North Pier (a fifteen-minute tram ride away), Mr Dawson at the gift shop on King Alfred Road and Mrs Ellis at the dance academy further up the street, which was where she was headed now – Joy's earnings wouldn't meet the expense of a bigger room with a more pleasant outlook. No, she must make do with things as they were.

Her spirits rose as she turned on to the deserted promenade. At this time in the morning seagulls ruled the silent world. They soared over the newly built concrete air raid shelters spaced out at regular intervals along the prom, curving effortlessly overhead, their wings flashing white, their orange legs tucked under sleek grey bellies. Oh, for the freedom of the sky – the ability to sail on an air current over golden sands fringed with lapping waves. Joy paused in the shadow of the Tower to survey Blackpool's three piers striding out into steel-grey water, with a conglomeration of buildings at the end housing yet more funfair attractions and a theatre for end-of-the-pier shows. She was one of those people who was afraid to walk on piers because of the gaps between the wooden planks through which you caught a glimpse of the restless sea below. One half-hearted attempt shortly after Joy had arrived in Blackpool as an evacuee had made her tremble violently and retreat, overcome with dizziness.

Giving herself a quick shake, she hurried on: a lone figure on the wide prom. When she reached the imposing Majestic Hotel, whose seafront entrance was currently barricaded by sandbags, she turned into King Alfred Road and walked past several smaller hotels that had been requisitioned by the government and converted into offices for civil servants – one for the Inland Revenue and one for the Department of Health. They had a gloomy look, with more sandbags piled near their entrances and blackout blinds pulled down. A street sweeper pushing a handcart was the only other early riser and he and Joy exchanged brief nods as their paths crossed.

Soon she came to the dance academy where she must start her day. Letting herself into the building with the key Mrs Ellis had given her, she used a second key to enter the ground-floor dance studio. It was a big room, some thirty feet long and twenty wide, with a dance barre along one side and floor-to-ceiling mirrors lining another. The sprung mahogany floor was polished to perfection. At the far end stood an upright piano and a table with an expensive, up-to-date gramophone.

Joy's first task was to collect her brushes, dustpans and dusters from a small side room next to the cloak-rooms close to the main entrance. This she did, catching sight of herself in the huge mirror as she set about sweeping. It seemed to her a nondescript image: a slight figure with thick, dark-brown hair tied back, wearing a short-sleeved white blouse and grey slacks. A wave of self-consciousness passed over her as she turned away and began her work until a faint tap-tap at the plate-glass window distracted her. Cocking her head to one side, she listened. Yes; there was another tap and the outline of a man's figure through the blind, so she decided to put down her broom and go to the front door to investigate.

'I'm sorry to bother you.' Rightly assuming that neither Lorna nor Sylvia would be up, Eddie had supposed that the cleaner would be the only person whose attention he could attract. 'You must be Joy.'

'That's me.' She peered cautiously through the half-open door.

'My name's Eddie Winter. Mrs Ellis mentioned that you arrive early to start your cleaning work.'

'Yes?' A visitor at this time in the morning was the last thing Joy had expected – however, the man looked respectable in his light raincoat, collar and tie, carrying a brown leather briefcase.

'Sylvia is my dancing partner,' he continued. 'She lost an earring at the Tower Ballroom on Saturday night. I went back yesterday to check in Lost Property and luckily it had been handed in.' Eddie raced through the explanation, aware that his visit had interrupted Joy's cleaning routine.

'I see.' Joy relaxed, opening the door wide and allowing Eddie to step inside.

'I'm on my way to work – I have to catch the next tram out to Squires Gate.' Delving into his coat pocket, he pulled out a small brown envelope containing the lost earring and handed it over to Joy. 'I was pretty sure Sylvia wouldn't be up yet. Could you please give it to her for me?' The cleaner struck him as a shy girl, very young and keen to avoid notice. A pity; she could make much more of her looks if she tried.

'Of course,' Joy said stiffly.

'And could you give her a message, please? Tell her the Halle Orchestra is on at the Winter Gardens tonight. I can get tickets if she would like.'

'She certainly would!' As if by magic, Sylvia appeared at the top of the stairs. No tousled hair and crumpled dressing-gown for her; oh no – though she'd only just got out of bed at the sound of voices below, she was fresh as a daisy in a pristine pale-blue housecoat with curls artfully piled on top of her head.

'Good. I'll go ahead and buy the tickets,' Eddie confirmed.

Sylvia skipped down the stairs and stood with her back to Joy, who had stepped aside to give her some space. 'What brings you here?' she asked Eddie.

'I brought your earring. You said you needed it as a matter of urgency.'

'I do.' She thrust her hand under his nose. 'Those pearl earrings go with the outfit I plan to wear today.'

'Very urgent.' Eddie's lips twitched into a faint smile that he hid by raising his hand to his mouth and clearing his throat. 'Are you going somewhere nice?'

'Never you mind. Come on, Eddie, I haven't got all day – where's the earring?'

'It's here.' Joy stepped forward with the envelope.

A small frown creased Sylvia's smooth brow as she snatched it from Joy's palm. 'For goodness' sake, why didn't you say?'

Joy retreated into the studio. Her face felt hot; Sylvia's sharp tone had stung.

'What time does the concert start?' Sylvia went on in her light, tinkling voice.

'At seven.'

'Seven, you say?' Sylvia was busy checking the contents of the envelope. 'I ought to be back from Lytham by then.'

'Right you are.' Eddie knew better than to expect a thank-you. 'I'll wait for you outside the Opera House at half past six.'

Through the open studio door Joy heard the click of the front door followed by light footsteps back up the stairs. She swept briskly, trying to make up for lost time, and didn't notice Mrs Ellis enter the room some minutes later.

'How soon will you be finished here?' Lorna carried a book of sheet music to the piano. She glided across the polished floor with the upright posture of a trained dancer, shoulders back and chin tilted slightly upwards. 'My first pupil arrives at eight.'

'I'll be done by half seven,' Joy promised.

'Make sure you're thorough.' Lorna ran a finger along the top of the piano, looking for dust but failing to find any. Then she dipped into her pocket and drew out a few coins. 'Here; I may as well pay you now.'

Joy took the money and thanked her.

'I shan't need you tomorrow or the day after,' Lorna informed her as she sorted through her record collection before placing one on the turntable. With a precise, delicate movement she swung the needle arm over the disc and lowered it – Silvester's 'You're

24

Dancing On My Heart' filled the room. 'Come back on Thursday, the usual time.'

'Yes, Mrs Ellis.' Joy took out a yellow duster and ran it along the dance barre. When she looked up again, Lorna was gone. The record played on – a smooth, violin-led quickstep that Joy recognized from listening to the wireless. Unable to resist, she swayed and hummed softly as she dusted. A quickstep went in 4/4 time; a combination of foxtrot and Charleston invented in the 1920s. It involved walks, runs, chassés and turns, and sometimes a hop, skip and a jump – hard to visualize from merely listening to Mr Silvester's description. Nevertheless, Joy couldn't help giving it a secret go – still clutching her duster and raising her arms into ballroom hold with an invisible partner, she ran and skipped a few steps in time to the music, pirouetted on one foot then danced on towards the mirror.

The trip to Lytham was a lie that Sylvia had invented to throw her mother off the scent. In fact, she had no intention of taking the bus to the refined neighbouring resort and having tea there with friends.

On this occasion, as on many others, Sylvia found it easier to keep her mother in the dark. Cliff Seymour, the man she'd arranged to meet, had something of a bad reputation in Blackpool. From time to time Lorna would make critical remarks about him – he was the wrong 'type', having worked in a Berlin cabaret during the build-up to the war, and he had returned home under a cloud. Sylvia would dismiss these comments, putting them down to simple, straightforward jealousy. Cliff's new dance studio on

North View Parade was up and coming, meaning that some of Lorna's pupils had drifted in his direction. 'Cliff Seymour spouts a lot of nonsense,' Sylvia's mother would grumble each time this happened. 'All that rubbish about running Hammersmith Palais when he was scarcely out of nappies – I don't believe a word.'

'He teaches the jitterbug,' Sylvia had remarked on one occasion. 'Not to mention the American smooth. Perhaps that's what young people want these days.'

Her mother had treated her to a large dose of scorn. '"Classes for the masses",' she'd quoted. 'May I remind you that Cliff Seymour isn't even Imperial School trained. He doesn't have a single qualification to his name.'

So when Sylvia had run into Cliff before Saturday's waltz competition at the Tower, she'd been cagey with him.

'Hello, hello, how's the best-dressed girl in town doing?' Cliff had caught her during the interval, when Eddie had been chatting to some recently arrived RAF officers from Squires Gate. 'Remember me?'

'Hello, Cliff.' Sylvia had played it cool. Of course she knew him from their schooldays, when Cliff had stuck out as an unpopular loner with an inflated sense of his own importance.

'Long time, no see. I take it you and Eddie have entered for the Lonsdale Cup in London this year? I've been watching you – you two would do well there, mark my words.'

Sylvia's ears had pricked up. 'Do they stick to the English style?' she'd enquired.

Cliff had spoken knowledgeably. 'Yes, with a dash of individual interpretation thrown into the mix; small side steps and other original touches.' He'd smiled and flattered. 'You especially, Sylvia – you've got all the poise in the world and your frame and posture are excellent. I'd be aiming for bronze at the very least if I were you.'

Eddie had interrupted them as the second part of the evening was getting underway. 'Ready?' he'd asked Sylvia with unusual terseness. 'The judges have taken their positions – the competition is about to begin.'

'First place – congratulations.' Cliff had sought her out again at the end of a successful evening while Eddie joined the queue for coats. 'Not that it was ever in any doubt. We should meet and I can tell you about the Allied North of England Championship. That's in Liverpool, so not far to travel.'

When? Where? Sylvia had seen no harm in meeting and chatting to Cliff. They'd settled on Monday afternoon at North View Parade. He would show her his brand-new dance studio and they could go from there to take tea in the north part of town – anywhere she fancied.

Now that the assignation was almost upon her, Sylvia began to experience cold feet. Had she been a fool in agreeing to meet Cliff? Had she been swayed more by his smooth good looks than by his knowledge of dance competitions?

Cliff based his style on matinee idols who currently graced the silver screen. The double-breasted jacket he'd worn on Saturday had been tailor-made (Sylvia recognized an expensive item of clothing when she saw one) and his starched white shirt, dark-blue silk tie and black patent dancing shoes had been immaculate. He wore his light-brown hair slicked back and with a side parting that emphasized his high cheekbones, straight, narrow nose and jawline (not too square but just right).

Maybe she had fallen for his charms, but so what? She knew how to look after herself if Cliff tried anything untoward, and in any case the meeting was happening in broad daylight.

With one last check in her dressing-table mirror, Sylvia paused to clip on her cultured pearl earrings and to pat a stray lock into place. As she'd said to Eddie earlier, the earrings went beautifully with her outfit – a pale-green, tight-fitting dress with short sleeves, a straight skirt and a narrow cream leather belt; shoes and handbag to match the belt, naturally. A quick turn to the side, pull in those tummy muscles, head up, and Sylvia was ready to go.

'Give my regards to Betty and Myra,' Lorna called from the studio as Sylvia made her way out.

'Will do,' Sylvia replied cheerily. A tram bound for North Pier was due any minute – she would have to hurry.

Cliff's studio was smaller than Sylvia had expected and the entrance was somewhat poky. It lay at the end of North View Parade furthest from the beach, between a tobacconist's shop and a greengrocer's. The sign above the door read 'Learn to Dance with Cliff' and underneath, in smaller letters, 'Live in Your Dreams'. The proprietor himself was waiting for her at the door, casually dressed in shirtsleeves and Fair

Isle knitted waistcoat, enjoying the last few puffs of a cigarette.

He greeted her with a broad smile and a mock cockney accent. 'Hello, princess – welcome to my humble abode.'

'Hello, Cliff. I'm sorry I'm late.' She'd missed the tram after all and had had to wait ten minutes for another. A strong breeze had played havoc with her hair.

'All fashionable girls are late, don't you know?' He swept Sylvia through the door, straight into the studio, which, to her surprise, was smarter than the exterior of the building had suggested. It was softly lit by rows of overhead lights with pearlescent glass shades and by matching wall lights, with a sprung floor that gave a little as she followed Cliff across the room. Photos of him in white tie and tails with various partners and against fancy backdrops lined one wall. More risqué images of him dressed as an MC during his Berlin cabaret phase, surrounded by long-legged girls in sequins, fishnet tights and ostrich feathers, were tucked away in an alcove behind the gramophone.

'What do you think?' He asked as if her opinion mattered.

'Very nice,' she commented.

'*Nice!*' he echoed. 'Do you know how much money I've spent on redecorations?'

'It's modern.' There was an art deco touch to the lighting and clean lines throughout. The walls were jade green. 'But where's your piano?'

Cliff waved away the question. 'Who needs a piano when you have the latest gramophone and dozens of dance records on tap? Bunny hug to lindy hop – you name it.'

'It saves the expense of hiring a pianist, I suppose. How much do you charge per lesson?' Sylvia sifted through the pile of records that Cliff had pointed to.

'That depends. I usually teach small groups of no more than six pupils and I also offer private lessons. Two shillings and sixpence is my top rate.' He eyed her carefully, trying to read her expression. 'Here's a leaflet with my prices in it; put it in your bag.'

Sylvia gave a light laugh. 'Why? I'm not planning to take lessons here, you know.' She scanned the front page of the brochure – 'We teach you quickly, well and cheaply' – before handing it back. 'Who's "we", by the way? Do you have an assistant?'

'No, it's just me at the moment, but "we" sounds better. Why – are you looking for a teaching job?'

She laughed again. 'You've got a nerve!'

'You can't blame me for trying.' Sylvia Ellis had always been the ice maiden, even at school, but she was slowly warming up. 'What do you say we go and find that cup of tea and a scone?'

'No scone for me, ta.' She followed him out of the door. 'I'm watching my figure.' Drat; here came that breeze again, ruffling her hair.

'You don't need to,' Cliff assured her, strolling along, hands in pockets and steering her towards a café that he knew would impress. *Hang the expense*, he thought; *this one is most definitely worth it.*

CHAPTER THREE

The Tower Ballroom took Joy's breath away. How could architects have dreamed up such a magical, fairy-tale palace – what, almost fifty years earlier? She wondered how much the whole thing had cost. An upper and lower balcony overlooked the dance floor, festooned with gilded plasterwork (so much gold leaf!) and the curved ceiling was painted with bright frescoes depicting chubby cherubs sitting on clouds and alluring maidens playing lutes and all manner of musical instruments. There was even a sliding roof that opened up on fine summer evenings to allow 'dancing under the stars'. At one end there was a stage with steps leading up to it and the whole floor was illuminated by two rows of magnificent, sparkling chandeliers.

Joy stood open-mouthed. Never in her life had she seen anything so grand.

'Here; take this.' Ruby Donovan, Joy's new, no-nonsense supervisor, handed her a broom and a dustpan and brush. 'Your first job is to smarten up the bar area – and mind you don't break anything.'

Coming down to earth with a bump, Joy set about the task. It was her first day as a member of the cleaning team employed to keep the ballroom looking its best; a job she'd acquired thanks to Tommy Rossi, who was a pal of Ruby's and had passed on news of the vacancy.

'Give it a go,' he'd told Joy. 'It'd be handy for you. After you've finished there at three, you can come straight across to the circus and carry on as usual.'

'I could do with the money,' Joy had admitted. The hours she worked for Mrs Ward and Mr Dawson were being cut back; she wasn't sure why. Perhaps everyone was feeling the pinch because of the war. At any rate, the chance to take a second steady wage from the Tower proved tempting.

'I've sung your praises to Ruby,' Tommy had assured her. 'I warned her not to judge by appearances.'

'What do you mean by that?' Joy had run into him on Monday, at the start of her circus shift. It had been the first time she'd seen him out of his clown costume and she'd been taken aback by how normal and pleasant he looked, with the dark, wavy hair she associated with Italians and with regular features and a more muscular build than she'd expected.

'Come off it; you don't exactly look as if you're cut out for hard graft.' Eyes twinkling and grinning broadly, he'd laid it on thick.

Joy had kept up her defences. 'Says who?'

'Says me. And don't take it the wrong way – I'm only saying you're far easier on the eye than your average char lady.'

Batting away the compliment, Joy had written down Ruby's details. The following day she'd applied for the job and got it.

'Starting this coming Friday,' Ruby had informed her. 'Twelve o'clock to three o'clock, five days a week.'

'I hope you're right about Joy Hebden,' she'd mentioned to Tommy when she next saw him. 'That girl is in need of a few extra helpings of porridge, if you ask me.'

And now Joy was busy with dustpan and brush behind the bar that ran the length of the ballroom, only glancing up when she heard organ notes issuing from enormous sets of pipes to either side of the stage. And, wonder of wonders, the Wurlitzer rose smoothly through a trapdoor in the centre of the stage and there was a man at the keyboard playing a familiar tune. He filled the vast ballroom with sumptuous music.

'Falling in love again.' One of Joy's fellow cleaners crooned the words in a strong German accent – 'Fallink in loff again'. She clutched her sweeping brush to her chest and twirled out into the centre of the ballroom. Two of the other girls joined in, giggling.

'You lot, stop messing about.' Ruby's half-hearted reprimand went unheeded and she herself hovered at the edge of the floor, as if tempted by the song from *The Blue Angel* – Marlene Dietrich at her husky, prewar best. Ruby's expression was dreamy, a smile curling the corners of her lips upwards as if the tune had transported her into a world of plunging necklines, ivory cigarette holders and satin skirts slit up to slim, shapely thighs.

The organist stopped abruptly then marked his sheet music with a pencil.

Joy emerged hesitantly from behind the bar. 'Is that Mr Dixon?' she asked her supervisor.

'The great man himself,' Ruby confirmed. 'Have you heard him on the wireless?'

'I have!' Joy enthused.

'Did you know they can listen to his programme in Canada, India, Africa, Australia – you name it? And that Wurlitzer was specially built for him.'

'You seem to know a lot about it,' Joy observed as the music started up again and she returned to her work behind the bar.

'Yes, and don't I love it? "Blue Is The Night" is my favourite. I get lost in that one each time I hear it.'

There was another pause while the famous organist wrote notes on his score.

Ruby broke out of her reverie and clapped her hands. 'Back to business, everyone.'

Grumbling, the girls resumed their duties while their supervisor ran a duster over the shiny bar top. 'I haven't seen you at any of the Saturday-night hops,' she mentioned to Joy as they cleaned.

'I don't dance,' Joy admitted quietly. *Only by myself, when no one's looking.*

'What do you mean, you don't dance? Everyone dances!' Ruby applied spit and polish to a dull patch on the counter. Her mid-length auburn hair was pinned back by a row of kirby grips and colour came into her freckled cheeks as she worked. Joy judged her to be in her mid twenties or perhaps a bit older. 'Take me: I carried on coming here twice a week even after my Douglas joined up. And don't look at me as if I'd committed one of the seven deadly sins.'

'I wasn't . . . I'm sorry.' Joy's mouth had fallen open but she clamped it shut and resolved to keep her reactions better hidden in future.

Ruby chatted on. 'Douglas doesn't mind me having a bit of fun while he's away. And where's the harm in the odd tango or foxtrot?'

'No harm,' Joy agreed warily as she stooped to sweep a small pile of cigarette butts into her dustpan. She had yet to get the measure of her new boss, who seemed more relaxed and open than Joy had expected.

They worked quietly for a while as Reginald Dixon began a new number that followed a strict tempo and filled the enormous space.

'You should give it a go,' Ruby suggested during another lull. 'Dancing does wonders for your mood, doesn't it, Tommy?'

Joy glanced up to see her clown friend peering over the bar at her on her hands and knees. She sprang to her feet and hastily tucked her blouse into the waistband of her slacks.

'Especially the up-tempo ones.' Making it obvious that he had time to kill, Tommy casually offered Ruby and Joy a cigarette. 'How are you getting on?' he asked Joy when she politely refused.

'Fine.' Just that; one word before a wave of shyness overcame her.

'She's fitting in nicely,' Ruby confirmed with a satisfied wink.

Tommy inhaled deeply then blew out a spiral of blue smoke. 'I couldn't help overhearing the word "tango". Don't tell me you've roped Joy into joining your dancing gang.'

'Not yet. I'm working on it, though.'

Tommy picked at a shred of tobacco that had got stuck on the tip of his tongue. 'Let me know how you get on.'

'I am here, you know!' Despite her embarrassment, Joy decided to speak up. 'Listen, I don't have time for dancing and anyway, I'm not interested.'

'You do and you are.' Ruby was the sort who refused to take no for an answer. 'And as for that old chestnut of not having anything to wear, one of the girls here will lend you something. What size bust and waist are you?'

Tommy grinned. 'I'll leave Joy in your capable hands,' he told Ruby as he strolled off.

'Well?' the supervisor demanded.

'Thirty-four and twenty-three.' Joy blushed furiously. This would be a big move for her if she went ahead with it; she was used to being the metaphorical child without pennies to spend, staring at jars of sweets in the shop window – always on the outside looking in. 'But honestly, you don't have to bother.'

Ruby waved away her protests. 'Mavis, you're a size thirty-four bust, aren't you?' she called across the ballroom to a tall, slim girl who was climbing a stepladder to dust lightshades on the lower balcony. 'You don't mind lending Joy your off-the-shoulder pink satin number, do you?'

'More bounce!' Pearl instructed. 'Come on, Bernie; you're not even trying!'

'I'm bouncing!' he protested. For God's sake, he'd arrived at the Pleasure Beach early on Saturday morning and was happily minding his own business when Pearl had pounced. 'Look: bounce-bounce, kick and spin!' He went through the motions in the deserted entrance to the waltzer ride.

'Not bad,' Pearl conceded. Having got wind of

another dance competition at the Tower, she'd checked and found that tonight was lindy hop night. 'That ten bob is as good as in our pockets!' she'd declared when she'd tracked him down.

Bernie had ummed and aahed. 'What's lindy hop when it's at home?'

'It's a mixture of salsa and tango, with lashings of energetic swings and underarm turns.'

'Talk to me in English,' he'd pleaded.

'Like the jitterbug,' she'd explained with exaggerated patience.

'Why didn't you say so?'

'I was trying to.'

Bernie was easily bored. Having bounce-bounced, kicked and spun, he wandered off through the empty funfair towards the dodgems, where his brother, Mick, was tinkering with one of the electric cars.

Pearl chased after Bernie. 'What's wrong? I've already told you you're a natural. All you need to do is learn the basic steps.'

They squeezed between the small, beetle-shaped bumper cars until they found a space where they could carry on practising. 'It's all about leg action,' she insisted. 'Forget about ballroom hold – you have to swing me out as far as you can then pull me back in. Then we break away and shake our hips, like so!'

Bernie swung Pearl with so much enthusiasm that she cannoned into Mick's crouching form. He pitched forward into the car he was working on.

'Bloody hell, watch where you're going!' Mick grumbled.

'Sorry.' Pearl helped him to his feet and dusted

him down. He was six years older than Bernie and nowhere near as easy-going. In fact, she'd always been wary of him because of his notorious temper. 'Mick Greene has had more fights than I've had hot dinners,' was the way Pearl's father described it. He was bulkier than Bernie and was known to throw his weight around as a foreman at the Vickers Armstrong factory. Here at the Pleasure Beach, most people knew to give him a wide berth.

'Just bugger off,' Mick mumbled, wiping his hands on a rag that he pulled out of the back pocket of his overalls. 'I'm talking to you, Pearl; Bernie has no use for the lindy bop or whatever you call it. He's got better things to do.'

Needled by his rudeness, Pearl retaliated. 'You checked with him, have you?'

'I don't have to.' Mick gave a vicious kick to the rubber bumper of the car he was working on. 'I know without asking.'

'So you're a mind reader now?' Honestly, he was the limit. 'If you must know, we're entering tonight's dance competition at the Tower Ballroom.'

Mick turned to confront his brother. 'You're doing what?'

'Just a bit of fun,' Bernie mumbled through gritted teeth. Best not to annoy Mick; Pearl should know that by now.

'Dancing is for bloody sissies!' Mick stuffed the rag back into his pocket. 'You hear me?'

'I hear you.'

Mick was working himself up into a lather. 'Bloody Tower Ballroom! You wouldn't catch me going within a hundred yards of that place. I'm telling you, Bernie—'

'All right, all right.' Bernie raised his hands in surrender before backing away.

'Go on, bugger off!' Mick told Pearl again, his face dark and glowering. 'I mean it – I won't have you leading my kid brother off the straight and narrow.'

'And Bernie doesn't have a say in the matter?' Once a bully, always a bully, but she put up one last, lukewarm show of defiance. 'Honestly, Mick, just let him make up his own mind.'

His scowl deepened and he turned his back; end of the matter.

With a sigh Pearl trailed after Bernie, back towards the waltzers. 'I hope I haven't got you into hot water,' she told him. 'I'd no idea Mick felt that way about the Fred Astaire business.'

Bernie shrugged. 'Neither did I. But if I keep my head down he'll soon forget about it.' He swung absent-mindedly at one of the empty carriages and set it spinning.

Pearl frowned as she watched it turn. 'About tonight . . .?' she began.

Bernie stuck his hands in his pocket and jutted out his chin in a mood of bold defiance. 'I'll be there,' he promised. 'Seven o'clock on the dot.'

'Come into the lounge.' Lorna invited Eddie to sit with her while Sylvia finished getting ready for their usual Saturday night out. Lorna had sensed a frosty atmosphere between the two of them ever since Sylvia's get-together with her chums in Lytham at the start of the week and was determined to root out the cause.

Eddie sat on a chair by the window and gazed down

at the busy thoroughfare, hoping to disguise the fact that he felt thoroughly miserable.

'Sylvia won't be long,' Lorna assured him. 'You know what she's like – never happy with the way she looks.'

Eddie smiled and flicked an invisible speck from his trouser leg. Good manners prevented him from saying what was on his mind.

'How is your father?' Lorna enquired after Dr Maurice Winter, a respected Blackpool GP, a widower and her frequent companion on theatre outings.

'He's well, thank you. He made a point of asking me to pass on his regards and says that he looks forward to seeing you at the opening night of *The Pirates of Penzance* – next week, I think.'

'Tuesday,' Lorna confirmed. 'Now, Edward; about Sylvia . . .' she began.

'It's good news about General Eisenhower taking charge in Europe this week.' Eddie made an unsuccessful attempt to change the subject. 'We've waited long enough for the Yanks to enter the fray.'

Lorna ploughed on regardless. 'Sylvia can be trying at times, but deep down she means well.'

'Quite – we've danced together for many years so I can safely say that I know your daughter very well indeed.'

'And long may you two continue as dance partners.' Lorna perched uneasily on the edge of the sofa. 'I see a great future for you both in the world of ballroom. Once you've achieved everything there is to achieve in the amateur sphere, it will be time to consider turning professional, your health permitting.'

Eddie flicked at the same spot on his trousers. 'No

need to worry about that, Mrs Ellis – touch wood, my asthma is well under control.'

'So what *are* you worried about? Has Sylvia done something to offend you?'

Eddie sighed. The seconds ticked slowly by and he felt the pressure to give an honest answer. 'If you must know, she stood me up on Monday night. I'd bought two tickets for the Halle.'

'And she let you down?' *Typical Sylvia!* 'Monday, you say? If I remember rightly, she visited friends in Lytham that afternoon.'

Lorna was racking her brains for a reasonable excuse for her daughter's unmannerly conduct when Sylvia appeared barefoot. She wore a flared navy-blue skirt with white daisies appliquéd on to the hem, teamed with a white blouse. Her hair was pulled back in a ponytail that made her look younger than her twenty-one years.

'Where were you on Monday evening?' her mother demanded without preliminaries.

Sylvia flashed Eddie an irritated look. 'I missed my bus back from Lytham and I had to wait ages for another,' she answered with brittle cheeriness before rushing to change the subject. 'Do you mind if I borrow your white court shoes, Mother? They go better with this outfit than my peep-toed sandals.'

Heaving a sigh, Lorna excused herself and went to fetch the shoes.

'Really?' Sylvia hissed angrily at Eddie. 'Did you have to put me on the spot like that?'

Eddie spread his palms. 'What did you expect? Your mother asked me what was bothering me and I told her; simple as that.'

'Thanks for nothing!' For two pins Sylvia would have stormed out of the room but that would only have attracted more attention to Monday night. In fact, she and Cliff Seymour had stayed longer than she'd intended at the Victoria Tearooms. There'd been so much to talk about amid the polite tinkle of spoons and the rattle of cups into saucers. After the pros and cons of Sylvia and Eddie entering the North of England Championships, she and Cliff had gone on to discuss some of the key trends identified in the *Dancing Times* and from there they'd exchanged views on the latest dance crazes. Cliff had opened her eyes to the extent of the American influence and they'd joked about the ISTD's stuffy response. Finally, Cliff had described his cabaret days in Berlin. 'Or rather, my nights,' he'd confided. 'Berlin only comes alive after midnight. I often didn't get to bed until dawn.' Sylvia had soaked up his colourful descriptions of the city clubs – low lighting, jazz music, scantily clad dancers and groups of young, blond German officers in the audience. 'I loved every minute of it,' Cliff had confessed.

Before Sylvia knew it, the café was closing its doors and she and her entertaining new companion had found themselves out on the promenade. It had been a warm, sunny evening as they'd wandered back to his studio. Cliff had insisted on demonstrating some complicated steps to the ever-popular Charleston – Sylvia had risen to the challenge and joined in. He'd praised her; she had the right slim, almost boyish figure and high kicks that other girls would die for. Time had flown.

'Out with the old, in with the new!' Cliff had declared as he walked her to the tram stop at last. 'If ever you fancy travelling down to London with me, I could introduce you to some of my contacts there.'

Sylvia was no fool; she suspected mixed motives behind Cliff's flattery. Still, she'd had a grand time and had arranged to return to his studio to learn the rumba.

'If you're interested in performing a Latin routine from far-off shores,' he'd suggested.

'Perhaps,' she'd replied with a non-committal shrug of her shoulders.

'Palm trees and sparkling blue seas.' With supreme self-confidence he'd cajoled and charmed his way through her apparent indifference.

'Very well, I'll do it.'

'Don't tell your mother!' had been his parting words as she'd stepped on to the platform at the back of the tram. He gave a wink and a wave. 'See you shortly, princess – bye-bye!'

Now Lorna returned to the sitting room with the shoes that Sylvia had asked to borrow. 'Isn't that skirt a bit short?' Lorna cast a critical eye over her daughter's appearance.

'No, not for the lindy hop.'

Lorna made a sour-lemon face. 'Oh, please!'

'Keep up with the times, Mother,' Sylvia chirruped as she led Eddie out of the room.

'By the by – have you had anything to eat this evening?' Lorna called after her.

'No time.' Sylvia skipped down the stairs. 'Come along, Eddie – we don't want to be late.'

'Not again!' Pearl jabbed Bernie with her elbow and glowered in the direction of Sylvia and Eddie as they made their grand entrance into the ballroom. 'They ought to be banned from these Saturday-night amateur competitions.'

Bernie had downed a couple of beers to loosen up before slipping quietly from the house. He'd met Pearl at the end of Empire Street. For the sake of the elusive ten shillings, he was ready to give tonight's dancing contest everything he'd got. In the meantime, he propped himself up against the bar and caught an eyeful of Sylvia in her short blue skirt and perky blonde ponytail. As for Eddie – well, he looked his usual stuffed-shirt self in blazer and collar and tie. Bernie had opted for a more casual look – open-necked blue shirt, blue slacks and brown suede shoes that he hoped would add bounce to his lindy hop when the time came.

Pearl dashed off to find Ida and Doris. The three friends would compare notes about the get-ups of other dancers and assess their chances of winning the prize money. She passed close to where Sylvia stood – directly under a sparkling chandelier – then climbed the stairs to the lower balcony where she collared her pals and complained loudly about public enemy number one: namely Sylvia Ellis.

'Just look at her!' she seethed. 'She thinks she's the bee's knees. But what's the betting she and Eddie come a cropper when they have to go out of hold.'

'So what are you worried about?' Ida leaned over the rail to wave to Thora. 'Yoo-hoo, down there!' Her sleeveless, green-and-white-striped dress was nipped in at the waist and flounced out over her hips, and when she bent forward she showed yards of starched white petticoat.

'Sylvia and Eddie aren't used to the Latin stuff,

that's all I'm saying.' Pearl picked out several people she knew huddled at the side of the dance floor. She waved at Mavis Thorne in her shiny pink dress before realizing her mistake – it was Mavis's frock all right but not Mavis wearing it. 'Who the heck's that?' she muttered to Ida and Doris. The mystery girl's figure was even slimmer than Mavis's.

'No idea. She's pretty, though.'

Tommy Rossi joined Pearl's small gang. He'd wangled a Saturday night off from the circus and had made his way into the packed ballroom without paying the entrance fee. 'Her name's Joy Hebden,' he informed the girls with a smug air. 'She happens to be a friend of mine.'

Pearl studied Joy more closely – the pink satin flattered her olive skin tone and dark hair, but she looked ill at ease. 'Does she now?'

'Yes; a friend,' he repeated with emphasis.

'You're a dark horse, Tommy Rossi,' Ida teased. 'Mind you, that one's probably a bit on the young side for you.'

'Ha-ha!' He walked off with a scornful laugh.

'Touchy!' Ida commented. 'Was it something I said?'

A sudden hush in the crowd below told the girls that the dancing was about to begin. All heads turned towards the stage and the crimson curtains parted to show the trapdoor sliding open and the gleaming, chrome-trimmed Wurlitzer organ rising from the depths with Reginald Dixon at the keyboard. There was a loud round of applause for 'Oh I Do Like To Be Beside The Seaside', his jaunty signature tune.

'See you later, alligator,' Pearl told Ida and Doris before rushing off to find Bernie.

Down on the dance floor, Ruby and her pals clapped along with the music. ' "When the brass band plays tiddly-om-pom-pom!" ' Ruby trilled. Standing next to Joy and shielding her from the push and pull of the crowd, she outlined some rules for the newcomer. 'They say you should always wait for the man to ask you to dance but that's not the way I look at it.'

'No?' Joy murmured faintly. Her mouth felt dry and her palms sweated. She kept tugging at her shoulder straps to make sure she was decent. Why, oh why had she agreed to wear Mavis's dress?

'No. I reckon a girl has the right to choose her own partner. If you wait to be asked, the chances are you'll end up with a bloke who has two left feet.' Ruby wore artificial poppies in her curled hair, carefully chosen to match the vibrant colour of her pleated skirt.

Joy felt faint at the idea of being the one to do the asking.

'Take him over there.' Ruby pointed to a regular in the corner – all spiky hair, jutting bones and angles beneath an ill-fitting suit. 'Avoid that one like the plague. But the one over there by the bar is a decent dancer.' Ruby gave Joy a small shove. 'His name's Neville. Go on; off you go.'

Joy feared that her heart would stop out of sheer terror. Mr Dixon's signature tune had morphed into a relaxed ragtime number intended to encourage dancers on to the floor. Couples formed and went into hold. There were swirls of red, blue, green, purple – all the colours of the rainbow – as Ruby gave Joy another shove in the back.

'Do you come here often?' a familiar voice said and

Tommy materialized out of nowhere. He took Joy's hand and led her into the middle of the floor.

'Oh!' she gasped. 'Oh, thank heavens!'

'Corny, eh – "Do you come here often?", "You're a smashing dancer", "You're not so bad yourself!"' Smiling broadly, Tommy parroted some common chat-up lines as he held Joy at a respectful distance, right arm around her waist and leading with his left. 'This is a foxtrot. The clue's in the name – all you have to do is trot along in time to the music. I lead, you follow.'

'I know what a foxtrot is,' Joy said with a touch of pique. She managed to keep up with Tommy even when he made a rapid turn and changed direction to avoid a couple who were throwing themselves into the first dance of the evening.

'Evening, Bernie,' Tommy said to the man in a blue shirt and brown shoes. 'Fancy seeing you here. Evening, Pearl.'

Joy recognized the girl who worked on the fish and chip stall near the Central Pier; she'd often noticed her as she passed to and fro.

'Evening, Tommy!' the pair chorused, eyebrows raised in approval at his choice of partner.

Pearl gave Joy the once-over. It was the stranger in pink, wearing Mavis's dress. Close up she was indeed delicately pretty, as Ida had pointed out – with big brown eyes and amazing cheekbones. 'Someone had better be on his best behaviour!' she cried as Bernie whisked her away.

'Ignore them,' Tommy said. 'You *are* a smashing dancer, by the way – no kidding.'

Joy was starting to relax. She let the music take

47

hold of her body and thrilled to the rapid forward motion. 'I bet you say that to all the girls.'

'No, I mean it. In fact, do you fancy entering tonight's competition and having a crack at that prize money?'

'With you?'

'Yes, why not?' He drew her close and skipped her across the floor.

Blushing furiously, Joy shook her head. 'I've never lindy hopped before.'

As the music slowed, Tommy whirled his blushing partner towards the rows of tables and chairs next to the bar. 'There's always a first time,' he said with a final flourish. 'Anyway, swing dances are dead easy for someone who has natural rhythm.'

'I'll think about it.' Joy sat down with a breathless, dizzy sensation, fanning her face with her hand.

'Drink?' Tommy suggested.

'Yes please – a lemonade.'

And before she knew it, he was pushing his way through the crowd at the bar and a man in Royal Navy uniform approached. He asked Joy to partner him in the Viennese waltz: a classic, old-school dance that she had practised in the privacy of her own attic room. God bless Mr Silvester – thanks to him she had no qualms in accepting the invitation.

'Just one dance,' she explained hastily as she took to the floor with her second partner of the night. 'Then I'll have to get back to my table. My friend is fetching me a drink from the bar.'

By half past eight, as soon as the interval was over, couples were gearing themselves up for the evening's highlight – the much-anticipated swing competition. An MC in a white dinner jacket took to the stage to announce the start. 'Ladies and gentlemen, here's a quick reminder of how the contest will work. There will be three judges: one up here with me and two who will mingle with couples on the dance floor. A tap on the gentleman's shoulder will tell you that you've been eliminated, until only five couples remain. At that point the roaming judges will come up on to the stage to confer with the third judge and then the winners will be announced. So please take your partners. Make sure not to hog the space in the centre and allow the judges to get a good view of all the contestants.'

'Ready?' Pearl asked Bernie.

The lure of a ten-bob note brought him to his feet. If they won, he would wave it under Mick's nose and crow to high heaven. *Who's the sissy now?* he would gloat.

Over by the bar, Tommy stood up and extended his hand to Joy. 'Yes?'

She took a deep breath and allowed him to lead her on to the floor. *Why not? What's the worst that can happen?*

'Relax – it's all about the swing,' Tommy assured her with the broadest of smiles. The feeling that he was really getting somewhere with Joy at last put a spring in his step as he picked a good spot for them to be seen by the judges.

Eddie and Sylvia waited in the shadow cast by the lower balcony. 'Well?' he asked. Her dancing had been under par tonight: lacklustre and slightly behind the beat. 'We don't have to if you don't feel like it.'

'Of course I feel like it,' she snapped. Everyone was looking at them. Head up, smiling, gliding, she walked ahead of Eddie to a spot right under the judges' noses.

Only thirty couples had entered the contest, which meant that many dancers had opted out. Older stalwarts had decided to leave the lindy hop to the more energetic youngsters, while some raw recruits to the world of ballroom feared being made fools of and instead of continuing to dance, they shuffled towards the bar.

The effect, when the music started, was electric. Sixty dancers sprang into action and the floor gave beneath their feet. Face your partner, step to the left and kick, step right and kick, join hands and step forward then back and forward again, all in preparation for the first exuberant swing.

'Now!' Tommy whispered to Joy before flinging her wide with his left arm then drawing her in again.

'Hard as you like!' Pearl hissed at Bernie. *Woo!* A good job he was strong and he'd kept tight hold of her hand; otherwise she could have ended up on her backside.

Eddie took care not to swing Sylvia too far. When he pulled her back in, he saw that her smile was fixed and her eyes glazed. Bounce-kick, bounce-kick; there was no energy there, no enjoyment. 'We'd better take it easy,' he murmured as the couples who surrounded them broke hold then leaned forward to shake their shoulders and wiggle their hips.

'That's grand!' Tommy beamed at Joy as he grabbed her again and improvised an underarm turn. There was no faulting her musicality and he should know:

he'd learned to dance when he was knee high to a grasshopper.

'Steady on!' Pearl gasped when Bernie launched her straight up in the air. He caught her around the waist then spun her – bend the knees, bounce, bounce, bounce, spin!

All was motion. Sylvia tried to focus on Eddie's face but the chandeliers above their heads created a bright blur and the frescoes on the arched ceiling seemed to melt into a swirl of reds, blues and gold. The notes from the Wurlitzer pounded inside her head. She gasped. Eddie failed to hold on to her and she sank to her knees, reaching for support as she fell. She touched smooth fabric and saw a blur of pink before collapsing in a dead faint.

Joy felt a tug on her skirt and looked down in alarm. Sylvia Ellis, of all people, lay senseless at her feet.

'Oh Lord!' Pearl saw what had happened. She let go of Bernie in mid-swing and rushed to the rescue. 'Everyone, stand back!' she cried as Eddie bent over his partner and patted her cheeks in an effort to revive her. 'Sylvia Ellis has fainted. Stand well back and give her space to breathe!'

CHAPTER FOUR

Next morning Pearl scanned the headline of an old newspaper as she and her mother prepared to open their stall at the entrance to Central Pier. It was true what they said: yesterday's news was indeed today's fish and chip wrapper.

'Why did we have to bomb Bremen in the first place?' she wondered aloud as she tore the paper in half. 'It admits here that we suffered losses.'

'Of course we did.' Maria dipped slippery cod fillets into batter, all the while keeping an eye on Elsie at play on the beach. The weather forecast was fine and a fair number of striped deckchairs were already set out on the sand. 'Fritz no doubt spotted our boys coming on his radar – he'd have been ready for us. Don't go too near those donkeys!' She yelled a sharp warning that Elsie blithely ignored.

'The papers never tell us the whole truth,' Pearl grumbled. 'Lord knows what's really happening there or in Egypt – or Malta, for that matter.'

Maria tested the temperature of the fat by dropping a spoonful of batter into the fryer. 'It's a waste of time trying to work it out. All I hope is that Hitler leaves us to get on with our lives here in Blackpool.'

The town had seen little action during the previous couple of years – no one knew why. There had been accidents: the previous year, a German pilot had crashed, been captured and sent to a POW camp. And then, of course, there had been the Seed Street raid the year before that, when Jerry had been returning to base after a raid on Manchester and had disposed of his remaining bombs over Blackpool. However, the town's record for air raids wasn't too bad, considering the RAF trained thousands of recruits at Squires Gate and would therefore seem an obvious target.

Pearl wished that she could be as relaxed as her mother appeared to be. How could Maria overlook the string of concrete air raid shelters along the Golden Mile, ack-ack guns on the beach and sand-bags shoring up the entrances to major buildings, not to mention the strict rationing (luckily fish wasn't on the list), blackout times, Vickers Armstrong factory and RAF troops stationed nearby? War stared you in the face wherever you cared to look.

'Elsie – donkeys!' Maria screeched a second warning.

'I'll go and fetch her,' Pearl decided. She skipped quickly down the steps to the beach, kicked off her sandals then ran through the warm, soft sand towards the donkey man and his group of hard-working animals, decked out with jingling bridles, rosettes, ribbons and well-worn saddles. 'Sorry – is she pestering you for a free ride?' Pearl asked the elderly man.

'No more than usual,' he replied with a toothless grin. Long exposure to the sun had lined his leathery face while his battered tweed suit, worn all year round, was a salt-and-pepper mixture of grey and fawn that merged with the donkeys behind him.

'Sorry.' Apologizing again, Pearl took Elsie by the wrist and marched her firmly along the beach. Yes; a sunny if breezy day was in prospect. When was it not breezy on the north-west coast? The tide was going out, exposing barnacles and limpets clinging to the pier's undercarriage and leaving thick strands of dark, salty bladder wrack swishing around its feet. 'You're not to bother him,' she remonstrated with her sister. 'You stay right here where we can see you and play with your bucket and spade, you hear?'

Back at the stall, Maria served her first customer of the day. 'One of each twice,' she confirmed as she thrust two portions of fish and chips across the counter and took payment. 'Next?'

Pearl rejoined her. 'You'll never guess what happened at the Tower last night,' she mentioned as they went on serving a steady stream of hungry holidaymakers.

'No, I'll never guess,' a phlegmatic Maria agreed. 'Salt and vinegar?' she asked a stout man with a knotted handkerchief perched atop his bald head.

'I'll tell you, then – Sylvia Ellis only caused a kerfuffle by falling down in a dead faint in the middle of the ballroom floor. It meant she and Eddie didn't win the competition for once.'

'Fainted, eh?' Maria cocked an ear. 'That'll be ninepence, please.'

'Yes – fell flat on her back. Eddie had to pick her up and carry her off. I thought at first she was having us on.'

Maria shovelled a portion of chips into a paper carton. 'Why would she do that, pray?'

'We were dancing the lindy hop. Sylvia probably knew she couldn't win. I know, Ma – I'm a horrible person for thinking that way. Actually, it turned out her fainting fit was genuine. She'd had nothing to eat all day – not even a scrap of toast for breakfast.'

'That would do it.' Maria wrapped the chips then took the money. 'So who did win?'

'Not me and Bernie, worse luck. We came third, though, and we've talked about taking a dance lesson or two so we can do better next time. Don't tell Mick, by the way. No, the money went to Tommy Rossi and his partner.'

'Tommy from the circus?' Maria hadn't been expecting this answer. She'd known the Rossi family since they'd first arrived in Blackpool in the early twenties and set up an ice-cream business on the South Shore. Young Tommy had his heart set on clowning his way to the top of the circus ladder; watch out, Doodles and Charlie Cairoli!

'Yes, that Tommy. He claimed winning was a fluke. He danced with a girl in a borrowed dress who lindy hopped the socks off everyone there and they won first prize. Now, what was her name again?'

Joy could scarcely believe the weekend's events: firstly, winning the Tower Ballroom competition with Tommy and now strolling along the beach with him in the morning sun! After the dance he'd walked her home and proposed the outing: 'Meet me tomorrow by Central Pier. Let's go for a walk.' *Somebody, pinch me and wake me up*, she'd thought. She'd accepted Tommy's invitation with a nervous thrill, then spent a restless night wondering how she felt. Was a walk just a walk, or did it imply more? What were Tommy's intentions? Was that a silly question? If only she had someone to talk to, someone who could help set her mind at rest. But Joy had no one.

'I've been thinking,' Tommy said in his jokey way as he took two half-crowns from his pocket. 'The old cogs have been grinding away inside this thick skull and I've decided I'd like you to have all of the money that we won last night.'

'Oh, I couldn't!' Waves breaking on the shoreline and steady blasts of fresh, salty air provided a background to her words. 'You won it with me fair and square.'

'Take it.' He pressed the coins into her hand, recalling the expression of disbelief on Joy's face when the MC had announced the winners – the wide eyes, the round O of her lips. And here it was again: a look of wonderment and innocence. 'Put them in your piggy bank and save them for a rainy day.'

Joy frowned at the words 'piggy bank'. Forcing the cash back into his hand, she drifted towards the water's edge then let the shallow waves curl around her bare feet. A flotilla of Merchant Navy ships sailed south along the horizon towards Liverpool.

'Sorry.' Quickly realizing his blunder, Tommy joined her. 'I didn't mean to put my foot in it. All I'm saying is you probably need the money more than me.'

'Honestly?' Joy spluttered. Her sunny mood had vanished behind a dark cloud. 'And that's you trying to be tactful?'

'It's true, though.' He proffered the coins one more time. 'Come on, don't be so thin-skinned.'

'Thin-skinned!' What was meant to be a pleasant stroll was turning out to be anything but. 'Don't talk down to me, Tommy Rossi. I don't need your money, so there.'

Shoving the half-crowns back in his pocket, Tommy stared intently at her flushed face. 'I'm really sorry,' he insisted. 'I'm an idiot.'

'You are,' she agreed hotly. 'I can fend for myself perfectly well without accepting charity.'

Wow, Joy was really something when she was annoyed! Better not tell her that, though. Tommy strode towards the pier, hands in pockets and paddling ankle-deep. 'I know you can. Anyway, I didn't do it out of the goodness of my heart. I offered you the money cos I hoped we could do it again – I mean, enter the odd competition here and there. And that might involve you taking a few dance lessons.'

'Oh.' Joy was taken aback. The breeze ruffled her hair and she raised both hands to brush stray locks from her cheeks.

'No offence,' Tommy went on. 'You're fine as far as the lindy hop goes, but natural ability's not enough when it comes to more complicated stuff like tango. It involves tricky flicks and kicks and no rise and fall; you need an expert to teach you that.'

'And you can do the tango without lessons, can you?'

'I've already had lessons,' he explained. 'From my mother when I was younger – to keep up the family tradition. My parents went to all the dances back home in Milan. She didn't have a daughter to teach so she roped me in instead.'

'Oh,' Joy said again. 'I didn't realize.'

'How could you?' Instead of walking straight on under the pier, Tommy cut across the beach towards the promenade. 'Fancy some fish and chips?' he called over his shoulder.

Joy ran to catch up with him. 'I don't know what's wrong with me; I don't usually fly off the handle.'

He halted at the steps to the prom. 'Money – it's a touchy subject. Yes or no to fish and chips?'

'No – thanks. I'm not hungry.'

'Right you are.' At the top of the steps Tommy paused to return Pearl's cheery wave from behind her stall.

('I've remembered her name – it's Joy Hebden,' Pearl informed her mother. 'It looks like Tommy has developed a crush on her.')

'Shall I walk you home?' Tommy was prepared to cut his losses. The stroll hadn't worked out as well as he'd planned; better to give Joy some breathing space until their paths happened to cross again.

She nodded then stooped to put on her shoes. 'You're right about the dance lessons,' she admitted quietly. Three bare-legged children armed with buckets and spades sped across their path, squawking in anticipation. 'I've been thinking the same thing myself.'

Tommy brightened. 'And we had a good time last night, didn't we? Mind you, we'll struggle to fit everything in if we intend to carry on – for a start, my boss isn't keen on me taking Saturday nights off.'

'But we could enter competitions elsewhere on a different night. I've heard there's a palais tucked away behind the Winter Gardens and another one on North View Parade.'

'That's not a palais exactly,' Tommy told her, 'that's Cliff Seymour's new studio; he's started holding competitions there once a month. There's one next Thursday.'

'Next Thursday?' Joy was surprised by how much in-the-know Tommy was. 'I wouldn't be ready by then; not if it was one of the formal dances.'

'It's not – I checked. Cliff favours Latin so it'll be the jitterbug.' They reached the corner with Silver Street and waited to cross the road. 'There's a possible fly in the ointment about this coming Thursday, though,' Tommy confided. 'My dad's applied for enemy alien status. That means the government has to issue a certificate to say he doesn't pose a threat. Otherwise they'll intern him on the Isle of Man for the rest of the war.'

Joy looked sharply at Tommy's face to check that he wasn't joking.

Tommy was deadly serious. 'He's Italian. I was born here so I don't have to.'

'That's a worry,' she commiserated.

'You don't know the half of it. If they did end up interning Dad, I'd have to take over the ice-cream business.' A tram rattled by, followed by a truck piled high with sandbags. 'I'd be forced to leave the circus.'

'But you love that job.' As they hurried across the wide road together, Joy caught hold of his hand.

'I do,' he agreed. 'I slap on the war paint and cavort around that ring every night hoping to make people split their sides laughing. What could be better than that?'

'Especially when there's a war on,' Joy agreed.

Tommy delved into his pocket with his free hand as they approached the green door of number 57. 'Do me a favour – take the money and buy those lessons?'

This time Joy accepted the two coins without comment. 'I hope your father's certificate comes through.'

'Me too,' Tommy breathed.

'See you tomorrow at the circus?'

'Yes.' He leaned in to kiss her cheek. 'Tomorrow.'

She felt the prickle of stubble on her skin. So a walk had turned out to be more than just a walk. A kiss on the cheek meant something, surely. Joy's heart pounded as she mounted the steps, turned her key in the lock and opened the door.

Sylvia stayed in bed all morning. Her mother brought in a breakfast tray – a cup of tea and two thin slices of buttered toast with blackberry jam on the side. Sylvia drank the tea and took a couple of bites of toast before pushing the plate away.

Lorna hovered by the bed. 'Try a little more,' she urged.

'No, thank you. I've had quite enough.' Two small bites was all that Sylvia could manage.

'You can't continue like this.' Lorna pulled a chair close to the bed. 'You need to eat to build your strength.'

Sylvia sighed and pulled the covers up to her chin. 'Please don't make a fuss.'

'Don't think I haven't noticed that a sparrow eats more than you do lately.'

'That's not true.' Trust her mother to nag. Sylvia would eat when she wanted to, full stop.

'Then why did you faint last night if it wasn't for lack of food?'

'It was hot, Mother. The lights were too bright and everyone was bumping into me. It was a nightmare.'

'What did you expect? Modern swing is called "dance madness" for a reason – all that vulgar kicking and spinning out of hold. You're giddy enough to give it a go, but I expected Edward to know better.'

Sylvia pulled the bedspread over her face, remembering the humiliating moment when she'd gone weak at the knees and collapsed. She'd come round to find Eddie carrying her from the ballroom down the stairs into the entrance hall and setting her down under a fan-shaped, stained-glass window. Joy had fetched a glass of water while the girl from the fish and chip stall had hovered anxiously in the background. Eddie had persuaded Sylvia to drink then she'd tried to stand; no, not possible. 'Take your time.' Eddie had been patience itself. He'd ordered a taxi and eventually accompanied her home.

Once there, her mother had flapped and fussed. Dear, thoughtful Edward – Lorna had thanked him profusely.

'I'll be fine,' Sylvia insisted now from under the bedspread. 'I just need to take it easy for a day or two.'

Lorna shook her head in exasperation. 'I wish you'd listen for once.'

'Mother!'

'If not to me then to Edward. He's worried about you too.'

'No need. There's nothing wrong with me.' *Please go away!* Sylvia screwed her eyes tight shut.

'I'll leave the tray beside your bed,' Lorna decided after a long silence. Receiving no response, she supposed that Sylvia had gone back to sleep and crept from the room.

Everyone had stared at her – and not in a good way. *Everyone!* Sylvia had seen strange, flickering patterns form inside her eyelids then felt the colour drain from her cheeks. Her knees had buckled. She'd tottered and reached out to save herself before drowning beneath a sea of shocked faces. *What a spectacle!*

And not only that; now her mother was fetching toast with extra jam and Sylvia was expected to eat it. Next it would be Sunday lunch of lamb chops and potatoes then a tea of fish-paste sandwiches followed by tinned peaches with Nestlé's condensed milk – starch and sugar and everything that was bad for your figure. With a sigh of disgust, Sylvia turned on to her side and drew her knees to her chest.

Random thoughts darted in and out of her befuddled brain. Her mother of all people should understand – potatoes and sweet things must be avoided. Everyone knew they piled on the pounds. A dancer had to be careful about what she ate. Sylvia must not be weak and give in to temptation. She was sure that Cliff Seymour would share her point of view. He'd seen the professional dance world from the inside and knew what it took to stay at the top. Cliff would never force food on to her that she didn't want to eat.

There was a knock on her door followed by Eddie's tentative voice asking if it was all right for him to come in.

Sylvia didn't answer. She decided she would talk to

Cliff about the starch and sugar problem when she returned to his studio on Wednesday to be taught how to rumba.

Eddie knocked again. 'Sylvia, may I come in? I've brought you some roses and a bar of Dairy Milk.'

Pushing back the cover and easing herself into a sitting position, she smoothed her hair and drew her bed jacket around her shoulders. 'Yes; I'm decent!' she replied in her light, sing-song voice. Eddie's roses would go into a cut-glass vase on her bedside cabinet but his gift of chocolate was destined for the bin.

CHAPTER FIVE

Eddie scarcely knew what to think. Sylvia had been behaving oddly since his Sunday visit, giving him the cold shoulder when he'd seen her out and about with her chums on Monday night and still refusing to talk about Saturday's fainting incident when he'd called in at the academy after work on Tuesday evening.

'Forget about it,' she'd snapped during a break in the lesson she was teaching on her mother's behalf as it had been Lorna's night to attend *The Pirates of Penzance* with Eddie's father. 'I'm perfectly fine, as you can see.'

She'd certainly looked fine; immaculate as usual in a sleeveless pink blouse and black slacks and with her hair tied up in the ponytail that she currently favoured. But her manner had been chilly and she'd refused to say whether or not they would go to the Tower Ballroom as usual this coming Saturday. 'I don't know if I'll be free,' she'd told him before clapping her hands to gain the attention of her young pupils then lowering the gramophone needle on to an Andrews Sisters recording – chin up, shoulders back, don't look down at your feet, smile!

So it had been left open, to be decided later in the

week. Oh well; Eddie was used to Sylvia blowing hot and cold. Theirs was a tricky relationship – they'd been dance partners from the age of nine, when Eddie's father had first sent him to Lorna for lessons. Eddie had been mesmerized by Sylvia from the start. She seemed to him like a ballerina pirouetting on top of a musical box: graceful, glittering and beyond reach.

Beginner Eddie had learned a wide variety of steps quickly and soon out-performed the other boys in his class. His pairing with Sylvia had been the obvious one – they were of a similar height and build, with outstanding potential, according to Lorna. Outside of dance classes they'd begun to spend time together with their parents' approval. They'd shared an interest in reading and music. Neither had sought other close friendships.

Then they'd reached what Lorna called the 'difficult age'. On his thirteenth birthday Eddie had lost interest in dancing and joined the school football team, where he'd displayed yet more natural ability. Lashings of mud and countless hefty tackles hadn't put him off – he enjoyed the thrill of sprinting down the wing and scoring goals. Meanwhile, Sylvia had fought off the attentions of half a dozen young admirers, none of whom could tango. Her mother had kept her on a tight rein and the boys had fallen by the wayside.

Then suddenly: disaster! Eddie's football team had been 2–0 up on a cold, foggy November afternoon and he'd been preparing to take a free kick when his chest had suddenly tightened and his airways had closed up. He'd taken rasping, shallow breaths and sunk to the ground. By good fortune his father had been among the spectators and had made an immediate diagnosis – Eddie was experiencing a serious asthma attack. Maurice Winter had used an adrenalin inhaler kit – a nebulizer that he kept in his doctor's bag in the boot of his car. Eddie had recovered and the crisis was over, but Maurice, realizing that his son lived under the cloud of further similar attacks, had declared that Eddie was barred forthwith from strenuous outdoor activity.

Of course, Lorna had welcomed Eddie back to the academy with open arms. Sylvia had seemed glad, too; Eddie's illness had brought out a softer, more solicitous side in her. She gave him gifts (a Bing Crosby record and a book about British birds), wrote him affectionate notes and agreed to go to the cinema with him. Kisses and confidences were exchanged.

But Eddie could also fall foul of Sylvia's perfectionist temperament. She would criticize his technique on the dance floor and treat him to an icy look that sent shivers down his spine. According to her, his clothes and hairstyle were behind the times and why would he never come clean and tell her how he felt? 'I'm not a mind reader,' she would say with a petulant toss of her pretty head. Eddie threw the criticism back at her: this was a case of the pot calling the kettle black. A frostiness would set in until she relented and called him 'Eddie, dear' and put her arm around his waist as they walked up King Alfred Road. She would kiss him on the doorstep to the academy.

And so it went on: hot one minute, cold the next, even after war broke out. Lorna was happy to encourage what she saw as a harmless first romance.

Regardless of dire government warnings about the threat of air raids, she put her golden couple through Imperial Society tests that they passed with flying colours. Despite strict petrol rationing, she entered them into competitions and drove them as far afield as Manchester and Liverpool.

Against all odds, ballroom dancing experienced a boom. Lorna's business prospered – after all, there was no shortage of young men in Blackpool, thanks to the RAF base at Squires Gate. Trainee pilots flocking into town in search of female company soon realized the advantages of being able to foxtrot their way across the dance floor with an attractive girl in hold. Eddie watched a fair few of them try it on with Sylvia.

He remembered one handsome older pilot in particular. What did they say about the green-eyed monster? Jealousy had certainly kept Eddie awake for a few nights until the flight lieutenant was duly given his marching orders.

Eddie recollected this as he spent his dinner break walking from the Vickers factory along Squires Gate Lane towards the airfield nearby. At first a breath of fresh air was all he had in mind, but activity on the runways – the take-off of three Coastal Command aircraft in quick succession – drew his attention. The day was warm so he took off his jacket, slung it over his shoulder then leaned against an anti-aircraft gun and watched the planes set off on patrol against German U-boats operating in the Atlantic. The pilots flew low over the brick control tower, close enough for Eddie to make them out in their leather helmets and flying goggles. The men were roughly the same age as him and risked their lives on a daily basis.

'Bloody asthma,' he muttered out loud, frustrated by his failure to play a more active part in the war effort.

He carried on along the lane until he came to a construction gang hard at work on a Bellman hangar. These things went up incredibly quickly; there were now over a hundred of the vast metal sheds, where once there had been flat green fields overlooking sand dunes.

Eddie was taken aback when a crane operator working nearby jumped down from his cab and strode across the uneven ground towards him. He shielded his eyes from the sun in order to make out the man's features.

'Now then, Eddie!' Bernie hailed him from a distance of twenty yards. 'What brings you all the way out here?'

Eddie jerked his thumb towards the factory behind him. 'I work there,' he explained.

Bernie nodded. 'Oh yes, Pearl mentioned it.'

'I'm taking a breather during my dinner break.'

'Good for you. And how's Sylvia? Has she got over falling flat on her face?'

'Sylvia's fine, thanks. Nice of you to ask.'

'I'm not being nice,' Bernie said with a dismissive laugh. 'Pearl will want to know, that's all.' The sound of more planes taking off threatened to drown out the tail end of his explanation so he raised his voice above the roar. 'She's roped me in to being her dance partner again this coming Saturday. If you two enter the competition she reckons we won't stand a chance.'

'I see.' Eddie smiled awkwardly as he noticed a second man in overalls heading in their direction.

'Well?' Bernie asked.

'Well what?'

'Will you and Sylvia be there or won't you?'

'I'm not sure yet.' Recognizing Bernie's brother and guessing by the look on the older man's face that he was annoyed, Eddie cleared his throat by way of warning. 'I'd better be off,' he mumbled as he set off back down the lane.

'Bernie!' Mick hollered.

Bugger it! Bernie gritted his teeth and turned to face the music.

'What the bloody hell do you think you're doing?' Mick challenged.

'Nothing.' Bernie hunched his shoulders and strode towards his crane.

'Don't give me that. I heard you yack-yacking with Mr Twinkle-toes back there – something about a competition?'

'No; you must be hearing things.' *Buggeration!* Bernie was sure that his weak denial wouldn't wash.

Mick realized that he'd jumped to the right conclusion. 'Pearl's not still pestering you about entering dancing contests, is she?'

'No; sod off, Mick.' As Bernie was about to haul himself up into his cab, he felt himself suddenly yanked back by his shoulder and before he knew it he was on his arse.

'Don't try to pull the wool over my eyes.' Mick jerked his brother roughly to his feet. He grew conscious of an audience – two members of his construction crew had downed tools and come close, eager to see some action. Well, Mick wouldn't give them the satisfaction. Instead of brawling in public with Bernie, he hissed at him through clenched teeth. 'I don't want you getting pally with Eddie Winter and his set of nancy boys – do you hear?'

'Eddie Winter's not a nancy boy.' Bernie dusted himself down. 'Anyway, what business is it of yours if I decide to go dancing with Pearl?'

'It *is* my business if you drag the family name into the dirt.' Mick stood with clenched fists, seething with anger. 'We'll sort this out later,' he promised as he shoved Bernie against the side of his cab. Then he turned to the spectators. 'Sorry, lads – the show's over. Everyone, get back to work.'

Pearl read the words of Henry Scott's new sign – 'Scott's Amusement Arcade' in bold red lettering and, underneath, the slogan 'Great Scott: you too could win the jackpot!' – which her father had concocted in what he considered to be a moment of word-play genius.

'Scott's Arcade – Great Scott – get it?' he'd crowed as the sign was erected.

It was certainly eye-catching – Pearl gave him that – and it seemed to be working at the end of this, their opening day. The sign sat within a frame of multicoloured electric light bulbs, winking on and off to attract the attention of couples strolling along the prom and of sunburned, bedraggled families coming up from the beach. It seemed they all had money to burn and the aptly named one-armed bandit was an ideal draw – a tanner to get into the arcade and then as long as they liked to insert coins into slots, hearing them land with a clunk before watching small balls rattle through metal mazes. It was mesmerizing stuff.

Pearl's job had been to encourage those who hesitated. 'Come on, sir – give it a go!' 'What have you got to lose?' 'Madam; you know you want to!' She'd taken over from her father while he went to slake his thirst at the Black Horse on Empire Street, a favourite pub with fairground men, market stallholders and circus performers. 'Keep 'em coming,' Henry had instructed Pearl. 'Show a bit of leg; tell 'em they can win a small fortune.'

'How much?' Pearl had wanted to know.

'Oooh, lots.' He'd promised to be back within the hour but no such luck. Three hours had passed and there was still no sign.

Come early evening, Pearl's heart was no longer in it. She knew that the only one making any money was her father and it felt mean to entice an innocent kid or an elderly granny into the arcade with false promises. The youngsters made a beeline for the Little Mickey machine while the pensioners went for Lucky Star. As for Playball – an overenthusiastic dad had jammed the mechanism and was demanding his money back when Bernie appeared out of nowhere and managed to unscrew the back of the machine, fiddle with its innards and fix it.

'Where did you spring from?' Pearl wanted to know after the angry man had departed with his winnings. Bernie looked dapper in fawn waistcoat and his beloved brown suede shoes.

'I came straight from our house. I saw your dad holding forth outside the Black Horse – looking the worse for wear, as it happens.'

'Tell me something new.' Pearl sighed then shrugged. 'Anyway, where are you headed?'

'Nowhere special,' he fibbed. 'I'm keeping out of Mick's way.'

'Why? What have you done wrong now?' Another of the machines paid out – there was a delighted cry as coins tumbled noisily into the metal dish.

'Nothing. You know what he's like – Mr Know-it-all.' Bernie was still sore about the row at the airfield. It had rankled with him all afternoon and he'd made a quick getaway at the end of his shift. He'd shot home and got washed and changed, determined to avoid the browbeating that would surely come, then set his mind on dropping in on Pearl. 'How long do you have to man the fort here?' he asked her.

'Until someone comes to relieve me.' She stared beseechingly into his eyes. 'I don't suppose . . .?'

'Don't look at me!' Spotting Ernie stuffing his face at Maria's fish and chip stall, he called his name and beckoned him across. 'It's your turn.' He snatched a chip from Ernie's carton. 'No arguments,' he insisted as he stationed the boy by the entrance to the arcade then whisked Pearl along the prom. 'There's no point fluttering those long lashes,' he joked. 'It won't wash with me.'

'It was worth a try.' She laughed and ran to keep up with him. 'Where are we off to, anyway?'

'It's Wednesday,' he remarked as he turned right at the Majestic and hurried her past a row of shops selling dresses that Pearl couldn't afford. 'It so happens that tonight's the night.'

'For what?'

'For you and me to have our first dance lesson. I've only gone and signed us both up at the Lorna Ellis Dance Academy.'

'You haven't!' She gasped at the turnaround. Until now it had been her putting the pressure on him. And Lord, she wasn't dressed for dancing – she was wearing the wrong shoes, the wrong blouse, the wrong everything.

'I have,' he insisted. A flame of rebellion had flared within him. 'Mick can get lost. Once we've polished up our moves we'll prove that we've got what it takes to win one of these competitions.'

'Are you sure?' Pearl pulled at Bernie's hand to slow him down. As they arrived at the studio entrance doubts gave her a bad case of the butterflies. 'Have you thought this through? Are you sure we're good enough?'

'Of course we are.' He oozed confidence. 'Move over, Fred Astaire and Ginger Rogers – make way for Mr Bernie Greene and Miss Pearl Scott, Blackpool's up-and-coming ballroom stars!'

'Good; that's more like it!' Cliff watched Sylvia rotate her slender hips in a figure of eight. 'Don't be shy – swivel like there's no tomorrow.'

Flushed by the exertion, Sylvia followed his instructions. She'd arrived early at Cliff's studio, read the sign that said 'Learn to Dance with Cliff – Live in Your Dreams' and almost changed her mind. Her mother would be furious at the betrayal and Sylvia could all too easily picture the disappointment on Eddie's face, too. *They'll accuse me of going over to the enemy*, she'd thought with a grim smile. *But what do I care? I'm a grown-up and free to choose.*

In this spirit she'd pushed open the door to find Cliff alone in his studio, practising a complicated series of chassés, hops and syncopated steps.

'Why, princess – I wasn't sure you'd come!' Cliff had exclaimed as he completed the sequence. 'I half expected you to back out.'

'Why should I?' she'd retorted. 'I'm more than ready to branch out into Latin. My mother refuses point-blank to teach me, so here I am.' She'd taken off her jacket and put on her heeled dancing shoes then launched straight into the lesson.

'More rotation,' Cliff demanded now. 'Thrust your hips forward and shift your weight – slowly, slowly. Swivel your feet, lead directly through the ball of your foot. Make it hot and steamy; that's the ticket.' He raised the needle from the record. 'Good job!'

Sylvia inhaled deeply. The rise and fall of rumba steps came naturally – they reminded her of waltz and foxtrot. It was the seductive hip rotation that bothered her because it felt unnatural and louche. Could a girl be called louche, or was it a word reserved for men? she wondered. Anyway, that was how it felt.

'Take a breather,' Cliff suggested. Sylvia was unaware of her potential. If only she could rid herself of an obvious prudish streak, she had the perfect body for dancing Latin: long legs that would flick and wrap around her partner and a sinuous torso with arm extensions and back bends to die for. She had perfect musicality and timing to boot. 'When you're ready, we'll try all that in hold.'

'I'm ready.' Sylvia convinced herself that she could succeed at whatever she set her mind to. She would get the rumba right if it killed her.

'Hip to hip, as if we're glued together,' Cliff instructed after he set the record spinning again. He slid his arm around her waist. 'Look me in the eye;

imagine we're about to make mad, passionate love; flick your right foot between my legs; keep to four/four time – perfect!'

Sylvia felt the heat from Cliff's body through her light summer dress. He wore a strong eau de cologne – presumably some kind of aftershave. She stared at his face as they danced until his sharp, angular features started to blur.

'This is a Cuban dance of seduction. You have to imagine it's scorching hot. There are palm trees, a bay with white sand, waves breaking on the shore.' Cliff painted a picture that was hard to resist. 'Now we go out of hold. Snake those hips, shake those shoulders.' He circled Sylvia as she danced alone then came back into hold and swept her round in a series of reverse turns. The music ended in a crackle and a hiss of static.

'Perfect,' Cliff murmured, his lips against Sylvia's cheek.

She felt his warm breath and then the touch of his lips on hers.

He pulled back a fraction to give her a questioning look.

She stared at him, her eyes wide and her heart fluttering wildly. Then, with a sharp intake of breath, she leaned forward and kissed him back.

There were several newcomers to Lorna's lesson that Wednesday evening but, to her surprise, far and away the best couple were Pearl Scott and Bernie Greene. The quickstep was by no means an easy dance to learn – three parts foxtrot and one part Charleston – a combination of short steps at a walk and a run, chassés, jumps and skips, but Pearl and Bernie had taken to it like ducks to water. Bernie, especially, had natural rhythm and fluidity in his movements that reflected his relaxed, cheerful temperament. Pearl had to work a little harder – she was over-eager and tended to rush at things – but she, too, had what it took to become an excellent ballroom dancer.

'I must say, I'm impressed,' Lorna confided during a break in proceedings. Her pianist, Angela Watson – a fair-haired, solidly built, taciturn woman – had gone upstairs to make herself a cup of tea and the studio was buzzing with noise and movement from assorted couples who leaned against the barre or sat catching their breath on a bench near the piano. 'It's not often that I see beginners with such promise.'

'You're kidding, right?' Secretly pleased, Bernie adopted a casual, couldn't-care-less air. He was longing for a ciggie and a pint.

'No, Mr Greene; I'm perfectly serious. I take it you have Pearl to thank for dragging you along?'

Pearl laughed. 'Actually, Bernie was the one who did the dragging.'

'No matter.' Lorna ran a cool gaze over the well-matched pair. Bernie was rough around the edges – and no wonder, given his tough upbringing in the streets behind the Tower. But he was slim and carried himself well; with the right clothes and haircut he could be made perfectly presentable. Pearl's appearance also needed work – it would be better if she grew her hair long enough to pin back in an elegant chignon and she needed to tone down the brash colours and bold floral prints to attain a more sophisticated look. But her face was perfect: heart-shaped and with exceptional grey-green eyes set off by almost jet-black hair. 'You'll come again, I hope?' she prompted. 'If you can master the quickstep, the tango shouldn't be a problem – or the Viennese waltz and the foxtrot, for that matter.'

'I'm not sure about that.' Thrusting his hands in his pockets, Bernie seemed cagey.

Lorna turned to Pearl for a reason.

'For a start, we're both busy people,' Pearl explained.

'Busy, busy,' Bernie echoed. 'Pearl's family run stalls on the Golden Mile and I work at the Pleasure Beach during my time off from Squires Gate.'

'Besides, Bernie's brother isn't too keen,' Pearl elaborated. 'He thinks dancing is for sissies.'

'Only, his word for it is worse,' Bernie added with a knowing wink.

'Then your brother must learn to move with the times,' Lorna said tartly. 'Tell him young men up and down the land crowd into the palais these days, especially on a Saturday night. If nothing else, it's the ideal place to meet people of the opposite sex.'

'I'll tell him,' Bernie promised with a grin. 'Be on the level with us, Mrs Ellis: are me and Pearl really any good?'

'Certainly.'

'Good enough to win competitions?'

Lorna considered her answer carefully. 'It's hard to say. Tonight you've taken your first, tiny steps as a couple and you've demonstrated definite promise.'

'But?' Pearl prompted.

'But, like anything else, success on the dance floor involves a good deal of hard work – on your posture, your timing, your floor craft and many other things.'

'That means lots of lessons before we start earning money, then?' Bernie's mood changed quickly – he was all for walking away.

'Money?' Lorna echoed. 'Forgive me; I assumed we were talking about you performing as amateurs.'

Pearl stepped in quickly. 'We are. Bernie was asking how long it might be before we won a few bob, say at the Empress or the Tower and other local dance halls.'

'Money,' Lorna repeated. Refreshed by her cuppa, Angela had returned and taken up position at the piano so time was short for Lorna to net these talented newcomers who would prove to be a feather in the academy's cap if they went on to succeed in local competitions. 'Let's cut to the chase. To win prize money you will indeed need more tuition from me. And before you say anything, I'm prepared to offer you lessons at a rate well below my normal charges; let's say one shilling.'

'Per couple?' Pearl shot back at her.

'Very well; per couple. For six lessons only. Then we'll reconsider.' Lorna extended her hand to Pearl. 'Oh, and one more thing.' She turned her piercing gaze on Bernie. 'In future, bring the appropriate footwear. Black patent is required for ballroom, so please get rid of the suede.'

CHAPTER SIX

Joy swept spent cigarette butts from under the seats on the lower balcony of the Tower Ballroom while on the floor below a hundred desk clerks and pen-pushers dressed in vests and shorts sweated it out during a PE class provided by their government employers. After a long day working for the Inland Revenue or the Department of Health, the men followed barked instructions with various degrees of enthusiasm – bend, twist, lunge – many with their minds fixed on a pint of cold beer at the Queen's Arms as a reward for their exertions.

'It's meant to be good for them,' Ruby said with a mischievous smile as she mimicked the activity below. ' "Step to the left, now to the right, twist, raise your right knee to the chest, now the left." You'd never think so to look at their faces – it's more "Tow that barge, lift that bale . . ." '

Joy stood up straight to ease the crick in her back. She was coming to the end of her Thursday shift at the ballroom and not especially looking forward to crossing over to the circus, where she would most likely bump into Tommy.

'Come and look at this,' Ruby invited. 'See the tall

one with the dark 'tache, over by the stage? I wouldn't say no to him if he offered.'

'You're married, remember?' Joy was learning not to be shocked by her larger-than-life supervisor's comments and to take everything she said with a pinch of salt.

'So?' Ruby spluttered with laughter as she flicked her duster in Joy's direction. 'I'm kidding. Remind me – how old are you?'

'Seventeen,' Joy replied.

'So you're young and fancy-free – what do you reckon?'

Joy watched the moustachioed man raise his elbows to chest level then twist his muscular torso to the right then left. 'He's all right, I suppose.'

'All right!' Ruby beat her chest with her fists. 'He's a Johnny Weissmuller – "You Tarzan, me Jane!"'

Ruby's chest-beating mime made Joy laugh too as she deposited the contents of her dustpan into a bucket.

'That's better. You've been going around with a face like a wet weekend for days now – I've been wondering what was up.'

'Nothing's up,' Joy fibbed. On Sunday Tommy had kissed her and arranged to see her the following day. But then on Monday, Tuesday and Wednesday he'd gone AWOL. With each day that passed, Joy had felt more confused. Was Tommy avoiding her? Was he waiting for her to make the next move or had he lost interest in following up what she'd felt to be a definite spark between them? In the end she'd resigned herself to the fact that she'd made too much of their brief encounter. *Forget it*, she told herself. *Forget the dance lessons and competitions; forget everything. And yet, and yet . . .*

'Seriously, what's up?' Ruby refused to let the matter drop.

Joy sighed. 'Tommy's been avoiding me,' she confessed. 'We went for a walk on Sunday and I've seen neither hide nor hair of him since.'

'More fool him.' Ruby polished vigorously as she talked. 'Not only do you and Tommy Rossi win the competition out of the blue last Saturday night but you were far and away the best-looking couple there.'

Joy blushed at the compliment. 'I was happy to split the prize money but he insisted on giving me his half – he said I should spend it on dance lessons.'

'That was nice of him.' Ruby waited to hear more.

'We chatted. He said how much he loved the circus and he told me things about his family – how his mother taught him to dance when he was young.'

'And did you kiss?'

Joy hesitated.

'I take that as a yes,' Ruby concluded. 'And now you say that Tommy's ditched you?'

'Yes – no – I don't know.'

'Hmm. Would you like me to have a word with him?'

'No!' Joy gasped. 'Please don't.'

'I will if you like.'

'No thanks; I'd rather let it drop.'

Joy was startled by a sharp blast on the PE instructor's whistle to mark the end of the class. As the weary men collected their belongings and drifted off, Ruby signalled to her team that they too were free to go. 'It's Tommy's loss, not yours,' she reminded Joy as they parted.

Reflecting on her new friend's words of wisdom, Joy hurried along the service corridor that connected the ballroom to the circus ring. Ruby was right: Joy should get over Tommy's disappearing act. In fact, she would go ahead with the dance lessons regardless – she resolved to book a block of six the next time she went to work for Lorna Ellis.

In better spirits, she collected her cleaning items from the cupboard then carried on down the steps towards the empty circus arena without acknowledging the small team of Polish trapeze artists – three men whose names Joy didn't know and two girls called Irena and Alina – gathered under the archway leading to dressing rooms beyond. Clad in figure-hugging rehearsal leotards, they bounded into the ring as Joy started to clean. Two of the men dipped their hands and feet into a box of chalky resin before scaling a vertical rope ladder to perch on narrow trapezes, swiftly followed by the girls. The other man stayed on the ground to check the safety net.

Joy did her best to mind her own business – while the acrobats executed breathtaking feats above her head, she cleared toffee wrappers from under the first row of seats. The men hung upside down from their trapezes waiting for Alina and Irena to catch hold of their hands. Then they swung, meeting in the middle to allow the girls to somersault in mid-air and switch partners before continuing the pendulum arc. The man on the ground stood hands on hips, casting a critical eye over the daredevil aerial routines.

'Not for a king's ransom, eh?' a familiar voice asked Joy.

She turned to see Tommy dressed in civvies – no tie and in an open-necked shirt and casual trousers. Her heart missed a couple of beats then fluttered back into action.

'Sorry if I made you jump.'

Alina lost her grip and plummeted into the safety net where she bounced awkwardly before steadying herself. The man on the ground ordered her back up the ladder. 'Again!' he yelled harshly.

'What's the matter? You look as if you've seen a ghost,' Tommy told Joy.

'I wasn't expecting . . .'

'I'm sorry I haven't been in touch. I was in Liverpool with my dad,' Tommy explained in a rush. 'The police mislaid our documents so we had to go in front of the tribunal in person to prove that he'd lived in England for more than twenty years.'

'I see.' Joy swallowed her surprise. 'Did it turn out all right?'

'Yes, eventually.' The experience had shaken Tommy. 'The panel wanted to look into Dad's possible links to the Italian fascists.' He shuffled uncomfortably as he watched Joy's shocked reaction.

'Surely not!' she cried.

'Dad denied it, but it was touch-and-go.'

'I see.' The conversation jerked forward. This was a serious matter and Joy scarcely knew what to think.

'Dad explained that he'd borrowed a fascist badge just once or twice, solely to gain entry to an event in one of the major dance halls in Milan. He swore he had no official links with the party.'

Joy nodded earnestly. 'Of course not.'

'He informed the tribunal that he'd joined the ARP here in Blackpool. He volunteers as a warden three nights a week to help enforce the blackout. He finished by demanding to know what more proof they needed of whose side he was on.'

'Such a worry for you all.' Joy gave a loud, sympathetic sigh.

'There was a two-day delay but in the end the panel classed Dad as Category B.'

'What does that mean?'

'No internment, thank God,' Tommy told her. 'They warned us they'd keep a close eye on him but he's free to carry on running his business for the time being.'

'So all's well.' Tommy wouldn't have to leave the circus after all. As the four acrobats reached the end of their routine and dropped safely into the net, Joy had a peculiar sense that her mood this past week had swung and jiggled as wildly as the abandoned trapezes above their heads. There'd been elation, confusion, despair and now there was a glimmer of hope. 'I'm glad,' she told Tommy.

'I've missed seeing you,' he confessed with a nervous smile.

'Me too.'

'I mean it.' He watched Joy's face turn pink as she went back to her work. 'I was scared you'd give up on me.'

'In what way?' She began to see that the habitual cheeky smile was a kind of mask that Tommy adopted to hide his feelings.

'You know – I wasn't around on Monday like I

promised so I thought you might go off and find yourself a new partner.'

'No, I didn't do that.' Joy felt a fresh flicker of disappointment. Is that all she was to Tommy: a dance partner?

'That's good, then. But I have to work tonight to make up for the shifts I missed, so any dance lessons will have to wait.'

'I could book one for tomorrow evening if you're free.'

'No, I'm not, worse luck. But we could take a short stroll after you've finished here, before my evening show.' Holding his breath, Tommy waited for her reply.

Joy nodded. Shoots of hope took root.

And that was how Tommy and Joy took their second walk, hand in hand, at the same time as animal trainer Vic Marsden led four of his elephants from their subterranean stables under the Tower, holding up trams, buses and cars as the stately beasts processed across the promenade then down the concrete slipway on to the beach for their evening exercise.

Joy stopped to stare at the magnificent, obedient creatures, each one's trunk curled around the tail of the one in front, their enormous flat feet plodding through the soft sand, huge ears slowly flapping. 'Am I dreaming?' she whispered.

'No, it's real.' Tommy squeezed her hand. 'You've seen elephants on the beach before, haven't you? And lots else besides. Come to sunny Blackpool and leave your worries behind – that's what the adverts say.'

Men and girls flew through the air; elephants

kicked up sand in their slow, sedate progress to the water's edge; waves lapped the shore and two young people delighted in each other's company. Who knew what tomorrow might hold?

'Yes; what do you want?' Sylvia glared at Joy as she opened the door and found their young cleaner hovering in the entrance to the studio. 'If you're waiting for your wage, I don't know anything about it. You must ask my mother.'

'No, it's not that.' Joy stepped to the side to let Sylvia pass. 'I've booked a ballroom lesson here.'

Sylvia was taken aback. 'Come again?'

Sylvia's look of astonishment seemed intended to cut Joy down to half her actual size. 'For this evening,' she faltered.

'So you're not here to work?'

'No, I did my job this morning. Mrs Ellis told me to come back for my first lesson at six o'clock.'

Taking in the information with raised eyebrows, Sylvia looked Joy up and down. According to Eddie, this was the girl who'd upstaged her by winning the lindy hop competition the previous Saturday, when she'd been almost unrecognizable with her hair pinned up and wearing a shiny pink dress. Someone must have waved a magic wand – gone was the colourless, dowdy nonentity and in her place had been a glamorous version swinging and twirling in the arms of Tommy Rossi, a circus performer whose name Sylvia vaguely recognized. Now her newest rival had arrived at the studio in a short-sleeved, pale-green blouse and a straight skirt that emphasized her slim waist and narrow hips – not showy but decidedly attractive, especially with her thick, dark hair swept back from her face. 'I take it my mother outlined the cost of the lessons?' she asked archly.

'Yes, thank you,' Joy replied stiffly.

'Then you'd better go in and join the others.' Sylvia carried on up the stairs towards the flat. With a twinge of guilt, she remembered that Joy Hebden had been one of the people who'd stepped in to help during the disastrous fainting incident. *Perhaps I ought to have thanked her.* The pang of conscience soon passed, however. If Joy proved to be a serious rival in the long term, it was better for Sylvia to keep her at arm's length from the start.

Inside the well-lit studio Joy encountered a gathering of equally nervous pupils – more girls than men – bunched together by the piano where a stout, straight-backed woman in twinset and pearls sat on a stool arranging her sheet music. Lorna Ellis was nowhere to be seen.

'It's Joy, isn't it?' One of the girls split away from the group and introduced herself. 'I'm Pearl – Pearl Scott; remember me from last Saturday? Is this your first time here?'

'It is,' Joy admitted shakily.

'This is my second. Great minds think alike, eh? Did you come with Tommy?'

'No – he has to work, worse luck.'

'That's a pity.' Pearl linked arms and dragged Joy across the room to introduce her to Bernie, who leaned against a wall smoking a cigarette. 'Feel free to borrow him,' Pearl encouraged. 'I mean it – he's yours any time you want.'

'Man for hire,' Bernie quipped, then grinned at an

anxious-looking Joy. 'Don't worry – it'll be a doddle,' he promised. 'If I can learn the old waltz, anyone can.'

Joy took a deep breath. She'd screwed up her courage to come here and running into Sylvia in the hallway had knocked what little confidence she had. She felt awkward and out of her depth despite Pearl and Bernie's friendliness.

'This is a big group,' Pearl rattled on with rapid-fire comments. 'Lorna and Sylvia Ellis must be making money hand over fist. They'll both be teaching tonight. Don't be put off – Bernie and I found during our first lesson that Lorna's bark is worse than her bite and as for Sylvia, just ignore the hoity-toity act and follow what she does.'

The door to the studio opened when Pearl was in mid-flow and their instructors entered. There was an immediate silence, followed by a trill of high notes from the pianist and an order from Lorna for everyone to select a partner.

As a girl of above-average height in a room where women outnumbered men, Joy expected to be partnered with one of the smaller girls and to take the man's role, but instead she was quickly claimed by a good-looking man in a patterned sweater and wide black slacks.

'Shall we?' he asked as he led her into the centre of the room. 'I'm Terry Liddle, by the way.'

'Joy Hebden,' she replied in a low voice.

'I'm a first-timer here,' he confessed with an amused glint in his clear grey eyes. 'We're about to find out if I have two left feet.'

Terry was tall – well above six foot – and he oozed

confidence. There was a man-of-the-world air about him; his fair hair was stylishly cut with a wavy forelock that was long enough to curl down over his forehead, and the zig-zag pattern on his blue-and-cream jumper was bold. Joy noticed his shoes: black and polished to perfection.

'It's my first time here, too,' she confessed. 'I've always wanted to learn but I never had the chance until now.'

Terry glanced around the studio to check that everyone else had found a partner. 'Keep those jitters in check,' he murmured under his breath. 'I'm sure we'll be fine.'

Sylvia and Lorna, both dressed in trim blouses, trousers and shoes with small heels, and with their hair worn high on their heads in classic dance-mistress style, took up position at the front of the room. 'Good evening, everybody.' Lorna projected her voice to fill the room. 'And a special welcome to those of you who are new here tonight. As this class contains many beginners, we will start with basic moves for the modern English waltz in which we move diagonally across the floor in a counter-clockwise direction. The tempo is a strict thirty bars per minute.'

As her mother reeled off the standard introduction, Sylvia stood nearby with a bored expression. Because of the number who had signed up for the class she'd been press-ganged into sharing the teaching at the last minute. 'I have other plans,' she'd told Lorna.

'Then cancel them,' had been the sharp retort.

With one hand resting lightly on the top of

Angela's piano, Lorna continued her usual spiel. 'The modern waltz involves undulations and rapid changes in speed; the man leads with a powerful body swing on the first beat of each bar, followed by a sway towards the centre of the turn, rising high on the toes during the second and third beats.'

'Blimey!' Bernie said under his breath to Pearl. 'What's she on about?'

'Behave yourself,' Pearl hissed. 'I'm trying to concentrate.'

'The basic figures are straightforward, changes of weight are regular and the tempo is slow.'

Sylvia raised a hand to her mouth to hide a yawn. At this rate they'd never finish on time for her to meet Cliff at eight.

'May I borrow you for a second?' Lorna chose the man closest to hand, who happened to be Terry. 'This is what we call a close hold.' She demonstrated by placing her partner's right hand on her left shoulder blade then stretching his left arm out to the side. 'Please copy,' she said as she returned Terry to Joy with a gracious smile.

'Willingly,' Terry said with a wink as he slid a hand around Joy's waist.

Sylvia stepped forward to adjust his hold. 'Higher,' she instructed sternly. 'Pay attention – hand on the shoulder blade, not the waist.'

'Whoops!' Terry pulled Joy closer and awaited further instructions.

'Turn the head to the side, chin up.' Sylvia moved on to correct Pearl's stance then concentrated on the next couple. Lord, people were such fools; unable to follow the simplest instruction!

'I'm browned off,' Bernie complained as Lorna lectured them on the finer points of the natural turn. 'This is bloody boring compared with last time.'

Pearl had to agree. She pulled a face and murmured an apology.

'What do you do here in Blackpool?' Terry asked Joy as they practised their first natural turn – one-two-three, one-two-three. Step forward, to the side, feet together and repeat. No beginner after all, he moved smoothly and strongly across the floor, all mention of two left feet forgotten.

'I'm a cleaner.' She hadn't expected to dance with a handsome stranger with twinkling grey eyes whose hand kept slipping out of position and who drew her closer with every step. 'What about you?'

'Oh, this and that,' Terry countered. 'As a matter of fact, I've just taken a job at the lido on South Shore – you know, near the pier. I'm new to town so these dance lessons are a way of getting to know people.'

Joy knew the open-air baths well from the outside, though she'd never swum there. They were said to be the biggest in the world and copied an Italian style of architecture that drew the crowds in huge numbers. 'I live on that side of town,' she mentioned as they executed a quarter turn.

'As it happens, so do I.' Terry steered Joy between two other couples who were fumbling and stepping on each other's feet. 'On Silver Street.'

'What number Silver Street?'

'Number fifty-seven; Iris Grigg's boarding house.'

Joy came to a sudden halt. 'Really and truly? Why, I live there too!'

' "Of all the boarding houses in all the towns in all

the world . . ." Or should that be "gin joints"?' Grinning, Terry turned her towards the floor-to-ceiling mirror. 'Actually, I know you do,' he confessed as he studied their reflections and found them satisfactory – Joy's natural grace and elegance was a good foil for his strong masculine style. 'I've seen you coming and going.' In fact, he'd observed from his first-floor room as Joy had stood on the doorstep with her diffident, dark-haired companion. The young couple had exchanged chaste kisses; very sweet. Tonight he'd recognized her straight away as she'd made her awkward solo entrance into the dance studio and he'd decided on the spot to become her dance partner for the evening.

'I haven't seen you there,' she told him.

'And now the reverse turn,' Lorna announced as couples mastered the basic steps. 'Gentlemen begin with the left foot forward, ladies with the right foot back.'

Sylvia glided between the dancers, adjusting Bernie's hold and nodding at Terry to acknowledge that he'd got the hang of it. She wondered who the newcomer was as she went on to the next couple. Joy's partner was strikingly good-looking and a smooth mover – quite the sophisticate. Tommy the circus clown was certainly no match for this tall, handsome stranger.

'What do you make of our landlady?' Terry had enjoyed Joy's open-mouthed astonishment. 'Personally, I'd rather do battle with Goering himself than cross swords with Iris.'

'She's fierce,' Joy agreed. 'When did you move in?'

'Just over a week ago. The new job started on Monday.'

'Very good, you two.' Lorna's eagle eye had picked out Terry and Joy. Then she seized on Pearl and Bernie for more praise. 'Excellent footwork and line,' she told them. 'A little more polish and better presentation are all that's required.'

'What did I tell you?' Bernie turned Pearl with extra flourish and zest.

'You've changed your tune,' she giggled.

'So what? Roll on the next competition is what I say.'

Pearl felt she was floating on air. After a slow start, Lorna's lesson had been crammed with tips on how to improve their technique. Of course, there was still a lot to learn in their five remaining sessions. 'You're glad we came?' she asked.

'Over the moon,' Bernie declared as the class drew to a close. It was true; dancing with Pearl had given his mood a big boost after the problems he'd been having with his brother.

'Wait outside – I'll join you in a tick.' Pearl headed to the ladies' cloakroom close to the front door where she found Sylvia surreptitiously changing from slacks and blouse into her pale-green summer dress. As Sylvia raised her arms to slip the dress over her head, Pearl was shocked to see the clear outline of her ribcage. *Too thin!* she thought with a slight shudder.

Meanwhile, Joy emerged from a cubicle to hear Pearl offering to help Sylvia with her zip. She'd nipped into the cloakroom after thanking Terry and attempting to say goodnight. 'Thank *you*,' he'd replied, all charm and smiles. He'd insisted on waiting for her and walking her home.

'Drat!' Sylvia remembered that she'd forgotten her

house key. 'If I go upstairs and Mummy sees me, she's bound to give me the third degree – where are you going at this hour, who with, when will you be back?'

'Here; take mine.' Joy removed the King Alfred Road key from her key ring and handed it to Sylvia. 'You can give it back to me the next time I see you.'

'Bless you.' Sylvia slipped the key into her bag before peering into the mirror and pinching her cheeks to create some colour. 'I'm sorry I was off with you earlier and, by the way, who was that dreamboat you were partnered with tonight?'

'His name's Terry Liddle. We live at the same boarding house on Silver Street.'

'Lucky you.' Sylvia moved on quickly. 'Now, girls; not a word to Mother about this little escapade if she happens to ask. I pretended I was going straight up to my room for an early night.'

'Cross my heart,' Pearl promised. *Too thin by half, too pale, too frantic.*

'Joy?' Sylvia prompted.

'I promise.' Joy reluctantly agreed to be an accomplice.

Leaving the cloakroom, the three girls were relieved to find that Lorna was still in the studio with Angela, discussing music for their next lesson. One by one they slipped out on to the street and merged with the steady trickle of holidaymakers heading towards the promenade.

Collaring Pearl, Bernie invited her to drop in at the Queen's Arms with him. 'My pal Joe Taylor just popped in there for a swift half,' he explained. 'With a bit of luck he'll buy us a drink.'

'Pull the other one.' Pearl wrinkled her nose. 'This

is your way of not having to face the music at home.'
The spectre of Mick obviously loomed large.

'What if it is?' Bernie shrugged. 'Actually, I've been thinking I might spend a few nights at Joe's place until the dust settles.'

'Is it as bad as that?' Pearl linked arms with Bernie and they sashayed down the street. 'Listen; if ever you want to back out of dancing with me, I'll understand,' she assured him.

'I don't,' he said in a flash. He wouldn't be bullied. Anyway, he'd experienced an unexpectedly pleasant feeling when he waltzed with Pearl. He liked the look on her face when he whirled her around: all gleeful and lit up like the Illuminations. 'I don't,' he repeated. 'I want us to carry on and to hell with Mick.'

'Right you are.' It was the answer Pearl had wanted to hear as they joined the short queue outside the pub. *Live for today and let tomorrow take care of itself.*

'Here you are at last!' Back at the door into the academy, Terry stepped forward as Joy emerged from the cloakroom. 'Here was me thinking you'd sloped off without me,' he said, making a show of offering her his arm.

'You really didn't have to wait.' Embarrassed, Joy fixed her gaze on the pavement.

'I didn't have to but I wanted to. Walking home will give us chance to get better acquainted.'

Sylvia slipped Joy a knowing look before picking up pace and threading through the crowd. After tonight she really must amend her view of their mousy cleaner.

'So, Joy, have you always lived in Blackpool?' Terry asked, smooth as silk. 'Do you have any brothers and sisters? Where do your parents live?' A fresh breeze blew off the sea and the evening sun cast a rosy light on the shop fronts, hotels and government offices that lined the street and on the sandbag barricade at the entrance to the Majestic Hotel. Joy's answers were monosyllabic but revealing. Terry learned a lot and gave nothing away.

Meanwhile, Sylvia took her sunglasses from her bag, perched them on her small, finely shaped nose then hurried on ahead of the crowd. It was one thing to be late for Eddie, who was used to her scatter-brained ways, but quite another to keep Cliff waiting. She glanced at her watch: ten minutes past eight. Getting changed had cost her a full five minutes.

Cliff sat in the green, open-topped sports car that he'd borrowed for the night from a garage mechanic friend who owed him a favour. 'Bring her back in one piece,' Bert Porter had insisted as he'd begrudgingly handed over the keys. 'She belongs to my boss; he'll have my guts for garters if there's so much as a scratch on her.'

Cliff had parked outside the entrance to the Majestic at eight o'clock prompt and passed the time by watching the comings and goings along the prom. Herds of holidaymakers paid their sixpences to pass through turnstiles for the end-of-the-pier show. *Like sheep*, Cliff observed as he flicked the stub of his cigarette into the gutter. He'd give Sylvia another five minutes, tops.

Good Lord – a shiny, racing-green Morgan! Sylvia spotted Cliff's car parked on the corner. The top was down and he lounged back in his seat with his head turned in the direction of the seafront. For a split second she hesitated. 'Meet me,' he'd cajoled at the end of their rumba lesson. And oh, the kiss, the sharp intake of breath, the tingle as their lips had touched! 'Tomorrow,' he'd whispered. 'We'll go for a spin in my car – up the coast to Cleveleys.'

She'd said yes in a flash but now she held back. Why? Cliff was here, as promised, at the wheel of a snazzy sports car, ready to whisk her along the coast road in the setting sun. What was wrong with that? *Nothing!* Sylvia decided as he spotted her in his rear-view mirror then leaned over to open the passenger-side door. She slid in gracefully, in full view of Pearl and Bernie queuing to go into the Queen's Arms and of Joy and her handsome new dance partner turning the corner on to the prom.

'Hello, princess.' Cliff flicked his lighter with his thumb and lit a cigarette. The small blue flame illuminated his sharp profile. 'What kept you? No, never mind – you're here now.'

He turned on the engine, pressed his foot on the clutch and rammed the gear stick into position before roaring away from the kerb. 'I chatted on the phone to Mitch Burns – an old friend of mine from London.'

'What about?' The Morgan dodged in and out of slower traffic.

'About you, princess. I said I'd found him the best little ballroom dancer in the North of England if he was interested.' With his foot hard down on the accelerator, Cliff glanced sideways to judge Sylvia's reaction – up through second and third into top gear.

'And was he?' She swayed towards him as the car took a bend at speed.

'Maybe,' he teased. 'Mitch said you sounded promising but he'd have to see you in the flesh before he made any decision. It turns out we won't have to travel down to London either – he said I should arrange for it to happen the next time he was in this neck of the woods.'

'Excellent!' Behind her sunglasses, Sylvia's blue eyes sparkled. *The best little ballroom dancer in the North of England.* Cliff was certainly no slouch in the flattery department. As for his 'old friend' Mitch; well, time alone would tell.

The road opened out as Sylvia and Cliff left the town behind. Semi-detached houses gave way to bungalows then to fields on one side and to cliffs dropping away vertically on the other, with white waves crashing on to dark rocks below.

CHAPTER SEVEN

Pearl and her family were up early. Saturday was the busiest day of the week for the Scotts, when day trippers arrived by the coach load to sample Blackpool's bright delights. Maria would be bound to sell out of fish and chips and Henry's arcade would be crammed with visitors queuing up to fling away their hard-earned cash.

'Wilf stole my sausage!' Elsie wailed as she and her two brothers wolfed down their breakfast.

'Didn't.' The culprit swallowed the evidence in two swift gulps. He jumped up from the table, grabbed his canvas bag full of newspapers and set off on his morning round. The door slammed behind him as their mother flipped her own sausage on to Elsie's plate.

Pearl gave a wide yawn and watched her father shave at the kitchen sink – he wielded a soft, soapy brush in his left hand and a cut-throat razor in the right. A small mirror was perched on a shelf next to canisters of flour, sugar and salt. Henry's braces dangled from his waist and his vest exposed his broad shoulders and hairy, muscular arms – an off-putting sight at the breakfast table, to be sure.

'You need a haircut,' Maria remarked as she dumped dirty plates in the sink.

'I'll get one later.' Henry scraped the razor down his cheek. 'Ernie, I want you on the door at the arcade this morning.'

'Why not Pearl?' Ernie complained.

'I'm busy, that's why not.' Pearl yawned again and stretched. She'd had a late night last night, out dancing with Bernie and afterwards drinking at the Queen's Arms. The two of them were getting on like a house on fire, spending more and more time in each other's company.

'Busy doing what?' Ernie demanded over a sudden, loud knock on the door.

'I'll get that,' Pearl said quickly. She dashed down the corridor to open it, only to be unceremoniously shoved aside by an angry Mick Greene.

'Where is he?' Mick stormed ahead of Pearl into the kitchen.

Henry carried on shaving without turning to greet their visitor. Elsie and Ernie slid out of the house by the back door while Maria faced Mick, hands on hips. 'Who are you on about?' she demanded.

'Come off it; you know who I mean.' Mick cast an angry glance over his shoulder at Pearl. 'That brother of mine has done a vanishing act, as if you didn't know.' He filled the small kitchen with his glowering, accusatory presence.

There was a series of quiet scrapes as Henry methodically drew the razor across his chin. Maria tilted her head to one side. 'And what makes you think we know where your brother is?'

'If you don't then she does.' Mick jerked his thumb towards Pearl. 'They're thick as thieves, those two.'

'Pearl?' Maria's voice was calm.

Pearl looked her mother in the eye. 'Search me,' she said with a shrug.

Maria advanced two steps towards Mick. 'You heard her.'

'She's a bloody liar! Bernie hasn't been home for days and I damn well know she knows where he's stopping. He's buggered off from work early two days on the trot, God knows where. All because he's turned sissy on me and started taking dance lessons with Miss Butter-wouldn't-melt here – I got that much out of him at least.'

Henry dipped his razor in a bowl of warm water, wiped it carefully then dabbed his face with a towel.

'Pearl?' Maria asked again.

'Yes, I go dancing with Bernie,' she conceded. 'But I'm not his keeper.'

'Bloody hell – see, she knows where he is!' Red in the face, Mick swung round to confront Pearl directly, knocking over a chair as he did so.

Pearl's eyes flashed. How dare he march in here with his muscles bulging and spittle forming on his lips?

'Spit it out!' Mick yelled.

Henry put down the towel then picked up the chair and carefully set it straight. There was another scrape as he pushed it under the table.

'Tell me where he's holed up or I'll—'

Henry moved swiftly. With the whiff of shaving soap wafting through the air, he came up behind Mick and

101

hooked his arm around his neck, yanking him back so savagely that he lifted him clean off his feet before dumping him on the floor. Mick lay sprawled against the table leg. Without saying a word, Henry hauled him upright then thrust him backwards out of the room and down the corridor. Mick wrestled free and threw a punch without landing it. Henry punched him back, smack on the chin, a blow that sent Mick reeling out of the front door where he toppled down the two steps on to the pavement and landed flat on his back.

Pearl and Maria heard the slam of the door.

'Bloody idiot.' Henry's two-word dismissal signalled the end of the matter. He stomped upstairs to finish getting dressed.

Maria went on clearing the table. 'Better warn Bernie that his brother's on the warpath,' she told Pearl in the same unruffled voice. 'And tell him your father's gone and made things worse.'

Pearl's first port of call was Joe Taylor's fruit and veg market stall. She found Bernie's good-natured pal transferring allotment-grown potatoes, rhubarb, cucumbers, tomatoes and lettuces from cart to stall, whistling as he worked. When he saw Pearl he picked up a spud and chucked it at her. 'Butter fingers!' he called when she fumbled the catch.

'Stop mucking about – I haven't got time,' a breathless Pearl protested. She'd flung on a cardigan over her cotton dress before dashing from the house. 'I'm looking for Bernie.'

Other market men went on preparing for the day's business. Most were in shirtsleeves and braces, many wearing flat caps tilted back on their heads. There was a general rumble of cart wheels over cobbles and the flap of canvas awnings as they set up their stalls for the day.

'If it isn't love's young dream.' Joe winked at Pearl.

'Lay off, Joe – I need to know where he is. Is he still at your house?'

Joe shook his head then lifted his cap to scratch his head. 'Search me. What do you want him for? Can't bear to let lover-boy out of your sight for five minutes, eh?'

'He's not my lover-boy and you know it.'

'If you say so.' Joe went on stacking lettuces.

'This is serious,' Pearl insisted. 'I need to warn Bernie that Mick came banging on our door. He's in a bad mood.'

'Tell me summat new.'

'Even worse than usual, because of us – Bernie and me – learning to dance.'

'Aye aye!' Bill Norton, Joe's neighbouring stallholder – a burly type with a rough, growly voice – barged in with a comment. 'A little bird told me that you'd been leading young Bernie astray.'

Pearl ignored him. 'Joe, I know that he's been staying with you since Thursday.'

'Aye, too frit to go home and face the music,' Bill grunted. 'Don't look at me like that – it's common knowledge.'

'Have you tried the Pleasure Beach?' Joe suggested helpfully.

'No, it's not open yet.' But it was an idea that Pearl would swiftly follow up. Thanking Joe, she dashed down a side street on to the promenade, where she headed south. Five minutes later she managed to charm her way past the nightwatchman who was handing over to the daytime security team at the funfair's entrance. 'I left my handbag here last night – not sure where – maybe under my seat in the casino – mind if I take a quick look?' On she sped with their blessing, straight past the low, white-fronted casino building then skirting the empty boating pool, with the rise and fall of the Big Dipper towering over everything. All was silent in the clear morning light.

'Bernie, are you there?' Pearl called out as she approached the waltzers. It was possible that he'd arrived early to do some maintenance work on the ride that he helped to run. She stepped up on to the undulating wooden platform and shouted his name again. There was no reply – only the screech of a row of gulls perched on top of the entrance to the ghost train – so Pearl sat down heavily in the nearest waltzer to catch her breath. Her weight made the car spin slowly. What next? Pearl closed her eyes and felt it spin faster and when she opened them again she was surprised to see Bernie doing the spinning and staring down at her.

'Don't – you'll make me dizzy.'

'That's the idea, isn't it?' Bernie spun again then jumped in beside her. He was his usual jokey self, with the light of laughter in his eyes and playing across his lips. He spread both arms along the high, padded back of the curved seat. 'What's up?'

The cup gradually slowed to a halt. Something disturbed the seagulls and they rose from the ghost train roof and flapped away. 'Mick is what's up.'

'Oh, blimey – what's he done now?' The smile vanished and Bernie moved closer.

'He came to ours at the crack of dawn looking for you. My dad thumped him.' Pearl didn't soften her account.

'Henry did what?'

'Thumped him,' she repeated. 'Mick threatened me, demanding to know where you were. I didn't tell him,' she added quickly.

'Thanks – I owe you one.' Bernie narrowed his eyes and nodded. His mind flashed through two obvious options. One, he could carry on lying low and wait for his brother's temper to cool, as planned. Two, he could come out into the open and thrash things out with him, after which Bernie would pack his belongings and find new digs. This was the better of the two choices, he decided.

'I've had a belly full of Mick ordering me about,' he told Pearl. 'And I won't stand for him barging into your house and making threats against you.'

'Are you sure?'

'Damned sure. I've been under his thumb for long enough – it's time I stood up to him.'

'But if you two fall out you could lose your job – he's your foreman; he could get you the sack from Squires Gate any time he wanted. And where would you live? Could you carry on staying at Joe's?'

'That's for me to sort out,' Bernie argued. 'Anyway, you see plenty of vacancies advertised in windows. I can easily find somewhere.'

'Wouldn't it be better to patch things up?' Pearl was against him making any rash decisions. 'Mick's all the family you've got.'

'Worse luck.' Bernie leaned his head back against the seat. 'Ever since we lost Mum and Dad in the accident, I've bent over backwards trying not to upset that damned brother of mine. He never really got over losing them; he just covers it up with the tough-guy routine and with drinking and throwing his weight around.'

The 'accident', two years earlier, was Bernie's way of describing the death of his parents, who had been unlucky enough to have been passing through Blackpool North Station late at night when Jerry dropped a dozen high-explosive bombs in the area. The theory was that the German pilot had flown in low and followed the gleam of the railway tracks, targeting the station but not much caring about accuracy. Robert and Glenda Greene had been among the victims.

'It can't be much fun,' Pearl sympathized.

'Mick and me will never see eye to eye.' Bernie had made up his mind. 'He's due here in an hour to do a stint on the bumper cars. I'll talk to him then.'

'I'm worried about how he'll take it. Would you like me to stick around?'

'No. What good would that do?'

She touched Bernie's knee with her fingertips. 'But if I hadn't roped you in to dancing at the Tower this wouldn't be happening. I feel that it's partly my fault.'

'You didn't rope me in to anything.' Putting his hand over hers, he lowered his voice to a murmur. 'I was as keen as you were.'

'Were you?' she whispered. *Were you really?* Pearl stared at Bernie, considering whether or not he was kidding. No, he was serious.

Her eyes were green as the sea sparkling in the sun;

a bloke could get lost in eyes like Pearl's. 'Yes; it meant I got to spend more time with you.'

Pearl gave a soft gasp of realization.

'I'll talk to Mick.' With an abrupt change of mood Bernie squeezed her hand then stood up. 'Where will you be later today?'

'I'm working at the arcade from noon until six.'

'I'll come and find you,' he promised. 'And don't worry; everything will work out just fine.'

'Edward, come in.' Lorna opened the door en route to her last teaching session of the day. She felt harassed after a long Saturday of dealing with scores of talentless young pupils whose mothers believed their offspring had a bright future in ballroom dance. 'Sylvia's upstairs,' she told Eddie. 'Be warned – she claims she's not feeling well, though I believe that may have been an excuse to get out of helping me in the studio.'

Eddie climbed the stairs to the apartment. He'd heard rumours that Sylvia ought to know about. The situation would have to be handled carefully, especially if she was feeling fragile, as Lorna said. 'Knock, knock!' he called as he tapped on the open door.

Sylvia appeared in a smart dress and matching jacket of her mother's. She'd altered the outfit by inserting shoulder pads, shortening the skirt and sewing extra darts in the bust and waist. Her face was fully made up and her hair arranged in an upswept French pleat that showed off her long neck. 'Eddie, hello.'

'Can I come in?'

'You may as well,' she replied ungraciously. On the

point of going out to meet Cliff, she'd received a last-minute phone call to say that he'd been held up in Liverpool. 'Sorry, princess; people to see, things to do,' he'd said vaguely as he'd cancelled their arrangement.

'What's wrong?' Eddie could see that Sylvia was on the verge of tears as she led him into the living room.

She sank wearily on to the sofa. 'Why should anything be wrong?'

'No reason. Anyway, I'm glad I caught you.' He sat down beside her and tapped his fingers on the arm of the sofa. 'I haven't seen much of you lately.'

'I've been busy.' Really, she didn't have the energy to soothe whatever hurt feelings Eddie was about to express. 'I hope you're not expecting me to drop everything and go to the Tower with you as usual?'

'No,' he said quietly. 'We hadn't arranged to do that and I know you like plenty of warning.' He carried on tapping. 'How are you, anyway?'

'Fine, absolutely fine.'

'You look tired.'

'Of course I'm tired,' she snapped. 'Mother expects too much of me and I have a life of my own to squeeze in between her demands.' Sylvia got up from the sofa and went to stare out of the window.

Eddie studied her silhouette. Sideways-on there was nothing of her; her curves were disappearing at an alarming rate. 'Are you eating enough?' he blurted out.

'For heaven's sake, you're as bad as my mother.' She crossed the room and took a cigarette from the silver case on the occasional table, lighting it with a lighter that she took from her pocket.

'When did you take up smoking?' Eddie asked

before raising his hands in surrender. 'All right, it's none of my business.'

Sylvia inhaled deeply. 'Why have you come, Eddie?'

'There's something I want to talk to you about,' he said uneasily. 'It's a bit awkward.'

A thin spiral of smoke dissolved into a filmy blue cloud above her head. 'You found out about Cliff and you're jealous,' she predicted icily.

'The whole town knows about you and Cliff Seymour and, yes, I'm jealous,' he admitted.

Sylvia bristled. 'When you say the whole town – does my mother know?'

Eddie shook his head. 'I don't think so.'

'Good – I prefer to keep it that way. If she found out that I'd been going to Cliff's studio for Latin lessons I'd never hear the end of it.'

'It's more than that, though, isn't it? You've been seen driving around with him in a sports car for a start. And before you tell me to keep my nose out, there are a couple of things you should know about Cliff Seymour. First off, that car doesn't belong to him. My guess is that he borrowed it specifically to impress you. Secondly, I happen to know that he's in hock to the bank to the tune of eight hundred pounds to cover the cost of refurbishing his studio. It'll take him years to pay off a debt like that.'

'How do you know all this?'

'My father has connections through the Conservative Club, but that's not the point. There's something else: when Cliff came back to Blackpool he was penniless, which makes me wonder what he did with all the money he'd earned at the Hammersmith Palais and at the glitzy Berlin cabaret that he talks about.

Worse, people say he left Germany under a cloud because of – how shall I put it? – the way he treated some of the dancers there.'

'Stop!' Beside herself with anger, Sylvia rushed at Eddie. 'It's all lies. You have no proof and you're only telling me this because you're jealous – don't deny it; you said so yourself.'

The sudden movement made her head spin. She stumbled into his arms and he took her full weight before lowering her gently on to the sofa. 'You're not well,' he murmured. 'Shall I fetch you a drink of water?'

'Yes please.' Suddenly meek and compliant, Sylvia bent forward and, with her head between her knees, waited for the world to stop turning.

Eddie brought the water from the kitchen. He crouched beside her and wrapped her fingers around the glass. 'Careful you don't spill. Sip it slowly – that's the ticket.'

The cold liquid trickled down her throat.

'Now, deep breaths.' Taking the glass, he kept watch as she slowly recovered. 'This is because you won't eat,' he said gently. 'You're wasting away.'

'Please don't fuss.' She made a gesture as if to push him away. 'It's all right for you – you can eat like a horse and not put on any weight, whereas I have to watch every morsel if I want to dance professionally.'

'That's not true – you're a perfect size.'

'No, I'm too fat.' She sighed. 'I need to lose a couple of pounds from around my waist.'

Eddie sat down beside her. 'I don't understand. If you look in the mirror the evidence is there, staring you in the face – not a spare ounce.'

'Just a couple of pounds,' she repeated. 'That way I can achieve what I want to achieve.'

'Which is?' He took her hand and stroked it with his thumb.

'Cliff has talked to a man called Mitch Burns about me. He's an old friend. Cliff wants me to audition for him.'

'Mitch Burns, you say?' Alarm bells rang loudly in Eddie's head. 'And where's he based? What's Cliff's link with him, exactly?' In order to spare Sylvia's blushes, Eddie had kept back some of the more lurid rumours surrounding Cliff's behaviour in Berlin, all of which increased his worry on her account.

'There you go – trying to throw a spanner in the works for me as usual.' Sylvia snatched her hand away. 'If you must know, Cliff says I'm the best ballroom dancer in the whole of the North of England. He has strong connections in the dance world.'

'I'm sure he has. But we need to know more about Cliff's friendship with this Mitch Burns fellow, don't you think?'

'Do you want me to succeed, or don't you?' Indignation brought hectic spots of colour to Sylvia's previously pale cheeks and her eyes filled with tears. 'Can't you just be happy for me, Eddie?'

Her plea made him soften his voice further as he placed his hand on her shoulder and felt her resistance melt away. 'I'm sorry – I didn't mean to upset you.'

She leaned into him, her lips trembling. 'I'm sorry too. I've not been feeling myself lately; I don't know why.'

'It's all right,' he soothed. 'We won't talk about

Cliff any more.' She was light and fragile as a sparrow. What on earth could he do to protect her and save her from herself?

'Or about my eating habits?' she whispered. Dear, reliable Eddie – he was strong and steadfast and would always be her friend.

'If you wish,' he promised.

Music from the studio below filtered into the room and Lorna's muffled voice issued instructions. 'To achieve a close hold in tango your bodies must touch at hip level. The man's right hand moves further across the woman's back – just so.'

'I do wish,' Sylvia insisted. 'There really is no need to worry about me, Eddie. Rest assured, I know exactly what I'm doing.'

CHAPTER EIGHT

Joy's new dance dress hung on a hanger on the back of Tommy's dressing-room door.

'Get changed in there,' he'd told her. 'Feel free – I'll stand guard in the corridor and make sure no one comes in.'

The clowns' airless dressing room smelled of greasepaint and stale sweat and was a riot of colour and sequins. Trumpets, French horns and trombones cluttered the cramped space, while blindingly bright costumes with swirling patterns hung from a rail that ran the length of the room. On the shelf below the make-up mirror Joy recognized the Charlie Chaplin-style bowler hat, false moustache and red nose worn by Charlie Cairoli, the most famous clown of all.

'How are you getting on in there?' Tommy called through the door. He'd finished his Saturday matinee performance and had waited for Joy to cross from the ballroom to the circus as usual. He'd suggested that she bring her dancing clothes to work to save her the bother of dashing back to Silver Street after she'd finished her cleaning shift and all had panned out nicely. Out in the corridor he leaned on the wall with his arms crossed, whistling quietly while he kept watch.

'Give me one more minute,' she replied hastily. She caught sight of herself in the mirror – the dress, made from peach-pink brocade with a cream chiffon bow to soften the neckline – flattered her skin tone in the way that Mavis's borrowed satin gown had done. Her hair was softly waved to frame her face and for once she was satisfied with what she saw.

Joy had bought the fabric from the market with coupons she'd been saving for just such a purchase. Iris Grigg had spotted her carrying the parcel into the house and had offered Joy the use of her sewing machine in her living room. 'No need to hand-sew when my Singer's standing there doing nothing,' she'd growled in a friendlier tone than usual. Joy had gladly taken her up on the offer and finished the dress in two evenings flat.

'Get a move on – Charlie and Paul will be here any minute.' Tommy warned her of the senior clowns' imminent arrival.

So it was on with the shoes and a quick last check in the mirror to make sure that the seams of her stockings were straight before Joy emerged from the dressing room to a whistle of approval from her dance partner for the night.

'Quite the bobby-dazzler!' Tommy offered Joy his arm and they paraded along the corridor together, using a back way in to the ballroom to skip the entrance fee that other dancers would have to pay.

'Is it allowed?' Joy's nervous question made Tommy laugh.

'Not strictly, but I'm pally with Edna in the ticket booth. She'll turn a blind eye even if she spots us.'

Tommy couldn't have cared less – the more people who saw him with Joy the better. He walked with a swagger up the stairs and into the ballroom, where chandeliers sparkled and gold leaf glittered.

Joy took a deep breath. The polished parquet floor reflected the lights and seemed to stretch for ever, inviting you to dance away to your heart's content. Tommy smiled at other couples gathered around the edge of the dance floor: hello to Pearl, looking gorgeous in a daringly short bright-green dress, and to Bernie, stylish in a blue double-breasted blazer and quick-talking and flippant as ever. Excitement mounted as the crimson curtains drew back to reveal an empty stage. An MC tapped a microphone and counted to three – 'Testing, testing . . .'

'Hello there, Sylvia.' Joy broke away from Tommy. Their arch rival sat near the stage dressed in a tailored, damson-coloured outfit consisting of dress and jacket with black velvet collar and cuffs. Eddie was with her.

Sylvia forced a smile. 'Hello, Joy – you look nice,' she conceded.

'Thank you.' Sensing a tense atmosphere, Joy smiled briefly at Sylvia's companion. 'Will you two be entering tonight's competition?'

'We're not here to dance,' Eddie replied quickly. 'Sylvia feels under the weather but I persuaded her to come and watch.' Not wishing to leave her alone after their fraught conversation, he'd persuaded her out of the flat with a promise that they would go to the Tower and sit quietly on the sidelines for once.

'I'm sorry you're not well.' Feeling a tap on her shoulder, Joy turned to find Terry Liddle standing too close and offering her his arm as if to claim her for the evening.

'If it isn't my favourite, peaches-and-cream dance partner, looking good enough to eat,' he said in his deep, mumbling voice. He greeted Sylvia with a casual nod, standing with his chest puffed out, seemingly aware that women's eyes followed him everywhere he went. There was a smouldering, mysterious presence about him, calculated to attract their attention.

Sylvia flashed Joy the look that said, *My, my; quite the conquest!*

'I'm sorry, Terry – I'm afraid I can't dance with you tonight.' Though startled, Joy quickly regained her composure. 'I already have a partner.'

He raised his eyebrows a fraction. 'Next time, perhaps.' Then he stepped away with a careless toss of his head.

'So who was that when he's at home?' A breezy Tommy joined Joy as the opening bars of 'I Do Like To Be Beside The Seaside' filled the room. Mr Dixon appeared as the spot-lit organ rose majestically into view.

'Nobody,' Joy replied as Tommy led her on to the floor.

Pearl and Bernie be-bopped like there was no tomorrow. They danced until they dropped – however anyone cared to phrase it – skipping their way through a lindy hop then throwing themselves into a Charleston, all up-tempo swivels and kicks. During the jitterbug, Bernie even attempted a daring leap-frog as Pearl leaned forward and braced herself, hands on knees – he was smoothly over in a flash and they continued to fling themselves about with gay abandon. Pearl's short skirt rose higher up her thighs, giving a glimpse of stocking tops as she kicked towards the ceiling – no matter, she was caught up in the music like everyone else, relying on Bernie to swing her out and draw her to him then rock in close hold, feeling the heat and sway of their bodies, exchanging brilliant smiles, dancing themselves towards exhaustion.

'A drink?' Bernie suggested as the music changed and couples formed a circle for the start of the hokey-cokey. The old-fashioned party dance didn't hold the same appeal as the Charleston and jitterbug, so they made their way to the bar.

'How did it go with Mick this morning?' Pearl used her hankie to mop her brow as she sipped her lemonade. It was a question she'd been dying to ask earlier but Bernie hadn't let her get a word in edgeways, babbling on about the fortunes of Blackpool FC and the fact that American pilots had finally arrived at Squires Gate and telling her about a programme on the Seven Wonders of the World that he'd listened to on the wireless; anything rather than address the elephant in the room, namely the problem between him and his brother.

'Fisticuffs.' One word covered it. Never mind that Bernie had tried his best to put across his point of view when Mick had arrived at the Pleasure Beach, Mick had railed on and on about nancy boys and pansies, how he wouldn't stand it under his own roof, how Bernie needed to toughen up and not be messing about with the bloody samba and cha-cha. 'Right you are.' Bernie had finally stood his ground. 'If that's how you feel, I'll get out of your hair.' He'd stormed off, intending to go straight home and pack a rucksack with bare essentials.

Mick had charged after him. 'What the bloody hell do you think you're doing?'

'Moving out.' He'd walked on without a backwards glance.

'Over my dead body,' Mick had snarled.

There'd been a struggle. Mick had tugged at Bernie's shirt collar then thrown the first punch; Bernie had ducked and Mick's fist had met thin air. Bernie had delivered an uppercut to Mick's jaw then the exchange of blows had been fast and furious until Bernie had twisted out of reach and run out through the gates, leaving Mick fuming and issuing unrepeatable oaths. With battered pride but more or less unscathed, Bernie had sprinted back to Joe's house and waited for him to come home from the market. Yes, Bernie could stay on with Joe until he found permanent digs – there was a room going on Silver Street, apparently. Bernie had promised to follow it up.

'And that's how things stand?' Pearl's hand grasped her glass more tightly. 'I take it you borrowed Joe's blazer for tonight?'

Bernie nodded. 'It's not really my style, is it? I'll collect my stuff from Empire Street when I know for certain Mick won't be there.'

'I could do that for you if you like.'

'No, ta – I'll do it.' Speaking about the morning's fight left Bernie feeling deflated. Bugger Mick – his hot temper and blinkered, set-in-stone views made him impossible to deal with. The situation was unlikely to change – Bernie felt cast adrift for good.

'I'll help,' Pearl insisted. 'Let me at least keep a lookout while you collect your belongings.'

They lapsed into a glum silence, watching the light-hearted dancers putting right arm in and right arm out; in-out, in-out, shake it all about. Pearl picked out a tall, distinctive figure who had taken up position behind Sylvia on the sidelines. His supercilious expression told her that he considered the hokey-cokey to be beneath him. 'Look who it isn't,' she said to Bernie.

'The bloke from our dance class,' he commented. 'The one who fancied himself rotten.'

'The very one.' Pearl turned to Joy, who was standing next to them at the bar. Tommy was busy ordering drinks before the interval rush. 'What did you find out about Blackpool's Clark Gable when he walked you home?'

'His name's Terry Liddle. He works at the lido.'

'Well, Bernie's right – he definitely fancies himself,' Pearl concluded as she watched Terry engage in conversation with Sylvia. As soon as the party dance finished and a waltz began, he swept her from her chair and led her on to the floor. 'He's got a cheek, pinching her from under Eddie's nose,' she remarked. 'He's a pretty good dancer, though.' This Terry bloke moved as if he knew his way around a dance floor; a match even for Sylvia as he led her in close hold into reverse turns and forward changes until, seemingly exhausted, she excused herself and returned to her seat. Terry scarcely missed a beat before selecting Ruby's friend Mavis as his new partner. 'Where did he spring from, anyway?'

Joy accepted her drink from Tommy. 'Lord only knows.'

'Tommy, what's the low-down on our friend Terry over there?' Pearl expected that the circus performer would have his ear to the ground. 'Other than that he works at the lido.'

Tommy reeled off facts gleaned from Irena, his Polish trapeze artist friend. 'Doesn't give much away about what he did before he showed up here. No friends that I know of. Likes a drink and is happy to spend time at the casino. Quite the night owl. Plus, he's made a name for himself by trying it on with a couple of the circus girls. Love 'em and leave 'em seems to be Terry's style.'

'And what brought him to Blackpool besides the job?' Pearl remained curious; Liddle was evidently a man who oozed charm. He had already moved on from Mavis to Pearl's chirpy friend Doris, whose brunette curls, smiley red lips and low-cut dress had clearly caught his eye.

'No idea.'

Their small group carried on watching the newcomer as the music ended and the MC announced the start of the interval. 'Tonight's competition will be the tango,' he informed his audience. 'Hold on to your hats, ladies and gentlemen – hot and steamy is the order of the day.'

'Hot and steamy' sent Sylvia and Eddie outside for a breath of fresh air.

'Would you rather stay or go?' Eddie was solicitous as always. The tango had long been one of their favourites – Eddie had quickly mastered the slow, predatory walk and progressive side step, while Sylvia's ability to arch her back and enter into the drama of the dance had come naturally.

Drained of what little energy she'd had by the heat of the ballroom and by dancing with Terry Liddle, Sylvia opted for home. 'Let me rest here for a few minutes before we set off,' she pleaded.

Back in the ballroom, three guitarists in flamboyant South American outfits had replaced the organist on the stage.

'I'll give it a go,' Bernie promised Pearl. 'I've never done tango before but I've watched it often enough.'

'Victor Silvester says you have to keep your legs bent and prowl like a tiger,' she advised. 'Slow, slow, quick – staccato.'

'If you say so.' He took her in hold and waited for the music to begin.

'Ever done this?' Tommy asked Joy as they followed Pearl and Bernie on to the floor.

'No, never.' She was flustered by the thought of the tango's provocative reputation but she had enough trust in Tommy to know that he would guide her safely through.

'It's mainly a slow walk, as if you're stalking your prey,' he said knowledgeably. 'Think tigers and lions.'

Up on the stage, the judges took up their positions, notepads in hand.

Nearby, Bernie drew himself up to full height and adopted his version of a sultry Argentinian stare, top lip curled and one eyebrow raised.

'Stop it!' Pearl giggled. The liquid run of guitar notes was amplified by loudspeakers all around the room. This was exciting! Straightening her features and arching her back, she was ready for action.

All of a sudden, a high-pitched siren shattered the mood – the unmistakable, ear-splitting wail that warned of an air raid. There was a gasp of disbelief and for a few bars the guitarists played on. Then they faltered and there was chaos.

'Evacuate the building. Find the nearest shelter.' The MC's announcement over the loudspeakers caused hundreds of dancers and musicians to flee in every direction. As long as the siren was intermittent, it meant they had a few minutes' grace. Once it changed to a continuous wail it meant that attack was imminent.

People piled out of the ballroom and elbowed their way towards the exit. A girl missed her footing on the stairs and was trampled on before being helped back to her feet. Tension crackled in the air and few words were spoken; the one aim was to get to a shelter before the siren changed.

Outside the building, dancers merged with members of the circus audience – parents with crying children and ashen-faced elderly couples stumbling as they fled for their lives. Realizing that performers would have had access to the underground storage area beneath the circus ring where they would stay safe in the event of an attack, Tommy was intent on going against the flow and dragging Joy in that direction, but the crush was too great. They were carried away from the Tower and along the pavement towards the nearest concrete bunker.

'Fingers crossed it's a false alarm,' Bernie muttered to Pearl as they joined the jostling stream.

A Civil Defence roof spotter stationed on top of the ballroom building gave a shrill warning blast on his whistle while at ground level wardens in helmets and dark-blue battledress appeared out of nowhere and took control.

'Red alert!' the roof spotter yelled – the on-off wail of sirens had switched to continuous and in the distance, several miles to the south, the black sky flared bright red. Fear thickened the air and became tangible.

More wardens appeared from back streets, wearing gas masks and stout canvas belts over their dark-blue battledress. They wielded torches and issued terse instructions to the terrified crowd.

'This shelter is full – move on to the next!'

'Women and children first!'

'Stay calm – don't shove!'

Joy's heart was in her mouth as more bright flashes lit the sky. *Please no!* This was how her sister and parents had perished, in unspeakable terror as bombs had exploded all around. Each flash was preceded by an ominous, dull thud, audible even at a distance, as the bomb hit the ground. Her panic increased when a warden signalled for her and Tommy to hurry on towards the next shelter, a hundred yards along the prom. They caught up with Eddie, who supported a dizzy, fragile Sylvia, and with Pearl and Bernie, running hand in hand.

'Squires Gate is going up in flames,' Bernie muttered under his breath.

Suddenly giant searchlights raked across the black sky, directed by anti-aircraft gunners on the ground close to the Vickers factory and the airfield. The siren continued to blare and the crowd grew ever thicker as residents emerged from seafront hotels, pubs and bingo halls.

Joy struggled to stay calm while people fought to reach the front of queues that had gathered at the entrance to each bunker, jostling and defying wardens' orders not to push. A man shoved her from behind. Tommy shoved him back. There was a scuffle, broken up by Bernie, who drew Pearl, Joy, Tommy, Eddie and Sylvia into a huddle outside the sandbagged entrance to the Majestic.

'There's a cellar under the Queen's Arms further up King Alfred Road – let's try that,' he suggested. 'Follow me.'

Pearl and Joy hurried with him, while Tommy lagged behind to help Eddie with Sylvia. At the fall of each bomb followed by the deadly riot of exploding earth, sparks and flames, she weakened and sagged. The two men supported her, one on each side, taking her weight and reassuring her that she would soon be safe.

'Down here.' Bernie heaved at the handle to a wooden trapdoor outside the pub. He opened it to reveal a ramp down into a vaulted cellar. The odour of beer and damp was strong. A bare electric light bulb told them that Bernie's idea wasn't original – the landlord and several of his regular customers, including Bernie's pal Joe, had already taken refuge there.

'Is there room for six littl'uns?' Bernie checked.

'The more the merrier,' came the reply.

So Bernie held out his hand to help Pearl and Joy down the ramp. Shortly afterwards, Eddie and Tommy carried Sylvia to safety.

'Batten down the hatches.' The bald, stout landlord, resplendent in crimson waistcoat and silver armbands with an emergency cigar tucked in his top pocket, issued a brisk order.

Bernie lowered the heavy trapdoor with a thud. 'Jerry's target is Squires Gate,' he announced. 'He probably tailed our RAF boys back from an attack on Dresden or Essen – it's one of those so-called spite raids.'

'Shift yourself,' Pearl told Joe, who was perched on an upturned barrel. 'Sylvia here needs to sit down.'

He moved immediately. 'Blimey, she looks like death warmed up.'

'I'll be all right,' Sylvia insisted, though all the evidence pointed to the contrary as she sank on to the barrel then leaned heavily against the damp wall with her head drooping forward.

'Is there a water tap down here?' Eddie asked the landlord. 'She needs a drink.'

'Don't we all?' Joe muttered. 'Something stronger than water would go down well.'

Joy closed her eyes and took a deep breath to ease her fear. Her heart raced at the disastrous turn of events: one minute she and Tommy had been preparing to tango, the next all hell had broken loose. And yet – so far, so good. Here they were, all in one piece and in relative safety. Water was produced for Sylvia and a nip of nerve-calming whisky for anyone who fancied it. When Joy dared to open her eyes, Tommy was beside her.

'This'll be a tale to tell your grandkids.' He smiled and squeezed her hand.

She squeezed back. Two weeks ago she'd had no one in the world to turn to. Now, against all her expectations, she had Tommy.

CHAPTER NINE

Soon after midnight sirens sounded the all-clear. When Bernie opened the trapdoor and led Pearl and the others out on to King Alfred Road, they found that a light rain had started to fall.

'Mind you don't slip on the wet pavement,' he cautioned Sylvia as she emerged, the last to join him, Pearl, Joy, Tommy and Eddie. Relief showed on all their faces after an hour and a half cooped up in the beer cellar.

'Take my hand.' Eddie stood by, ready to support Sylvia if necessary.

'I don't need any help, thanks.' Gulping in a breath of fresh air, she made her way with Pearl and Joy to the promenade.

Pearl halted by the Majestic and scanned the seafront to reassure herself that the orange glow in the sky hadn't spread beyond Squires Gate. Closer to home, the three piers and all attractions remained intact, including the Tower buildings and the Pleasure Beach beyond. 'Jerry didn't target the town itself, thank goodness.'

'I hear that one of our boys brought down a Dornier Do 217 – a *Schnellbomber*,' a jubilant passer-by reported. 'Serves Fritz bloody well right.'

Up and down the promenade people emerged from shelters to inspect the damage. More rumours did the rounds – the Dornier pilot had parachuted into the drink and two other enemy planes had collided in mid-air, exploding in a ball of flames. One of the runways at Squires Gate had been badly damaged.

'Let's hope they can rebuild it in double-quick time.' Joy kept her fingers firmly crossed. She and Pearl had fled from the ballroom without coats or jackets and the rain was carried in on a stiff breeze that cut right through her. The three girls huddled together for warmth.

'I don't fancy going through that again in a hurry,' Pearl confessed. 'You read about these blasted air raids in the papers and you'd think we'd be used to the idea by now, but this one was too close for comfort.'

'How scared were you?' Joy asked under her breath as Eddie, Bernie and Tommy joined them.

'Petrified,' Pearl and Sylvia admitted as one. Pearl's heart still pounded and Sylvia trembled from head to toe.

'I thought Hitler's plan was to leave us alone,' Sylvia complained. 'Once he's invaded, his men are supposed to come goose-stepping down the prom and turn the town into the Führer's own personal playground. Goebbels intends to fly the swastika flag from the top of the Tower.'

'You can't believe everything you read,' Pearl reminded her. 'For now, I'm just glad we're all in one piece.'

'Keep calm and carry on, eh?' The raid had brought

out hidden qualities in Bernie. Yes, he'd been scared witless just like everyone else, but he'd kept his head and come up with the Queen's Arms idea unaided.

'I was far from calm,' Sylvia admitted. 'I was convinced we were all about to breathe our last down in that awful cellar.'

Pearl gave her a reassuring grin. 'Did your whole life flash before your eyes? What did you see?'

'Truthfully? I thought about my mother.' Sylvia's eyes pricked with hot tears. 'She was in her dancing prime and holding aloft a national trophy for the Viennese waltz.'

'What about you?' Pearl asked Joy.

'I closed my eyes and tried not to think of anything.' Joy had had Tommy by her side. His arm around her shoulder had seemed to shelter her from the worst that might occur. 'How about you?'

'I pictured Elsie riding a donkey on the beach,' Pearl replied, 'with the sun on her little face and grinning from ear to ear.' This image was an actual snapshot of her sister that she kept in her purse and it represented pure glee. 'She loves those donkeys, bless her.'

'And yet here we all are, without a scratch.' Joy turned to Tommy with a smile. 'Tomorrow's a new day.'

'Tomorrow is already today,' he informed them with a glance at his watch. 'It's gone midnight.'

'Past our bedtimes.' Bernie offered to accompany Pearl to Empire Street but she declined.

'It's out of your way and, besides, you might run into Mick. Joy and Tommy are heading in my direction; I'll walk with them, if that's all right?'

'Fine by me,' Tommy agreed.

'And I'll escort you to your door before you get thoroughly soaked,' Eddie assured Sylvia.

Their group separated with buoyant, relief-filled goodbyes. 'Bernie and I will see you on Tuesday for our next lesson,' Pearl called after Sylvia.

'Likewise,' Joy added. 'Tommy and I will be there, too.'

'Champion; I'll see you then.' Though done in by the night's events, Sylvia paused to watch Joy and Pearl turn the corner. 'They're nice girls when you get to know them,' she remarked with an expression that registered faint surprise.

'Very nice,' Eddie agreed with a wry smile.

'And not bad dancers either,' she added. It was early days and Pearl definitely lacked polish, while Joy still needed to build up her confidence, but in Sylvia's opinion the two girls' first steps into the world of ballroom dance had shown distinct promise. 'I like them both, warts and all,' she decided airily.

Eddie smiled to himself. 'Warts and all,' he repeated under his breath as they reached the academy and Sylvia dipped into her handbag for her key. He kissed her on the cheek and said goodnight. Breathtakingly lovely and little-girl-lost rolled into one; that was Sylvia. Eddie's heart ached for her as he walked off down the street – a silent, solitary figure passing through dark, damp shadows – for he adored every silky hair on Sylvia's beautiful head, loved her more than she would ever know.

During the weeks following the air raid, Pearl and Joy's dance lessons at the Lorna Ellis Dance Academy

129

went swimmingly. Over and over again, Lorna corrected their posture and refined their footwork. 'More poise, more energy!' she urged Joy during the quickstep. 'Keep your chin up and smile at Tommy – that's much better!'

'Allow Bernie to lead,' she would remind Pearl as she tapped a nearby wall chart to illustrate what she meant. 'And please stick to the standardized footwork for the tango walk – there's no room for individual interpretation in this dance. Step back with the right foot without lowering the heel on the first beat. *Now* lower the heel then step back with the left foot.'

Pearl would sigh and roll her eyes at Bernie but she meekly followed instructions and lapped up Lorna's praise at the end of each session.

Progressing to the cha-cha, Pearl found that this was more her cup of tea. 'Saucy, fun and carefree.' It was a Friday evening in mid-July and Sylvia had boldly seized the chance to sneak in a cha-cha lesson while Lorna enjoyed another theatre trip with Eddie's father, Maurice.

'This will suit you, Pearl,' Sylvia predicted. 'Joy, please don't worry – it's a very easy dance based on three linked steps – the chassé coincides with the accented beats in each bar. One, two, three, four and one – with the accent on four and one!'

Angela struck up a spirited Cuban tune on the piano and Sylvia counted them in. 'Bernie, must I remind you that the close hold in cha-cha does not involve body contact?'

'Worse luck.' Taking a step back, Bernie grinned at Pearl, who laughed and was reprimanded by Sylvia.

'Sorry, miss.' Pearl cleared her throat and promised to concentrate.

'Don't worry – it sounds more complicated than it actually is,' Tommy assured Joy as they attempted an underarm turn to the right. 'Just relax.'

She swallowed hard, put her best foot forward and mastered the technique in no time at all.

Towards the end of the lesson Sylvia brought Eddie on to the floor to demonstrate a complicated move. Up until this point he'd been quietly observing from the sidelines, but now he slid an arm around Sylvia's waist then crouched low, supporting her as she kicked high. Her arms were raised and her fingers splayed in the style of a flamboyant flamenco dancer.

For ten minutes Pearl and Bernie and Joy and Tommy, along with a dozen other couples, made valiant attempts to copy the exuberant move.

'Phew, I'm dead beat!' The lesson ended and Pearl followed Joy to the ladies' cloakroom to compare notes. 'I don't know about you, but everything aches – we must have used muscles we didn't even know we had,' she said as she peered into the mirror above the washbasins. Her cheeks were flushed and wisps of damp hair stuck to her forehead.

'It was a challenge.' Joy felt as if she'd learned a lot – but yes, she admitted that she was exhausted. 'Sylvia's a hard taskmaster.'

'She certainly knows how to crack the whip.' After another busy week of helping her father and mother on their seafront stalls, Pearl's energy was flagging but she was still up for a good gossip. 'By the way, how are you and Tommy getting along – and I don't mean only on the dance floor?'

Joy made eye contact with Pearl in the mirror. 'He's lovely,' she murmured, blushing furiously.

'Not good enough – more, please!'

'He wants me to meet his parents.' The invitation had come out of the blue during one of Joy's cleaning shifts at the circus.

'You don't say!' Pearl's eyes widened as she turned to look directly at Joy. 'When?'

'This coming Sunday. I'm worried about what to wear.'

'It doesn't matter – you'll look the bee's knees in anything you choose. Tommy's mum and dad will take to you right away.'

'But really – shall I wear a dress or slacks?'

'A dress, definitely – maybe your peachy one with the chiffon bow.'

'It won't look as if I'm trying too hard?' For rookie Joy, the rules governing a visit to a sweetheart's parents were a minefield. All she knew was that the Rossis lived in a flat above their ice-cream parlour at the southern end of the Golden Mile.

'Maybe,' Pearl admitted. 'I've got one you could borrow – it's white cotton with a rosebud pattern – very fresh-looking. Call in at Empire Street tomorrow and I'll show you.'

The arrangement was made as the girls rejoined Tommy and Bernie on the pavement outside the academy.

'Things must be getting serious between you two,' Pearl teased Tommy. 'A little bird tells me Joy's had a formal invite to meet your ma and pa. I've promised to lend her a dress for the occasion.'

'Pearl, please!' Wishing that the ground would

swallow her up, Joy elbowed her treacherous friend out of the way.

Laughing, Tommy took hold of Joy's hand. 'Ignore her,' he said as they strolled away.

'Trust you,' Bernie remarked quietly. He and Pearl set off in the opposite direction towards the Majestic.

'Why, what did I do?' All innocence, she swung his arm as they walked past the gaudy window display of Dawson's Gift Emporium, dominated by a giant teddy bear surrounded by racks of postcards, sunhats and beach towels.

'You put Tommy and Joy on the spot.'

'They didn't mind.' Pearl was full of breezy confidence and chatter. 'Anyway, I was right – anyone can see that those two are falling for each other. They need a little shove in the right direction, that's all.'

'And you're the one to give it.' The rattle of an approaching tram meant that Bernie and Pearl had to wait before crossing the broad promenade and taking the steps down on to the beach by Central Pier. Shadows were long and families were packing away towels, picnic hampers and sun umbrellas prior to heading back to their hotels.

'What's up?' she asked as he waited for her to take off her shoes before they strolled towards the water's edge with the setting sun in their eyes. 'You don't seem your usual self.'

'What are you on about?' Head down and with his free hand jammed into his trouser pocket, Bernie batted away Pearl's question. They came to a halt at the edge of a shallow, sparkling pool left by the ebbing tide.

'I mean it, Bernie – what's up?'

'If you must know, Mick has got me the sack at Squires Gate,' he admitted glumly. He'd kept this to himself so as not to spoil the evening but now the secret wormed its way into the open.

'What did I tell you?' Pearl yelped.

'He nailed me for my poor timekeeping – arriving late and leaving early, according to him, but I was only doing that to keep out of his way. And I took Wednesday morning off to move into my new digs on Market Street; Mick reckoned I never asked his permission. The bosses believed him and handed me my cards.'

'Market Street?' Pearl echoed. 'I thought you went after the vacancy on Silver Street?'

'I did but it had already been taken by Terry Liddle.' Bernie had followed up the room that Joe had recommended without success. 'I don't mind Market Street – it's handy for the Pleasure Beach. There's a chance there'll be more work for me there.'

'But honestly, how could Mick do that to you?' Bernie's news had stunned Pearl. 'To his own brother!'

'You know what he's like.'

A fresh, nerve-jangling thought struck Pearl – the maintenance work at the funfair that Bernie had mentioned might not be considered as essential to the war effort. 'And does this mean you could be conscripted?' she asked.

'It might do,' Bernie admitted. 'I'll face that hurdle when I come to it. For now, I'm hoping Mick won't queer the pitch for me with the gaffers at the Pleasure Beach like he did at Squires Gate.'

Quick-thinking Pearl came up with a short-term

134

solution. 'If he does, you could come and work for us on one of our stalls. Dad needs an extra pair of hands in his amusement arcade.'

Bernie nodded. 'Ta for that – I appreciate it.' Stunned by how suddenly his life had taken a turn for the worse, he felt bereft of ideas. 'I'll need some sort of a job to pay the rent at Market Street.'

'And all this because you took up ballroom dancing!'

He gave a hollow laugh before skirting the pool and striding across the wet, ribbed sand to where waves lapped at the shore. Out to sea, a small convoy of merchant ships headed north – tiny specks on the glittering horizon. 'Mick's a hothead and no mistake.'

'And a bully,' Pearl insisted. She stood beside Bernie, lost in thought. 'This mess you find yourself in because of dancing – is it worth it?' she asked at last. 'What would happen if you backed down? Would Mick be able to get you your old job back?'

'Probably not.' There'd been too much swearing and hollering, too many insults and an avalanche of ill feeling between them. 'Anyway, I wouldn't want to work with him again.'

Ignoring this, Pearl held to her line of thought. 'Say you gave up coming to the Tower Ballroom with me and started playing footie or whatever else it would take to get back into your brother's good books—'

'You're not listening.' Bernie cut her off. 'I've had it up to here with Mick; full stop.'

'But dancing's only a hobby,' she protested. 'And the chance to earn a few bob every now and then.'

'Can't you see? It's more than that.' The feeling of

135

pressure in Bernie's chest threatened to explode. If only he had the words to express it. In an effort to keep control, he strode swiftly under the pier and out the other side.

Pearl ran after him – from sunshine to shadow and out again. 'But it would make sense in the long run,' she insisted. 'What's the odd lindy hop and quickstep compared with what you're giving up right now?'

Bernie veered off up the beach towards the prom. Frustration flickered across his face. 'Bloody hell, Pearl – do I have to spell it out?'

'Spell what out?' Normally Bernie was easy to read – but not now.

He stopped short and turned to face her with unusual intensity. 'It's not about the dancing, you idiot.'

She cannoned into him and dropped one of her shoes.

He picked it up, tipped out the sand then handed it to her. 'It's about us – you and me.'

They stood very close. Trams trundled along the prom, children's voices called, two lads stacked deck-chairs against the sea wall. Pearl didn't notice anything except Bernie's face staring intently at her.

'Don't you see?' he murmured.

Suddenly, yes she did! Her earlier inkling was trans-formed into solid-gold certainty.

'I don't mind about the dancing. It's you I care about.'

It was as if the soft petals of a flower had opened in the sunlight, filling the world with beautiful scent. Pearl took a deep breath.

'Say something,' Bernie pleaded.

'What?'

'Do you feel the same way?'

'Yes,' she breathed. *Yes, yes!*

'That's all right, then.' The low sun lit their faces with a golden glow. Their kiss was like a breeze caressing their lips – a gentle, longing touch before they took a step back and held hands for a moment that blossomed into a future full of promise. 'Thank God for that.' Bernie grabbed Pearl and lifted her clean off her feet. He spun her round.

'Bernie, I'm dizzy!' she cried. 'Stop – put me down or else!'

'Two days on the trot!' Sylvia gave vent to her exasperation soon after she arrived at Cliff's studio. 'Really, my mother is the absolute limit. On Friday she went to see yet another Gilbert and Sullivan with Dr Winter and last night it was *The Merchant of Venice* at the Grand.'

'Leaving you to teach Blackpool's masses how to quickstep,' Cliff commiserated, with one eyebrow raised ironically.

'You've no idea! I didn't mind the first one so much – there are some couples in the Friday-night class who pick things up easily and I've grown friendly with two of the girls – Pearl Scott and Joy Hebden. We spent hours cooped up in a cellar during the last air raid and got to know each other better. But yesterday I had to deal with an unruly bunch of American GIs. They all chew gum and have two left feet.'

Cliff smiled as he switched on the gramophone and selected a record. 'You could always send your unruly GIs here for me to teach – I wouldn't mind one bit.'

'Hmm – I'll bear that in mind.' Sylvia had been on time for once, expecting to meet the famous Mitch Burns at last. She'd spent ages beforehand deciding what to wear. Evidence of having made too much effort would make her seem unsophisticated but too little would look as if she didn't care enough about the opportunity on offer, so she'd chosen one of her sleeveless blouses and an apple-green, knee-length skirt that flared when she turned. Her hair was in a high ponytail and she wore her pearl earrings with a necklace to match. In the event, however, the mysterious Mr Burns had pulled out at the last moment so she and Cliff were alone in the studio.

'Come on, princess; forget about your mother,' Cliff suggested as a big-band swing number filled the studio. 'Concentrate on why you're here.'

But Sylvia's bad mood was slow to lift. 'I thought I was here to dance for Mr Burns and further my career,' she complained with an impatient flick of her wrist. 'Anyway, what are his connections, exactly?'

'Why, he puts on dinner dances at the London Ritz and he stages competitions at the Hammersmith Palais where I used to work, among other things. Everyone who is anyone goes to Mitch's dos – royalty, singers, film stars; you name it.'

'What else?' Sylvia demanded more information, keeping Cliff at arm's length when he tried to take her in hold for the jitterbug. 'I looked him up in a copy of *Modern Dance and Dancer* – he doesn't appear in the ISTD list.'

'That's because he doesn't *teach* dance, silly,' Cliff explained with exaggerated emphasis. 'He goes around the country selecting dance partners for

Lord-this and Sir Percy-that. He opens the door into a brave new world of luxury you can't even dream of – parquet floors, oak panelling, crystal chandeliers, professional dance bands with gleaming brass instruments, beautiful ball gowns everywhere you look. Listen – are we going to learn this dance or not?'

'Of course we are. I just feel let down, that's all.'

'Me too.' Cliff moved on swiftly to the matter in hand. 'Now, as you no doubt already know, jitterbug builds on familiar swing steps like those you see in similar American crazes like Truckin' and Susie O, where there's plenty of room for solo performance. Kick as high as you like, loosen up and shake those hands and hips.'

An hour's practice brought Sylvia to a level where Cliff was satisfied and he suggested adjourning to the Seaview tearoom – a change of venue from their previous outing.

'I would love to,' she replied as she changed her shoes then gathered her belongings, 'but I'm afraid I've run out of steam.' In fact, she was dead on her feet and uncertain how she would even make it back to King Alfred Road.

'Are you sure I can't persuade you, my lovely princess?' Cliff caught hold of her hand and bestowed a winning smile.

Flustered by his flattery, she was on the point of changing her mind. 'Do you have your car?' *His or someone else's?* Sylvia recalled Eddie's warning.

'No, but Seaview is just down the road.'

'I really don't have the energy,' she decided.

Cliff pushed a stray strand of hair back from her cheek. 'Oh, come on – humour me.'

Memory of the kiss that they'd shared flashed back into her consciousness – his half-closed eyes and the softness of his lips. Sylvia willed it to happen again.

'One little cup of tea,' he whispered in her ear.

She felt his warm breath on her cheek and turned her face towards him.

He pulled away with a questioning look. 'Well?'

No kiss, then. Sylvia felt a thud of disappointment in her chest. 'Sorry to turn you down,' she said. 'Please can you call me a taxi? I have to go straight home to bed.'

On her way to the Tower to meet Tommy on her day off, Joy gave way to an urge to enter Madam Rosie's fortune-telling booth – a bold move that gave her butterflies but one that she'd been promising herself for a long time. Pearl's borrowed rosebud dress suited Joy and gave her confidence a boost as she walked along the sunny promenade and approached the curious black-and-white sign depicting a palm with mysterious symbols that enticed her in.

'Sit,' the woman instructed as Joy entered the tiny, dimly lit room – not much larger than your average pantry. The sickly-sweet smell of incense greeted Joy and the airless, stuffy atmosphere did little to settle her nerves. 'Place your right hand on the table, palm up.'

Joy followed the instruction. No gypsy earrings, silver bangles or fringed shawl were in evidence – in fact, this teller of fortunes looked distinctly average in her fashionable summer dress and neatly waved dark hair. Her face was thin and stern, her eyebrows heavy, and she wore a dark-red lipstick that served to make her look even more severe.

Rosie studied Joy's palm for a few brief seconds. 'You lack confidence,' she reported without looking up. 'You are not born to lead. However, you possess sympathy and grace. I see that you live an independent life and are without family.'

Joy was surprised that so much accurate information could be gleaned from studying a person's palm. She gave a small gasp and her eyes widened in astonishment.

'At a deeper level I see courage and creativity. There is ambition, too.'

Edging forward on her stool, Joy felt her heartbeat quicken. True enough, dance demanded creativity and the courage to perform in front of others. And yes, the hidden desire to be the best had emerged when she and Tommy had won the lindy hop competition.

'The heart line is strong but it is broken – you have already seen tragedy in your young life – in your family,' the fortune teller intoned with a quick glance at Joy's flushed face.

'My mother and father were killed by a bomb,' Joy confirmed. 'My sister, too.'

Madam Rosie gave a sympathetic nod. 'A fork in your head line tells me that you face a change in your career.'

'But about the heart line?' Joy prompted.

With a slight rise of her eyebrows, the woman ran cool fingertips across Joy's palm. 'It is long and straight, showing idealism. You feel things deeply. There is only one fork, showing the disaster you have already undergone. I see no future heartbreak.'

Joy experienced a sudden spurt of hope, followed

by a flicker of doubt and a suspicion that fortune tell-
ers must prophesy a similarly rosy future for all their
customers – how else would they ensure that the sixpences kept rolling in? 'What else do you see?'

'The line of life is long.' Pushing Joy's hand away
with unexpected suddenness, Rosie rested back on
her stool and stared hard at Joy's face – young and
eager, hopeful, delicate and decorative as sugar icing
on a cake. Summing up her client, she spoke in a
softer tone. 'Don't let a lack of confidence spoil your
chances of a happy and successful life. Be bold.'

'I will.' Joy nodded earnestly. It became obvious
from the hardening of the fortune teller's expression
that their session was at an end so she pushed a small
silver coin across the table, stood up and mumbled
her thanks, pushing aside the heavy curtain that
covered the doorway and stepping out on to the
prom. Blinking in the strong sunlight, she squared
her shoulders. *Be bold!* This was the message she
would carry with her.

'My, my – what have you been up to?' Tommy's
voice broke into her thoughts. Exiting through a side
entrance to the Tower, he spied Joy emerging from
the booth and broke into a run. 'Madam Rosie hasn't
been telling your fortune, by any chance?'

'She has,' Joy confessed.

'And did she say that you would marry a rich man
and have five children?' Fresh from a matinee performance, Tommy was in high spirits. There was an
extra spring in his step as he took Joy's hand and they
walked together past the hum and bustle of countless
kiss-me-quick stalls and amusement arcades. 'That's
Rosie's usual line – marriage and kids for the girls,

money and fast cars for the few boys daft enough to stump up a tanner to have their lives mapped out.'

Joy bridled slightly. 'There was nothing of that sort. Anyway, I wouldn't have fallen for it.'

'Of course not – you're far too sensible.' *And clever and independent and looking extra-specially pretty today in your rosebud dress!* Tommy couldn't wait to show her off to his mum and dad.

'How did your matinee go?' Joy chose safer territory.

'Oh, the usual fun and games.' He'd played a solo tune on the trumpet – 'Oh My Papa' – then cavorted across the ring performing pratfalls to gales of laughter. He'd chucked pretend buckets of water at the front row and showered the audience in confetti instead of liquid. Oh, how the old ladies had squealed and shaken their fists! He'd juggled two balls high in the air, then four, then six, somersaulted through flaming hoops then teased and tormented the great Cairoli before being carted away in a wheelbarrow, legs kicking, arms waving wildly. From the clowns' dressing room, as he'd wiped off his make-up and changed out of his sequins, he'd heard lions roar and elephants trumpet. Rounds of applause for the animal acts had followed him along the corridor out on to the street. And now here he was, striding towards the South Pier with his sweetheart on his arm. Joy with a capital J and joy with a small one.

'That's our place, right opposite the pier.'

Joy made out a green-and-white-striped awning and a wooden sandwich board displaying a giant cone piled high with scoops of pink and white ice cream. The sign above the shop read 'Rossi's Genuine Italian Ices'. There was a short queue at a hatch serving passers-by and next to it there were wide glass doors into a bright interior where tables were covered with pristine gingham tablecloths. The café was bursting at the seams with customers enjoying their delicious Sunday treat.

'Come in,' Tommy said to Joy as they reached the doors.

She took a deep breath. *Be bold!* Before she could step inside, a small, round-faced, busty woman wearing a green apron over a white overall bustled towards her. '*Entra, entra!*' she gushed. '*Prego entra!*'

'Mamma, meet Joy. Joy, this is my mother, Lucia.' Tommy's fingers were firmly crossed as he made the introductions.

Lucia was all smiles and hugs. 'My Tommy's young lady, please follow me. We look forward so much – Tommy's father and I. We hear good things about you.'

'Thank you for inviting me.' *Be bold!* The shyness that usually held Joy back melted away in the face of Mrs Rossi's gleeful greeting. She followed Tommy's mother across the ice-cream parlour into a narrow hallway with a staircase at the far end.

'*Seguimi*,' Lucia gushed as she led the way up the stairs. 'Follow. We are so happy. You are nice girl – very pretty. Come!'

The first-floor living room was cosy and cluttered. Lucia's net curtains were pristine, the cushions on the comfy armchairs were brightly embroidered and there were lace doilies on every available surface. Fancy glass vases adorned the windowsill – translucent ruby red and emerald green glinting in the sunlight.

Lucia beamed at Joy. 'Tommy's father – he comes.'

Footsteps sounded along a corridor then Tommy senior appeared – an older version of his son, with the same thick, wavy hair and lively brown eyes. Framed in the doorway, he tilted his head to one side and took a moment to study Joy.

She exhaled softly. Would she pass muster?

'*Bellissima!*' The verdict came with a broad smile and a wink in Tommy's direction. '*Ciao, signorina; prego siediti.*' Pointing to a seat by the fireplace, he invited their visitor to sit down.

The talk was light and sunny – Blackpool was the best place in England for summer holidays. Nowhere else had such lengths of golden sand and its fairgrounds and end-of-pier shows were second to none. No wonder holidaymakers flocked here in their thousands. And they always wanted ice creams; the Rossi business was booming.

'And our boy is at the circus.' Lucia puffed out her chest when she spoke of young Tommy's skills. '*Acrobata, giocoliere, pagliaccio.*'

'In English, Mamma, please,' Tommy junior reminded her.

Lucia's laugh was throaty and warm. 'I forget. She looks like Italian. Her eyes are brown like hazelnut. My Tommy, you are lucky man!'

'You will eat ice cream?' Tommy senior left the room and ran downstairs without waiting for Joy's answer. He returned minutes later with a glass dish piled high with the stuff. 'Strawberry,' he told Joy. '*Mangia, mangia!*'

'Eat,' Tommy translated. He dipped Joy's spoon in the ice cream and fed it to her.

The ice cream melted in her mouth. 'Delicious,' she murmured.

'My Tommy says you dance like Latin girl.' Lucia beamed at Joy. 'The cha-cha, the samba, the rumba . . .'

'I try my best,' Joy answered modestly. 'We've paid for a few lessons but I pick up most of the steps from Tommy.'

'Yes – very good dancer.' Like his wife, Tommy senior was proud of his son. 'And kind and funny. You are lucky girl.'

Joy blushed. The conversation moved on, skipping through Joy and Tommy's ambitions in the dance world and the competitions they might enter, touching on food rationing and clothing coupons. 'I have dresses for dancing,' Lucia volunteered. 'From Italy, when I was young.' She wouldn't take no for an answer. 'If they are too old, we cut them and make new.' She made a snipping motion with her fingers. And yes; Joy would be delighted to accept Lucia's offer – they would squeeze their sewing sessions into their already busy schedules, come what may.

'I knew you'd get on like a house on fire,' Tommy told Joy after she'd said her goodbyes to his parents and he walked her home.

Bathed in late-afternoon sunshine and delighted by Lucia's welcoming chatter and Tommy senior's pride in his son, Joy felt that the visit had gone better than she could ever have expected. 'I like them.' She squeezed Tommy's hand as they turned into Silver Street. It was time to part. *Be bold!* 'They're lovely. Thank you for inviting me.'

He hesitated outside the door of number 57. What now?

'*Prego entra*,' Joy whispered with a smile. 'I'd like you to see where I live.'

With her heart in her mouth, she led him up the steps and along Mrs Grigg's dingy corridor, up the stairs past Terry Liddle's room on the first floor, up another flight of stairs to her attic with the dim skylight and the picture of her lost family on the mantelpiece. 'It's not much,' she apologized as she opened the door.

Tommy's height meant that he had to stoop under the sloping ceiling. Joy's dresses hung from a hook on the door. The fire grate was empty and the rug was threadbare. Her bed was pushed under the eaves. He thought of all that he could give her and all that she deserved before the photograph drew him like a magnet.

'This is you?' he asked quietly.

'Yes, and that's my sister, Margaret, and my mum and dad.' She pointed out each one. 'We once came to Blackpool on our holidays.'

The little group in the picture stood in front of a fairground ride complete with a string of electric lights and a painted sign over their heads that read, 'Oh Girls!' A beaming Margaret posed between her father and mother while Joy stood slightly apart dressed in sandals, white ankle socks and a coat with a velvet collar. She wore two white ribbons in her hair. Her head was dipped and she wasn't smiling for the camera.

'My dear girl,' Tommy murmured and drew her close.

Joy sank into his embrace and let out a sigh.

'Are you sad?' he asked.

'No – I'm happy,' she replied. This was how it felt to soar like a bird high in the blue sky, to ride the air currents without a care. This was love, pure and simple.

CHAPTER TEN

Wearing the right dance shoes was vital, Sylvia declared. They could make the difference between competition success and failure. Shoes that were too high or too tight restricted movement; too low and they made a girl seem less elegant.

Joy and Pearl listened to the voice of the expert after their latest lesson at the academy had ended and Bernie and Tommy had sloped off ahead of them to the Queen's Arms.

'It's important,' Sylvia insisted as she inspected Joy's shoes and found them lacking. 'Those heels are not high enough.'

'But I'm tall,' Joy pointed out. 'I don't want to tower over my partner.'

Sylvia dismissed her objection as she stooped to fish out a spare pair of shoes from a cupboard behind the piano. She stood up too quickly and had to steady herself against the wall. 'Tommy is tall too. He can take your extra height. Here, try these.'

'Go on; humour her,' Pearl encouraged.

So Joy slipped her feet into the shoes that Sylvia had produced – strappy ones with a slim, three-inch heel. They fitted perfectly.

'You *shall* go to the ball!' Pearl crowed, her voice carrying through the empty studio.

'Borrow them for as long as you like,' Sylvia urged with unwonted generosity. 'They'll make all the difference.'

Joy thanked her and popped the shoes into her bag.

'Where's your mother this evening?' Pearl asked Sylvia as she and Joy prepared to join the boys in the pub. 'We haven't seen much of her lately.'

'Oh, she's at a concert with Eddie and his father.' As Sylvia wafted the question away, she lost her balance again. This time Pearl and Joy paid more attention. Pearl reached for the piano stool and made Sylvia sit for a moment to catch her breath.

'Don't fuss.' Sylvia responded with her usual refrain. 'I'm perfectly fine.'

Pearl frowned at Joy. 'She doesn't seem fine, does she?'

Sylvia's face was drained of colour and her expression was dazed. 'You look poorly,' Joy confirmed.

True to form, Pearl tackled the problem head-on. 'This is to do with you not eating, isn't it?'

'Oh, please . . . not you as well!' Sylvia attempted to stand but found that she lacked the strength. She sank down on to the stool with a loud sigh.

'Pearl's right,' Joy insisted quietly. 'You've lost too much weight. It's not good for you.'

'I'm feeling a little dizzy, that's all.' Sylvia let her shoulders slump and her head drop forward so that her face was hidden. 'It's my time of the month.'

Pearl and Joy crouched beside her. 'Why won't you listen?' Pearl asked. 'I'm sure we're not the first to have noticed how thin you are.'

Sylvia sighed again. 'Oh, my mother goes on and on at me – Eddie, too. They don't understand.'

'What don't they understand?' Joy prompted, gentle as ever.

'Anything!' Tears welled up. 'I eat when I want to. It's nobody's business except mine.'

'But why starve yourself?' Pearl sat on the floor next to Sylvia and drew her knees to her chest. The sun shone at an angle through the plate-glass window, casting long shadows over the polished floor. A reflection in the tall mirror showed three girls huddled together in close conversation.

'I won't weaken,' Sylvia warned. She pushed her hair back from her face, brushing away the tears that had started to fall. 'Whatever you say to me, I won't change my mind.'

'Even if it makes you poorly?' Joy persisted.

'If I eat what I like and the pounds pile back on, I'll never get where I want to be,' Sylvia reasoned. 'It's obvious.'

'To you, maybe,' Pearl argued. 'But not to us.'

'What Pearl means is, if you lose any more weight you'll make yourself seriously ill and then what?'

'You won't even try to understand!' Sylvia's cry was from the heart. 'A new world is opening up for me – Cliff has promised to introduce me to an impresario.'

'An impresario?' Pearl repeated sceptically.

'Yes, a man who introduces girls to men in fashionable circles – people with titles and money who wish to find highly trained partners to dance with them at the Ritz.'

The thud of cynical disbelief in Pearl's stomach was

almost audible. 'You're kidding! How come Little Lord Fauntleroy can't find his own dance partner?'

Sylvia's expression grew pinched and petulant. 'Mr Burns isn't looking for any common-or-garden girl. His gentlemen seek expert dancers who can impress judges and help them win competitions.'

Joy raised a warning finger to shut Pearl up. 'That's all well and good,' she soothed. 'But dancing is a strenuous business – it takes stamina and that means you have to keep your strength up.'

Sylvia shook her head impatiently. 'Don't you see? This is my chance to leave Blackpool and make my mark in London.'

'We do see,' Pearl said with a grimace. 'We see exactly.'

'Cliff is all for it,' Sylvia insisted.

'I'll bet he is,' Pearl muttered under her breath.

'Hush!' Joy warned.

'He's teaching me all the Latin dances that my mother refuses to countenance, so I'll be more up to date when Mr Burns asks to see me.'

'Oh, Sylvia.' With a sigh Pearl stood up and straightened out the creases in her skirt. 'I hope you know what you're doing.'

Joy helped Sylvia to her feet. 'How do you feel now?'

'Perfectly all right.' Pleased that she'd stood her ground, Sylvia glanced at her reflection and pushed back more stray hairs from her forehead. 'I'm not stupid,' she told Pearl. 'I can see why you might have reservations about Cliff; I had a few myself at first. But he really doesn't take advantage – quite the opposite.' Since their solitary, brief kiss it was noticeable that Cliff had made no further moves. This was a novel situation for Sylvia and one that confused her and nibbled away at her confidence. Why was Cliff Seymour seemingly immune to her charms?

Pearl raised her hands in a gesture of surrender. 'Come along, Joy – we can't keep the boys waiting any longer.'

'Thank you for the shoes.' Joy followed Pearl towards the door but before she left the studio she glanced over her shoulder and saw that Sylvia had already dismissed them from her thoughts and was studying her reflection. She turned this way and that, inspecting herself from every angle. Joy felt a sharp stab of concern which she dismissed with a quick goodbye as she stepped out into the street.

Too thin – what nonsense! Sylvia inspected herself sideways on. Wasn't it Wallis Simpson who said that a woman could never be too thin or too rich? 'Never explain, never complain' was another of her sayings that Sylvia had read in a magazine. People had been so unfair to the American divorcee when she'd married the Duke of Windsor, but Sylvia had always admired the woman's elegance and single-mindedness. Besides, her dress sense was second to none.

Sylvia drew herself upright and took a deep, shuddering breath. Then, for no reason at all, she began to cry. Sobs rose from beneath her diaphragm, threatening to choke her as they reached her throat then bursting out in an uncontrollable surge. What on earth was the matter with her? Her frame was racked with sobs and she sank back on to the stool, covering her face with her hands and crying hot tears until she was exhausted.

It was most unlike her and Sylvia had no idea what had brought it on. Drawing a handkerchief from her trouser pocket, she noisily blew her nose then took several deep breaths to regain control. Then, gathering her last ounce of energy, she went upstairs and straight to bed before her mother got back. *Pearl Scott – of all the cheek!* Sylvia thought as she put on her nightdress. *What does she know about anything – a girl who serves behind a fish and chip counter!* Sylvia removed her make-up with a swab of cotton wool. *Pearl didn't even know what the word impresario meant.* Firm swipes with the cotton wool took away the bright-red lipstick. *Likewise Joy Hebden, who means well but simply follows where Pearl leads. They know nothing about the wider world, either of them.* But Sylvia would make them eat their words. She would put on a perfect performance for Mr Burns. Cheerio, Blackpool and hello, London. She would sparkle and impress, rise to the heights. There would be no limit to what she would achieve.

After the surprise air raid early in the month, July rolled smoothly on. Crowds continued to flock to Blackpool to soak up the sun and enjoy all that the town had to offer. There were queues at the entrance to the Pleasure Beach and outside the lido, snaking along the wide prom. Seafront stalls sold out of sunhats, ice cream and candy floss, while at night the circus and theatres were full to overflowing.

'What did I tell you!' Henry crowed to his wife and Pearl, plus anyone within hearing distance. 'I'm raking it in with the Allwins; making money hand over fist.'

Maria said nothing and went on dipping fish in batter. It was coming up to five o'clock on a Friday evening and the rush for fish and chips was about to start.

Henry stood in shirtsleeves and waistcoat on the baking-hot pavement, leaning his elbow on the counter and acknowledging passers-by with a good-humoured nod.

'Did you hear me, oh ye of little faith?' he said to Maria. 'The arcade is a runaway success.'

'How about raising my wages, then?' Working alongside her mother, Pearl sliced through raw potatoes, ready to put them in the fryer.

Henry acted as if he hadn't heard. 'As a matter of fact, I'm thinking of opening another one on the north shore.'

'Come again?' Maria stopped what she was doing.

'I'm ready to expand my business,' Henry boasted. 'What's wrong with that? If a man doesn't take a risk then he'll never get anywhere. The only thing stopping me is finding a reliable chap to run it.'

Pearl ceased chopping, knife poised over the board. 'I can think of someone.'

'Who?' Henry cocked his head to one side.

'Bernie.'

'Bernie Greene?'

'Yes – that Bernie. He's been looking for work ever since Mick got him the sack at Squires Gate.'

'Hmm.' Her father gave the idea serious consideration. 'He's got his head screwed on – unlike that lout of a brother.' Everyone in Empire Street had fresh tales to tell of Mick getting drunk, starting fights and getting himself banned from the Black Horse. Just last night he'd passed out in the entrance to Mason's yard and had to have a bucket of cold water chucked over him to bring him round. Neighbours said it was a miracle that he managed to hang on to his foreman's job at the airport and that he was going to the dogs in a big way.

'And Bernie's a decent mechanic – he knows how to fix the slot machines if they go wrong.' Pearl spoke rapidly then held her breath. Bernie had admitted only yesterday that he was only just scraping a living by helping Joe on his market stall and doing as many hours as possible at the Pleasure Beach. It meant he was hard pushed to pay his rent and keep up with the dance lessons that they'd lined up. There was also the small matter of a possible call-up into one of the armed services that bothered her.

Maria – never one to beat about the bush – added her support. 'Pearl's right – Bernie would do a good job.' Hot fat sizzled as she lowered battered fillets into the fryer. 'Knowing you, you'll go full steam ahead, whatever I say. So find your new premises and do what Pearl suggests: give Bernie a go.'

'Please, Dad!'

Hard-headed Henry laid down his first condition. 'I wouldn't be able to pay him much – not until we're up and running.'

Maria gave a snort that said it all.

'Say yes,' Pearl pleaded. 'I'm seeing him later. Shall I ask him to have a word with you?'

Henry growled and grumbled about setting-up costs but in the end he agreed. 'Aye; tell the lad to come and talk to me this evening.'

Pearl filled the wire basket with freshly cut chips then lowered them into the fryer where they sizzled happily. 'Champion.' She leaned over the counter and gave her father a peck on the cheek. 'Ta, Dad – you've made my day!'

The Wards' house in the north of the town was Joy's last cleaning job of the day. It meant taking a tram from the lido along the seafront to the family's modern, semi-detached home in a cul-de-sac well away from the tourist throng.

Joining the queue for the tram, Joy found herself standing directly behind Edna Ward, her employer's twenty-five-year-old daughter – a lively, chatty type with flaming red hair – who straight away engaged Joy in conversation.

'Phew, I'm boiling!' she declared as she fanned her freckled face with a magazine. She was dressed in a sleeveless yellow sundress with a square neckline. 'I don't know how you manage to clean houses in this weather.'

Joy envied Edna her easy manner. 'It'll cool down in a bit,' she assured her.

'I can't stand the heat.' Edna craned her neck to look for the next tram. *Nothing doing.* Bathers with towels rolled under their arms emerged through the lido turnstile and joined the end of the queue.

Following Edna's gaze, Joy spotted the unmistakable figure of Terry Liddle, head and shoulders above the crowd, wearing a pale-blue sports shirt and dark-blue slacks. As soon as he spotted Joy in the queue, he made a detour in her direction.

'Long time no see,' he said as he approached. 'Why has Blackpool's answer to Hedy Lamarr been avoiding me?'

Edna gave Joy a curious glance.

157

'Hello, Terry,' Joy replied in a neutral tone. 'I haven't been avoiding you. I've been busy, that's all.'

'But not too busy to come dancing with me tomorrow night, I hope?' Bold as brass, not thinking for a second that she would turn him down, he held her in his dazzling gaze. 'Tower Ballroom – I'll pay for your ticket. You watch – we'll wipe the floor with the other contestants.'

Joy shook her head. 'I'm sorry – I can't. I've arranged to go with someone else.'

Edna gave a gasp of disbelief.

Terry's smile faded. 'Tell her she doesn't know what she's missing,' he said to Edna with a shrug and a conspiratorial wink before abruptly turning away and resuming his original course towards Silver Street.

Relieved to see his back view, Joy let out a sigh. It was true that their paths had rarely crossed and she'd been perfectly happy with that.

'Oh, I say!' Edna's eyebrows had shot up during Joy's brief conversation with her fellow lodger. 'Most girls would give their eye teeth—'

'Here comes a tram,' Joy interrupted curtly.

'What did you say his name was?' Edna shuffled forward expectantly.

'Terry – Terry Liddle. He works at the lido. Why?'

'Nothing – only, I could've sworn I recognized him from when I worked in Blackburn.' Edna squeezed into the crowded tram ahead of Joy. 'But if I remember rightly, the fellow I'm thinking of was called Anthony or Tony something or other. It must be a case of mistaken identity.'

'Move along, please!' The conductor's impatient bark and the increasing crush in the tram's central

158

aisle broke up the conversation. A middle-aged man gave up his seat to Edna, who sank gratefully into it, while Joy held on to the overhead luggage rack and swayed as the tram jolted into action again. Dismissing Terry from her thoughts, she turned her attention to more pleasant matters – to Tommy and their arrangement to meet at the ice-cream parlour next day.

'I'd prefer for you to stay in tonight,' Lorna warned Sylvia from the kitchen as she prepared snacks for an evening at home with Maurice and Eddie. 'If you have anything else planned, please cancel it.'

'I don't, as it happens.' Sylvia's off-hand reply filtered through from the living room. She sat with her feet up on the coffee table and her head resting against the back of the sofa. A magazine lay open and unread on her lap.

Lorna entered the room with a tray. She'd arranged her hair and chosen her dress with her usual care. 'It's not too much to ask, surely.'

'Don't go on – I've already agreed to stay in.'

'Move your feet, please.' Lorna put down the tray. 'Hurry up and get changed – our guests will be here any minute.'

Sylvia overcame a heavy lethargy to heave herself upright. 'I thought I'd stay in these clothes.'

Her mother looked askance at the blouse and skirt Sylvia had worn all day. 'At least comb your hair and freshen up your face.'

'Really, Mother – we're expecting Eddie and Maurice, not royalty.' Nevertheless, Sylvia sloped off to her room and chose the pale-green dress that she brightened up with sparkling costume jewellery. When the doorbell rang and her mother ran downstairs to welcome their guests, Sylvia was making last-minute adjustments to her hair.

'So kind . . . not too much trouble?' Maurice Winter stepped inside.

'Not at all; please come up.' Pleasantries drifted through Sylvia's half-open door.

'Is Sylvia able to make it?' Eddie asked as the trio mounted the stairs.

'Yes; she wouldn't miss it for the world,' Lorna assured him.

Gathering her resolve, Sylvia joined them in the living room.

Maurice Winter was courtesy itself. 'Sylvia, dear – how nice to see you. It's been far too long.'

She accepted a kiss on the cheek from both men.

'Please take a seat, everyone.' Lorna had choreographed the evening perfectly. Maurice was to sit close to the open window while Sylvia and Eddie sat side by side on the sofa. Music played softly in the background – a mellifluous violin arrangement that wouldn't interfere with conversation. Lorna poured dry sherry. Everyone leaned in and chinked their glasses. 'Cheers.'

Eddie noticed that Sylvia took the smallest of sips.

Maurice, on the other hand, quickly finished his glass and accepted a refill. He was a distinguished-looking man with thinning grey hair and handsome, even features. His voice was reassuring and his manners were perfect, if a touch suave. He confessed to having had a busy week at work: full surgeries with many referrals to hospital, followed by meetings at his club in the evenings. A senior member of the town's Civil Defence team had suggested that Maurice join them in the control room on a voluntary basis, but for a busy GP lack of time was always a problem. 'Besides, a man needs to relax occasionally; don't you agree?'

'Wholeheartedly.' Lorna perched on the edge of her seat, nodding vigorously.

Eddie offered Sylvia a plate of savoury titbits, which she refused. Though they sat within touching distance, she stared ahead with a glassy expression, refusing eye contact.

'So, Sylvia, what's this I hear about you branching out into Latin?' Maurice said out of the blue. 'Rumba, samba, and this new thing imported from America that they call the jive.'

Lorna froze, sherry glass in hand. Eddie raised his hand at his father as if stopping traffic. Sylvia rocked back in her seat and shot Eddie an accusatory look.

'Not guilty,' he whispered through clenched teeth.

Maurice cleared his throat. 'Oh dear, forgive me – it seems I've spoken out of turn.'

'Surely you're mistaken – Sylvia is strictly modern – waltz, foxtrot, quickstep and tango. We never stray into Latin at the Lorna Ellis Dance Academy.' Lorna was adamant. 'Back me up, Edward dear.'

'It's true – you don't,' he said faintly, fearing what was to come.

'I'd like to know who's spreading this rumour,' Lorna said with slow deliberation, her eyes flicking from Eddie to Maurice before finally resting on Sylvia's face. 'Have you any idea who it might be?'

Sylvia fought for breath. Her head was spinning and she found no words of explanation.

Gallant Maurice jumped to what he thought was the rescue. 'Let me settle this for you. I overheard a chance remark by a patient in my surgery waiting room – forgive me if I don't provide a name. Sylvia was mentioned in a flattering context: how talented she was. I could have sworn the words lindy hop and jitterbug were used but I'm obviously mistaken.'

'Sylvia?' Lorna demanded, her voice keen and cutting as a knife.

Three or four half-formed excuses flitted through Sylvia's head before resentment killed them off. 'Oh for heaven's sake, Mother – yes, I've been learning Latin; with Cliff Seymour, if you must know!'

'Cliff Seymour?' Lorna put down the sherry glass with a stricken look, then without saying another word, she rose from her chair and stalked from the room.

'My sincere apologies.' Seeing that the evening was ruined, Maurice stood up, ready to leave. 'Had I realized . . .'

'No – you weren't to know,' Sylvia said faintly.

'I'm so sorry.' Eddie, desperate to offer comfort, could only apologize on his father's behalf.

Maurice sought to downplay emotions. 'Perhaps Lorna will come round to the idea, given time.'

'I think not,' Sylvia whispered as she stood to see them out. She'd gone against everything that her mother stood for – and behind her back, at that; the betrayal was too great.

Softening his tone, Maurice took his young friend by the shoulders and looked her in the eye. 'My dear, I've known you for a good many years,' he reminded her gently, 'and during that time I've grown very fond of you. I think of you almost as a daughter and I have no wish to see you hurt.'

Eddie bit his lip uneasily but said nothing.

'I feel duty-bound to offer advice regarding Cliff Seymour,' Maurice went on.

Sylvia waited with mounting dread.

'I must warn you to be very careful about any promises that Mr Seymour might make,' Maurice continued. 'I don't only mean promises on a professional level but on a personal one as well.'

Panic fluttered to the surface. 'What do you mean? I don't understand.'

'It's delicate.'

'Father, perhaps not now?' Eddie tried to intervene but without success.

'Professionally the man might be everything he claims. He may well be an excellent teacher and possibly has useful connections in the dance world – who knows? But on a personal level, when it comes to a relationship between a man and a woman, all may not be as it seems.'

Still the penny refused to drop. Sylvia frowned and shook her head, as if bothered by an insect.

Maurice cut through the web of confusion with language that he hoped she would understand. 'Cliff Seymour is not the marrying kind,' he told her softly.

'Ah!' *But the flirtatious compliments, the drive in his sports car, the solitary kiss! Surely not?!*

'You take my meaning?' Maurice prompted.

'Yes.' Feeling as if the entire world had shifted beneath her feet, Sylvia offered no resistance as Eddie eased her on to the sofa.

'Mr Seymour may pretend otherwise, as men of his

persuasion must do.' Maurice ended his explanation with an apology of his own. 'My dear, I'm sorry if this comes as a shock.'

'Yes, it does.' *But then no, not entirely.* Sylvia recalled Cliff's passing references to blond German officers at his Berlin nightclub and to gum-chewing American GIs whom he would welcome to his studio with open arms. God; she'd been a naive fool! How easily Cliff had pulled the wool over her eyes.

'You go, Father,' Eddie said. 'I'll stay here with Sylvia.'

'If Sylvia wishes?'

'Yes, please,' she murmured, grasping Eddie's hand. The room still tilted at an odd angle and her vision was blurred. His hand was warm and solid.

'Very well; I'll show myself out.' With a formal nod, Maurice left the room.

'Not the marrying kind,' Sylvia repeated. 'Hand on heart, it didn't cross my mind.'

'Why should it?' Eddie asked. 'Cliff puts on a good act.'

'I thought he . . .' *The kiss, for goodness' sake!* 'But no, it turns out that he's only interested in me as a dancer.'

Eddie stroked her hand. The sound of Sylvia's mother returning made him hold it more firmly.

'How could you go behind my back?' Lorna burst back into the living room, her cheeks flushed with rage. 'Edward, did you know about this?'

Sylvia snatched her hand away. 'Leave Eddie out of it. This was my choice and no one else's.'

'Your choice!' Lorna fumed. 'Your choice to lower yourself to the level of every common soldier, sailor

164

and fairground worker in town. I've seen the way they grab hold of their partners and barge around and bump and kick their feet about. The girls are as bad – showing their underthings and letting themselves down.'

'It's just people having fun, and why not?' Knowing deep down that she had little chance of winning the argument, Sylvia's defence was weak.

'And for you to cheapen yourself and throw away your chances of making a real career out of entering bona fide ISTD competitions is sheer madness. Tell her, Edward.'

'You'd better go,' Sylvia told him before he could be dragged in. 'Please – this is between my mother and me.'

'If you're sure?' Reluctant to leave her to Lorna's mercies, Eddie nevertheless bowed out.

Lorna waited until she heard the click of the downstairs door latch then changed tack. 'How could you do this to poor Edward – and with Cliff Seymour, of all people?'

'There's nothing going on between me and Cliff.' Sylvia shuddered as she spoke the stark truth.

'I don't believe you. You've betrayed Edward as well as me. You fling his devotion back in his face.'

'Mother – please.' Lorna's lapse into melodrama forced a grim smile from Sylvia. She stood up from the sofa. 'I'm tired. I'm going to bed.'

'Not so fast!' Lorna barred her way. 'I need to know that you'll give up this Latin nonsense; now, this minute.'

Mother and daughter faced each other, eye to eye and burning with fury.

'Well?' Lorna demanded.

'No,' Sylvia replied fiercely. 'You can't force me.'

Lorna was the first to blink. 'What do you mean: no?'

'I mean, I'll carry on taking Latin lessons. Whatever else Cliff may be, he's a good teacher and I wish to learn from him.'

Lorna's eyes widened in disbelief then narrowed into a stubborn expression of steely anger. 'Do as you please,' she said as she stepped aside. 'But understand this: if you follow the Latin path there will no longer be a place for you to teach at the Lorna Ellis Dance Academy. Do you understand?'

'Perfectly.' Sylvia hovered in the doorway.

'I shall be forced to focus my energies on Edward's future instead,' Lorna threatened. 'His potential to reach the top, with or without you, is what I must concentrate on. I will find him a new partner – perhaps Joy Hebden or Pearl Scott.'

Lorna had forced Sylvia's hand and her mind grew crystal clear. 'Have it your own way. I'll be out of your hair as soon as I can find new lodgings.'

'Wait!' Lorna's stomach lurched at the sudden, unexpected shift. She reached out and caught hold of her daughter's arm. 'You don't have to move out of the apartment. It's not what I meant.'

'Get out of my way, Mother.' Sylvia wrenched free. 'I'm leaving home and nothing you can say or do will stop me.'

CHAPTER ELEVEN

'Blimey, what a mess!' Pearl stared in dismay at Bernie's scattered belongings. It was her first visit to his new room on Market Street and she noticed that shirts and trousers lay crumpled on the floor and shoes had been flung into a corner next to the bed. Socks and underthings had at least got as far as the top of the dilapidated chest of drawers. Faded curtains hung limp from their hooks, the dingy green walls were unadorned and ashes from the previous winter's fires were heaped in the grate.

'If I'd known you were coming, I'd have tidied up.' Unconcerned, Bernie made a move to shift a pile of football magazines from the one chair in the room.

'Fibber!' she said with a laugh. Bursting to deliver her news, she picked her way between articles of clothing then seized his hand. 'Guess what – Dad is thinking of opening a second amusement arcade.'

'So what?' Bernie drew her to him. Amid the chaos of the room, Pearl glowed. She brought light and fun wherever she went, and boy, was he glad to see her!

'So he'll need someone to run it. I've put in a good word on your behalf.'

'You don't say.' He kissed her long and hard.

Pearl struggled free. 'Did you hear what I said? Dad may have a job for you. He wants to talk to you before he makes up his mind.'

Bernie went in for more kisses but as the news sank in, he drew back. 'A job?' he repeated.

'Yes – running the new arcade.'

Bernie popped his lips. 'Listen, I know your dad of old. Are you sure this isn't just pie in the sky?'

'No – he means it. For once he's making decent money and he intends to expand. He wants to see you right now, this minute.' Pearl fastened the top button of Bernie's shirt. 'But first you have to tidy yourself up. Put on a tie and a smart jacket.'

He went to the chest of drawers and rummaged for the single tie that he owned. 'Heck, Pearl – you could've given me a bit more warning. Do I need a shave?'

Running her fingers over his chin, she shook her head. 'Remember: let Dad do the talking. All you have to do is nod in the right places and convince him that you're the man for the job.'

'But am I, though?' Bernie obediently tilted back his chin and let Pearl adjust his neckwear. Truth to tell, his row with Mick, loss of job and recent move out of Empire Street had dented his confidence. 'When you say "run the new arcade", what would that entail exactly?'

'I don't know the details – you'll have to ask Dad. But Mum's already given you her seal of approval and that's a good thing.'

'Is it?' He reached for his best jacket then ran a comb through his hair.

Pearl brushed stray hairs from the shoulders of the

168

jacket. 'Yes; it might not look like it but she's the real boss in our house. There; you'll do.'

Before Bernie knew it, they were out on the street and heading across the market square in the direction of the Black Horse, where Henry held most of his so-called meetings. Sure enough, they found him propping up the bar, regaling fellow drinkers with exaggerated tales about his latest business success and boasting of his ambitions to expand.

'Amusement arcades are the future,' he proclaimed. 'These modern Allwins attract punters by the hundreds. All you need is the right premises and a bright sign above the door, flashing lights and all.'

'And the right people working for you.' Pearl popped up next to her father. 'Here's Bernie, like I promised.'

Henry cast a cursory glance at the applicant. 'What do you think, lad – are you up to the job? And before you answer, I hope Pearl explained that your wage will depend on how much profit we can rake in. No profit means no wage at the end of the week, *comprendo*?'

Pearl pulled a face but Bernie didn't blink. 'Fair enough,' he acknowledged.

'It'll be seven days a week to start with, working alongside Pearl for the rest of the summer season, and don't expect nine till five – we stay open till late in the evening. You'll keep track of the entrance money and top up the cash payouts in the machines. And don't stand any nonsense; if a customer kicks up a fuss, you boot him out, no messing.'

'Yes, sir.' Bernie grew keen. The responsibility appealed, as did the prospect of working with Pearl and rising to a new challenge.

Pearl's frown deepened. Seven days a week including evenings wouldn't leave Bernie and her with time for dancing – or for anything else, for that matter – something that hadn't crossed her mind until now.

'Well?' Henry demanded. 'You start as soon as I find premises.'

'Done,' Bernie agreed.

The two men shook hands then Henry turned to his pals and launched straight into a story about how much he'd won on a horse that he'd backed at Aintree. 'Mother's Pride, named after the new-fangled sliced bread. Came in at fifty to one.'

'Come along.' Pearl tugged at Bernie's arm and they left the pub, pausing on the pavement to take in what had just happened.

'What's up? Aren't you going to congratulate me?' he asked.

'Yes, well done. But boo-hoo, this'll mean no more dancing at the Tower on a Saturday.'

'No more lindy hops for the time being,' he agreed. 'And no dance lessons during the week either.' Seeing her dejected expression, he slid an arm around her waist and walked her down the street. 'Never mind; at least it's a job. And maybe we won't be tied up for long. Once the arcade is up and running, your dad might get us an assistant, then we'll take some evenings off.'

'And pigs might fly.' Pearl couldn't hide her disappointment.

'Listen.' Bernie drew her under the arched entrance of the derelict stable yard. 'Officially I'll be your boss.'

'Is that right?' she teased. 'Let's see how that works out, shall we?'

Bernie made a grab for her and kissed her hard. 'Yes. Don't worry – I'll give you time off so you can carry on having dance lessons without me.'

'No, it wouldn't be the same.'

'But it would be better than nothing. Then you could teach me all the new moves, for when I do wangle a few free nights for myself. We'd be ready to take on all-comers again.'

His attempt to cheer her up was interrupted by a ruckus outside the Black Horse and the sight of Bernie's brother being forcefully prevented from entering.

'Get it into your thick head, Mick Greene; you're banned!' the barman yelled, as Mick staggered backwards against a lamp-post then sank to the ground, legs splayed and head lolling. Two men stepped over him on their way into the bar.

Bernie swore then rushed to the rescue. He crossed the street, followed by Pearl, and together they set Mick back on his feet and dusted him down. Pearl jammed his cap more firmly on to his head, recoiling at the foul smell of tobacco smoke and alcohol on his breath.

'Let's get you home,' Bernie muttered as he supported his brother and guided him towards the house. 'God knows you don't deserve it, but I can hardly leave you lying there.'

Grunting and swearing, Mick tried to shove Bernie away. 'Keep your hands to yourself.'

The slurred words made Pearl see red. Really, Mick Greene was a loathsome, disgusting nuisance best left to his own devices. 'Leave him,' she told Bernie. 'Let him make his own way home.'

'That's right,' Mick growled. 'You heard the little lady; go and practise your fancy footwork with the other ponces.'

Bernie gritted his teeth. 'Let's get you into the house. Come on – that's the way. Up three steps; one, two, three. Through the door . . .'

Once inside, Mick jerked free then slumped to the floor. The thud of his body hitting the boards caused a shudder of exasperation to run through Pearl. 'Now will you leave him?' she demanded.

Bernie covered his brother with a coat that he took from a hook in the hallway then made a pillow with a rolled-up woollen scarf. 'He's going from bad to worse,' he sighed, staring down at the inert form.

'Yes, but let's go.'

Once outside, they drew deep breaths then strolled back in the direction of the Black Horse. 'Should we pop in and celebrate me getting the job?' Bernie asked.

Pearl shook her head. 'I'd rather it was just us celebrating, you and me together.'

'To my place, then?'

'Not if you're expecting me to tidy up.' Never cast down for long, she jabbed her elbow into his ribs.

'I wouldn't dream of it.'

'Come on, then.' Pearl took the lead across the empty square and into the deep shadow of the Tower, where young lovers clung to each other under shop awnings and raucous gangs of lads and lasses roamed. Faint strains of a popular song drifted from the Pleasure Beach – 'Tangerine' by Jimmy Dorsey.

' "When she dances by, Señoritas stare . . ." ' Bernie sang under his breath. 'I haven't got anything to celebrate with,' he warned Pearl. 'No bottles of beer or even sherry. Shall we buy some from the off-licence?'

'Let's not bother.' She snuggled up to him and felt the warmth of his body.

'Right you are.' They reached Market Street. It felt like a now-or-never moment – Pearl would come up to his room, knowing there was nowhere for them to sit except the bed. And from there they both knew what was likely to happen. 'You're sure you want to?' he asked.

'No,' she confessed with a shy smile. 'Are you?'

'Yes.' He unlocked the door and led her up the creaking stairs. Opening the door into his room, he went quickly to pull down the blackout blind and turn on a bedside lamp. Then he shifted the stack of magazines from the chair. 'If you'd rather?'

'No – here's fine.' Pearl sat on the bed. This was the occasion that nobody talked about; a first time for them both. Sure, you saw the build-up in films – low lighting, a swell of violins, a soft-focus lens, the glint of a pearl earring, a fully clothed embrace. Yes, in the privacy of your own bedroom you might rehearse what the occasion would be like in real life, but on the silver screen there were never socks strewn across the eiderdown and a creased shirt at the end of the bed. She laughed out loud.

'What's funny?'

'This – everything!' The mess was Bernie's mess and she loved him for it. 'I am sure now, but I'm still not going to tidy up.'

'I'm still not asking you to.' Laughter summed up Pearl – brightness and happiness. She was irresistible. He sat beside her on the bedsprings that poked through the thin mattress. She smelled of something sweet, a flower that he couldn't name. Her neck when he kissed it was warm and smooth.

'Will you give up working the waltzers?' she murmured.

'Yes, I'll have to.' He kissed her cheek then swung her legs on to the bed. They lay side by side, staring at the ceiling.

'So no more free rides – Elsie will be heartbroken.'

'She'll get over it.' It felt like the most natural thing in the world to be lying next to Pearl and, without embarrassment, Bernie said what was uppermost in his thoughts. 'I've never gone all the way before.'

'Me neither.'

'Do you want to?'

'Yes.' Pearl turned towards him with a longing that melted every limb. The outside world didn't exist – it was just the two of them: her and him. 'With all my heart.'

This kiss in this room on this bed and in the midst of his muddle was the beginning of a tender, loving journey that would bind Pearl and Bernie together for better or worse and remain in their memories for the rest of their lives.

Sylvia wasn't certain what time Joy would finish her cleaning shift at the circus. All she knew was that it was Saturday and Joy would be in a rush to go home and get changed into her dance things. Running into Tommy in his spangled clown regalia in the corridor that overlooked the circus ring, Sylvia said she hoped she hadn't missed her.

'No; she's in there.' Tommy jerked his thumb towards the clowns' changing room. He was surprised to see Sylvia in these rough-and-ready surroundings. She was in her usual finery – high heels and frills, with her hair in a sleek ponytail – but there was something different about her that he couldn't put his finger on. 'Joy's getting changed into her dance togs,' he explained. 'It's easier than her trekking all the way back to Silver Street.'

'I'll wait here,' Sylvia decided. She found Tommy's sequinned pantaloon costume, dunce's hat and painted face disconcerting – it was only his voice that was recognizable. 'If you don't mind, that is,' she added.

'Feel free.' Ah yes; the difference wasn't in what Sylvia wore or the way she styled her hair but in the jerkiness of her movements and the forward slope of her shoulders. And bloody hell, she was thin as a rake. 'Will we see you and Eddie at the ballroom later?' he asked to pass the time.

'Yes, although things are rather difficult between us at the moment,' Sylvia replied stiffly.

'Since when?'

'Since yesterday, if you must know.' After the furious row between mother and daughter, Lorna had quickly recovered from Sylvia's shock announcement about leaving home then wasted no time in picking up the telephone and explaining to Eddie that she had washed her hands of her rebellious daughter. Standing in the doorway, Sylvia had heard only her mother's side of the conversation – Lorna's decision was final: Sylvia had betrayed her and there would be no going back. She was no longer part of the Lorna Ellis Dance Academy; from now on Eddie would be dancing with a new partner.

Sylvia had withdrawn to her room feeling sick at heart. She and her mother had not spoken since.

'You two have had a tiff?' Tommy asked with genuine concern.

Sylvia shook her head. 'Not me and Eddie. The problem is between me and my mother and I fully expect him to take her side.'

At this moment Joy emerged from the changing room to find Sylvia deep in conversation with Tommy while down below animal cages were being erected in the ring in readiness for the evening performance. There was the clang of metal, the sound of men whistling and a general sense of busy anticipation.

'There you are!' Seeing Joy in her peach-coloured dress and the heeled shoes that she'd lent her, Sylvia broke away from Tommy. 'Oh good – I hoped to catch you. I wanted to ask you if you knew of a vacancy in any of the boarding houses on Silver Street.'

Joy was taken aback. 'Who wants to know?'

'A friend.' Sylvia's fib fooled nobody. 'I'm asking on behalf of someone who's in urgent need of somewhere to live.'

Joy glanced at Tommy, who shrugged. 'There's no room at number fifty-seven – I know that for a fact. But I do remember seeing a vacancy sign in the window of number twenty-five.'

'Number twenty-five,' Sylvia repeated. For the first time in her life, she was forced to contemplate independent living and the prospect terrified her. She'd turned to Joy for help because she was the only girl Sylvia knew in similar circumstances. 'How much should my friend expect to pay for lodgings in that part of town?'

'It depends. Rooms at the front of the house are always more expensive. Your friend should expect to pay less for one overlooking the backyard or up in the attic.'

Sylvia was aware that lack of money would come near the top of her list of problems. She would have to rely on her meagre savings and start to earn a wage as quickly as possible. 'Thank you – I'll pass that on,' she murmured with flushed cheeks and a refusal to look Joy in the eye.

'I'll leave you girls to it.' Feeling the tension, Tommy made a tactical withdrawal into his changing room.

Joy let a silence develop as she steered Sylvia along the dark, tiled corridor out into an open area containing a ticket office and a tearoom, complete with potted palms and ferns. Sun poured in through fan-shaped stained-glass windows and Joy chose a ledge in a shady corner on which to perch. 'Tell me the truth – this room you mentioned is really for you,' she prompted.

Sylvia's woes came tumbling out – the secret lessons with Cliff, the argument with her mother, the decision to cut loose and fend for herself. 'I planned not to say anything until after I've sorted myself out. I didn't want to burden you.'

'You're not,' Joy assured her. 'But are you sure that leaving home is the right decision?'

Sylvia grew animated. 'I don't have a choice. If I

stay, my mother will have won hands down – I'd have to do exactly as she tells me. And I'm twenty-one years old! Why shouldn't I make my own decisions? I don't have to stick to what she teaches – where's the harm in learning Latin, for goodness' sake?'

'I can see that,' Joy agreed. 'But this is a big step to take and Pearl and I are already worried about you.'

'There's no need but thank you anyway.' Spurred on by Joy's kindness, Sylvia fell deeper into confessional mode. 'If I let you into another secret, will you swear not to tell?'

'I swear.'

'It's about Cliff.' She took a deep breath. 'I have it on good authority he's . . . well, he's not interested in girls in the romantic way.' Colour deepened in Sylvia's cheeks as she leaned forward and struggled to express herself.

'Why not?' *Not interested in girls?* The simple phrase left Joy puzzled.

'He prefers men,' Sylvia explained bluntly. 'I suppose I ought to have guessed but honestly it never crossed my mind.'

Thunderstruck, Joy's eyes opened wide – she'd never even heard of such a thing. 'That can't be right!'

'It is. That's how some men are, apparently. And it explains a lot about the way Cliff acts – why he doesn't have a sweetheart, for a start.'

'But I thought *you* were . . .'

'What?'

'His sweetheart. So did Pearl. To be honest, we both felt a little sorry that you seemed to have dropped Eddie.' *So some men prefer to be in a relationship with another*

178

man – good Lord above! It took time for Joy to make sense
of the information that had fallen into her lap.

'Tell no one.' Sylvia heaved a deep sigh. Why was
life so complicated? She glanced at her watch then
stood up. 'Talking of Eddie, I've an arrangement to
dance with him here tonight.'

Joy's head whirled with shock and disbelief. 'Does
he know . . .?'

'About Cliff? Yes; his father was the one who broke
the news to me, and Eddie was there at the time. I'm
not sure if he'll show up – not after a nasty phone call
that my mother made. But I hope he does.'

'I'm sure he won't let you down.' Steadying herself,
Joy accompanied Sylvia down the stairs then out on
to the pavement. 'We'll see you later, with or without
Eddie?'

'Yes.' Sylvia decided there and then that going out
for the evening was better than staying in and suffering her mother's sullen silence. 'And remember: not
a word.'

'Ernie, make sure Elsie is in bed by eight and, Wilf,
don't go further than the end of the street,' Pearl
instructed as she got ready to leave the house.

'It's not fair – why do I have to babysit?' Ernie
complained.

'Because Mum and Dad are still at work and I'm
going out.' Pearl brooked no argument. She'd made
a special effort to look her best by washing her hair
and putting on her shiniest, tightest Latin dress,
determined to make the most of the leisure time she
would have with Bernie before they started their new
jobs. She'd scrutinized her face in the mirror as she'd

179

dabbed on her lipstick. Did she look different after last night? Surely a girl's appearance should alter after she'd taken the momentous step into woman-hood. But no one seemed to have noticed, except perhaps her mother, who had stared hard at Pearl over the breakfast table but said nothing. Anyway, she certainly felt different, wearing her secret like a halo, spreading light wherever she went.

She closed the door behind her and floated down Empire Street on a cloud of well-being. Bernie greeted her on the corner and they walked hand in hand to the ballroom where they met Tommy and Joy, who were waiting for them outside the main entrance. It was a cloudy, sultry evening with little wind. The sea was dark grey, the beach almost deserted.

'Are you ready for the contest?' Tommy led the way inside. 'It's the cha-cha; all saucy chassés and high kicks.'

'Ready!' Bernie and Pearl chorused as they joined the ticket queue.

'And let's hope Herr Hitler doesn't spoil our fun this time,' Tommy added with a wry grin.

Joy kept a lookout for Sylvia among the colourful crowd. The girls who came to compete wore close-fitting dresses of turquoise, scarlet and gold, with skirts split high up the thigh, teamed with fishnet tights and high heels. Soon Joy picked out Sylvia in a daring halter-neck dress of crimson satin trimmed with black lace, and she was relieved to see Eddie standing next to her, a little ahead of them in the queue. Joy ventured forward to say hello.

Eddie returned the greeting as Sylvia flashed her a sharp look: *I hope you've kept your word!*

'Sylvia, can I pick your brains about the cha-cha?' Joy invented a pretext as she secretly gave Sylvia's hand a reassuring squeeze. 'Where does the musical accent come?'

'On the count of four and one; cha-cha-cha,' Sylvia reminded her with a grateful smile.

She'd been badly on edge as she'd got ready to come out. Luckily her mother had been busy in the studio and Sylvia had been able to slip away unnoticed. The nerves had increased as she'd walked down King Alfred Road and on to the prom – the bruised, black sky had reflected her mood. It was only when she'd seen Eddie waiting for her at the ballroom entrance that she'd relaxed a little. 'Thank heavens you're here,' she'd breathed.

He'd kissed her on the cheek. 'Why would I not be?'

'I heard what Mother said to you on the phone. She's washed her hands of me and I thought you might do the same.'

Eddie had shaken his head. 'You know me better than that.'

'She's too stubborn to back down,' Sylvia had warned him.

'Like mother, like daughter,' he'd teased as they'd joined the queue.

'Is Tommy with you?' Eddie asked Joy with a glance over his shoulder.

'Right here!' Tommy gave a wave. 'Watch out for our smooth chassés, cha-cha-cha!'

'That means the whole gang's here.' Pearl added her voice. 'Bernie's got his eye firmly on tonight's cash prize, as per usual.'

'You betcha.' Bernie offered a thumbs-up.

'May the best man win,' Eddie replied.

'And the best girl,' Pearl chipped in.

The queue shuffled forward. Once they bought their tickets there was a whole hour of sedate waltzes and elegant foxtrots before the cha-cha competition got underway. First the crimson curtains would part and Mr Dixon would rise on to the stage with his Wurlitzer. The crystal chandeliers would sparkle and the opulent 'Wonderland of the World' would work its unique magic.

Sylvia, Pearl and Joy gathered with their partners in the centre of the dance floor. They clapped as the organ rose into view then they eased into a quickstep – bright music, tricky combinations of walks and chassés in 4/4 time.

'Life doesn't get much better.' Bernie spoke softly into Pearl's ear as he held her close and they promenaded diagonally across the floor. It was dancing that had brought them together – the whirl, swirl and twirl had gone to their heads and they'd fallen in love. *Grand!*

She smiled and sneaked a quick kiss. Gliding and swaying in time to the music, they made an eye-catching couple.

'Oops!' Ruby Donovan backed into Joy and Tommy then apologized. 'My husband, Douglas – *two left feet!*' she whispered, indicating her lanky, uniformed partner as they executed a clumsy turn.

Nearby, Mavis Thorne had more luck in the shape of Terry Liddle, oozing charm and showing off his skilful footwork. He winked at Joy as he whirled his partner round in one pivot turn swiftly followed by another.

Careful to protect Sylvia from bumps and trips, Eddie guided her safely into gaps between dancers. A quarter turn followed by smooth chassés followed by a nifty lock step; slow-quick-quick-slow. They were in their element, lost in the music and able for a few precious minutes to push aside their cares.

'Did Mother tell you: I'm leaving home?' Sylvia mentioned as the organ segued from quickstep to lilting, languid waltz – swing out on the first beat of the bar then sway into the centre of the turn, rising high on the toes; one-two-three, one-two-three. Simple and smooth.

Eddie held her close. 'No,' he murmured. 'I haven't seen Lorna since my father put his size ten foot in it.'

'I'm looking for lodgings. Will you keep your ears open for me?'

He hid his surprise with a gently teasing reply. 'Yes – if you promise to take better care of yourself than you have been lately.'

'Eddie!' She tapped him lightly on the shoulder and frowned.

'Sorry,' he breathed. 'I can't help worrying.' They swung and swayed in unison, past Tommy and Joy and Bernie and Pearl, weaving across the dance floor to the romantic swell of the organ.

All was smiles and chat as the evening wore on until the MC went to the microphone to announce the start of the night's competition. 'Ladies and gentlemen, the moment you've all been waiting for. You know the drill; judges will come among you, eliminating couples with a tap on the shoulder until only five finalists remain. Now, please take your partners for the cha-cha.'

'This is it!' Bernie's mood turned serious. 'The gloves are off,' he warned Joy and Tommy, who approached the challenge with determined expressions.

More musicians made their entrance – including a trumpet player, a bongo drummer and a man with a set of cowbells. Cha-cha was Cuban, with a strong rhythm created by the percussion instruments.

'Can't wait.' Tommy's voice was clear and confident.

Joy thrilled to the first compelling notes. Her partner loved the big, extravagant moves of this Latin dance and she hoped to do it justice. She arched her back in readiness and pointed her left foot to the side. One-two-three-four-and one . . .

. . . Two-three-four. Sylvia threw herself into the dance with all the energy that she could muster. Underarm turn to the right, left fingers flexed. Spot turn then underarm turn to the left.

Eddie guided and supported his partner with effortless ease, his hands at her waist or in the small of her back as she flicked her feet, flexed her spine, bent her knees and kicked higher than his shoulder.

Judges took note. One by one couples were eliminated, including Ruby and her soldier husband, until only a dozen remained. Terry and Mavis were still going strong and so were Tommy and Joy. Pearl and Bernie had also impressed. Sylvia was visibly tiring and she and Eddie were the next to go.

'Bad luck,' Joy whispered as they left the floor.

'Best not to overdo it.' Eddie found a seat for Sylvia and went to buy her a drink at the crowded bar.

While Eddie was gone and the contest entered its final stage, Cliff materialized out of nowhere. He wore a black satin shirt open at the neck and his light-brown hair was slicked back with brilliantine. Without waiting to be asked, he pulled up a chair and sat down next to Sylvia. 'I see you ran out of steam,' he commented as he slid a cigarette from a silver case and lit up.

She sat uneasily on the edge of her seat, staring straight ahead.

'What's the matter?' he asked through a cloud of smoke.

'Nothing. No – really.' Or everything; depending on her response to what she'd learned about Cliff's private life. Aware that she was faced with a difficult dilemma, Sylvia faked a display of sangfroid to give herself some breathing space. 'Who's your partner tonight?' she asked as casually as she could.

'No one in particular.' Cliff watched the remaining contestants with professional interest. 'My money's on Terry and Mavis.'

'They're very good,' Sylvia agreed as the judges eliminated three more couples. 'Terry's a dark horse – he arrived at the academy claiming not to know a thing about ballroom dancing, but look at him now.'

'He came to me for Latin.' Cliff dropped in the remark with slow emphasis, giving himself time to judge Sylvia's reaction.

Glancing sideways, she sensed a strong, unspoken undercurrent. *He knows I know!* Call it instinct, sixth sense, intuition – Sylvia was one hundred per cent sure.

She knows! Cliff interpreted her altered behaviour – wary where once she'd been flirtatious, guarded instead of gushing. 'Terry and I hit it off straight away,' he continued in the same deliberate manner.

Terry Liddle, of all people! Picking up on the unspoken message, Sylvia was beyond astonished. Terry, the swaggering night owl, with his love-them-and-leave-them reputation had put everyone off the scent. However, sensing that Cliff was testing her, she kept her cool. After all, she reasoned, what did it really matter what two men did in private? Even though it was against the law, it was still their choice to make. It was only a pity that they were forced to hide the truth from the world. There; she'd reached her decision! With a slow shift of weight, she turned in her chair to look Cliff in the eye.

'I need new teaching work,' she announced. 'Mother and I have parted company, due to my branching out into Latin.'

'Have you now?' Thoughtfully Cliff stubbed out the remains of his cigarette. Somehow Sylvia had learned his secret. He'd acknowledged it and, by George, she'd come up trumps! Good for her. 'I can give you a few hours each week and pay you the princely sum of two bob an hour, starting Monday evening. How does that sound? Basic samba, rumba, cha-cha – the RAF boys are beating a path to my door, not to mention civil servants and GIs.'

'It's a deal,' she agreed. Eddie was on his way back with the drinks, picking up pace when he noticed who she was talking to. 'Oh, and I'm looking for new lodgings too, if you hear of something.'

'I'll keep my ears open.' Cliff gave up his chair to Eddie as he delivered his parting shot. 'Very well,

186

Sylvia – I'll see you at the studio on Monday at five o'clock sharp. Everyone's mad keen to learn jive, but we'll start with a simple tango and move on from there.'

CHAPTER TWELVE

'And after careful consideration of the merits of our finalists, the winners of tonight's competition are . . . drum roll, please!' Up onstage the MC paused while the entire ballroom held its collective breath. '. . . Miss Pearl Scott and Mr Bernard Greene!'

Pearl clapped her hands and jumped for joy. Bernie turned to her for confirmation. 'That's us,' he muttered in disbelief.

'It is!' She hugged him and laughed.

The MC justified the win. 'Our judges have awarded this couple top marks for their excellent poise, musicality, foot and leg action and presentation.'

'Congratulations!' Joy and Tommy patted Bernie and Pearl on the back then shoved them towards the stage to collect their winnings.

Everyone clapped and cheered. Clouds of confetti showered down from the ceiling like coloured snowflakes, fluttering on to the heads of contestants and landing on the polished parquet floor.

'Heck; that stuff gets everywhere – on the balconies, under the seats, behind the bloomin' bar. We'll be sweeping it up for days,' Ruby grumbled to Mavis.

The winning couple shook hands with the MC and pocketed their prize.

'Well done, both of you.' Sylvia made a special effort to push through the crowd. 'You were worthy winners.'

'Thanks to you,' Pearl reminded her. 'We couldn't have done it without your expert teaching.'

Ditching Mavis with unceremonious haste, Terry made a beeline towards the victors to congratulate them. 'Latin suits you,' he conceded. 'The rest of us had best be on our toes in future.'

'But don't let it go to your heads.' Cliff appeared at Terry's side with a quiet word to the wise. 'There's still room for improvement.'

'"Learn to dance with Cliff"!' Terry quoted the phrases displayed above Cliff's studio door. '"Live in your dreams!" for half a crown a lesson.'

'We'll think about it,' Pearl said, though in reality she knew that she and Bernie wouldn't have the time for extra tuition.

Victorious Bernie beamed and vigorously shook everyone's hand. 'We did it!' he crowed. 'We won the blasted thing!' So much for Mick's put-downs; this would show his brother that ballroom dancing was worth pursuing.

After the excitement of the competition had died down, Reggie Dixon's old-school Viennese waltz held less appeal. Many of the younger dancers called it a night and drifted away from the ballroom, including Eddie and Sylvia, Joy and Tommy and Pearl and Bernie. The group said their friendly goodnights outside the main entrance.

'Thanks again,' Pearl told Sylvia. 'We might not

have appreciated it at the time, but you set us on the right road with your "Heads up, shoulders back and smile"!'

'You and your ma scared the living daylights out of us,' Bernie confessed. 'But it sure was worth it.'

'There'll be no stopping any of us now,' Tommy assured Sylvia and Eddie. 'It'll be our turn to win again next week; you'll see.'

'Over my dead body!' Bernie threatened.

Their laughter rose above the crashing waves of the incoming tide and the muted strains of organ music from the ballroom. It was time to part – Eddie and Sylvia to King Alfred Road and a chaste kiss on the doorstep; Tommy and Joy to Silver Street, where their more tender kiss would be spoiled by Terry's rude interruption as he pushed past them outside number 57 with a casual 'Sorry to spoil your fun'. Meanwhile, Pearl and Bernie headed to his lodgings on Market Street for the second night in a row.

Bernie led the way up the stairs and opened the door to his room with a mock fanfare. 'Ta-da!'

'You tidied up,' she gasped. Shirts and jackets were hung on hangers from a row of hooks behind the door, shoes were set in pairs under the bed and the top of the chest of drawers had been cleared.

'For you, Miss Pearl – anything!' he declared, dropping to one knee and placing a hand on his heart like a knight of old paying court to his damsel.

'Get up, you idiot!' She yanked Bernie to his feet and they tumbled sideways on to the bed, arms and legs entangled. Tonight there was no hesitation, no questioning looks; only a shared longing to be together as they breathed warm kisses on to cheeks, necks and lips. Losing focus, seeing only a flutter of dark eyelashes and hearing a soft groan from parted lips, they gave way to desire.

On the north shore an army of cheerful volunteers were on the beach filling sandbags and slinging them on to the back of a lorry parked nearby. It was Monday morning and an early sea fret swathed the men in grey mist as Henry, Bernie and Pearl came to a halt close to North Station's vast glass canopy. They'd stopped at a spot overlooking the pier, a crazy-golf course to one side and a deserted boating pool beyond.

'What do you think?' Henry demanded with a broad sweep of his arm.

Pearl wasn't sure what to say. The north shore had a different flavour to central and southern Blackpool; it was more family-oriented, less kiss-me-quick, with a couple of pricey hotels that catered mainly for wealthier visitors.

'Well?' Henry turned to Bernie for an answer.

'What exactly are we looking at?'

'Follow me.' Pearl's father crossed the promenade then strode on along the length of the Victorian pier, past elaborate cast-iron shelters towards a conglomeration of stalls and cafés at the far end. 'I've already borrowed the cash from a pal and shelled out six months' rent up front,' he informed them, 'so it makes no difference what you think.'

Pearl ran to keep up. 'Trust him,' she muttered to Bernie. A couple of hopeful gulls whirled overhead, hovering over a fisherman's basket as he baited his line then with a quick flick of his wrist cast out to sea.

'This is it.' Henry stopped outside a boarded-up

stall with an uninspiring, faded sign that read 'North Shore Amusements'.

'This is what?' Pearl queried.

'My new premises. I didn't even have to lay out any money on slot machines,' Henry boasted. 'We'll make do with the old ones.'

Bernie's and Pearl's hearts sank. Besides being in the wrong part of town, the machines were likely to be old-fashioned and the stall itself would need a good deal of redecoration to bring it up to scratch.

'I thought we were buying new Allwins,' Pearl complained as her father unlocked the door then forced it open with his shoulder. The interior was worse if anything: dingy in the extreme and lined with dust-coated one-armed bandits that looked as though they belonged in the ark.

Bernie used his jacket sleeve to wipe away the dust from the nearest machine. It turned out to be a Chip or Bust: an original Allwin with a spiral layout and a red, blue and green background. 'Not bad,' he conceded.

'There are three Jackpots and four Little Mickeys.' Henry pointed out the more popular machines.

Bernie spotted an up-to-date Spitfire close to the entrance. It had a picture of the famous fighter plane against a yellow background. Beside it was an automatic payout Wizard. Maybe the amusement arcade had potential after all.

'All it needs is a lick of paint, a bit of spit and polish and a new sign outside the entrance saying "Great Scott's Amusements".' Henry turned to Pearl. 'We'll be up and running by the start of next week if you both put your backs into it. Bernie, you can fettle

192

these machines and make sure they're all in working order, right?'

'Yes, sir.' Determined to look on the bright side, Bernie inspected the machines one by one. 'I can do that.'

'Good lad. I'll leave you to it.' Henry rubbed his hands eagerly as he prepared to depart. 'Let me know if you come across any snags.'

Leaving the door swinging open, Henry swaggered back along the pier, whistling all the way; Mr Blackpool from head to toe.

Snags like woodworm and dry rot, a leaking roof and birds nesting in the rafters . . . Pearl looked around helplessly at her depressing surroundings. 'Honestly, my father is the absolute limit,' she groaned.

'Don't worry.' Bernie put an arm round her shoulders and tilted her head back to give her a quick kiss. 'We'll show him,' he vowed. 'If we work hard, we can make a go of this, I swear.'

Terry's footsteps clattered downstairs in hot pursuit of Joy, who was leaving the Silver Street house for work. He was dressed for the weather in a short-sleeved shirt and shorts, looking a picture of health with his smooth, tanned skin and lithe physique.

'What's the rush?' He slid ahead of her in the narrow hallway and made a show of opening the front door in gentlemanly fashion. 'By the way, I'm sorry if I put a stop to the billing and cooing with what's-his-name last night.'

'His name is Tommy Rossi,' she replied coolly. After Terry's interruption she and Tommy had parted with blushes and fond words.

Terry kept pace with Joy down the street. 'You have to watch these Italians,' he advised in his characteristic mumble, designed to make the hearer pay special attention. 'They're all *ti amo* and *ti adoro* until they get what they want. Afterwards it can be a different matter.'

Joy winced at the tasteless remarks. 'And you would know, would you?'

He shrugged off her challenge. 'It's common knowledge. Your young man could be the exception that proves the rule, but if not, trust me: I'll be waiting in the wings to pick up the pieces.'

Irritation scratched at the surface of Joy's shiny, optimistic mood. She'd got dressed with a smile on her face, remembering the pleasures of the previous Saturday: the thrill of dancing the cha-cha with Tommy and her unselfish delight when Pearl and Bernie had won first prize. The look of astonishment on their faces had been priceless. Now, though, Terry's sly digs were undermining her sense of well-being.

'Don't look like that – I only meant I'd be standing by to be your new dance partner,' he explained. 'If and when you two love birds break up, you'll need someone to fling you about in the jitterbug. Well, look no further.' He spread his arms invitingly as they reached the prom.

Joy gave him her frostiest stare. 'Standard dances are more my style,' she informed him. 'Tommy favours Latin but I prefer foxtrot and quickstep.'

'Whichever.' Terry shrugged again. 'Just bear my offer in mind.'

Breathing a sigh of relief as they went their separate ways – Terry to the lido and Joy to the tram stop – she recalled a brief conversation she'd had the day before with her landlady.

'A word to the wise,' Iris had said when Joy had been using the sewing machine to run up a new pinafore for work. 'I've got a feeling something's not quite right with our Mr Liddle. Take my advice – his type is best avoided.'

Joy had expected an explanation but her landlady had grown tight-lipped. The machine had whirred and the needle had flown in and out of the flowered cotton fabric. Joy had nodded in agreement. 'Don't worry, Mrs Grigg – I intend to steer well clear.'

Now, as she hopped on to the next tram, she wondered again what Iris had meant by 'not quite right'. Sylvia's recent revelation about Cliff Seymour was impossible to ignore, like grit in Joy's shoe, and, unlikely as it seemed, she wondered if the phrase 'not quite right' was linked in some way with Sylvia's 'not interested in girls'. The mystery played on Joy's mind during her ride along the prom and still bothered her when she alighted and made her way to the Wards' house, where she let herself in and dealt with a bad-tempered greeting from the family's pet corgi.

As she shooed the yapping dog into the kitchen, Edna Ward drifted downstairs in hair curlers and dressing-gown.

'Don't mind me,' Edna said in her friendly fashion. 'It's my day off. I intend to have a lazy time doing nothing at all.'

'It's all right for some,' Joy commented under her breath.

'Be quiet, Buster!' Edna called to the dog as Joy

wheeled the Hoover from the under-the-stairs cupboard. Buster took no notice. Edna sat on the bottom stair and took out a packet of cigarettes. 'I enjoy watching other people work,' she teased. 'By the way, I've remembered where I saw that Terry chap before.'

Joy turned on the Hoover and ran it over the hall carpet. 'Come again?'

'Quiet, Buster!' Edna lit her cigarette. 'I remembered where I saw your friend, Terry.'

'He's not my friend,' Joy said over the whine of the vacuum cleaner. Her interest was piqued, nonetheless. *Not quite right* – the phrase shot to the forefront of her mind.

Edna went to quieten the dog then came back. 'It came to me the other evening when I was in the bath. I used to work as a clerk in Blackburn magistrates' court, dealing mostly with unpaid speeding fines, drunk and disorderlies, and so on. But sometimes I came across a juicy divorce case involving adultery, desertion, insanity . . .'

Joy switched off the Hoover to concentrate on Edna's account. The hairs at the nape of her neck prickled in anticipation.

'Well, that's where I saw your Terry: in the divorce court. It sticks in my memory because he was so darned good-looking. He was the respondent. The wife was claiming desertion. Apparently, he'd walked out on her just before the start of the war, without giving a reason. He denied it but the magistrates granted the decree.'

'Are you sure?' Joy was taken aback. 'Didn't you say it must have been a case of mistaken identity?'

Edna shook her head. 'You don't forget a face like

196

that, not to mention the Mr Universe physique. It was definitely the same man but going under a different name. I telephoned my friend who worked in the court with me and asked if she remembered the case. She did and her memory is pin-sharp. She recalled the name: Tony Lincoln.'

Joy frowned. 'That doesn't make any sense. Why would Terry change his name unless he had something to hide?'

'To make a clean break from his past, I reckon.' Edna gave her imagination free rein. 'Just suppose he owed money to some unsavoury characters and left Blackburn because of it. Or else the deserted wife wanted revenge – a woman scorned, and so on. Or maybe Tony Lincoln was in serious trouble with the law; that would be a good enough reason for him to vanish without trace.'

'He kept the same initials,' Joy remarked. The sound of her employer's voice calling from the back garden reminded her that she wasn't paid to gossip. 'I'd better get on,' she told Edna hastily.

Mrs Ward appeared with a bunch of yellow roses that she handed to Edna. 'Put these in a vase for me, there's a dear. Mind the thorns. And Joy, when you've finished with the Hoover, I'd like you to dust the ornaments in the front room, please.'

'Yes, Mrs Ward.' Joy switched on the vacuum cleaner and Edna took the roses from her mother.

'The Mysterious Case of the Lido Lothario!' she sang out as she disappeared into the kitchen. 'Agatha Christie would have a field day with this one!'

*

Sylvia's suitcase lay open on her bed. She'd packed most of her day clothes but had left her dance dresses hanging in the wardrobe – a shiny, colourful reminder of the break she was about to make. Her mother hadn't spoken a word to her since Friday night. It was now Monday afternoon and the silence between them had settled like a mid-winter frost.

Finding a place to live was still Sylvia's top priority, along with securing more paid employment to top up the two shillings per hour that Cliff had offered her. Tommy and Joy were on the lookout for vacant rooms for her but so far she'd heard nothing from them. Cliff, too, had said he would keep his eyes peeled. Meanwhile, she'd scanned the small ads in the *Gazette* and written down a few addresses that merited further investigation. But before that she would teach her first Latin lesson then find out exactly how many sessions Cliff could offer her at North View Parade. Glancing at her watch, she saw that it was time to leave.

From the studio Lorna heard Sylvia come down the stairs. She went to the window to watch her daughter step out on to the sunny street in her sleeveless white blouse and wide, high-waisted black slacks. She wasn't carrying a suitcase – only her string bag containing her dance shoes – and she seemed to be in a hurry. A frown creased Lorna's brow. What was the betting that Sylvia was rushing to meet up with Cliff Seymour? The very name left a bitter taste in the older woman's mouth and she turned away in disgust.

Across the studio Angela sat unobtrusively at the piano, quietly sorting through sheet music for the lesson that was about to start. She, too, had heard footsteps on the stairs and the click of the door latch. 'Won't Sylvia be joining us today?' she enquired with a hint of worry in her voice.

'No, not today,' Lorna replied, pressing her lips together and inhaling deeply. 'But Edward will be here later to lend a hand if necessary.'

'I see.' Passing no further comment, the pianist laid out her scores, folded her hands in her lap and waited.

The tram to North View Parade rolled to a smooth halt as Sylvia reached the stop. Rushing had left her short of breath so she sank gratefully into the nearest empty seat and gathered her energy during the slow ride along the prom. Lorries trundled down the beach loaded with sandbags. The donkey man roped together his string of weary donkeys, ready to lead them home. Children flew kites, dogs chased balls and shallow waves curled around the iron legs of the North Pier.

Soon it was time for Sylvia to alight. Stepping down on to the pavement and hearing her name called, she spotted Pearl waving from the turnstile entrance to the pier and heading in her direction – Pearl, with her ever-ready smile and petite figure, with a touch of the tomboy in her dark, pixie-cut hair and easy, loose-limbed way of moving. *What now?* Sylvia wondered.

'Fancy seeing you here!' Pearl declared. 'Ignore the way I look – I've spent all day cleaning Dad's new amusement arcade, on my hands and knees scrubbing floorboards while Bernie worked on the slot machines.'

'Good for you.' Pearl's gaiety was as good as a tonic for Sylvia. 'I don't know where you find the energy.'

'Where are you headed?' Pearl noticed the dance shoes in Sylvia's bag. 'Let me guess: you're going Latin on us again at Cliff's studio.'

'Yes; we'll discuss more details about my teaching there. And I'll be late if I don't get a move on.'

'Teaching?' Pearl was wide-eyed. 'How will your mother feel about that?'

'She won't be happy but I don't care; it's a free country. Now I have to dash.'

Off Sylvia went, breaking into a run up North View Parade and arriving at Cliff's studio at the same time as a tall, dark-haired man with a paunch, a clipped moustache and gold tiepin. He was dressed in a formal, pinstriped suit that was unsuitable for a hot summer's day.

'After you.' Looking her up and down, the stranger stepped aside to allow Sylvia to enter first.

Inside the studio a bunch of eager pupils had gathered. The few girls were easily outnumbered by a score of young men from government offices who had followed the trend to learn the basics of ballroom as a way of enhancing their social lives. Sylvia's entrance attracted admiring glances and two or three low wolf whistles.

Cliff hurried forward to greet her. 'There you are! Let's throw you in at the deep end. You know where the gramophone is,' he added with a casual wave of his hand. 'Begin with the basic tango walk out of hold then move on to progressive side steps – nothing too tricky.'

'You want me to start teaching now, this minute?' Sylvia's mouth went dry as she surveyed the room. All eyes were trained on her – did Cliff mean to leave her to it?

'Go ahead,' he urged.

'By myself?' she asked faintly.

'Yes. Afterwards I'll introduce you to Mitch, who has dropped by unexpectedly.'

Sylvia swung her head towards the tall stranger by the door, who acknowledged her with a slight dip of his chin. The famous Mitch Burns was here in person!

'We won't be breathing down your neck,' Cliff promised. 'I'll take Mitch for a drink and a quiet chat. See you in an hour.'

There was nothing for it but to take up position at the front of the studio and begin. 'We start with our feet together and weight on the right foot for the gentleman and on the left for the lady. Gentlemen, pass the left foot forward across the body.' Despite her nerves, the words came easily and Sylvia was able to demonstrate clearly. 'Copy me,' she instructed as she lowered the needle on to the record.

Her motley crew of clerks, map readers and telephone operators did as they were told.

'That's right,' Sylvia encouraged. 'Slowly repeat the walk. Don't lower the heel until the second beat. Gentlemen, bring the ball of your right foot to the instep of your left. Ladies, mirror your partner's movements – very good!'

The concentration in the room was intense and time passed quickly. After sixty minutes and many false starts, everyone had achieved the basic prowling tango walk.

The lesson ended and verdicts were returned as the pupils dispersed.

'Harder than it looks.'

'Miss Ellis makes it seem easy but it's not.'

'When do we get into hold?'

'It takes two to tango, sure enough.'

Sylvia turned off the gramophone and was returning the record to its paper sleeve when Cliff and his VIP visitor returned – and with them Sylvia's nerves. Her heart raced as she tucked her blouse into her waistband and smoothed her hair.

'Let's dispense with the formalities, shall we?' Mr Burns's deep voice boomed across the emptying studio. A gold signet ring on his right hand and the diamond-studded pin on his dark-blue tie glinted under the studio lights. 'Cliff has been singing your praises, young lady,' he said as he approached.

'Pleased to meet you.' Sylvia blushed under the impresario's cool scrutiny: head to toe, as if examining an item before purchase. She could almost feel his podgy fingers turning her this way and that.

'She's the right height,' he commented. 'However, some men prefer a curvier model. I expect that could be achieved?'

Sylvia jerked her head to one side as if receiving a slap to the face. Her stomach lurched and she shot a look of concern at Cliff, who avoided her gaze.

'You won't find a more assured ballroom dancer,' Cliff told his associate. 'Sylvia has been taught by her mother since she was knee high to a grasshopper. Lorna Ellis is a leading light in the ISTD and, besides, I've seen for myself that Sylvia picks up new routines extremely quickly.'

'She's elegant enough for the dinner-dance circuit, certainly.' Mitch Burns continued his assessment before asking Sylvia a direct question. 'Might you consider putting on a little weight?'

She swallowed hard before offering an evasive answer. 'I could try.'

'And might you agree to performing onstage if the opportunity arose?'

'I haven't considered it,' she admitted with burning cheeks.

'Then you should. There's money to be made in cabaret – Cliff knows that better than most. It provides a more regular income than hobnobbing at the Ritz and suchlike. Most of my girls move on from competition dancing to performing within a very short space of time – unless they snag a wealthy patron, that is.'

'First things first.' Cliff quickly moved things on. 'Can you link Sylvia up with the high-society circle and find her a partner?'

'Without a doubt,' Mitch confirmed. 'There's always a call for competent ballroom dancers. It would be under the usual terms and conditions – I would secure lodgings and make the introductions. Dancers provide their own attire and meals are not included. Their fee is paid directly by the client.'

'Understood,' Cliff confirmed under his breath, still refusing to look at Sylvia.

'Well?' Mitch demanded. 'Are the terms agreeable?'

Her thoughts whirled. 'Don't you want to see me dance first?' she asked.

'Not necessary – I trust Cliff's judgement. I only wanted to be sure that you looked and sounded the part.' Burns tucked his red silk handkerchief more firmly into his top pocket then glanced at his watch.

'No need to make a decision immediately,' he told Sylvia. 'Talk through the details with Cliff here – he knows how to contact me with your answer.'

Mitch Burns's steel heel tips clicked across the floor as he departed with Cliff in tow. There was a minute's pause as the two men talked outside on the pavement before Cliff returned to find Sylvia sitting on the floor with her back against the wall and her knees drawn up under her chin.

He sat down beside her. 'Ought I to have given you advance notice?' he asked with a sympathetic wrinkle of his nose.

She nodded. 'Mr Burns caught me off guard.'

'He's not everyone's cup of tea.' Cliff offered Sylvia a cigarette, which she took. 'But he knows how to pull strings and make things happen.'

'Would I really have to put on weight?' Strangely, this was the issue that stuck in her craw, not Mitch Burns's unsympathetic manner.

'It might be for the best.' Cliff reached for her hand. 'I've seen what happens when a girl refuses to eat. It doesn't end well.'

'And would I lodge with other girls or would I be by myself? How would a client choose me as his partner?'

Cliff sighed at her naivety. Shipping Sylvia off to London would be like sending a lamb to the slaughter. 'You don't have to say yes,' he cautioned.

'But it would be too good an opportunity to miss,' she sighed. 'And now would be the perfect time.'

Until now, every girl he'd approached on Mitch Burns's behalf had quickly cottoned on and had accepted the proposition with their eyes wide open. But innocent Sylvia took everything at face value.

'Listen.' Cliff swung her round to face him then chose his words carefully. 'You know that I've seen more of this world than you have. You've recently guessed, or else someone has told you, about the life I lead.'

She nodded and held his gaze, content to let his hand rest on hers.

'It didn't turn you against me,' he went on. 'Why not?'

'Because it's none of my business.'

Her answer – brief and direct – surprised him. There was more depth to Sylvia Ellis than he'd expected. 'Thank you. Not everyone feels that way.'

'Shame on them.' She spoke from the heart, raising her voice so that it filled the studio. 'People are too quick to judge.'

Cliff pulled away and leaned his head against the wall before drawing deeply on his cigarette. He seldom had the chance to talk openly about his situation and, now that it arose, he felt a strong desire to unburden. 'It would be a big relief if I didn't have to pretend.'

'Like you did with me when we first met?' she asked. *The flirting, the kiss – a false trail to put her off the scent.*

'Yes – I'm sorry about that. You are a very attractive girl, by the way. Why hasn't someone snapped you up? Many have tried, I suppose?'

'A few,' she conceded.

'Including Eddie Winter?'

'Yes, but Eddie and I have known each other for years. We've grown up together so there's no spark between us.'

205

Cliff leaned sideways and gave her a friendly nudge. 'Then perhaps you should put the poor bloke out of his misery. Tell him once and for all that you have no interest in him, romantically speaking.'

Sylvia bristled. Yes, she understood that her mother would quickly find a new dance partner for Eddie and knew with a sinking heart that she would pick at the scab of this unwelcome fact until it bled. But, given the circumstances, Sylvia could scarcely object. 'No need – my mother will soon partner him up with someone else. Eddie's a catch. The new girl will fall in love with him, he will reciprocate, and that will be that.'

'Don't accept Mitch's offer,' Cliff said out of the blue, as the blade of guilty conscience cut through him. 'Don't go to London. Stay here.'

Astonished at the turnaround, Sylvia stared at him. 'And do what, pray?'

'Accept my offer to teach here with me for as many hours as you like. Then you and I can enter Latin competitions together all over the North of England, as far afield as Liverpool and Leeds.' Cliff could see it now: he would snatch Sylvia from Mitch Burns's grasp and the pair of them would swing, lindy hop and mambo their way to victory.

'But where would I live?'

'Here, on North View Parade. I know of a spare room above the tobacconist's next door.' Cliff stood up and pulled her to her feet, smiling invitingly and charming his way through her defences. 'Come on, princess – what do you say?'

CHAPTER THIRTEEN

To reach North View Parade on foot, Joy and Pearl chose a shortcut across the market square then on through alleyways and down side streets in the less salubrious part of town. They passed behind the Winter Gardens building with its high glass dome then nipped down cobbled Euston Street with its jumble of poky terraced houses, small businesses, warehouses and a working men's club where, as luck would have it, they encountered Mick Greene and a few of his workmates from Squires Gate. The men, including Sam Grigg, Fred Salter and Howard Reynolds, were dressed in faded blue overalls and lounged against the wall by the entrance to the club. They were armed with pints of bitter and shrouded in a cloud of tobacco smoke. Howard whistled as Pearl and Joy approached.

Pearl's heart sank at the sight of Bernie's brother. 'Keep going,' she hissed at Joy.

But Mick had no intention of letting the girls pass unchallenged. 'If it isn't Cyd Charisse and Rita Hayworth!' he mocked. 'Hey, girls – give us a twirl!'

There was rough laughter and a pincer movement to surround Joy and Pearl and block their progress.

'Let me introduce myself – my name's Sam Grigg.

Yes, that's right; I'm Iris's lad,' one of the men told Joy as he attempted to grab her around her waist. He had the landlady's skinny build and similarly sharp features, with a receding hairline and the same sour expression. 'I'll jitterbug with you any day of the week.'

Joy pushed him away. Sam tripped on the kerb and overbalanced, spilling his beer in the process. Swearing followed and more raucous laughter at Sam's expense.

Mick stepped menacingly in front of Pearl. 'So you've got what you wanted – our Bernie is well and truly under the thumb.' His speech was slurred and he was unsteady on his feet. 'He's joined that bunch of pansies at the Tower.'

Pearl refused to be intimidated. 'Bernie isn't under my or anyone else's thumb and he's no pansy either.'

'Pull the other one.' Mick sang from the same old song book. 'Any bloke who prances about a ballroom floor in a tight shirt and a pair of dancing pumps fits the bill. Isn't that right, Fred?'

'Too true, Mick – too true. It's downright unnatural. Why, I even heard tell of a couple of GIs dancing together. Apparently, they were flinging each other around the floor like there was no tomorrow.'

'I know what I'd do with 'em if I got half the chance.' Mick practically spat the words.

Joy and Pearl had heard enough. They pushed past the uncouth gang and turned the corner to catcalls and ironic wolf whistles.

'Why didn't you tell him that Bernie's had to give up dancing for the time being?' Joy had recently learned that it was an ongoing bone of contention between Pearl and her father, who had insisted that

Bernie give every hour that God sent to getting the new arcade up and running.

'Because I didn't want to give Mick the satisfaction.' Argue as Pearl might, Henry had refused point-blank to let Bernie have the night off, which was why she was without a partner as she and Joy hurried to Cliff Seymour's dance studio for their first lesson in Latin.

Joy remained doubtful as they hurried along. 'Are you sure we're doing the right thing?' she wondered. 'Ought we to be going behind Mrs Ellis's back like this? After all, she started us on the right path and she's an excellent teacher.'

'But a lousy mother,' Pearl reminded her. 'She practically threw Sylvia out for "betraying" her. It was either English style or Latin as far as Lorna Ellis was concerned – and never the twain shall meet.'

'That's according to Sylvia,' Joy said. 'We haven't heard Mrs Ellis's side.'

Pearl stopped dead. 'Sylvia's account rang true,' she insisted. 'I got it from the horse's mouth yesterday – she was lugging her belongings off the tram just as me and Bernie finished work in the new arcade. We helped her to carry her two suitcases to Ibbotson's tobacconist's shop. She was in tears, poor thing, saying how her mother had issued an ultimatum and it wasn't fair for Lorna to lay down the law in that way. I promised we'd back her decision by switching to Latin and here we are.' Pearl set off again with an impatient tut.

Joy trotted to keep up. 'I suppose we can carry on taking lessons from Mrs Ellis as well as Mr Seymour. We need to improve in both Standard and Latin if we want to compete.'

'Latin is the future,' Pearl maintained. The warren of back streets opened out on to a square containing a wine lodge and several hotels, and beyond that the start of North View Parade. 'Lorna Ellis is a stick-in-the-mud and she'll be left behind if she's not careful. Mark my words – we won't be the only ones to desert the Lorna Ellis Dance Academy for Cliff Seymour's classes.'

There was no more time to talk as the girls approached Ibbotson's window display of assorted meerschaum and briar pipes and big black and gold tobacco canisters. Sylvia was waiting for them with an edgy smile.

'Here we are, ready to be put through our Latin paces,' Pearl announced cheerily. 'Bernie couldn't make it, though.'

'Neither could Tommy,' Joy added. 'He hoped to come but one of the other clowns felt poorly so Tommy had to step in at the last minute.'

'So it's just us girls.' Curious to see the inside of Cliff's studio, Pearl forged ahead. 'How do you like your new room?' she asked Sylvia in passing. 'Have you unpacked your stuff?'

'Most of it,' Sylvia replied. 'I'll go back to King Alfred Road later for my dance dresses and a few other things – if I decide to stay.' Right now her move felt temporary, forced on her by her mother's unforgiving stance. Despite her misgivings over Mitch Burns and Cliff's tempting offer of teaching work, longer-term decisions were still up in the air.

Joy brought up the rear, entering the studio and pausing to admire the stylish modern decor. 'Might you move back in with your mother after all?'

'Oh no.' Sylvia was adamant on this front. 'But an

opportunity has opened up for me to go to London in the near future.'

'Woo-hoo!' Pearl teased. 'Here's me scrubbing floorboards at the end of the North Pier and Joy polishing the beer pumps in the Tower Ballroom, while you swan off to the capital!'

'I haven't said I'll go,' Sylvia cautioned. 'Cliff wants me to teach here instead, even though London was his idea in the first place.'

Pearl opened her bag and took out her dancing shoes. 'See – he's sweet on you!'

'No.' Sylvia threw Joy a warning glance. 'That's not the reason.'

'So what's stopping you, Dick Whittington?' Pearl asked as she too changed her shoes. 'I would've thought you'd jump at the chance.'

Sylvia lowered her voice. 'They say I'd have to gain weight,' she confided. 'Silly, isn't it?'

Pearl and Joy hid their surprise by stooping to fasten the straps of their shoes.

'Quite ridiculous,' Sylvia continued. 'You see girls far thinner than me up there on the silver screen, so elegant and beautiful. And their pictures are in all the magazines as well.'

'No,' Joy countered carefully. 'It's the other way round – you're much skinnier than the current crop of Hollywood stars.'

'And this is what's stopping you from saying yes?' Pearl was incredulous. 'You'd give up the chance to go to London because you'd be expected to put on a few pounds?'

'That's one reason.' Sylvia was aware that more people were arriving – three chattering teenage girls chaperoned by an older woman, two embarrassed boys in school blazers and grey flannel trousers and the instantly recognizable figure of Terry Liddle.

Joy was unsettled to see that Edna Ward's Lido Lothario was here in the flesh and she hoped very much that she could avoid him.

'Here comes another deserter.' Pearl pulled Joy to one side while Sylvia crossed the studio to introduce herself to the new arrivals. 'Is it a case of rats leaving the sinking ship?'

'I heard something very strange about Terry yesterday,' Joy confided. She noticed that Cliff had appeared from a side room and was talking with Terry Liddle alias Tony Lincoln. 'It seems he may not be who he says he is.'

'You don't say!' Dragging the story out of Joy, Pearl reacted with loud gasps and exclamations – the magistrates' court, a divorce under a different name. 'The rotter! How could he?'

'Edna was certain it was the same man.'

'It's not likely that there are two Tarzans matching his description within thirty miles of here – and with the same initials to boot.' Pearl loved nothing better than a good scandal.

Yet there he was, finishing his chat with Cliff and striding towards them and, to Joy's dismay, laying claim to her as his dance partner.

'What's the matter? Aren't you pleased to see me?' he asked teasingly but with a hint of suspicion. He looked from Joy to Pearl then back again. 'Should my ears be burning?'

'I don't know; should they?' Pearl queried with mock innocence. 'Actually, we're curious, Terry;

where did you live before you took up your job at the lido?'

A faint frown appeared on his tanned face. 'You know what curiosity did.'

'Yes, but we're not cats,' Pearl retorted. 'A friend of a friend reckons she knew you in your previous life. That's the problem with standing out from the crowd – it's impossible to stay incognito for very long.'

'Your friend of a friend is wrong.' The frown disappeared and Terry was back to his smooth, undentable self. 'Before I came to Blackpool I was serving under Montgomery in Egypt. Yes, that's right – I was a Desert Rat until I was invalided out of the army with a heart murmur.'

'Ladies and gentlemen, the lindy hop!' Cliff brought their conversation to a halt by lowering the gramophone needle on to a recording of Duke Ellington's 'Take The "A" Train'. 'Sylvia and I will begin by demonstrating the basic moves,' he explained. 'Note the bounce and the kick. Listen to the beat. *And* one, two, three . . .'

Summer heat was intense as July gave way to August. The air was unusually still and the sky a brilliant, unbroken blue. Holidaymakers with picnic baskets and parasols continued to flock to the beach, where they managed awkward changes into swimming costumes, exposing glimpses of lily-white flesh beneath skimpy towels. Business boomed for Clive Rowse, the donkey man, and for Rossi's ice-cream parlour, which was where Joy was headed, full of anticipation, on the morning of the first Saturday of the month.

She and Tommy had made plans to fit in an hour's dancing rehearsal in the small yard behind the café. They were both free that evening and wished to be ready to take on all-comers in the upcoming quick-step competition. Pearl and Bernie wouldn't be taking part and neither would Sylvia and Eddie, so the field was wide open and Joy and Tommy felt they had every chance of winning the prize.

'We're out of practice,' Pearl had lamented when Joy had mentioned that week's competition. 'Bernie claims he's forgotten every single thing he learned in Lorna Ellis's classes and, anyway, Dad is putting on the pressure for us to open the new arcade. We'll both be working late on Saturday.'

'I haven't seen Eddie since I left home.' Sylvia had dismissed Joy's query about him with an airy wave of her hand. 'Although he tried to convince me other-wise, I can only assume that he's taken Mother's side and wants nothing more to do with me.'

Joy had doubted that this was true but only time would tell. In any case, she and Tommy continued to have high hopes that their practice session would stand them in good stead later that day. Slow-quick-quick-slow. She rehearsed the quickstep rhythm in her head as she drew near to the ice-cream parlour. Dancers should be light on their feet, anticipating the quarter turn followed by a lock step then a nat-ural pivot turn. Caught up in rehearsing the steps in her head, she failed to see Tommy emerge from under the parlour's striped green awning then hurry towards her.

She only noticed him when he stopped abruptly within six feet of her. A glance along the promenade told her that there were no tables and chairs with bright tablecloths set out in front of the café and that the hatch serving ice-cream cones was closed.

'Tommy, what's wrong?' Her heart jolted. Something terrible must have happened to transform him from his happy-go-lucky self to the worried figure who stood in the blazing sunshine without uttering a word as families laden with beach paraphernalia traipsed past.

Tommy's face was pale and drained of expression. He tried to speak but no words came.

'Tell me.' Joy feared the worst.

'It's Dad,' he stuttered.

'Is he ill?'

'No.'

Taking him gently by the hand, she led him to the nearest shelter and sat him down on a bench overlooking the beach. Suddenly their surroundings seemed to belong to an alien world – the bright parasols and sunburned faces, the sound of laughter as children jumped over incoming waves or built castles on the golden sand. Only the grey concrete bunkers lining the promenade reminded Joy of the grim reality of the times they were living in.

'The police came and arrested him.'

'Surely not! When?'

'First thing this morning, while we were still in bed. They carted him off to the station.'

'Whatever for?'

'The Home Office changed its mind – they've decided he's a fascist after all.'

Joy's chest tightened with dread as she began to make sense of the situation. After initially being let off the hook by the Liverpool officials, someone higher up the chain of command must have taken a second look at Tommy senior's paperwork and as a result his Italian background had come under scrutiny. 'Who's "they" exactly?'

'People at the central internment tribunal in London. They withdrew Dad's Category B card without warning and issued him with a new one – a Category A. It all happened in a flash: a knock on the door, two police officers – a sergeant and a constable – a piece of paper shoved in Dad's face telling him he was regarded as an enemy alien and his being at liberty constituted a danger to the state.' Tommy recited the exact wording with a hollow laugh. 'This is my dad we're talking about. You couldn't find anyone who poses less of a threat to this country.'

Joy shrugged helplessly. 'We both know that. But what made them change his category?'

'It must have been the bloody fascist badge he borrowed soon after he met Mamma in Milan.' Tommy hung his head in an attitude of despair. 'Just once or twice, to gain entry into a dance and give her a treat. Dad was never an actual member of any party. But it's a blot on his record, written down in black and white – and that's why the Home Office has changed its mind.'

Joy imagined the shock of the knock on the door, the disbelief as the police had charged Tommy senior. 'But where will he end up?'

'The sergeant said they'll hold him at the police station overnight then put him on a ship to the Isle of Man first thing tomorrow. He'll have to stay in a prison camp there until Hitler surrenders.'

'"Collar the lot!"' Joy quoted the phrase that had been bandied around at the start of the war. Mr Churchill himself had come on to the wireless and said it. All enemy aliens had been forced to register and there'd been a wave of bad feeling against anyone with a German- or Italian-sounding surname. Property had been destroyed by so-called patriotic gangs who had taken the law into their own hands. But that had been two years previously and Joy had fondly imagined that public hostility had died down since then. 'Isn't there anything we can do?' she asked.

'No.' Tommy sighed. 'Mamma can't take it in at the moment – it's all too much.'

Joy stood up with fresh resolve. 'We should go to her.'

Tommy agreed and they walked together towards the café. 'I left her in her bedroom, crying her eyes out. She and Dad have never spent a night apart since they were married. She'll be lost without him. I've already told her I'm willing to give up the circus job and help with the business but she just cries and cries.'

Joy quickened her pace and arrived at the café entrance at the same time as a man dressed in sandals and baggy khaki shorts with a brood of five children in tow. They'd been attracted by the 'Genuine Italian Ices' sign and were disappointed to find that the blinds were down and there was no sign of life. They went away empty-handed, complaining loudly.

Tommy's hand shook as he unlocked the door and gestured for Joy to follow him up the stairs to Lucia and Tommy senior's room, where they found his mother curled up on the bed, crying her eyes out.

Her blue dressing-gown was crumpled and her dark hair spread loose against the white pillow.

Joy sat down on the edge of the bed. 'There, there,' she murmured. 'Everything's going to be all right.'

Lucia buried her face in the pillow. '*Scusami, per favore.*'

'There's no need to apologize.' Tommy's mother's world had collapsed without warning and Joy's heart went out to her. 'Cry as much as you like – get it out of your system. Tommy and I are here now.'

'My Tommaso – they took him away.' Lucia's voice was muffled by the pillow. '*Due carabinieri* – two policemen take him to prison – *una cella di prigione* – to a small room with locked door. How will he sleep alone? What will he eat?'

'The Isle of Man may not be so bad as you think,' Joy soothed. 'There will be others there in the same boat. I'm sure Tommy's dad will make friends and find ways to pass the time.'

'*Due carabinieri,*' Lucia repeated. She eased herself on to her elbows, allowing Joy to see her swollen face and the desperate fear in her eyes. 'They take him and shoot him?'

'No,' Joy insisted. 'They'll keep him in a prison camp until the war ends then they'll let him return home.'

'There now, Mamma – sit up.' Tommy eased her into a more comfortable position. 'That's better. Joy's right – Dad won't come to any harm. And I'm here. We'll keep going for his sake.'

Lucia grasped his hand. 'You are good son – the best. *Insieme* – together we wait, we work, we carry on.'

'That's right – *insieme*: together.' Tommy took a

218

deep breath. He'd made a promise and he would keep it, but the struggle showed in his eyes as he glanced at Joy. 'I'll leave the circus and help you run the ice-cream parlour, Mamma.'

'*Sì! Sì*, my Tommy!' Lucia held his hand more tightly and drew it to her chest, kissing his fingers and shedding more tears.

'A cup of tea,' Joy announced brightly. She went downstairs, finding her way around Lucia's neat kitchen – tea caddy, teapot, sugar and milk – while Tommy helped his mother to calm down. Joy was arranging milk and sugar on a tray when he joined her.

He came up behind her and put his arms around her waist, kissing her gently on the back of her neck. 'Thank you,' he whispered.

'No need to thank me.' She turned and put her arms around his neck. 'Your mum is lovely – I can't bear to see her so sad.'

'She's the best mother a son could wish for – I'd do anything for her.'

'And you're lovely, too.' Joy kissed Tommy then drew back so that she could see his face more clearly. 'You know you don't have to leave the circus.'

'But I do,' he lamented. 'Mamma can't run the place without my help. This is the busiest time of year.'

'And you love what you do,' she argued. 'The music, the juggling, the tumbling and clowning around, making people laugh – the circus is your life. It would break your heart to give it up.'

'I'll manage somehow.' Tommy had already resigned himself to the inevitable.

'What if . . .?' She hesitated. Was she overstepping the mark? *Be bold!* Madam Rosie had read reticence in Joy's palm and this had been her parting shot. *Take the initiative. Seize the day!* 'What if I were to step in and help your mother instead?' There; she'd said it!

Tommy took a step backwards and collided with the kitchen table. 'What about your cleaning work?'

At least he hadn't dismissed her idea out of hand. 'I'll give it up. Your mother can pay me a small wage to serve in the café. And perhaps I'll be able to fit in an hour or two's cleaning here and there. I'm sure we can work it out.'

'You'd do that?'

'I would – I will!' Joy had never felt more certain.

'For us? For me?'

'Yes.' *Be bold. Speak what's in your heart.* She drew him close again. 'Because I love you.'

Four small words – the most important she would ever say. The calm, contented world that had disintegrated when Tommy had shared his news in the shelter overlooking the beach took on a new shape – it was peopled by Tommy senior, Lucia and Joy's own Tommy, by a family who loved and laughed, worked and ate together. Joy was no longer alone.

'I love you too,' Tommy declared with a grin that spread from ear to ear. He picked her up and whirled her round in the tiny kitchen. The kettle boiled. Lucia's footsteps were heard on the stairs. 'I love you, Joy Hebden. You're the best girl in the whole world!'

CHAPTER FOURTEEN

Eddie knew that Sunday was Sylvia's day off. In the old days he would have arrived unannounced at King Alfred Road, making his way there after church. Lorna would have invited him in then chivvied Sylvia to get dressed and join them in the living room. There would have been pleasant chit-chat before Eddie suggested a stroll along the prom. Depending on Sylvia's mood, she would have agreed or turned him down flat. 'Yes, that would be lovely,' or, 'I can't, Eddie – not today.' Hair-washing or filing her nails would have been the perfunctory excuse.

However, now that Sylvia had moved out of her mother's place into the room above Ibbotson's, Eddie thought that his best option was to hover in the vicinity of North View Parade until she ventured out on to the street.

'How long are you prepared to hover?' Pearl had demanded with typical bluntness when he'd mentioned this plan in passing. She and Eddie had bumped into each other the previous evening at a tram stop by the North Pier. 'You could be hanging around outside the tobacconist's for hours. Why not take the bull by the horns and march straight in?'

'Shops are shut on Sunday,' Eddie had reminded her.

'Then bang on the door until someone comes. Throw stones at Sylvia's window to attract her attention.' Pearl's suggestions had grown more outlandish. Admittedly, she'd gone over to Latin as far as dance was concerned, but in the battle royal between Eddie and Cliff as Pearl saw it, she was firmly in the Eddie camp. 'Do something before Cliff Seymour makes his next move.'

Eddie had shuffled his feet and looked uncomfortable. 'I'm not worried about that,' he'd insisted without offering a reason.

'You should be.' Pearl had been exasperated. Sometimes polite and well-brought-up chaps like Eddie Winter could be slow on the uptake. 'Cliff isn't my type but he's the bee's knees as far as most girls are concerned – a good-looking, smooth-talking charmer who can dance; it stands to reason.'

Eddie had cleared his throat then moved swiftly on. 'But what if Sylvia doesn't care to talk to me?'

Pearl had continued to huff and puff. 'Why ever would she not?'

'I haven't spoken to her for over a week.' Sylvia's sudden move out of King Alfred Road had taken Eddie by surprise and this latest decision to move in next door to Cliff had floored him completely. 'She most likely assumes that I've taken her mother's side.'

'All the more reason to get in there with the Romeo act – wherefore art thou, blah-blah. Climb on to Sylvia's balcony with a rose between your teeth and go down on bended knee.'

'Not my style, I'm afraid.' Eddie had ended the

conversation where it had started – he would hover on North View Parade and hope for the best.

In the event, his patience paid off. The cloudy morning saw fewer families than usual make their way down to the beach as Eddie took up position in a bus shelter opposite Ibbotson's. He read the newspaper headlines about yet another heavy incendiary attack on Hamburg and the ongoing stalemate at El Alamein, every now and then glancing up at the tobacconist's doorway. At last, after an hour of tedium, Sylvia emerged. She wore a lilac-coloured dress that Eddie hadn't seen before and an Alice band held her shoulder-length hair back from her face. She looked achingly young.

Eddie sprang to his feet and ran across the road, dodging between a bus and a taxi then taking her by surprise as she set off down the street. 'Do you mind if I walk with you?' he asked.

The tilt of her head as she continued to walk said yes, she did mind. 'I'm busy, Eddie. Mother's out for the day visiting friends so I'm on my way to King Alfred Road to pick up some more of my stuff. What do you want?'

'I just needed to check that you were all right.'

'As you see . . .' She walked on, head in the air.

'Good, good.' Guiding her around a sign directing day trippers towards the crazy-golf course, Eddie stuck like glue. 'Your mother is worried—'

'Don't!' she warned. 'Seriously – don't!'

He quickly changed tack. 'Angela sends her best wishes.'

Sylvia nodded. 'Tell her that I'm sorry I didn't have time to say goodbye.'

'And you have everything you need?'

'Once I've collected my dance dresses, yes.' Reaching the prom, Sylvia slowed her pace. 'What do you really want?'

He held his breath and dug deep for an answer. 'Don't think I've abandoned you,' he said quietly. 'I care about you – that's why I'm here.'

'Eddie . . .' Touched by his sudden sincerity, she linked arms with him. 'You've a funny way of showing it,' she chided, 'staying away for I don't know how many days.'

'I know – I'm sorry. I wasn't sure what to do. The situation with Cliff threw me somewhat. I was surprised you wanted anything to do with him after my father's revelation.'

'It was hard to take in at first,' Sylvia admitted. 'In fact, I was flabbergasted. Don't pass this on, but in a moment of weakness I let Joy in on the secret – yes, Joy of all people. I regretted it the moment I opened my mouth – the poor girl almost fainted from shock.'

'Yes, that was an error on your part.' Eddie could easily imagine what effect the information would have had on Sylvia's unworldly friend.

'Don't worry – she swore not to breathe a word and Joy's the type to keep her promises. Likewise, I've vowed to keep my mouth shut in future.'

'Probably for the best,' Eddie agreed.

Sylvia walked on slowly towards the pier, where a Salvation Army brass band had gathered, cornets, trumpets, tambourines and French horns at the ready. 'Don't you feel a little bit sorry for Cliff?' she wondered.

'Not really. Why – do you?'

The band began to play 'Onward Christian Sol-diers'. A motley crowd of dog walkers, children and penniless tramps gathered to listen. 'With the cross of Jesus going on before.'

'I do,' Sylvia asserted. Having had more time to think it through, she'd remained firmly on Cliff's side. 'I'm sure he can't help the way he is.'

'Tell that to the Sally Army,' Eddie commented as a member of the band came round with a collection box. 'I don't believe General Booth's charity extended as far as Cliff Seymour and his ilk.'

'Well, it should.' She was adamant. 'Imagine hav-ing to spend your life pretending to be someone you're not, setting up smokescreens so people don't suspect, living in fear of being discovered. Anyway, Cliff's private life doesn't alter the basic facts – he has the contacts and the experience in Latin that I need.'

Sylvia's mixture of moral indignation and cool pragmatism amused Eddie. 'I understand that. But be careful – please.'

Sylvia tapped his arm impatiently. 'For your infor-mation, I've met Mr Burns at last. It seems I can go to London any time I like.'

The naive boast reminded Eddie of their early days on the dance floor when she'd been full of shiny con-fidence and they'd won every competition they'd entered. Now, though, the prospect of the capital city swallowing her whole alarmed him. 'I mean it, Sylvia – look before you leap.'

'Aren't you pleased for me?' she asked with a touch of her old petulance.

'Yes.'

'Say it as if you mean it.'

'No; if you must know, I'm not pleased.' Truth burst through the veneer of good manners that Eddie worked hard to maintain at all times. 'I don't want you to leave Blackpool. I want you to stay here and for things to be the same as they were – for us to be dance partners and more.'

Sylvia shook her head. 'We can't go back in time. My mother would never have me back for a start.'

'Then where does that leave us?' he asked with mounting trepidation. 'I accept that we may no longer be dance partners, but I'm hoping that we can still be friends.'

She frowned. 'Friends – yes.'

'But?'

Sylvia recalled Cliff's advice that she should put Eddie out of his misery. 'But don't expect anything more.'

'Does that mean you don't have the same feelings for me as I have for you?' His stomach tightened in anticipation of a killer blow.

Sylvia spoke gently. 'This may sound odd, Eddie, but you're too careful and cautious for me. You weigh everything up before you act or speak. You never do anything on the spur of the moment or stand up for yourself when I behave badly. I've come to realize that your inexhaustible patience isn't good for me.'

He grimaced before acknowledging the truth of her words. 'I can change,' he promised. 'I can be more spontaneous – just give me a chance.'

'Look at us!' she pleaded. 'Standing here on the promenade on a Sunday morning with nowhere private to go. We've known each other for years and never progressed beyond the first stages. Compare us with Pearl and Bernie. It was the same for them – they grew up together just like we did. The way Pearl tells it, Bernie took the plunge and declared his feelings to get to where they are now. That's the difference.'

Eddie grew indignant. 'What do you think I'm doing now? I'm risking everything to have this conversation with you. I've said I'd like us to be more than friends.'

'And still you're polite, still you're more kind to me than I deserve,' she said with a long, drawn-out sigh.

A bitter taste formed on Eddie's tongue. 'Since when was being kind and patient considered a crime?'

'It's not – of course it's not. But that's my point, Eddie. The fact is, I began a new stage in my life this week. It was a massive step for me to move on from the academy.'

Eddie raised his hands in a gesture of surrender. 'And have you moved on from me, too?' he asked, drawing her to one side under a newsagent's awning. The Salvation Army played on and the busy world hurried by while he waited for what seemed like an age for her answer.

Sylvia sighed and squeezed his hand. 'Yes,' she murmured gently. 'Dear Eddie; I believe I have.'

'Roll up, roll up!' Henry drummed up custom for his new end-of-the-pier attraction. 'Try your luck, ladies and gentlemen, boys and girls. Don't be shy!'

Sun, sand and sea – the ingredients were there; now all it needed was for customers to enter the brightly lit portal.

Pearl sat behind a desk inside the doorway to the arcade, fresh as a daisy in a pink-and-white-striped frock and white sandals, waiting to take the entrance money. Bernie had come up with the bright idea of playing music to entice customers inside, so Pearl had bought a second-hand gramophone and loud-speakers then chosen upbeat records from her own collection to set the mood. But still; would strollers along the pier be willing to part with their hard-earned cash? she wondered.

Henry stood under the brand-spanking-new Great Scott's North Shore Amusements sign, shirtsleeves rolled up ready for action. Everything was spotless and in working order, thanks to Bernie and Pearl's hard graft.

'Only a tanner to get in!' Henry's confident cry rose above the general hum of voices and the occasional shriek of gulls. He spread his arms to greet his first eager customers – three lads in their teens with identical cowlicks of hair curling on to their smooth, sunburned foreheads. 'That's right, gents. We have the mighty Spitfire machine right here by the door and more – much more – inside! Chip or Bust, Little Mickeys and Wizards – roll up!'

Pearl took their money with a sigh of relief. Give her dad his due, he certainly had the gift of the gab.

'Ladies – this is your lucky day!' Henry collared two busty, middle-aged women wearing stiff corsets under their flowered dresses. 'Come inside – the jackpot is yours for the taking!'

More sixpences rattled into Pearl's till and the arcade quickly filled. Soon every machine was taken and a queue started to form at the door. Bernie put on an Andrews Sisters favourite. Pearl grinned at him and returned his thumbs-up. Nodding and smiling at customers, he made his way towards her.

'So far, so good,' he said over the harmonious trill of 'Don't Sit Under The Apple Tree'.

Pearl nodded her agreement as she crooned the words to the jaunty song. ' "With anyone else but me". That means you,' she reminded him. 'You're not to walk down lovers' lane with anyone else but me.'

'No, sirree,' Bernie promised.

'Five of you? That'll be half a crown, please.' She took more money and admitted a family into the gaily lit space. At the flip of a trigger, balls ricocheted through miniature mazes to much crossing of fingers and holding of breath. An occasional yelp of triumph signalled that not everyone left the penny arcade disappointed.

'You're the manager here,' Pearl reminded Bernie. 'What do you say we introduce small prizes as well as payouts?'

'Such as?'

'A bar of chocolate or a few sweeties for the kids. Maybe a big teddy bear as a star prize. We could sit him in a glass case under some fairy lights.'

'Hmm; there'd be an outlay up front but it might pay off. I'll think about it,' he said.

'Families will be our biggest customers on this side of town – it would attract more of them.'

'Maybe, but we shouldn't try to run before we can walk,' Bernie cautioned.

Outside on the pier, Henry had worked up a thirst. 'Pearl, Bernie – I'm taking a break,' he called. 'Back in two ticks.' He was gone before they could object.

'Two hours, more like,' Pearl said with a laugh. Towards the back of the arcade one of the Mickey machines paid out – ker-ching!

'That'll be sixpence to you, sunshine,' she told the next customer in the queue – a ten-year-old lad with a mop of curly red hair.

'I'll take over where your dad left off.' Bernie strode out on to the pier, shielding his eyes against the sun. Those three Andrews girls warbled on like songbirds. The pure blue sky was reflected in the sparkling sea. Yet more punters queued to gain entrance to their new attraction. 'Roll up, roll up!' he cried. 'Come along, gents – you're on holiday. Why not throw caution to the wind!'

Pearl carried on taking the cash. Ker-ching. Had it been worth all the scrubbing and scraping, the painting and polishing? Her dad's gamble certainly seemed to be paying off. Ker-ching, ker-ching. Silver sixpences tumbled one after another into her till. She glanced out at Bernie, who beamed as he waved his arms like a traffic policeman, directing new customers into the arcade.

But there would be no more jitterbugging with her sweetheart for the time being, worse luck. Pearl's smile faded. It was a shame but they would have to make the best of it.

At least Mick would be pleased, she reflected. Recognizing that blood was thicker than water, she embraced the notion that the warring brothers would kiss and make up once Mick found out that Bernie had abandoned the ballroom floor. Admittedly it was a long shot – about as likely as winning the jackpot on the Spitfire machine. In any case, Pearl felt sure that Bernie was better off staying in his new lodgings, well away from Mick's bad temper and heavy drinking. Better still, Market Street gave them all the privacy they needed now that they were an established couple. Both revelled in their uninterrupted nights of passion and clung to their newfound intimacy.

'Two shillings, please,' she told the next in line – four lads in Boy Scouts uniforms. 'Bernie!' She leaned out of the doorway to attract his attention.

He hurried inside. 'What's up?'

'The record's finished. Can you choose a new one?'

Bernie selected a disc that he'd snuck into the rack without her knowing. After a scratchy start, frenetic notes from George Formby's ukulele replaced the dulcet tones of the Andrews Sisters.

Leaning on a blooming lamp-post! Pearl raised her eyebrows and Bernie chuckled. ' "Do do do dah dah dee dee dee . . . Oh me, oh my; I hope the little lady comes by." ' Her sweetheart was perfect in many ways but he had one definite fault – his taste in popular music left a lot to be desired.

In spite of big changes in their lives, Pearl, Joy and Sylvia danced on regardless.

The waltz and quickstep became second nature to Joy. Loyalty drove her back to lessons at the Lorna Ellis Dance Academy, which she squeezed in between cleaning shifts at the Tower and waiting at tables in Rossi's – '*Sei magnifica!*' a resilient Lucia told her as she scooped ice cream into glass dishes. Back at the academy, under Lorna's watchful eye, Joy thrilled to romantic violins and glided in Eddie's arms; a perfect picture of cool elegance.

Meanwhile, encouraged by her new teacher at North View Parade, Pearl concentrated on jitterbug and lindy hop – bounce and spin, bounce and swing. 'That's right – go wild!' Cliff instructed. She kicked her legs like a Tiller Girl, high above shoulder level, and swayed her hips back and forth for all she was worth. 'Wilder still!' he commanded. Swing dancing gave Pearl the freedom to express herself. After a hard day's work in the arcade, she would rush to Cliff's studio to be swung and spun into oblivion by eager RAF men or an ever-willing Terry.

If Sylvia regretted her switch from Standard to Latin, she gave no sign. Instead, she committed herself to teaching cha-cha and tango, whose basic figures she demonstrated with Cliff. 'Have you decided about London?' he asked her more than once. Her answer was always, 'No, not yet.' *Not if it depends on me gaining weight,* was the unspoken subtext.

Before leaving home, she'd started a graph to chart her weekly loss – two pounds then one pound (disappointing) then, on a particularly good week, three whole pounds. She felt pleased and proud as she pencilled in the downward slide.

On the second Thursday of August Cliff and Sylvia held a jitterbug contest with a prize for the winning pair.

'First prize is a whole guinea!' Pearl informed Joy over an afternoon treat for young Elsie at Rossi's. Melted ice cream dribbled from the bottom of her sister's cone. Pearl caught the drops in a paper napkin and carried on enthusing over Sylvia and Cliff's recently announced competition. 'I jumped at the chance!'

'What about Bernie?' Joy asked with a quizzical stare.

'He has to work, worse luck.' Pearl turned down the corners of her mouth. 'My slave-driver father refuses to give him the night off.'

'And Bernie doesn't mind you entering without him?'

'No – why would he? What about you and Tommy – will you give it a go?'

'He's working at the circus tonight and, anyway, I'm not keen on jitterbug,' Joy reminded her.

Pearl caught more dribbles in her napkin. 'Don't be such a fuddy-duddy – jitterbug is fun.'

'It's not so much the dance that I object to. It's being flung about by Terry Liddle.'

Elsie turned her cone upside down then sucked noisily from the bottom while Pearl reassured her friend. 'Don't worry, you'd be safe – Terry has offered to dance with me tonight.'

'Even so.' Joy decided not to go.

So Pearl made a solo appearance at North View Parade, full of *joie de vivre* and excited at the prospect of winning the guinea prize. She wore a white blouse with frills, a flared cherry-red skirt and a matching bandanna in her dark hair. After weeks of summer sunshine, she had a deep, even tan and a healthy out-doors glow.

'You look Spanish.' Terry greeted her with an exuberant flamenco flick of his wrists and a stamp of his feet.

'Huh. I was aiming for American.' She glanced dubiously in the studio mirror.

Terry hailed a group of GIs who had arrived without partners. 'American or Spanish?' he asked, gesturing towards Pearl.

'Mexican,' one replied with a thumbs-up.

'That'll do,' she decided, assessing other contestants as they chose their partners. Pleased to see indomitable Doris and Thora approach two good-looking, crew-cut GIs, she waved and wished her friends luck.

'They'll need it.' Terry flashed his smile and whisked Pearl into the middle of the floor, ready to begin. 'What?' he asked with wide-eyed innocence. 'I'm only stating the obvious – everyone knows that you and I are far and away the favourites.'

Sylvia overheard his comment. 'Don't forget I'm one of the judges.' She arched her delicate eyebrows and treated Terry to one of her long, dismissive stares. 'You know what they say – pride comes before a fall.'

'Not tonight,' he retorted. 'Hey, Cliff!' He raised his voice above numerous murmured invitations to dance. 'Ready when you are!'

Cliff lowered the needle on to the record he'd chosen – a Glenn Miller number that began with a trill of piano notes.

Twenty couples counted themselves in. Jazz trumpets upped the tempo as Terry placed a hand on the top of Pearl's head and spun her like a top to begin their routine.

'That's right – whip the hips!' Cliff called out to all contestants. 'Stamp those feet and boogie-woogie.'

Terry and Pearl threw in a couple of shoulder stops then pirouetted out of hold. They held hands as they pecked their heads back and forth like chickens then separated again, jumping clear of the floor, pulling their legs up beneath them and clapping, landing with a skip before linking hands.

'Ready?' Terry signalled their next daring move.

Pearl nodded and he slid her between his legs. She stayed in a low crouch while he swung his leg over her head and back again. The tempo quickened, led by a fast, insistent drumbeat. He pulled her to her feet then stooped forward and sent her sailing over his rounded back. Everything was on show – Pearl's petticoat and a pair of red knickers that matched her skirt.

'Boogie-woogie, stamp and kick!' Cliff's eyes were on the GI partners of Thora and Doris. Jitterbug was in the New Yorkers' blood – they bopped and jived like professionals as the music reached a crescendo. Terry and Pearl had better watch out.

One by one the competing pairs were eliminated until only Doris and Thora with their GIs and Terry and Pearl were left on the floor. The music picked up speed, the swings and turns grew bolder, the jumps higher, until Cliff and Sylvia declared Thora and her American partner the winners.

'It was only fair,' Sylvia commented to Pearl afterwards. 'Cliff could hardly pick Terry, could he?'

'Why ever not?' Pearl was mystified. Perspiration trickled down her face as she decided to head to the door for a breath of air.

Drat! Sylvia regretted her slip of the tongue and hid it by attending to the gramophone while everyone filtered out of the studio.

'What did Sylvia mean – Cliff couldn't choose you?' Pearl asked Terry, who was outside on the pavement, smoking a cigarette.

'Don't ask me,' he replied airily. 'Let's try again at the Tower this coming Saturday.'

'I don't know if I'll be free – I'll have to check with Bernie and my dad first.'

'Oh come on,' Terry cajoled, drawing her close and landing a quick peck on the cheek. 'Live a little.'

Pearl broke away but Terry followed her down the street. He overtook her then seized her in ballroom hold and kissed her again: this time full on the lips. 'We make a perfect pair,' he insisted as he whirled her round. 'We both know it.'

Whoosh! Terry was pulled away and Pearl reeled sideways. From out of nowhere Bernie came at Terry like a whirlwind, shoving him against the plate-glass window of Ibbotson's and yelling in his face.

'I saw that!' he roared. 'Lay another finger on her and I'll punch your bloody lights out!'

Pearl regained her balance as a small crowd gathered, including Bernie's friend, Joe Taylor, and Iris Grigg's son, Sam, together with a bunch of his drinking mates and the GI who had won the competition. She and Bernie had arranged to meet for a drink after he'd closed down the arcade and she'd finished at the dance studio. What she hadn't bargained on was him seeing her and Terry kissing in the street followed by this sudden flash of jealousy on Bernie's part.

'Leave off!' She tried to come between them but was pushed to the ground then helped to her feet by Joe.

Terry kept Bernie at bay. 'Calm down, pal. You've got the wrong end of the stick.'

'Don't "pal" me! You swine, I saw you kissing her with my own eyes!' Bernie landed a punch to Terry's stomach. Terry, urged on by bystanders, retaliated with a swift uppercut.

'Stop them!' Pearl pleaded with Joe. The two men were evenly matched and threatened to do each other serious damage. More blows were exchanged. Sylvia and Cliff emerged from the studio and Cliff rushed to intervene.

'Hey, guys; break it up.' The GI entered the fray. He swung a punch at Bernie and sent him staggering against a wall. Seeing red, Joe piled in to help his friend. Soon it was an out-and-out brawl.

'Somebody stop them!' Pearl cried. The crack of knuckle against bone made her feel sick. 'Bernie, for God's sake!'

'Guys, guys, give it a rest.' The American shoulder-charged Terry, who stumbled backwards into the tobacconist's shop doorway.

Sam grunted a derisive comment about big-headed Yanks before delivering a kick to the small of the GI's back. Pearl tried again to intervene but Sylvia held her back. More punches, kicks and oaths were exchanged.

'I'll call the police,' Sylvia decided. There was a phone box nearby and she rushed to dial 999.

'No – don't do that!' Pearl followed her across the street. 'If Bernie lands in trouble with the police, he could lose his job on the arcade.'

'But this is all nonsense.' Reluctantly, Sylvia allowed Pearl to drag her away from the phone box. 'You have to convince Bernie that Terry isn't interested.'

'In me?' Pearl quizzed.

The fight showed no sign of stopping. Bernie's shirt collar hung loose. Joe was having to restrain the GI while Sam rugby-tackled Terry to the ground. Cliff dragged Terry free before Sam could land a kick. On discovering that his nose was bleeding, Sam faded into the background.

'Yes; in you or any other girl.'

At this moment Pearl noticed Cliff take out his handkerchief and use it to dab at a gash on Terry's forehead. A single, tender gesture plus Sylvia's unguarded comment was all it took. Pearl gasped and gripped Sylvia by the wrist. 'You mean to say . . .?'

'No – no, of course not!' Sylvia attempted to backtrack.

Pearl ignored her. 'They . . . the two of them: Terry and Cliff!'

'Oh Lord!' Sylvia gave up any attempt to deny it.

Of course! How could Pearl not have realized?

'Yes, but please don't say a word,' Sylvia pleaded.

Sloping by with his mates, Sam overheard the girls' conversation and memorized every word.

'If you do, God knows what will happen,' Sylvia warned Pearl. 'Me and my big mouth – I've already let Joy in on part of the secret.'

Cliff and Terry. Terry and Cliff. 'Hang on a minute.' Pearl's mind ticked over slowly as she watched the two men disappear into the studio together. Meanwhile, Joe pulled the GI off Bernie and remonstrated with him. 'Terry started his job at the lido soon after Cliff landed back in Blackpool,' she remembered. 'The timing has to be more than coincidence.'

Sylvia waited in silence for Pearl to come fully up to speed.

Both men were showy and flirtatious, quickly earning themselves reputations with the girls. 'Clever beggars – they hid it well,' Pearl muttered. 'And you say that Joy already understands the situation?'

'She knows the Cliff part of the story.'

'But not Terry's involvement?'

'No.'

'I discovered there was a big mystery surrounding Terry Liddle,' Pearl confided. 'Joy found out that he used to go by the name of Tony Lincoln. Now I realize there was more for him to hide than a wife and a divorce.'

The cogs turned slowly as Pearl and Sylvia conferred and the crowd that had gathered to witness the fight dispersed. The GI straightened his cap and shook hands all round, while Joe dusted Bernie down.

Returning without Terry and seeing Sylvia huggermugger with Pearl, Cliff hurried across.

'Is everything all right?' he asked Sylvia warily.

'Yes, perfectly fine,' she said in her best cut-glass voice.

'Pearl?'

'Yes, ta – everything's champion.'

A shame-faced Bernie joined them. 'Sorry about that,' he mumbled.

'And so you should be, you idiot!' Pearl retorted. 'I hope you're not going to get into a punch-up every time I dance with someone else. Tell him, Sylvia. I never did a thing to encourage Terry – it was all perfectly above board.'

'Perfectly,' Sylvia echoed stiffly.

'And Terry and I didn't even win the prize.' Pearl sighed as she straightened Bernie's collar. 'Thora and the Yank stole it from under our noses. There, you daft clown; put that in your pipe and smoke it.'

CHAPTER FIFTEEN

Clothes moths had had a field day among the dance dresses in Lucia's trunk, as Joy discovered when she held one up and found it full of holes.

'*Mio Dio!*' Lucia's hands flew to her cheeks. 'How is this?'

'Moths.' Joy looked to Tommy for help in translating.

'*Tarme,*' he explained.

'Some are not so bad.' Joy pulled out a heavily beaded pearl-grey silk gown that had escaped the worst ravages. 'We can alter this one to make it fit me. Or this blue taffeta one.'

So, while Tommy headed off to work at the circus, the two women brought the salvageable blue dress down from the attic and set about the alterations. They snipped at the stiff, lightweight fabric and sewed contentedly, remarking on the busy day they'd had in the ice-cream parlour and on the letter that Lucia had received from Tommy senior.

'The food they give him . . .' Lucia pulled a sour face. 'It is meat and potatoes; no pasta. The bed he sleeps on is narrow like this.' She measured out the width with her arms.

'But he's well,' Joy said with a smile. 'And no doubt missing the comforts of home.'

'*Sì, sì.* I tell him do not worry – you help now with ice cream. You work well. We sell plenty. Tommy is happy at the circus. *Tutto bene.*'

Tutto bene – as far as Joy was concerned, the expression said it all. The shift from full-time cleaning to working part-time in the café had gone smoothly. Her private employers had accepted her resignation with regret, while Ruby had begged her to stay on at the Tower for three afternoons a week. Joy had grown fond of her workmates there so the compromise suited her very well.

'I can't believe that I landed on my feet,' she'd confided to Sylvia when she'd sought her out at Cliff's studio to inform her that she intended to carry on taking lessons at the Lorna Ellis Dance Academy. Sylvia had just finished teaching a jive class and had been pleased to see her. 'I love helping at the ice-cream parlour and spending time with Tommy's mum,' Joy had explained.

'Lucky you.' Sylvia had sighed and drawn a contrast between their current situations. 'How the tables have turned – you being welcomed into the Rossi family with open arms; me with not a soul in the world who cares about me.'

Joy had assured her that things would soon change for the better. 'Anyway, plenty of people care.'

'Who?'

'Pearl and me, for a start. And Eddie.'

Sylvia had put Joy right on that score. 'Not Eddie – not any longer.'

'Cliff?' Joy had ventured. 'Bearing in mind the . . . circumstances.'

241

'Yes – Cliff cares for me in his own way,' she'd conceded. 'He wants me to stay here in Blackpool.'

Joy had refrained from expressing her opinion and returned to the original reason for her visit. 'So you're sure you don't mind me continuing with classes at King Alfred Road – or the fact that your mother intends to pair me up with Eddie for the big competition coming up at the end of August?'

'At the Tower?' Sylvia's query had been a touch sharp. Then she'd immediately softened her tone. 'No, of course I don't mind – what right would I have to object? Mother has a good eye for selecting dancers who work well together and Eddie's technique is faultless. You'll be an ideal pairing for waltz and quickstep.'

Now, as daylight faded and Joy and Lucia altered the taffeta dress, Joy went back in a roundabout way to the same subject. 'The skirt of this one will hold its shape nicely when I dance the quickstep. That's my favourite of all the dances I've been taught.'

'Quickstep is beautiful,' Lucia agreed. 'But my Tommy – I teach him cha-cha and samba, not quickstep.'

'That's why my dance teacher has suggested a new partner for me for a big competition at the Tower. His name's Eddie Winter and he specializes in the English style.' Joy sat with her needle poised over the fabric, awaiting Lucia's reaction.

There was a short silence then, 'My Tommy – he knows this?'

'No, not yet. I'll tell him as soon as I get the chance.'

'Soon,' Lucia urged. 'My Tommy, he deserves to know.'

242

'He won't object to my dancing with Eddie,' Joy assured her. 'Tommy and I can still have fun dancing together whenever he gets time off from the circus.'

Silence again.

'You suppose he'll be jealous?' The notion sent a shiver through Joy's slender frame. 'I won't do it if Tommy doesn't want me to. Do you think I ought not to? I'd hate to upset him,' she babbled.

'*Calmati.*' Lucia snipped her thread and put the sewing aside. 'Be calm. Tell him. Listen well to what my Tommy say.'

'How many times?' Bernie asked Pearl. 'I'm sorry, I'm sorry, I'm *sorry* for scrapping with Terry Liddle – all right?'

Rumours about the fracas still ricocheted around the town's fairground workers and stallholders twenty-four hours after the event. There'd been a punch-up involving the younger Greene brother. No – not the older one, which would have been no surprise to anyone. The brawl had taken place outside the dance studio on North View Parade. Bernie had thrown the first punch at the good-looking chap who'd been brought in to run the lido. Sam Grigg reckoned Bernie might as well have saved himself the trouble – Terry Liddle had no interest in Pearl Scott, or in any other girl for that matter. No interest in girls? Blackpool pricked up its ears. What was Sam on about? Everyone had Liddle marked out as a lady-killer, so no wonder Bernie had had a go at him for making a move on his girl.

'It's true.' On the Friday night, Sam held court in the Black Horse. 'I was there. I saw Cliff Seymour being all lovey-dovey with Terry Liddle. I heard Sylvia Ellis yoke their names together – Cliff and Terry, Terry and Cliff.'

'What did I bloody well tell you?' Mick crowed as he banged his empty glass down on the bar then demanded another pint. 'No man worth the name goes within a mile of the Tower Ballroom.'

'Yes, Mick – we know.' The barman had heard it all before. 'Now take it easy, there's a good chap.'

'I don't rate Seymour's chances of making a go of his new dance studio – not after this gets out,' was the general opinion around town. 'People don't like that kind of carry-on. It's not natural.'

So Bernie's apology missed the mark as far as Pearl was concerned. 'Don't you see?' she asked as they closed down the arcade after another busy day. 'It's not the fight I'm bothered about – it's the damage this does to Cliff and Terry's reputations.'

'But how was I to know what those two got up to behind closed doors?' Bernie protested. As the gossip had taken hold, Pearl had dumped the blame on him. She'd kept her distance, avoided eye contact and complained about every record Bernie had chosen to put on the gramophone, nit-picking her way through the entire day. Assuming that apologizing for the umpteenth time would do the trick, it turned out that he was wrong. 'Are you telling me you knew all along?'

'Not about the two of them being a couple, so to speak. But I can't say I'm surprised.'

Following Pearl out of the arcade, Bernie locked the door. It was dusk and the sea was calm, the pier practically deserted. 'Bloody hell,' he said with a sigh. 'It's a right mess.'

'You can say that again. And not helped by you doing what you did yesterday,' she reminded him. 'Lord knows what happened when Terry showed up to work today – *if* he showed up!'

'I won't lose my rag again,' Bernie promised. There was no excuse for his behaviour and he knew it.

'Are you sure?'

'Yep.' Feeling miserable, he walked a little apart from Pearl, head hanging and hands in his pockets.

'All right, let's forget about it.' Relenting at last, she linked arms. 'I arranged to meet Dad in the Black Horse – he owes us a week's wages.'

The prospect cheered them up as they walked along the unlit prom, past sandbagged hotels with their blinds down and the row of squat, concrete air raid shelters extending as far as the eye could see. Stars twinkled in a cloudless sky and a silver moon hung low over the watery horizon. Bernie and Pearl took their time, stopping occasionally to congratulate each other on the success of the new arcade and to whisper sweet nothings.

It was almost closing time when they reached the pub. Joe and a few of his friends left as they arrived.

'You had a narrow escape,' Joe told Bernie. 'Mick and his gang have just gone.'

'Have they heard about Cliff and Terry?' Pearl asked.

Joe nodded. 'Who hasn't?'

'Ought I to warn Cliff next time I see him?'

'No, stay out of it,' Joe advised her, clapping Bernie on the back before carrying on up Empire Street. 'You too, pal. In future, steer well clear.'

Promising to stay out of trouble, Pearl and Bernie went inside the Black Horse to collar her dad.

'You just missed him.' The barman glanced around the dimly lit, smoke-filled room. Two old market men finished a desultory game of darts while a third cleared away an unfinished game of dominoes. 'He was here a minute ago.'

'There he is.' Pearl spotted her father as he emerged from the gents. 'Over here, Dad!' she called.

Henry ambled over to join them, looking the worse for wear after a solid night propping up the bar. His top button was undone, his tie hung loose and grey stubble shadowed his chin and upper lip. 'I suppose you want your money,' he grumbled.

'Bullseye,' Pearl confirmed. 'I worked out the profit for this week and by my reckoning you owe us two pounds ten shillings each.'

Henry chuntered on. 'Five whole quid – how the hell do you work that out? Remember I've got overheads – rent, licences, repaying what I borrowed to set the place up, et cetera.'

Pearl held out her hand, palm uppermost. 'Dad!'

He patted his pockets in an absent-minded way. 'I haven't got the cash on me. You'll have to wait until tomorrow.'

'Now, Dad!'

'We've done our bit and more,' Bernie reasoned with him. 'We're making a go of it and now you have to pay us what you owe.'

Henry continued to fumble in his pockets without success.

'And give Bernie one night off a week,' Pearl added. 'That's right, Dad – he deserves a break, starting tomorrow night. You'll have to step in and take the door money yourself.'

'Or else what?' Henry's lame challenge only prolonged the agony.

'Or else Bernie goes back to his job at the Pleasure Beach and I go back to helping Mum on the fish and chip stall. Cough up, Dad, and get it over with.'

Muttering complaints, Henry produced four crumpled pound notes and two ten-shilling notes from his waistcoat pocket and handed them over. 'Daylight robbery . . . my own flesh and blood . . . hard as nails, just like her mother.'

Bernie and Pearl clutched the notes in triumph. 'And every Saturday night off, starting tomorrow?' Bernie insisted, polite but firm.

'Yes, damn it.' The cheeky so-and-sos had Henry over a barrel.

'Quick, before he changes his mind.' Pearl pocketed her money then grabbed Bernie's hand. 'This calls for a celebration,' she exclaimed as they dashed outside.

'My place?' Bernie suggested with a broad grin.

'Honestly, my dad – it's like getting blood out of a stone.' She laughed breathlessly as they reached Market Street and Bernie searched for his key. 'But you know what this means?'

'With Saturday nights free we can take up where we left off with the fancy footwork,' Bernie answered. It had been a sticky twenty-four hours but things had worked out well in the end. 'Tower Ballroom, here we come!'

'How's Terry?' Plucking up the courage to approach Sylvia and Cliff after she'd spotted them together in the Tower Ballroom the following evening, Pearl blurted out the question at the forefront of her mind.

There was the usual buzz of anticipation as dancers waited for Reginald Dixon and his organ to appear. All the familiar faces were there. Ida, Doris and Thora, dressed up to the nines, had bagged themselves a handsome RAF man apiece, while Ruby and Mavis circled the room looking for likely partners. Pearl had come with Bernie on his first night off, while Joy and Tommy – love's young dream – sat in their own little bubble at a table close to the bar.

'Terry's off work,' Cliff replied abruptly. He turned his back on Pearl and engaged in conversation with one of the American soldiers who regularly attended dance classes on North View Parade.

'Best to let it drop,' Sylvia warned Pearl, while Bernie drifted off to chat with Tommy and Joy. 'Cliff's made it clear that the subject of Terry Liddle is off-limits, even for me.'

Pearl sighed. 'Would it make any difference if I got Bernie to apologize to Terry face to face?' she wondered.

'It's too late for that.' Sylvia didn't mention to Pearl that ever since the fight Terry had been holed up in Cliff's flat above the studio, refusing to go anywhere or see anyone. 'The damage is done. Cliff has received nasty phone calls and notes through his letter box calling him horrid names. People have stopped coming to his classes. To be honest, it's a disaster.'

'And Cliff refuses to discuss it?'

'What is there to say?' Sylvia shook her head. 'It's partly my fault. This wouldn't have happened if I'd kept my mouth shut.'

'You weren't to know how nasty people would be,' Pearl pointed out. 'Or how these rumours would spread.'

'They're more than rumours,' Sylvia reminded her, one eye on Cliff, who had moved on from the GI to speak to the MC for the night. 'And people round here aren't prepared to live and let live. They want everyone to follow their rules – men should go to the pub, follow football and play darts, or else.'

'Not all people.' Pearl preferred not to believe it and yet she only had to think of Mick and his gang to know that it was largely true. 'Would it be best for me and Bernie to make ourselves scarce?'

'What? No; stay and enter the competition. If you left now it would only set tongues wagging again.' Sylvia was distracted by the sight of Cliff having a heated discussion with the MC – a pompous, middle-aged man in a white dinner jacket and red bow tie. She excused herself then threaded her way towards the two men in time to catch the tail end of their conversation.

'I work part-time as a clerk in the council offices,' the master of ceremonies proclaimed. He was a solidly built, broad-faced man, standing with his feet wide apart, as if ready to take on all-comers. 'And I know for a fact that Liddle's name is mud there. The powers that be are worried about him being in charge at the lido after what's happened. They say they can't afford to take risks with a man of his sort.'

'You're telling me that they intend to sack him?' Cliff was incredulous.

The MC was unmoved. 'Not to put too fine a point

on it, there are young lads running around that pool with hardly any clothes on . . .'

Sylvia gasped with shock and Cliff swayed backwards. *Of all the rotten, unfeeling jobsworths . . .*

Cliff was within a hair's breadth of retaliating when she intervened. 'Come along,' she whispered as she guided him towards the nearest staircase leading to the lower balcony. Once there, she sat him down on one of the seats and gave him time to draw breath. Down below, the evening got underway with the appearance of the celebrated organist, accompanied by his familiar theme tune.

Cliff lowered his head and rubbed his temples. 'What can I do?' he groaned. 'I can't fight it – I just have to bite my tongue and try to live with it.'

Couples gathered on the dance floor for a quickstep. All was movement and bright colour under the frescoed ceiling and glittering chandeliers as daily cares dropped away.

'And now I have to go home and tell the man I love that he's about to be hounded out of his job.' Cliff's mood grew gloomier still.

There were no words of comfort from Sylvia; only a sympathetic smile. 'How long have you two known each other?'

'Not that long. There was a gap of a few months between me leaving Berlin and coming back to Blackpool. I was in London, saving money while I worked for Mitch Burns, and that's when I met Terry. His wife had found out about an "affair", as she liked to call it; actually, Terry had been in a two-year relationship with an army sergeant. Anyway, she found out about it and divorced Terry then the army chucked him and his sergeant out for immoral conduct. Terry had been rattling around London at a loose end when he turned up at a tea dance at the Savoy that I went to too. You could call it love at first sight.'

'For both of you?' Sylvia asked.

'More me than him at first,' Cliff admitted. 'I made most of the running – Terry was still raw after being dragged over the coals in the divorce court. And anyway, look at him – how could I resist?'

'He is very good-looking.' She wondered whether this had been part of Terry's problem. To be too handsome could turn out to be a curse rather than a blessing. Sylvia had experienced this herself – always the golden-haired princess in the fairy tale, never a real, flesh-and-blood girl.

'It was me who persuaded him to come to Blackpool,' Cliff went on. 'We both knew we'd have to be careful and not give anything away. Tongues will always wag.'

This tongue in particular! Sylvia was stricken with guilt. She'd broken trust with Cliff when she'd tittle-tattled, first to Joy and then to Pearl. She hadn't meant to – she was just silly and inexperienced. 'It was me,' she confessed in a whisper. 'I'm the one who gave away your secret.'

'There may be trouble ahead . . .' On the dance floor below, couples executed neat quarter turns and lock steps to an Irving Berlin tune. 'Let's face the music and dance.'

'You?' Cliff thumped the padded arm of his seat with his fist – once, twice, three times.

'Me,' she repeated with a sinking feeling. 'It's my fault.'

He shot out of his seat then strode up the steps to the back of the balcony. She ran after him.

'Stay away from me.' Cliff pushed her away with savage force. 'I might have known that you wouldn't be able to keep your trap shut.'

'I'm sorry. I didn't mean—'

'Don't waste your breath apologizing to me!' He pulled her up savagely. 'Say sorry to Terry – he's the one who stands to lose his job, who can't face leaving the house.'

His anger tore through her fragile self-esteem. 'I honestly had no idea about Terry at first,' she cried. 'Not until you and I had our talk. But no one else guessed the truth until I blabbed to Pearl.'

'Yes, Terry puts on a good show – he ought to have been on the stage. I tell him so whenever I see him flirting with girls and them falling head over heels in love with him.'

'He certainly had us fooled.'

'But not any more.' As the conversation drew to a grim conclusion, Cliff buttoned up his jacket then strode the length of the balcony before disappearing down the stairs. The music played on. Couples glided and turned.

Sylvia didn't move. Weariness weighed her down as she picked out Pearl dancing with Bernie and Joy in Tommy's arms. She was tired of it all – the back-biting, her own mistakes, the fall-outs with Eddie and her mother and now this: the row with Cliff that would no doubt put paid to her plans to become his teaching assistant. There was nothing left for her here. Tomorrow she would collect the very last of her belongings from King Alfred Road and the day after she would telephone Mitch Burns and accept his offer to work in London. Yes; this is what she would do – she would buy a one-way train ticket and leave Blackpool for good.

CHAPTER SIXTEEN

'If you ask me, someone slipped last night's judges a back-hander,' Tommy complained as he and Joy strolled along the Golden Mile. It was early on Sunday morning and the beach was deserted except for dog walkers. The sun had risen into a duck-egg-blue sky and all seemed pristine – few footsteps marred the smoothness of the wet sand and wavelets broke white and frothy on to the curved shore as far as the eye could see. 'Just kidding,' he confessed. 'Ida and her RAF pilot were worthy winners.'

Joy thought back to the previous night's competition. She and Tommy had done their best, but cha-cha wasn't her forte and they'd never been in real contention. Still, she'd had a happy, carefree time on the dance floor and afterwards, too, when Tommy had walked her home and kissed her on the doorstep and told her between each lingering kiss that he loved her.

'Stop saying that!' She'd laughed and attempted to push him away.

'Why?' Yet another kiss – this time on the side of her neck. 'I love you, I love you, I love you!'

'Because!' She would swoon if he carried on and

she would give herself up completely to his caresses. 'People will see.'

'Which people?' A snatched kiss on the other side of her neck.

'Mrs Grigg, for a start.' She'd turned Tommy's face towards her then kissed him softly on the lips. 'I'd better go in,' she'd whispered.

She'd left him with a last peck on the cheek and a promise that they would walk on the beach next morning, before the hordes of day trippers arrived.

'Look over there – one of our favourite sights,' Tommy said now, pointing to a spot beyond the pier, to the water's edge, where Vic Marsden tended his elephants during their morning stroll. He stood and watched six huge African animals lumber into the cold Irish Sea, heads raised and trunks waving, while their keeper splashed their sides and used a long-handled broom to scrub them down. 'Joy; look,' Tommy said again.

Following the direction of his pointing finger through the tall iron legs and criss-crossing girders of the pier, she smiled absent-mindedly. 'Actually, I've got something to tell you.'

'Uh-oh.' Tommy doubted that it could be anything serious. He held her hand as they walked on towards the pier.

The longer Joy had waited, the harder this had become. For days it had been the last thing she'd thought about before falling asleep and the first thing that had come to mind when she'd woken up. Now she fumbled her way towards the topic that had preyed on her mind ever since her conversation with Lucia. 'I hope you won't mind what I'm about to say.

255

You must be honest and tell me if you do,' she beseeched him.

'Mind what?' As they came to a halt under the pier, Joy's nervousness set Tommy on edge. 'Come on – spit it out.'

'I can easily tell Mrs Ellis that I'd rather not.'

'Rather not what? Don't tell me there's trouble brewing in our little paradise.' *Stay calm*, he told himself. *Make light of it, whatever it is.*

'You know that Sylvia has fallen out with her mother?'

'Yes – so what?' Tommy began to see where this was going.

'Sylvia's gone over to Latin so Eddie is left without a dance partner for waltz and quickstep.' Joy teetered on the brink.

'Lorna Ellis wants you to dance with Eddie?' Tommy hazarded a guess.

Joy held her breath. 'Yes, but only if you don't mind. She'd like the two of us to work towards a big competition at the end of this month. Our first official practice is arranged for midday today but I haven't said yes yet. Would you – *do* you – mind?'

Tommy took a step back to consider his answer. 'No,' he decided in two seconds flat. 'I don't mind one bit.'

'Honestly and truly?' She couldn't quite believe it.

He grinned at her. 'My name's not Bernie Greene, you know. And Eddie Winter is no Terry Liddle, either. Besides, I'll have a lot on in the next few weeks. Harry Skelton broke his arm during yesterday's matinee; I've been asked to cover for him.'

The sense of teetering on a cliff edge vanished and

Joy took a long, thankful breath before speaking. 'You're right – Eddie is a gentleman. And Mrs Ellis says this is an opportunity for me to make my mark in the competition world.'

'Hush!' Tommy stopped her with a kiss. Salt water dripped from girders over their heads, splashing into shallow pools. The sound of the elephants trumpeting their presence to the town's sleepy hotel guests made him smile again. 'You and I are made for each other – we both know that. You dancing with Eddie and me working overtime at the circus won't change a thing.'

Joy's brown eyes shone with relief. 'Then your mother and I had better get sewing,' she cried. 'It'll be all hands on deck if my blue taffeta dress is to be ready on time.'

'We were robbed,' was Bernie's first comment when he answered the door to Pearl's knock and invited her upstairs to his room. His hair was tousled, his eyes still hooded with sleep.

'When? Who by?' She pulled a face at the sight of a pair of Bernie's shoes kicked off and left in the middle of the room and dirty shirts tossed into a corner. Old habits died hard, it seemed.

'Last night at the ballroom, by the judges.' He made a half-hearted effort to straighten the bed-clothes as he spoke. 'Tommy and me both reckoned they took a back-hander.'

'Rubbish. Ida and the pilot deserved first prize.' Pearl plonked herself down on the edge of the bed. 'Anyway, it's time Ida had a bit of luck. Her brother was on convoy duty on HMS *Eagle* when she was hit by a torpedo – Bob Jonson ended up clinging to an upturned lifeboat until a Maltese fishing boat rescued him from the drink. He was luckier than most but, still, the news hit Ida hard.'

Bernie sucked his teeth then apologized.

'For the mess in this room or for being mean about Ida?' she asked.

'Both.'

'Listen; I can't stop long – I've promised to look after Elsie this morning. I just wanted to know if you've made up your mind about entering the big competition at the Tower – the one the MC announced last night?'

Bernie looked into the mottled mirror above the mantelpiece and ran a hand through his untidy hair. 'Not if it's Viennese waltz or any of the fuddy-duddy stuff.'

Pearl grimaced. 'Someone got out on the wrong side of the bed.'

He made an effort to sound more positive. 'I'd enter like a shot if it was jive or jitterbug.'

'It'll be both types,' she explained. 'The first section will be ISTD stuff – foxtrot, tango, waltz and quickstep. The second half will be swing, which will suit us down to the ground.'

'What's the prize money?' Bernie wanted to know.

'I'm not sure but I'll find out from Sylvia. She and Eddie won first prize for their foxtrot last year.' Pearl watched Bernie kick the cast-off shoes under the bed. 'Seriously, what's up with you today?'

'Nothing – sorry.' He sat down next to her. The bed sagged and creaked. 'The competition is at the end of August, right?'

'Yes, the twenty-ninth.'

'All right, count me in.'

'That's more like it!' She gave him a peck on the cheek. 'We'll have to find time to practise if we want to stand a chance of winning. It won't be easy.'

Bernie stood up with a distracted grunt. He crossed the room to fiddle with the blackout blind. 'This roller's been sticking ever since I got here,' he grumbled before prodding his finger into the spongy wood of the windowsill. 'Bloody rotten. Floorboards, too – riddled with woodworm.'

Pearl sailed along regardless. 'I reckon we can fit it in. There's only two weeks between now and then but we'll use every spare minute when we're not working at the arcade. We might even be able to squeeze more time off out of my cheapskate dad. Ernie's of an age where he can help out now that the place is up and running and I'll get Mum to convince Dad that he has to pull his weight too.'

'Good luck with that.' Bernie wandered restlessly around the room then came to a halt beside the chest of drawers, where he seemed to reach a decision. Opening the top drawer, he pulled out a brown envelope then thrust it towards Pearl. 'I came home to find this on the mat last night – hand delivered.' It had been gone midnight when he and Pearl had parted and everyone with any sense was tucked up in bed. The only living soul Bernie had seen had been an air raid warden on patrol. 'The envelope had been ripped open and stuck back together with tape.'

Her heart skipped several beats as she removed the printed form inside. She read an official heading – 'National Service Acts' – and underneath, in capital letters, the dreaded words: 'Enlistment Notice'.

'No!' Refusing to read on, she placed the paper face-down on the bed.

'Yes.' Bernie picked it up again and thrust it in her face. 'It's from the Ministry of Labour and National Service Regional Office. This is my name and old address. The postmark says it was posted two weeks ago. Mick must have opened it then kept hold of it before he finally got someone to push it through this letter box.'

'Dear sir,' she read now. The typewritten words seemed to dance and blur. 'In accordance with the National Service Acts you are called upon to serve—'

'And there's the date.' He cut her off by pointing to a handwritten section. 'Monday, September the seventh, nineteen forty-two. They'll send me to a training camp in Scotland with a travel warrant to get there.' Now that Bernie had spoken the words out loud, the call-up notification became shockingly real. 'It's not as if I wasn't expecting it,' he admitted.

'But you can't go!' Pearl's thoughts flew wildly hither and thither. 'We need you here. They can't make you. They sent it to the wrong address. You can pretend you never received the papers.'

Bernie shook his head. 'It won't wash. And there's no point arguing that working in the arcade is essential war work, is there?'

Pearl continued to grasp at straws. 'Put it off. Tell them it's too soon – you didn't get the letter straight away. You need more time to get ready.'

A second shake of Bernie's head brought Pearl to a grinding halt and they sat in silence for a long time. In the top corner of the window, a brown moth beat its wings helplessly against the dirty pane. A milkman

260

delivered bottles to doorsteps below then rattled on along the cobbles in his electric float.

'It's my call to action,' Bernie said at last. 'It can't be helped.'

'No.' Pearl couldn't bear to lose love so soon after finding it. If Bernie came to harm on the front line, her heart would shatter like glass. 'No.'

'Yes.' Bernie placed his hand over hers and looked into her eyes. 'Let's face it – I have to go and do my bit.'

With Tommy's blessing Joy stuck to her arrangement to meet with Eddie and Lorna. She had butterflies in her stomach as she approached the King Alfred Road dance studio; stepping into Sylvia's shoes wouldn't be easy and though she knew that Eddie would be encouraging, she was less sure that she would measure up to her strict dance mistress's exacting standards.

From inside the studio Eddie spotted Joy hovering anxiously on the doorstep. He went out to welcome her with a bright smile. 'There you are. Lorna isn't back from church yet but come in and we'll wait together.'

This gave Joy breathing space and a chance to master her nerves. Meanwhile, Eddie's mind turned to music for their lesson.

He flipped through a rack of records. 'Which do you fancy – Silvester or Glenn Miller?'

'I don't mind – you choose.' Joy reflected again on how much things had changed in the last few weeks. Here she was in the place that she once swept and dusted and polished, a shadowy presence quietly going about her job. And now she found herself thrust into the limelight. Far from being overlooked, Lorna and Eddie were pinning their competition hopes on her.

'Glenn Miller it is, then,' Eddie decided. He watched Joy take off her cardigan then change her shoes. 'Have you seen Sylvia lately?' he ventured to ask as he placed the record on the turntable.

'I saw her last night, but only from a distance.'

Joy's cautious answer didn't satisfy Eddie. 'How did she seem?'

'To be honest, she didn't look well.'

'Thin as ever, I presume?'

'Yes.' Unsure of her ground, Joy hesitated. 'I'm sorry if I've spoken out of turn.'

'No – thanks for being honest.' He reflected on Joy's comment as Lorna popped her elegant head around the studio door. She was wearing a pale-blue, narrow-brimmed hat perched at a stylish angle on the back of her head.

'Sorry I'm late. I'll be with you as soon as I've taken off my outdoor things,' she assured them before hurrying upstairs.

'I'm sorry, Joy; I've put you in a difficult position.' Eddie cleared his throat awkwardly. 'I ought not to have mentioned Sylvia – you two have become good friends lately. She and I are no longer on speaking terms, as you know.'

'Perhaps in time . . .' Joy hated to see Eddie looking and sounding so downhearted. 'There might be a way for you to patch things up.'

'No, I don't hold out any hope of that sort.' He dismissed the idea. 'I do still worry about her, though.'

'Yes; it's only natural.'

'One can't just forget. And I wish she'd look after herself properly.' Hearing footsteps coming down the stairs, Eddie broke off.

Lorna entered briskly. Eager to get on with the business at hand, she quelled the mix of emotions that the split with Sylvia had caused. She regretted it, of course, but the sharp sting of betrayal and the hot anger that had followed hard on its heels had remained with her and made her all the more determined to push ahead with this new partnership. 'Let's begin with the basic quickstep steps, shall we? Now, Joy, the key is to move easily around the floor in a happy, upbeat mood. Start in close hold. Ready?'

Happy and upbeat. As Eddie took her in hold, Joy repeated the words to herself. Her partner was as tall as Tommy but not as broad in the shoulders.

'Forward steps using a heel lead, followed by two more steps on the balls of the feet – this is the basic move. And one, two, three!'

They were off! Eddie whisked Joy on a diagonal across the studio floor, soon incorporating lock steps and then chassés according to Lorna's precise directions. Joy managed to keep a clear head, even as the tempo increased, appreciating Eddie's perfect balance and impeccable hold. Up close, his features were undeniably attractive, especially those clear grey eyes framed by eyebrows that were darker than his mid-brown, wavy hair. Feeling safe in hold with him, she relaxed into the swift movements and danced fluidly, mirroring his smile as they turned – slow, quick, quick, slow.

Outside on the street, Sylvia was surprised to hear music coming from the studio. She'd expected her mother still to be at church when she'd planned this quick visit to King Alfred Road after a miserable, sleepless night full of regret. 'Careless talk costs lives' – the government's propaganda poster was as true at a personal level as it was nationally. Sylvia knew she should have borne this in mind before gossiping about Cliff to Joy and Pearl. Two unguarded moments meant that everyone was now as wretched as could be and the only way out was for Sylvia to close the door on everyone and everything that she knew. The certainty had sat like a dead weight on her chest as she'd stared at the ceiling all night long.

Now she stopped at the door to the academy, trying to muster enough courage to enter. The strain of music emanating from the studio was 'Tuxedo Junction', a Glenn Miller instrumental number that Sylvia and Eddie had danced to many times. Drawn like a moth to the flame, she peered through the window to glimpse Eddie and Joy taking instruction from her mother: Eddie without his jacket, dressed in a crisp white shirt and dark trousers, Joy in a jade-green dress with a flared skirt that swung out as she turned. Sylvia gasped and stepped back as if stung by a bee.

'Good, Joy – well done.' Lorna was satisfied with her pupil's technique. She lifted the needle from the record to comment in more detail. 'Your timing is excellent but your presentation leaves room for improvement. We need a little more snap in your syncopated running steps and more confidence in your posture – shoulders back, chin up.'

More snap, more confidence. Taking the instructions to heart, Joy waited for the music to begin again.

'Eddie, are you ready?' Lorna asked sharply.

He jerked himself back into the moment. Was that Sylvia's face that he'd glimpsed at the window? She'd been there for a split second – no more. The sight had shattered his concentration. What was she doing here? Why hadn't she come in? Hadn't the others been aware that she was here? 'Forgive me,' he mumbled to Lorna. 'I need a moment – a breath of air.' With that, he walked swiftly out of the studio and on to the street.

Despite Joy's well-intentioned warning, Sylvia hadn't been prepared to witness Eddie dancing with Joy and it had thrown her off balance. All thoughts of retrieving her belongings from the flat had fled in an instant and she'd turned tail and run. She'd reached Dawson's Gift Emporium when she heard Eddie calling her name.

'Sylvia, wait!'

She turned to see him running after her.

'What's wrong?' he demanded as he caught her up.

'Everything!' She was unable to contain the misery that had been building up for days. The final straw had been the sharp pang of jealousy that she'd just experienced and she recoiled from it. Left out, let down, alone in the world. 'You and Joy, Mother, Cliff and Terry – everything!'

'Take a deep breath.' Eddie resisted an impulse to take her in his arms. 'Surely it can't be that bad.'

'I only came to collect my last few things,' she sobbed. 'I didn't realize anyone would be there.'

'Is there anything I can do?'

'Nothing. This is all my fault. I deserve to be miserable.'

'Sylvia – please.'

'Don't tell Mother,' she pleaded as she brushed away her tears. 'Go back, pretend you haven't seen me. Carry on as before.'

'I will in a moment. But listen – surely it doesn't have to be this way.' Eddie felt helpless in the face of Sylvia's flood of emotion.

'It does,' she insisted. 'I've done and said things that can't be mended. I didn't mean to.'

'Hush – I know you didn't.'

'I'm a bad, bad person.'

'That's not true.'

'It is – look at the way I've treated you, Eddie. Over all these years I've kept you dangling on a string, knowing that you'd always be there.'

'That was my choice – I was willing to wait.' Eddie's hope was that she would talk her way through the crisis as she had done many times before.

'And now Cliff; I've ruined his life by my careless-ness.'

'I wish Dad had never told you about Cliff Sey-mour's private affairs – a fact like that weighs too heavily.' It was unjust that a person's whole future could pivot on a loose word; his father, with all his medical knowledge and experience of the world, ought to have known this.

'It's not fair!' Sylvia pulled a handkerchief from her pocket and roughly dried her tears. 'People are horrid. Cliff is a good teacher – he deserves to succeed.'

'No, it's not fair,' Eddie agreed. 'We have to hope that it will be a storm in a teacup. Before too long those horrid people you mention will find something and someone new to talk about.'

Sylvia hardly seemed to hear. 'That won't help Terry when he loses his job at the lido. Yes, that's right – the town council wants to dismiss him. Oh, I know he seemed too big for his boots when he first arrived, but what harm has he done – really, when you stop to think about it? It must have been as hard for him as it was for Cliff to keep their secret.'

'I agree.' As Eddie sifted through the facts, a new thought struck him. 'I expect your name is mud with Cliff now?'

Sylvia nodded. 'He's angry with me, and who can blame him? That's why I've decided to move away.'

Eddie's chest tightened. 'Are you sure?'

'Yes – leaving Blackpool is the decent thing to do under the circumstances.'

'You've made up your mind – you're going to London to work for Mitch Burns?' Eddie's raised voice attracted attention from passers-by. 'Please, Sylvia; I've said before – look before you leap in that direction. You could land yourself in all kinds of trouble.'

'Keep your voice down,' Sylvia hissed. 'People are staring at us.'

A woman pushing a pram looked askance as she crossed the road. Suspecting a lovers' tiff, she walked on towards the seafront.

'I mean it, Sylvia. I've got a funny feeling about this so-called offer. What do we really know about Burns and his network? And you'd be alone in a big city. Who would you turn to if something went wrong?'

'I can look after myself.' She answered with more confidence than she felt. 'Anyway, nothing will go wrong.'

'At least discuss it in more detail with Cliff. Find

267

out as much as you can about Mr Burns,' Eddie urged. Aware that he'd been away from the studio longer than he'd intended, he glanced up the street to see Lorna standing in the doorway.

His advice fell on deaf ears. 'There's no point – my mind is made up.' Sylvia, too, caught sight of her mother. 'I have to go,' she said hastily. 'Goodbye, Eddie.'

With no way to stop her from jumping off this latest precipice, Eddie was forced to watch Sylvia hurry away. She disappeared around the corner without looking back.

I will go! She repeated the three words to herself. *I will go and no one can stop me.* One phone call stood between her and the capital city, with its swanky hotels; between her and the best big bands, the gilded dance halls and their suave, sophisticated denizens. In London she would make her dream come true.

It was only when Sylvia alighted from the tram at the end of North View Parade that an obstacle occurred to her. She didn't know Mr Burns's telephone number. The problem stopped her in her tracks. She could hardly ask Cliff for the information she needed and she didn't suppose that any of the national dance organizations would be able to supply it. She wondered how many Mr M. Burnses there would be in London's telephone directory then thought that perhaps she should wait until Cliff had gone out and seize the opportunity to slip into his studio. She was sure that he kept a book of addresses and telephone numbers on a shelf under the gramophone.

Deciding that this was the best course of action, Sylvia was hit by a second, much larger obstacle: Mr

Burns's harsh comment about her lack of curves. Her heart sank. What if a successful career in London was over before it had even begun? She pictured meeting the impresario for a second time, perhaps as she stepped off the train into the clamour, smoke and steam of King's Cross station, and seeing him register the fact that she hadn't gained a single pound. In fact, the opposite might well be the case – recent stresses had resulted in Sylvia eating even less than before. Disaster loomed.

She glanced at her image in a shop window. In her opinion she didn't look too thin, but then she'd noticed that several of her dresses didn't seem to fit her as well as previously. And there was also her distinct lack of energy and a tendency to burst into tears at the drop of a hat, not to mention the downward slope on the graph on her wall that provided the concrete evidence that was needed. Perhaps she could take steps to alter this . . . perhaps, perhaps.

'Watch out, miss!' A lad riding a bicycle close to the kerb screeched to a halt as Sylvia drifted off the pavement. 'Look where you're going.'

Perhaps . . . A newsagent's on the corner of North View Parade was open for business. It would no doubt sell sweets. As if in a trance, Sylvia dipped into her handbag to find her booklet of food coupons then entered the shop.

'Vital Supplies Reach Malta!' 'Eighth Army Advances in Egypt.' Patriotic headlines were emblazoned across the tops of newspapers displayed on a wire rack next to the till. A small woman with round glasses and grey hair scraped back into a bun thrummed her rheumatic fingers on the glass countertop. Behind her was a shelf with big jars of dolly mixtures, barley sugar twists, black jacks, sherbet dabs and liquorice allsorts: a riot of coloured, sugary treats.

'I'd like a quarter of the dolly mixtures, please.' Sylvia's voice didn't seem to belong to her as she made her request.

The shopkeeper weighed out the sweets then tipped them into a paper bag. Sylvia paid for her purchase, her coupon was stamped, then she carried the dolly mixtures out of the dingy shop that smelled of tobacco and newsprint. For the woman behind the counter it had been an everyday exchange; but not for Sylvia, who took the sweets to her room above the pipe shop where she methodically laid them out on her table – pink ones to the right, yellow ones to the left and chocolate-flavoured ones in the middle. She stared at them for a long time before she finally overcame her revulsion – *Disgusting dolly mixtures; nothing but dreaded sugar and nasty food colouring!* – and chose a pink-and-white children's sweet then tentatively raised it to her lips.

CHAPTER SEVENTEEN

'Bernie's right – it can't be helped.' Maria left no room for doubt as she doled out a supper of cod and chips to the little ones and Pearl moped around the kitchen. 'If he's received his papers, he's duty-bound to do his bit.'

'You wouldn't say that if it was Ernie who'd been called up,' Pearl snapped as she stole a chip from Elsie's plate then went to stare out of the window at her father's heap of mangled metal and timber in the backyard.

'Ernie's not old enough.' A literal-minded Maria rattled knives and forks on to the table. 'Don't eat with your fingers,' she scolded Wilf.

'That's not the point, Mum. I'm saying if it was your nearest and dearest in the firing line you wouldn't shrug it off so easily.'

Maria stood her ground. 'War is war. We all do as we're told.'

'Why now? Just when the new arcade is up and running and we've persuaded Dad to give Bernie some time off.' Pearl's complaint was accompanied by a loud sigh.

'Eat up – I don't want to see anything left on your

plate,' her mother told Elsie before she drew Pearl out into the corridor. 'You're setting a bad example,' she warned in a low voice, scarcely moving her lips. 'I don't want them to hear you moaning on like this. Go out and get some fresh air. Pull yourself together.'

Scowling deeply, Pearl flounced out of the house without any thought of where she might end up. Her mother hadn't even tried to understand how she felt, but then what had Pearl expected? Bernie himself had clammed up after he'd shown her the call-up papers and she'd left him in his room stewing over the implications. She'd arranged to see him tomorrow before work at the arcade after they'd both had time to cool down.

Where was the easy-going Bernie that she loved? she wondered as she made her way through the maze of back streets then walked along the prom in the evening sunlight. Of course, her mother was right; Pearl must come to terms with the fact that it would take more than her sweetheart's quick wit and devil-may-care attitude to keep him out of uniform. The familiar sight of the Pleasure Beach with its big wheel and roller coasters brought with it the memory of taking Elsie to ride on the waltzers for her birthday treat – the fun of it, the thrills, the squeals of delight, with Bernie spinning them faster and faster ('Hold on to your hats!'), in the innocent, carefree days before Pearl and Bernie had tripped the light fantastic and before their lips had touched. *If Bernie and you dance together, will he be your boyfriend?* Elsie's naive question came back to Pearl as she strode on along the seafront. *Definitely not – no kissing; hand on heart.* Pearl's smile was wistful as she recalled her broken vow.

Before long she found that she was approaching Rossi's ice-cream parlour. Its awning was raised and the blinds were down, but Pearl spotted Joy emerging from South Shore Terrace on to the prom and heading in the same direction as her. She called her friend's name then hurried to intercept her.

'Why so glum?' was Joy's first question. 'What's happened?'

'Bernie's been conscripted, that's what.' Pearl's voice was flat and her whole body conveyed dejection. 'Walk with me,' she pleaded. 'Tell me not to worry; by the time he's done his training, the war could be over.'

Joy's shrug showed that she was unconvinced. 'Is it happening because he lost his job at Squires Gate?'

'Yes; if it wasn't for Mick . . .' Pearl trailed off. Together she and Joy crossed the road then leaned against an iron railing and stared out to sea. The wide, perfectly flat horizon reminded them how vast the world was and how little they as individuals figured in the grand scheme of things.

'One day at a time,' Joy advised quietly. 'Easy for me to say, I know.'

'There I was, excited about the idea of us entering the competition at the end of the month, and all the while Bernie was keeping schtum about his call-up papers. I'm an idiot.'

'No, you're not.' A breeze blew off the sea, pushing the girls' hair back from their sad faces and ballooning their light cotton skirts out behind them. The setting sun cast long shadows across the pavement. 'When you stop to think about it, we're all living for the moment, not knowing what the future holds.'

'At least you can be certain that Tommy won't be

called up, not as long as the circus is allowed to continue. The government line is that entertainment is good for morale – look at ENSA and the Glamour Girls, look at Adelaide Hall singing about hanging out the washing on the Siegfried Line.'

Joy squeezed Pearl's bare arm. 'I'm sorry,' she whispered. 'But chin up – and remember: Bernie will need your support.'

Pearl had the grace to blush. 'Not only am I an idiot but I'm a selfish cow, too. My first thought was that I couldn't bear it if anything were to happen to Bernie. But you're right – I'll pack up my troubles in my old kit-bag . . .'

'And smile, smile, smile.' Joy completed the line from the Great War marching song. 'That's the spirit.' The girls stared out to sea, mesmerized by the magical sight of a red sun sinking and seemingly melting like liquid gold into the horizon.

'Thank you,' Pearl murmured as the burning orb disappeared.

'What for?' For a brief moment Joy chose to ignore the sound of Lucia calling her name from the doorway to the café.

'Just thank you.'

'Joy, *mia cara*; come inside. There is tea, there is cake; *torta di noci* – enough for two girls!'

'Shall we?' Joy asked Pearl.

'Yes indeed.' A smile appeared like sun from behind clouds as Pearl linked arms with Joy. They turned and crossed the promenade with fresh energy in their step at the promise of Italian cake and a cup of good, strong British tea.

*

'What, no Sylvia?' Pearl arrived at Cliff's studio the following Tuesday evening to find a smattering of GIs and assorted secretaries and shop girls; it was a sparser gathering than she'd expected to see. She counted fifteen or sixteen pupils rather than the usual thirty. Bernie had got there before her and was enjoying a quick smoke in the alcove behind the record player while Cliff selected discs for the jive lesson.

'No, it's just me tonight.' Cliff's answer was terse. In fact, he'd only seen Sylvia once since their row on Saturday night, when he'd walked into the studio and caught her flicking through the pages of his address book. She'd coloured up and made excuses before scurrying away with her tail between her legs. Though nothing had been said, he had assumed that she wouldn't show up for any further teaching sessions – well, so be it. 'I wasn't sure you two would put in an appearance, either.' Cliff glanced sideways at Bernie, who pinched out the lit end of his fag before inserting the remainder in his shirt pocket.

'Say if you don't want us here,' Pearl offered. 'We'd understand.'

'It makes no difference to me whether you go or stay, as long as you pay your money and don't expect us to kiss and make up.'

'We're just here to learn,' Bernie assured him. 'It won't be for long, in any case – I've been called up at the end of the month.'

Cliff flicked another quick glance in his direction but his expression gave nothing away. 'Good for you,' he muttered before taking up position at the front of the class while as usual the Americans grabbed the best-looking girls as their partners. Tonight's lesson would be like taking coals to Newcastle as far as the GIs were concerned.

'Jive belongs to the swing dance group,' Cliff reminded everyone. 'It's a combination of salsa, swing and tango, as lively as you like.'

Pearl and Bernie found a space, ready to follow instructions. Pearl was doing her best to follow Joy's advice and take one day at a time. Privately, Bernie had a different name for it: burying their ostrich heads in the sand. Either way, they were both determined to make the most of the little time they had left and that was why they were here, swinging and turning under the bright lights, bumping hips and grinning frenetically, clicking their fingers and dancing like there was no tomorrow.

At the end of the lesson Cliff singled them out. As the studio emptied, he ushered them into the alcove where the photographs of him performing in the Berlin cabaret had started to curl at the corners and come unstuck from the wall. 'About the fallout after recent events,' he began in his usual suave manner as he opened his cigarette case and offered it round. 'This isn't a peace offering,' he warned. 'This is me bringing you up to date with what's going on between me and Sylvia – and Terry, too, for that matter.'

Pearl's heart sank as the men lit up and spirals of smoke wafted clear of the alcove. Bernie shuffled uncomfortably from one foot to the other as Cliff continued.

'Pupils are leaving in droves.' His matter-of-fact tone concealed any emotions he might be going through. Only dark shadows under his eyes and an occasional nervous tic in one of his jaw muscles gave him away. 'I

276

had to cancel a class last night because hardly anyone showed up. The RAF boys have been told to stay away and it won't be long before the same thing happens with the civil servants.' He smiled grimly. 'Perhaps the top brass think that what I've got is catching.'

'That's not funny,' Pearl murmured.

'No, but it's true. Now that word is out about me and Terry, people will avoid this dance studio like the plague.'

'And Sylvia?' Pearl asked with mounting dread.

'I've a hunch that she'll take up the offer to go to London before too long. In fact, I'm not sure what's holding her back.'

'I'll try to find out,' Pearl promised.

'Do it soon; before it's too late,' Cliff urged. The worm of guilt continued to gnaw at his innards but as yet he'd lacked the courage to tackle the problem directly. Besides, it was Terry, not Sylvia, who came top of his list of current concerns.

'What about Terry?' Bernie prompted uneasily. They'd come to the crux of Cliff's problems and he expected the news to be bad.

'How's the cut on his forehead?' Pearl demanded specifics.

'Forget about the cut – time will heal it. The fact is, he says he can't face anyone – just can't do it.' Cliff massaged his temples and went on speaking with his eyes closed. 'Terry took a massive risk coming to Blackpool. He'd managed to leave his past behind by relocating to London and taking on a new name and everything. Coming back up north was a gamble but he did it for my sake. It hasn't paid off, worse luck.'

Pearl winced but was silent.

'It turns out that I've got a thicker skin than him – maybe because I've been in this living-a-lie game longer than he has; all my life, if you must know. But Terry was married before, pretending to lead a so-called normal life. Now he says he can't stand the shame of being found out. Can't – face – it!' Cliff stubbed out his cigarette with three vicious stabs.

'Where is he now?' Bernie asked. Guilt made it seem as if he was dragging his feet through thick mud.

'He's still in my flat. I'll borrow the Morgan later this week and drive him back to Silver Street. He's not prepared to risk showing his face in the daylight.'

'Sorry to hear it,' Pearl whispered. None of it fitted with the version of the Terry she'd assumed she knew – the brash show-off, the smooth-talker brimming with confidence. 'What will he do?'

'I don't know – he hasn't decided.' Cliff's spent cigarette lay crushed in the ashtray. 'It's all up between us, though; I do know that much. Terry's made it clear that it's over.'

As the conversation ground to a halt, all Pearl could do was sigh and shake her head while Bernie attempted to make amends by promising to drum up new custom for the dance studio.

'You can try,' Cliff grunted as he walked them to the door. 'But I doubt it'll do any good.' In his experience, the bubble of reputation, once pricked, was burst for good.

'At least let me try.' Bernie stepped out of the studio ahead of Pearl, who gave one last sigh. 'I'll tell everyone how good you are, that swing dances are all the rage and waltz is old hat. I'll make it happen – you watch.'

*

The days dragged for Sylvia now that she had no classes to teach. She spent them cooped up in her room, reading dance magazines and dreaming of her new life in London. She saw no one and desperately tried to make herself eat what she knew was bad for her – potatoes and bread; anything with lots of starch and as much sugar as her coupons would allow. It took an immense effort of will to overcome the revulsion she experienced as the food went down. Once or twice she'd even leaned over the toilet bowl and thrust her fingers down her throat to force it back up. But the lure of London was stronger; she would follow the dream at any cost. So, gone was the graph charting her weight loss and in its place above her bed she stuck up Mr Burns's telephone number, which she'd stolen from Cliff's address book.

The scrap of paper with the number written on it represented escape and she thought of little else, blocking Pearl's attempt to establish contact by pretending that she was out when Mr Ibbotson called her name from the bottom of the stairs.

'Miss Ellis, you've got a visitor – a Miss Pearl Scott to see you.'

Sylvia didn't answer.

'Miss Ellis?'

Silent and still as a trapped mouse, she stayed back from the window in case Pearl glanced up. She prayed to be left alone. Catching sight of herself in the dressing-table mirror, Sylvia realized that she hadn't combed her hair or put on any make-up for days.

'Miss Ellis!'

Silence.

'I'm sorry, miss – she appears not to be in,' the tobacconist's muffled voice reported to Pearl.

Sylvia heard nothing from Eddie and nothing from her mother. Endless hot, sticky days ticked by and she spoke to no one, went nowhere, did nothing. She forced herself to eat.

On the Thursday evening she ventured out to buy fish and chips. She waited until it was almost dark and all activity had ceased in the dance studio next door. Creeping downstairs, she was dismayed to discover that she'd timed it badly – a familiar green sports car was parked at the kerb with its canvas hood up and the boot lid and driver's door open. The passenger seat was occupied by a hunched figure whose trilby hat was pulled forward to hide his face. Before Sylvia had time to step back inside, Cliff came down the stairs then out on to the pavement carrying a suitcase.

Seeing her, he deliberately turned his back to put the case in the boot then, still stubbornly ignoring her, he sat in the driver's seat and turned on the engine.

'Wait!' Recognizing the passenger as Terry Liddle, and overcome by a wave of strong emotions, Sylvia rushed forward. She ran round the front of the car then peered in at the man whose life she'd ruined. He turned his head away and pulled his jacket collar up. The message was clear – he didn't want to talk. 'No, please – wait!'

Cliff revved the engine. Sylvia held on to the door handle. She heard Cliff swear and tell her to let go then Terry spoke.

'Let her have her say,' he muttered as he wound down his window.

Cliff cut the engine. 'Make it snappy,' he told Sylvia.

She crouched beside the car, aware that daylight was fading fast and the blackout was in force. The street was deserted. 'Terry, I'm sorry for everything.'

'Is that it?' His hat hid the gash on his forehead but not the look of defeat in his eyes. There was no glimmer of hope and not a sign of the confidence that had once oozed from every pore.

'What will you do now?' Sylvia whispered.

He fired a question back at her. 'What's it to you?'

She blinked in the face of his anger. 'I'm so sorry! I didn't mean any harm.' Words came out in an incoherent rush. 'I had no idea . . . people are so narrow-minded . . . nobody's business—'

'That's enough.' Terry put a stop to Sylvia's flow of remorse. 'It was only a matter of time before someone gave the game away. It just so happens it was you.'

Sylvia fought to recover her presence of mind. 'You could lie low for a while,' she suggested. 'Wait for the fuss to die down.'

'And live on fresh air?' Bitterness crept back in. 'I lost my job at the lido. Who will employ me now?' Terry gave a signal for Cliff to switch the engine back on. 'I have to shoulder part of the blame,' he confessed to Sylvia. 'I overdid the playboy act – it was meant as a smokescreen but I drew too much attention to myself. My coming on strong made Pearl's sweetheart jealous – I hold my hands up to that.'

'Your act worked at first, though.' Her mind flew back to the initial impression they'd all had of Terry; how he'd been charming and annoying in equal measure, a seemingly unstoppable force of nature.

He shook his head. 'Time to move on to pastures new, eh, Cliff?'

'Not in my case.' Cliff pressed his foot on the accelerator and made the engine roar. 'Blackpool's my home. I'm in debt up to my ears and my only way of paying it back is to make a go of this studio.'

'Just me, then.' Terry gave a resigned sigh. The prospect of constructing a new set of lies, of changing his name for a second time and cutting all ties with the past, filled him with despair.

'No – me as well,' Sylvia informed them. 'I'm leaving for London soon.'

Cliff took his foot off the pedal and leaned forward to scrutinize her face. 'Does Mitch know that?'

'Not yet. There are a few things to sort out before I telephone him.'

'Such as?' Cliff got out of the car, slamming the door before striding round to her side.

'Things.' She waved her hand vaguely.

Cliff frowned and thrust his hands deep into his trouser pockets. 'How long before you make that call?'

'I'm not sure – a few days, I suppose. I'm not rushing into it, if that's what you're afraid of.'

'Good.' Cliff kicked absent-mindedly at the front tyre. Now was the time to warn Sylvia off completely – to give her the lowdown on exactly what to expect if she went to London, to make it plain that the 'gentlemen' on Mitch's list wanted much more than a dance partner and that they would discard her after use like yesterday's *Daily Telegraph*. He imagined the look of horrified disbelief on her beautiful, naive face if he told her the truth. 'Take your time.' Still he prevaricated.

'I'm close to getting what I've always wanted,' she reminded him with a defiant tilt of her head. 'To enter the world of professional dance and show my mother that I can do it without her. It's my dream.'

The choice, as ever, was crystal clear. He could come clean. *Dress it up how you like, Mitch Burns is a pimp – no more, no less. And I, Cliff Seymour, have been his accomplice, scouting for likely girls with a talent for dancing that allows them entry into the upper circles of society. Until now, every single one of those girls knew what they were signing up for.* Though Cliff wasn't proud of his lucrative sideline, it had provided him with a steady flow of cash that would be needed even more now that takings at the dance studio were down.

Or else he could bite his tongue and let Sylvia go ahead with her plan. This way he could continue his connection with Burns and the money would keep rolling in.

'Hurry up, let's go!' Aware that a gang of rowdy men – six or seven of them – was approaching on the opposite side of the street, Terry leaned out of the car and spoke urgently.

Cliff noticed the hoodlums, beer bottles in hand and chanting a crude song. The moment had passed, damn it, and there was no time to lose. He jumped back in the car and started the engine.

Meanwhile, Terry leaned out of the window and extended his hand to Sylvia. 'Shake?' he offered with a rueful smile.

'Yes; shake.' She took his hand, sensing that it might be the last she'd see of him. As Cliff eased away from the kerb, she stepped back into the shadow of the tobacconist's doorway. One of the drunken men lurched on to the road, into the path of Cliff's car. There was a squeal of tyres as Cliff braked just in time.

'You were bang on the nail, Sam – it's them nancy boys!' The first man slurred his words as he stooped to gain a better view of the car's occupants. 'We're on to you, you pair of dirty bastards!'

Others joined him, jeering as they surrounded the car. One hammered at the windscreen while another smashed his empty bottle across the bonnet.

Sylvia heard names above the fracas – Mick, Fred and Howard. The men moved as a pack; when one started to beat his fists against the car hood, the others copied. They snarled and swore viciously as they rocked the Morgan from side to side.

'Bloody disgrace!'

'Dirty buggers!'

'You've got it coming!'

Unable to move forwards, Cliff slammed into reverse and careered backwards along the street, taking his tormenters by surprise. They reeled sideways, toppling into one another, swearing and staggering. Sylvia held her breath as the borrowed sports car reversed down a side street where it braked then shot forward out on to North View Parade and from there towards the prom, leaving the gang of angry men standing. Within seconds it had swerved wide around an oncoming tram and disappeared from view.

CHAPTER EIGHTEEN

Joy waited for Tommy in the corridor overlooking the circus ring where Alfred Court's famous lions and tigers thrilled the crowd. The poster behind her advertised 'Twenty Monarchs of the Jungle – the most ferocious group ever presented together in one cage'. Perched on their colourful podiums, the tamed beasts dwarfed the moustachioed, leotard-clad trainer as they squatted on their hindquarters and, dog-like, raised their enormous paws to beg for a reward.

Rather him than me. Joy didn't envy the animal trainer – or the monarchs of the jungle, for that matter. She hoped that Tommy would change quickly out of his clown costume after his evening performance so they could be on their way. Seeing such magnificent creatures cooped up inside a circular cage sent a shiver down her spine. Worse still, instead of roaming free in the wild, these poor lions and tigers were kept in stables below ground and rarely saw the light of day.

The crowd seemed to have no such qualms. They oohed and aahed at every crack of the trainer's whip, applauding loudly at each new trick then sitting in edge-of-the-seat suspense as the male lion prowled around the circumference of the ring, shaking his ragged mane and baring his yellow fangs at front-row members of the audience.

Joy had rushed to meet Tommy after another successful quickstep lesson on King Alfred Road. 'You're making excellent progress,' Lorna had told her. 'Your syncopation is much improved and your natural pivot turn is well-nigh perfect.' Eddie, too, had praised her. At this rate they'd be more than ready to compete at the end of the month.

'Boo!' Tommy had crept up behind Joy and now he pinched her waist with both hands. He'd appeared out of nowhere and played one of his favourite tricks.

Joy gasped and turned. 'You scared the living daylights out of me!' she hissed as she wiped a smudge of white greasepaint from his cheek.

'Quiet back there!' a man in the audience grumbled loudly.

So Tommy grasped Joy's hand and they strode along the corridor together, out into the first-floor area with its ticket booths and giant potted palms, then down the wide stairs and out of the arched main entrance on to the prom. Even though it was nine o'clock, there was still enough daylight for them to enjoy the silvery glimmer of water stretching to the horizon and the last blush of sunset in the clear sky.

'How did your lesson go?' he asked once they could speak freely.

'All right,' she replied.

'More than all right, I bet.' Tommy often teased Joy about her modesty. '*Prima in assoluto* – nothing less than perfect.'

'Mrs Ellis was pleased,' she conceded.

286

'And Eddie hasn't swept you off your feet yet?' Tommy joked.

'No – both feet are firmly on the ground.' It had been a long day, starting with a busy morning serving ice cream with Lucia, followed by a cleaning session at the ballroom then the lesson at the academy.

'Come on – let's get you home.' Circling her waist with his arm, Tommy shortened his stride to match Joy's. They talked of this and that – about Joy and Lucia's continuing efforts to get her taffeta dress finished and about reports of the ongoing repair work on the bomb-damaged Squires Gate runway. Before they knew it, they'd reached the turn-off on to Silver Street, where they met Sam Grigg hurrying towards them.

'Now then, you two.' Sam's hasty, low-key greeting was drowned out by the sound of a passing tram. 'Watch out – it's pistols at dawn at number fifty-seven,' he quipped, scarcely breaking his stride.

Puzzled, Joy turned to study his scrawny back view. 'What did he mean by that?' Sam had obviously been visiting his mother. Had there been an argument between them or between Iris and one of her lodgers?

'We'll soon find out.' Anticipating trouble, Tommy resolved not to say goodnight on the doorstep as usual but to see Joy all the way up to her room.

However, nothing out of the ordinary seemed to be happening as they arrived at the house and Joy turned her key in the lock. The blinds were down and all lights at the front of the building were switched off except for one in the landlady's sitting room.

'Everything's fine,' Joy assured him in a whisper.

'Are you sure?' Tommy was tired too – the extra performances to cover for Harry Skelton were catching up with him. On the other hand, the prospect of accompanying Joy up to her room was tempting.

'Yes!' She kissed him firmly on the mouth. 'Go!'

He kissed her back, lost in her sweet smell and the softness of her lips. Tommy sighed and kissed her again.

'Go,' she repeated, turning him around and gently shoving him from behind.

He gave in, blowing her more kisses from the pavement.

Joy smiled then closed the door. She was halfway up the first flight of stairs when her sour-faced landlady emerged from the front room in hairnet, dressing-gown and slippers.

'Oh, it's you,' Iris tutted. 'I heard noises and I thought it was him.' The 'HIM' came out in large capital letters. 'I mean him in the room below you who wants us all to think he's God's gift but now the whole town knows the truth.'

Joy's heart sank as she rested her hand on the banister. Looking up, she glimpsed a narrow shaft of yellow light under Terry's door.

Iris beckoned for her to come back down the stairs. 'My Sam's told me everything,' she hissed in a conspiratorial voice. 'Well, not every last detail because I'm his mother and he wanted to spare my blushes. It beggars belief what two men will get up to behind closed doors.'

'Mrs Grigg, please!' Joy looked anxiously up the stairs.

Her landlady raised her voice defiantly. 'I don't

care if the whole house hears me. It's shocking; and the idea that it might've happened here, under my roof . . .' She shook her head in disgust then ranted on. 'I went straight up there and gave his lordship his marching orders. Sam backed me up. I told Liddle he's got until Monday morning to pack his bags and move out – not a moment longer.'

Joy pressed her lips together and remained silent. So this was what Sam had meant by pistols at dawn.

'Until then, you'd be well advised to stay out of his way,' Iris told her. 'Anyone who's seen talking to HIM is likely to be tarred with the same brush.'

'Thank you – I'll bear that in mind.' Sick at heart, Joy continued on her way. She closed her attic door firmly behind her, leaning against it and taking several deep breaths while she considered her landlady's heartless action. Taking off her jacket, she paced up and down, unable to settle as she imagined Terry trapped in his first-floor room, presumably reeling from the fresh shock of being made homeless.

Not fair – especially after all he's been through lately. She gave a long, drawn-out sigh and kept on pacing, wondering about the wife in Blackburn who had divorced him and Terry's subsequent attempts to make a new life: first in London and now here. Admittedly, she didn't understand what had driven him into another man's arms – the concept was too far beyond her own experience – but still it bothered her that he should be punished for private actions that did no one any harm. It wasn't as if Terry had flaunted his affair with Cliff. Quite the opposite; they'd done everything possible to conceal it. Round and round she went in circles, always coming to the same point: *It's not fair!*

A faint noise from below drew her attention – the sound of a heavy object being scraped along floorboards. Silence followed and a growing sense of unease. Why shift furniture at this time of night? Joy waited and listened. She thought she heard the rasping sound of a sash window being opened, which meant that Terry must have turned out his light and raised his blackout blind beforehand. Her uneasiness escalated to alarm and yet she held back. Ought she simply to mind her own business and go straight to bed?

No; hang Mrs Grigg's advice – Joy's gut feeling was that she should investigate. So she crept downstairs to Terry's room and knocked quietly. There was no answer. She knocked a second and then a third time before nervously turning the knob and opening the door.

All was dark. A dressing table stood in the middle of the room, at an angle to the open window, and a net curtain billowed in the breeze. She made out Terry, half obscured by the curtain, crouched on the windowsill, naked from the waist up. He stared at her, arms braced against the window frame.

Joy froze. Terry had shifted the dressing table to give him access to the window and it was obvious why: he intended to jump, come what may.

Without saying a word he turned his head to stare into the blackness of the night. The white curtain danced in the breeze. He perched, ready to spring.

'Terry; please.' She edged towards him. Though a fall from this height might not kill him, it was likely to do serious damage. 'Please don't.'

Crouching, tilting forward, staring down at the yard below. There was nothing to live for – no hope.

'Let me help.'

Terry closed his eyes. *Jump, jump into the abyss.* Put an end to voices that hissed, mouths that sneered, society that demonstrated its disgust through insult, innuendo and worse.

Joy reached out her hand as she saw him lean further out of the window. 'Those men are not worth it. Don't let them win,' she murmured.

Don't let them win. These were the four short words that got through to him. Slowly Terry's determination to end it all weakened and, inch by inch, he rocked back on his haunches until he felt Joy's cool fingertips brush the bare skin of his shoulder.

The crucial moment had passed. *Breathe!* 'That's right – easy does it.' Joy held the curtain and watched him swing his legs to the floor. 'Take no notice of Mrs Grigg or that son of hers, or anyone else who has it in for you. Remember: you're miles better than them.' The tormented man's feet touched the ground. She took his arm and supported him towards his fireside chair, sat him down and fetched him a blanket from the bed, offering to wrap it round his shoulders.

Don't let them win. 'I can manage,' Terry said weakly, though his legs were like jelly and his hands shook uncontrollably as he tugged at the blanket.

'You *can*!' Joy echoed, kneeling beside him.

'I'm sorry.' He slumped in the chair, head lolling, chest heaving, sobs rising. 'I've nowhere to go. Mrs Grigg intends to throw me out on to the street.'

'Who in their right mind wants to stay here anyway?' Joy challenged. 'Look around you – threadbare rugs, a lumpy mattress, peeling wallpaper.'

Terry let out a long breath – somewhere between a sigh and a dry sob. 'Right,' he groaned.

'It's time to find you new lodgings in a better part of town.'

His throat hurt and his heart raced – but he was alive, thank God.

'Miles better than any of them,' Joy repeated as she rested a hand on his arm. Terry Liddle had hit rock bottom and had survived. 'You're young and strong and you can dance. You could get a job in any theatre, audition for film musicals, make your way to the very top, if you set your heart on it.'

Alive and with a future; still dim and blurred but a future, nevertheless. Terry pulled himself upright in his chair while Joy closed the window.

'Sylvia, Pearl and I will help you look, starting tomorrow.' Speaking on behalf of her friends, Joy threw a lifeline to the drowning man. 'Who needs poky Silver Street when there are boarding houses all along the Golden Mile? We'll find you a sunny room with a sea view, within a stone's throw of the Grand Theatre or the Winter Gardens or the Hippodrome.'

A possible way forward slowly took shape. It was illuminated by footlights and framed by a proscenium arch, peopled by a chorus of smiling dancers who, like him, knew how to hide heartbreak beneath a thick layer of greasepaint. 'Yes,' Terry agreed. 'I'll find new lodgings and make a fresh start.'

Sylvia recognized Eddie's familiar rat-a-tat, tat-tat knock on her bolted door. Lying in bed and reaching for her alarm clock, she saw that it was not yet eight o'clock.

'Mr Ibbotson said we could come straight up,' Eddie informed her. 'Are you decent? May we come in?'

'Who's "we"?' She sprang out of bed and scrambled for her dressing-gown.

'Your mother's here, too. She wishes to speak with you.'

'At this hour?' Sylvia pulled up the blind to let in the daylight. A visit from Lorna was the last thing she was expecting. 'Go away, Mother. Mr Ibbotson had no right—'

'Please!' Lorna spoke over her. 'We must talk.'

'There's nothing to talk about.' Sylvia approached the door but didn't open it. 'Really – what would be the point?'

There was a long pause and mumblings between the visitors before Lorna continued. 'I can't sleep for worrying about you, especially since I heard about the fight outside Mr Seymour's studio. A most unsavoury business.'

Unsavoury! The choice of word brought a wry smile to Sylvia's lips; it was so typical of her prim, ladylike mother.

'Sylvia, can you hear me?'

'Yes, loud and clear.'

'Please open the door.'

Not likely. Allowing them to enter would be like taking her finger out of the dyke and letting in a flood of unwanted emotions. 'Once and for all, Mother – nothing you can say could patch things up between us.'

'But I want to tell you how truly sorry I am.' Lorna's muffled voice grew desperate. 'I can't let you leave for London without at least trying to make amends. I would never forgive myself.'

Sorry! Now here was a plain little word that rarely passed her mother's lips. Sylvia was so astonished that she slid back the bolt and opened the door to find Lorna with her hands clasped in front of her and Eddie standing close behind. 'Good Lord!' she exclaimed. 'Miracles do happen.'

'Oh!' Lorna rushed at her daughter and threw her arms around her. 'You look painfully thin.'

'Thank you, Mother.' Sylvia released herself and retreated into the room. 'You don't look too hot yourself.' Though dressed immaculately in a lilac two-piece and white gloves, with not a hair out of place, Lorna's face was drawn and there were dark shadows under her eyes. Eddie, too, looked as if the tension of the past few weeks had taken its toll. 'Whose idea was this, anyway?' Sylvia asked.

'Mine,' Lorna insisted as she took in her surroundings. Sylvia's dresses hung from rails in the alcoves to either side of the chimney breast and though all was clean and tidy, there was a forlorn, impersonal air to the mismatched Victorian furniture and absence of paintings and ornaments. Two suitcases were perched on top of the mahogany chest of drawers and Sylvia's shoes were arranged in a neat row under the iron bedstead. 'Edward kindly offered to accompany me.'

'I can wait downstairs if you'd prefer.' His eyes flicked from Sylvia to Lorna then back again, the picture of uncertainty.

'Yes, you do that,' Sylvia decided. 'If you wouldn't mind,' she added more softly as she followed him out on to the landing. 'Talk about putting your head into the lion's mouth,' she teased quietly.

Eddie managed a faint smile. 'Just clear the air between you,' he encouraged before making himself scarce.

'Dear Edward,' Lorna sighed when Sylvia returned. 'He misses you most dreadfully.'

'Don't!' Like a cricketer on the boundary, Sylvia fielded the guilt and lobbed it straight back. 'We're not here to discuss Eddie. You came to apologize – I'm all ears.'

'I was too harsh,' Lorna admitted as, sighing heavily, she placed her handbag on the bed then removed her gloves. 'It came out of the shock of learning that you'd been taking Latin lessons behind my back. If only I'd stopped to think then moderated my language, we might have reached an agreement.' So far, so good, but Lorna's resentment soon bubbled to the surface. 'Why on earth didn't you tell me what you were up to?'

'Because!' Sensitive as ever to her mother's choice of words, Sylvia homed in on the accusatory phrase. 'I wasn't "up to" anything, as you put it. I was simply eager to learn new dances and I knew full well how you'd react. Lord knows, you told me often enough.'

'Yes, and that doesn't change,' Lorna admitted. 'I'm Imperial Society through and through. Dance for me is to do with poise and elegance not exuberance and individual expression.'

'Stop right there,' Sylvia interrupted. 'I've heard it all before. Besides, that may have been part of the reason for our difference of opinion, but deep down it had more to do with you and Cliff being arch rivals.

Standard versus Latin, old school versus modern – you were jealous of him.'

'Not jealous,' Lorna countered. 'But I do admit that I see that young man as competition and I was frightened of the detrimental effect his new studio would have on our business. Yes; frightened – and rightly, as it turns out.'

'Stop pacing around and sit down, please.' Sylvia's tone softened as she watched her mother take a seat by the window then waited for her to continue.

'I've worked so hard and for so many years.' Lorna gave a weary sigh. A shaft of sunlight exposed crow's feet around her eyes and a downward turn to the corners of her mouth that Sylvia had never noticed before. '*We've* worked so hard,' she corrected herself. 'You and I, together – ever since you were a small girl. And you were all I had in those early years. Becoming a mother made me determined to pull myself out of the hole I found myself in after your father—'

Thrown off balance by Lorna's frank tone, Sylvia cut in quickly. 'I understand.'

'You don't – not really. How could you? I was young when you were born: the age you are now. I'd broken all the rules, become an outcast and brought a halt to a promising career. But I didn't regret it, not for a moment. I was certain that I could manage somehow.'

'You've never said any of this before,' Sylvia murmured. 'Not a single word about my father – ever.'

Lorna was in so deep that a full confession flowed from her lips. 'I scarcely knew him. I met him here in Blackpool, at the very first dance festival held at the Empress. He was an older, married man from London – an ISTD judge for the foxtrot competition, no less. I suppose you could say that he swept me off my feet – quite literally.' Lost in memories of those days, Lorna gazed out of the window.

'And did he offer to help when he found out about the fix you were in?'

Lorna shook her head. 'I dithered, but in the end I did write to him. After several weeks he wrote back to wish me well and say that I should hand the baby over to be adopted. That affected me quite badly, I must say.'

Sylvia gasped at her mother's understatement. Those endless, nail-biting weeks of waiting for a reply must have been agony, only to be denied help at last and cast aside as an inconvenient nuisance. 'And that was it?'

'Yes. Two years later I learned that the poor man had been killed in a car accident. But I couldn't afford to dwell on any of that. I had you to look after, and once the scandal of your birth had died down I adopted the title of Mrs and managed, little by little, to build my reputation as a teacher of dance.'

'People gossiped?'

'Naturally.' Lorna turned her head to look steadily at Sylvia. 'But I didn't take any notice; I was too busy. And quite soon they forgot.'

'Yesterday's news,' Sylvia said with a sympathetic sigh.

'Quite.' Lorna allowed her ramrod posture to relax an infinitesimal amount. 'It helped that you were a beautiful child who melted hearts wherever you went. I'm afraid that I let people spoil you because of it.'

'I don't remember.'

'Trust me – it's true.'

'Why haven't we talked of it before?' Sylvia demanded hotly.

'Because digging up the past isn't my way,' Lorna explained. 'I'm only telling you now because there are certain parallels – an ambitious girl, an older man from London who might take advantage.'

Sylvia bristled. 'I take it Eddie has been gossiping?'

'He may have mentioned Mr Burns's name in passing.' Lorna brushed Eddie's contribution aside. 'I've made numerous telephone calls but none of my Imperial Society colleagues have any knowledge of a Mitchell Burns.'

'Mother, I've been through this with Eddie – Mitch Burns doesn't teach dance; he merely makes introductions. After that, it will be up to me to find the most suitable partner then enter the right competitions – to make my own way.'

Lorna swallowed an unreasonable desire to leap up and, with Eddie's assistance, forcibly drag Sylvia back to King Alfred Road. 'Exactly when do you intend to do this?'

'Soon.' *Lack of curves and the gaining of extra weight are all that's holding me back, damn it! And the dratted business of forcing more food down me is proving far harder than I expected.* Suspecting that her mother was likely to go to extreme lengths to prevent her from carrying out her plan, Sylvia made a swift move towards her bed to remove the tell-tale telephone number taped to the wall.

'What's that?' Lorna crossed the room but had no time to read and memorize the number before Sylvia took it down. 'I wish you would think again,' she pleaded. 'Now that we've cleared the air, why not come home? Believe me, I won't mind if you continue with Latin – it will be up to you. What do you say?'

Sylvia knitted her brows. Lorna's revelations had forced her to view her mother in a fresh light; she saw determination to succeed where once she'd seen stubbornness, courage in place of a desire to control. 'We're very alike,' she admitted.

'We are.' Lorna's smile was conciliatory. 'So come home and start afresh.'

Seconds ticked by. London was Sylvia's lure and dancing was her hook. 'No,' she said at last. 'I'm glad we've had this talk, Mother, but you're not the only person who's asked me to stay in Blackpool. Let me tell you what I told them – Mr Burns is offering me my big chance to step up in the world and I won't – I can't – turn my back on that. I intend to go to London as planned.'

CHAPTER NINETEEN

There was no time to lose. Joy flew through her early-morning chores – helping Lucia to lay clean tablecloths and set out fresh flowers (crimson sweet williams) to brighten up the café – before liaising with Tommy. It was settled that he would help his mother with the morning rush then Joy would be back in time for him to set off for his Saturday matinee. With this established, Joy dashed out to round up Pearl and Sylvia.

'It should only take a couple of hours,' Joy promised Pearl when, having overcome her lifelong dread of piers, she arrived unannounced at the entrance to Great Scott's North Shore Amusements. 'Terry is desperate to find new lodgings. I promised we would help.'

Pearl didn't hesitate. 'Hold the fort while I'm gone,' she instructed Bernie on her way out, firing questions at Joy all the way along the pier before the eager pair crossed the prom then hurried along North View Parade as far as Ibbotson's. Why? What's happened? Trust sour-puss Iris Grigg to kick a man when he's down. Had Terry really intended to end it all?

'Come on, Sylvia; get a move on.' Pearl refused to take no for an answer after she and Joy had run up the stairs and knocked on their friend's door. 'Helping us to find new lodgings for Terry is the least you can do.'

Having just recovered from her mother and Eddie's visit, Sylvia appeared flustered but she soon agreed to join them. 'What right does his landlady have to throw him out?' she demanded as she followed Joy and Pearl out on to the street. 'No, don't tell me – suddenly he's *persona non grata.*'

'*Persona non* what?' Pearl led the charge towards the nearest tram stop. 'Never mind. The fact is Joy prevented Terry from jumping out of a first-floor window last night. It's lucky she was there.'

'Well done, you.' A tram drew up and Sylvia was the last to step up. 'How did you talk him out of it?' she asked as the tram lurched on, turning the corner on to the prom then heading south. The sky was grey and the air humid. Heavy clouds threatened thunder later in the day.

'Somehow I convinced him life wasn't all doom and gloom; that there was light at the end of the tunnel.'

'Joy was the right person in the right place at the right time.' Pearl summed it up neatly. 'Now, you two, we need a plan of action.'

'Let's get off at the Tower then begin our search,' Sylvia suggested. 'There are always vacancies in the rabbit warren of streets behind the market.'

'But preferably somewhere decent with a sea view.' Joy was mindful of her promise.

'Tricky,' Sylvia pointed out. 'I speak from recent experience; rooms on the seafront are rare as hens' teeth.'

'We'll ask around. Joe Taylor has dozens of contacts

301

through his market stall; he might be able to offer us a lead.' Standing on the open platform at the back of the tram, Pearl was impatient to begin. 'My mother is another good bet. Let's start with her then try Joe. Failing that, we'll have to trawl the streets looking for vacancy notices in windows.'

'Will we tell people that we're looking on Terry's behalf?' Sylvia wondered.

'Best not,' Pearl decided. 'It would make our job twice as hard.'

'I think we should be honest,' Joy countered. 'It wouldn't do for Terry to turn up on the doorstep with his belongings, only to be turned away once his new landlord found out who he was.'

'Joy's right,' Sylvia agreed.

With the entrance to the Tower building in sight, the three girls hopped off the tram then headed straight for Maria's fish and chip stall. Did she know of any landlord who was broad-minded enough to take Terry Liddle as a lodger, bearing in mind recent events? Not too expensive but respectable. A boarding house along the seafront, perhaps?

Maria fended off the quick-fire questions. 'That's a tall order,' she warned as she filleted fish. 'And why isn't your new friend Mr Liddle doing his own looking?'

'Daft question, Mother.' Pearl sounded exasperated. 'Tell her, Sylvia – a gang of thugs is after him. He can't venture out for fear of being set upon.'

'That's right, Mrs Scott – I saw it with my own eyes. They threatened to overturn the car he was in.'

Maria held her filleting knife aloft. 'Was our friend Mick Greene involved, by any chance?'

'It was getting dark so I didn't recognize faces.' Sylvia tried to recollect the details. 'I did hear the name Mick mentioned, along with Fred and Sam and a few others.'

'I thought as much.' Maria nodded then went on with her work. 'Bernie's brother is heading for a fall. In fact, Henry reckons Mick will get his comeuppance pretty soon unless he sorts himself out.'

'This isn't getting us anywhere.' Joy reminded Pearl and Sylvia that time was pressing. 'If you hear of anything, Mrs Scott, please let us know.'

Crossing the wide road, they skirted the red-brick Tower building and entered an alley leading to the bustling market square, where they sought out Joe at his fruit and veg stall. Their presence attracted wolf whistles and compliments from stallholders and customers alike.

'To what do we owe the pleasure?' Joe asked Pearl, who once more led the charge. He weighed out a pound of Bramley cooking apples then tipped them into his elderly customer's basket.

Pearl picked up one of the apples from the display, tossed it in the air then deftly caught it. 'We're looking for new lodgings for a friend of ours. You've got your ear to the ground, Joe. Do you know of any vacancies?'

'Ta, Dorothy. See you next week.' Joe smiled and took the money for the apples. 'Who is this friend?' he asked Pearl with a guarded expression. 'Do I know her?'

'It's a him.' She leaned across the stall and spoke in a whisper. 'If you must know, Iris Grigg has thrown Terry Liddle out on his ear.'

'Whoa!' Joe took a step back. 'I wouldn't say that name too loud if I was you.'

'Too late – I heard what she said,' Bill Norton, his neighbouring stallholder, growled before spitting into the gutter. At the age of sixty-five his broad face was heavily wrinkled – he was a man whose opinions had been formed and fixed when Queen Victoria was still on the throne.

'See?' Joe busily rearranged his selection of salad vegetables.

'Yes, but you're different, Joe.' Pearl buttered him up. 'You're modern and broad-minded and you helped Bernie out in his hour of need. Well, our "friend" is in dire straits – he'll be minus a roof over his head come Monday unless we find him somewhere to live.'

A new customer elbowed her way in between Pearl and Joy, demanding three sticks of rhubarb and half a stone of spuds. 'And make it quick,' she added, glowering at the three glamorous girls who had obstructed her.

'This is hopeless,' Sylvia sighed. While Joe weighed potatoes, she, Joy and Pearl put their heads together. 'I vote we split up and look for vacancy signs ourselves. We may have to lower our sights and forget about the sea view.'

'Good idea – I'll try Market Street,' Pearl decided. 'I've an idea there's a vacancy at number twenty-two, where Bernie rents a room.'

'And I'll try Empire Street,' Sylvia said.

'No, not Empire Street,' Pearl said quickly. 'That's where Mick lives.'

'All right, then – King Street.' Sylvia was eager to continue their search.

Joe's grumpy customer paid for her purchases then went on her way. 'Talking of King Street . . .' Pearl directed an appealing glance at Joe.

'Whoa!' he said again. 'Don't look at me.'

'Why not?' Pearl wheedled. 'You have a spare room since Bernie moved out.'

'Yes, Joe – why not?' Sylvia and Joy chimed. The three of them linked arms and turned on the charm.

'Blimey, it's the bloomin' Andrews Sisters!' From across the square a man in overalls and a flat cap who sold spare parts for broken wirelesses grinned at their performance.

'Please, Joe!' Pearl begged. 'You were there that night when my Bernie threw a punch at poor Terry and everything ran out of control; you even tried to break up the fight.'

'"Poor Terry" now, is it?' Joe lifted his cap and scratched his forehead.

'Yes; surely you've heard? He's *persona non* . . . what was it?' Pearl turned to Sylvia.

'*Grata.*' Sylvia detected signs that Joe was wavering. 'Mr Taylor, you'd be doing Terry an awfully big favour if you let him have your spare room. He's had a dreadful time of it lately but Joy here has promised to help him get back on his feet.'

'Nay, lad – I'd think twice if I were you,' Bill warned. 'You'll have half of Blackpool on your back if you do what they're asking.'

'And the other half admiring you for doing the right thing,' Joy insisted. 'What do you say?'

'Say yes,' Pearl pleaded.

'But I don't even like the bloke,' Joe pointed out. 'He's far too big for his boots.'

'That was all an act,' Joy assured him as a small group of bystanders gathered. 'When you get to know the real Terry, you'll change your mind.'

'Nay, lad!' Bill repeated his warning.

'For what it's worth, I reckon everyone deserves a second chance.' The wireless man sauntered across the square. 'I know what they're saying about Terry Liddle and Cliff Seymour but who really gives a damn, eh?'

'That's right,' a young, homely-looking woman holding her small daughter by the hand agreed. 'I can't see that they're doing any harm.'

Joe continued to scratch his forehead.

'Each to his own,' someone else commented.

Sylvia nudged Joy and held up her tightly crossed fingers.

'Personally, I don't mind what they get up to behind closed doors,' Joe conceded. 'As it happens, I went to school with Cliff and saw how he was bullied day in, day out for being a sissy. I was never in favour of that.'

'That's because you're a decent sort.' Pearl's expression grew more earnest. 'You helped my Bernie out a few weeks back, so how about doing the same for Terry?'

'Yes, why not?' a new voice volunteered. 'Like him or loathe him, he didn't deserve to be sacked from his job at the lido.'

Joe played for more time by rearranging lettuces and cucumbers. 'How long would it be for?'

'Just until he gets back on his feet,' Joy assured him. 'He's keen to lie low for a while, so he wouldn't be any bother.'

'Go on, Joe – what are you waiting for?' the wireless man said.

'Yes, Joe; give the bloke a break.'

'We won't think less of you if you do.'

Joe held up his hands in surrender. 'All right – you win,' he told Pearl, Joy and Sylvia. 'Tell Terry he can move his stuff in tomorrow afternoon. We can talk about rent once he's settled in.'

'By heck!' Bill grunted in disbelief. 'Talk about sticking your neck out.'

'Champion!' Pearl clapped her hands and danced on the spot.

'Thank you, Joe!' Sylvia beamed.

'Let's go straight to Silver Street and give Terry the good news,' Joy said as the knot of interested observers dissolved. 'Thank you, Joe – you won't regret it.'

Dizzy with success, the three girls hugged their Good Samaritan then dashed away. Sadly there would be no sea view, but everything else had fallen into place. By the end of tomorrow Terry would be ensconced in King Street, ready to begin a new chapter in his life.

In the dash to Silver Street Joy shared the future she'd envisaged for him: dance training followed by auditions at local theatres and then a small role in a musical, slowly building to bigger, better parts.

'Yes, I can see him in top hat and tails in a chorus line at the Empire.' Sylvia delivered her seal of approval. 'He'd fit in perfectly there.'

'And who knows; he and Cliff might kiss and make up,' Pearl suggested as they drew near to Silver Street.

'Don't bank on it,' Sylvia warned. 'Cliff told me that it's over between them.'

Joy offered no opinion. 'You'll notice a big change in Terry,' she warned.

'In what way?' Pearl felt a flicker of fresh concern.

'You'll see.' Joy turned her key in the lock of number 57. 'Moving him into new lodgings is a step in the right direction, but don't expect miracles. There's a long way to go before we see the old Terry Liddle back on the streets of Blackpool.'

'Dancing bucks me up no end.' Ruby whirled around the ballroom floor in the arms of a GI from Squires Gate. She winked at Joy and Tommy then was gone, lost among the frills and sequins of a Saturday night at the Tower.

'Shall we?' Tommy offered Joy his hand then escorted her on to the crowded floor. Overhead, the chandeliers glittered and the roof was open to the stars. A brief thunderstorm late in the afternoon had cleared the air and now the night sky was sprinkled with a million pinpricks of silvery light.

'What do you say we live for today and forget about tomorrow?' Bernie led Pearl on to the floor.

Sitting at his Wurlitzer, Reggie Dixon began to play the ever-popular Irving Berlin number that invited couples to face the music and dance.

Pearl wore her favourite flared red skirt, teamed with a short-sleeved white blouse that left her free to twirl and swing to her heart's content. 'Wild horses wouldn't stop me,' she answered.

Eddie held his breath as he approached Sylvia, who was sitting under the balcony with her long, slim legs crossed, smoking a cigarette. 'For old time's sake?' he ventured.

Sylvia slowly stubbed out her cigarette. 'Why not?' she agreed.

Up onstage, a crooner in a white dinner jacket and black bow tie warned of trouble ahead.

' "Music and moonlight and love and romance".' Bernie mouthed the lyrics.

Pearl gazed into his eyes. ' "While we still have the chance",' she sang softly. For them the words were bitter-sweet but they smiled as they swayed and turned.

Joy and Tommy didn't speak as they danced. All was perfect: the music, the stars of the night sky, the nearness of their bodies.

'Thank you.' Eddie held Sylvia close, as if nothing had changed.

'What for?'

'For saying yes just now. For everything.' His voice was heavy with regret. By this time next week, she could be in London and he would be entering the last-Saturday-in-the-month competition with Joy. The world went on turning, everything changed, despite all his efforts.

'Silly!' Sylvia tapped him lightly on the shoulder; her characteristic reprimand. 'I'm the one who should be thanking you.'

The crooner sang of teardrops to shed. 'Why?' Eddie asked.

'For putting up with me all these years. For building bridges between me and Mother. For being my best friend.'

What more was there to say? Didn't she realize that his heart was broken in two – that holding her in his arms, breathing in her perfume and gliding across the dance floor with her was a torture that he could scarcely endure?

'Ladies and gentlemen, after that classic song from *Follow the Fleet* there will be a short interval.' The MC's announcement came as the last bars faded and the singer handed over the microphone.

Ruby parted from her GI with a quick kiss on the cheek, intent on beating the rush to the bar where she joined Mavis. 'My Yank was a bit of a let-down,' she confessed as they ordered their drinks. 'He may look the part but, to be honest, he has two left feet.'

'Better luck next time.' Mavis had been happier with her partner: a civil servant who had a regular sweetheart back home in Bristol. 'Mine didn't say much, but he had rhythm to spare.'

Back in the centre of the dance floor, Sylvia, Pearl and Joy gathered with their partners. Deciding that the bar was already too crowded to make it worth-while queuing, they all made their way towards the exit then out on to the deserted promenade where the sound of breaking waves and the feel of cool air on their flushed cheeks soothed them.

'Bernie and I have decided not to hang around for the competition tonight,' Pearl declared. 'We don't fancy the tango and, anyway, we both have an early start at the arcade tomorrow.'

'But count us in for next week,' Bernie declared. 'That'll be our very last chance to win a prize before I'm shipped off to Scotland.'

'Don't remind me.' Pearl quickly changed the sub-ject. 'Will you two hang on here?' she asked Joy and Tommy.

'Yes; the night is young.' Tommy's cheery reply was drowned out by the sudden, sickening wail of sirens followed soon after by the blast of whistles as ARP wardens appeared out of nowhere.

'Oh no, not again!' Sylvia's stomach churned and she clutched Eddie's hand.

'Make your way to the nearest shelter.' A female warden wearing a tin hat marked with a large white W swung her wooden rattle in their faces. 'Move along in an orderly manner, please! Everyone move along!'

The sirens split the night air as dancers poured out of the building. There was no panic, only a determination to obey orders and reach safety before the bombs fell.

Eddie kept firm hold of Sylvia's hand. He glanced towards Squires Gate – surely the Luftwaffe's intended target yet again. All was dark. Out to sea, there was no sound or sight of approaching planes and no searchlights raked the sky from the anti-aircraft bunkers that lined the Golden Mile.

'False alarm?' Tommy voiced what the others were hoping.

'Move along!' the warden insisted above the drone of sirens. On-off, on-off, on again – the intermittent signal indicated that they still had a few minutes to find shelter.

'Follow me.' This time Tommy was set on retreating to the underground area beneath the Tower where the circus animals were stabled and many of the performers had their dressing rooms. He went against the flow and led the way back through the main entrance, along a corridor then down a narrow concrete staircase into the bowels of the building.

The strong, acrid stench of animal urine made Sylvia hold her nose. The air down here was foul and

the dimly lit passageways were cluttered with paraphernalia belonging to clowns, acrobats and animal
trainers. Horses neighed from their stables while the
roar of unseen lions scared the life out of Pearl.

'I'd rather risk the bombs,' she muttered to Joy,
who clamped her hand over her mouth and tried not
to breathe.

Undeterred, Tommy found them a safe place
behind the enormous cogs and gears of the engine
that operated the rise and fall of the tank that filled
the circus arena with water for the Enchanted Cas-
cade, the grand finale of each performance. The
well-oiled miracle of Victorian engineering regularly
made audiences gasp as fountains shot high in the air
and the Valmar Trio performed aquatic acrobatic
feats. 'Everyone keep your heads down,' Tommy
instructed. 'You'll be quite safe here.'

Meanwhile, horse riders in Cossack costumes
darted along subterranean corridors to check on
their animals or to smoke strong cigarettes in dark
corners. A man in a Tarzan outfit hurried by with
three chimpanzees.

'Am I awake or is this a dream?' Sylvia clung to
Eddie's arm.

'It's real enough.' He strained to hear sirens but all
sound from above ground was deadened. There was
nothing for it but to sit it out until they got the
all-clear.

'Oh, the pong!' Pearl wasn't one to complain, but
really!

'Look at it this way – it'll be a good yarn to spin in
years to come.' Bernie laughed at the face she was
pulling.

One of Vic Marsden's elephants kicked at its metal door with a mighty clang. 'Good Lord!' Joy closed her eyes and prayed.

'False alarm!' Without warning the wiry elephant trainer came clattering down the stairs in his crimson costume, complete with gold braid and wearing a tall military-parade hat.

Sylvia, Pearl and Joy heaved sighs of relief and immediately regretted it. The stench, the stench!

'Panic over,' Vic informed them. 'All sirens have stopped – Firebomb Fritz won't be leaving his calling card after all.'

After the sirens had ceased Pearl and Bernie walked the short distance back to his Market Street lodgings. Neither said much as, hand in hand, they breathed in fresh air and negotiated the maze of cobbled streets and alleyways.

Each knew what was at the forefront of the other's mind: there were eight brief days between now and their separation; eight rising suns, sixteen high tides, one hundred and ninety-two fleeting hours of togetherness before war wrenched them apart.

Pearl brought to mind old King Canute and how he had stood on the shoreline trying to turn back the incoming tide. He'd worn his golden crown and furred robes, commanding the waves not to rise, only to get his feet thoroughly soaked. The lesson? The power of kings was as nothing against the forces of nature and time. 'What wouldn't I give to stop the clock from ticking?'

'Come again?' Bernie emerged from his own reverie.

'Why can't we stop the clocks? Why can't life stay as it is, right now?'

They paused at the corner of Empire Street to gaze up at the stars, aware of every sensation – her warm hand cradled in his, the scent of her perfume and his hair cream, the sound of their slow, easy breaths.

'Who'd have thought it?' Bernie asked, craning his neck to take in the whole of the night sky. 'You and me. Me and you.'

'Never in a month of Sundays.' They'd tumbled about the streets together for as long as she could remember; ridden bicycles, played football, got filthy, banged their heads and scraped their knees, hung around under lamp-posts sneakily smoking stolen cigarettes. Bernie had been the wisecracking joker while Pearl had been the leader of her girl gang, the rip-roaring adventuress. Romance hadn't entered their heads. 'Any regrets?' she murmured, nestling close.

'Dozens,' he teased. 'Actually, no – not one.'

'Me neither.'

They were about to walk on when Mick and Sam emerged from the Black Horse. Hoping not to be noticed, Bernie and Pearl drew back under the entrance to Mason's yard.

The two men stood on the pavement telling lewd jokes and laughing loudly then barring the way of three women who tried to enter the pub. Eventually they stood aside and made leering remarks – 'Get an eyeful of that!', 'Nice pair of pins!' Then, quickly losing interest, Mick took out a packet of cigarettes.

'Give us one, tight arse,' Sam demanded as Mick lit up.

Pearl and Bernie considered sneaking away but decided not to risk a confrontation.

'None left.' Mick showed Sam the empty packet before crushing it and throwing it into the gutter.

Eventually more noisy customers came out of the pub, causing a busy distraction that allowed Pearl and Bernie to slip away. Holding their breath, they emerged from the archway and quickly turned the corner.

'For God's sake!' Bernie muttered. He was ashamed of his brother's behaviour and how little effort he put into keeping up appearances. 'He's a damned disgrace.'

'He looks like a tramp.' Pearl remarked on Mick's unkempt appearance. He'd worn a baggy jacket and collarless shirt, and even from a distance she'd been able to see that his hair needed cutting and he hadn't shaved for days. She felt anger, not pity.

'Forget about him.' Unable to follow his own advice, Bernie scowled and picked up his pace, thrusting his hands in his pockets and striding ahead of Pearl. 'He's a bloody traitor for getting me the sack,' he muttered. 'I'll throttle him – I swear!'

'Calm down.' Pearl ran to catch up. 'What's done is done. Don't let him spoil the little time we've got.'

'All right – I won't throttle him.' Bernie defused the situation by jutting out his chin and making a joke. 'I'll let someone else do that when he gets into his next fight. Or else the coppers can nick him and lock him up for good – see if I care.'

'That's better.' She took his hand and walked beside him. 'You'll write to me?'

'When?'

'When you're in Scotland.' She dared not think further ahead than that.

'Every day,' he promised recklessly as they reached Market Street. ' "Dear Pearl, My sergeant major shouts at me for not polishing my boots, my uniform itches and the food's lousy. I love you. Best wishes, Bernie." '

'I'll write back: "Dear Bernie, Stop bleating on about your bloomin' boots. I love you too, you idiot. Love, Pearl." '

He took out his key and opened the door. 'Will you stay tonight?'

'All night?' They would make love then sleep. In the morning she would return to Empire Street and face the music; her mother dishing out the breakfast, her father shaving at the kitchen sink. *Where have you been, as if we didn't know?*

'It could be our last chance.'

'All right,' she murmured, her heart beating fast.

They went upstairs to the chaos of his room. Men were like children when it came to tidiness. Whose fault was that? Mothers', probably. Pearl picked up the usual crumpled shirt from the floor and flicked it at Bernie, who caught a sleeve and tugged her towards him. Laughing, they fell on to the bed, tangled up with the shirt. There were no silk sheets and monogrammed pillowcases with Japanese prints of snow-capped mountains on the walls, no silver cigarette-holders and cherry, Cupid's bow lips.

'I mean it – my sergeant major will yell at me and I do love you.' Bernie pressed his lips against her hair.

'I'll think about you every waking minute,' she promised. She'd visited the town library and looked

316

in an atlas to work out the number of miles between Blackpool and Bernie's training barracks in Perth, where conscripts would be subjected to six weeks of square-bashing. The barracks were over two hundred and forty miles away, an impossible distance. 'I'm dreading you leaving,' she confessed.

'It'll be fine – *we'll* be fine.'

'Will we, though?' She drew back so that she could see him properly in the gathering darkness: his dear face against the white pillow and a gaze that seemed to see into her very soul.

'Yes – you'll carry on at the arcade and before you know it Herr Hitler will wave the white flag and I'll be back here with you.'

Pearl ached for it to be true. 'I love you. I'll miss you.'

Their voices were no more than whispers and soon their bodies said all that needed to be said; skin to skin, tenderly embracing, kissing – his lips on her neck and shoulders, her hands on his broad, smooth back.

'We're getting good at this,' Bernie said when it was over.

'Practice makes perfect,' she agreed with a mischievous smile.

They lay in the dark, breathing deeply, looking up at the ceiling. Pearl expected him to reach for a cigarette but instead he said, 'Let's get married.'

She sat up with a jolt and drew the sheet up to her chin.

He sat up beside her. They stared straight ahead. 'Say yes.'

'We can't – you're leaving next week.' Her head was dizzy; she thought he might be kidding.

'Not now, silly. We can get engaged before I go then get properly hitched when I come back. Go on; say yes.'

'You want to marry me?' Pearl was incredulous. 'We're having too much fun,' she pointed out. 'Getting engaged is serious.'

'*I'm* serious. I'll buy you a ring to prove it. What would you like – emeralds, sapphires, diamonds . . .?'

'Stop!' Soon he would go on the train all the way to Perth and write letters. She would make a success of the arcade in his absence. 'Let me think.'

'Come on, what is there to think about?' He loved her, she loved him – it was as simple as that.

'Do you really mean it?'

Bernie groped for his lighter on the bedside table then flicked it on so he could see Pearl's face in the slim blue flame.

'I do,' he murmured.

Really there was no need for her to think it through. 'I'd like a big ruby,' she decided. 'With two small diamonds to either side.'

'You don't want much.' Bernie's grin split his face in two before he extinguished the light. 'So you're saying you'll put up with me till death do us part?'

'Hush.' She held him in the darkness as if she would never let him go. 'Yes; yes, you daft ha'p'orth – of course I'll marry you.'

CHAPTER TWENTY

Perhaps she'd scribbled it down wrong. Sylvia stood in the telephone box at the end of North View Parade, staring at the scrap of paper showing Mitch Burns's telephone number. Should the six have come before the two or was there one nought rather than two in the middle?

The operator in the Blackpool exchange informed her that there was no reply.

'I wish to speak to Mr Mitchell Burns,' Sylvia repeated insistently. 'Do I have the right number?'

'Hold the line, please.' There was a pause while the operator consulted her directory. 'The number is correct. There was no reply. Please try later.'

Frustrated, Sylvia abandoned her latest attempt then made a beeline for the underground public conveniences where she intended to weigh herself. The toilets, which doubled as an air raid shelter, were situated on the prom, opposite the entrance to North Pier. Looking around to make sure that no one paid her any attention, she went down the steps with her copper coin at the ready. Feeding it into the machine, Sylvia stepped on to the metal platform and anxiously watched the arrow move around the dial. Hallelujah, she'd gained weight – two whole pounds in a week! There was no mistake – it was the usual time of day (ten o'clock in the morning) and she took care to wear exactly the same clothes each time she weighed herself. Two pounds; she ought to be pleased, but in fact she experienced a loathing that was hard to conquer. Still; if this was what it took . . .

She climbed the steps and went back to the phone box to try again. The same operator took her call. Sylvia pressed the receiver to her ear and listened to the ring tone. Once again, no one answered. Please try later.

I've been trying! Sylvia slammed down the receiver with a petulant frown. *Four times already this Monday morning, at an hour when one would expect any self-respecting businessperson to be in his office.* She crossed the road then strode along the pier to talk to Pearl.

'He's not answering his phone,' she fumed.

'Who's "he"?' Pearl stood in the entrance to the arcade, arms folded across her chest. They were due to open to the public in half an hour, but as yet there was no sign of Bernie. 'Calm down, Sylvia. Take a deep breath.'

'Mr Burns, that's who! I wish to accept his offer and go down to London right away.'

'I see.' Pearl studied her friend carefully. Her cheeks were unusually flushed and the breeze had disarranged her curls. Otherwise, she was her usual stylish self in wide white linen trousers and a forget-me-not-blue blouse that brought out the colour of those startling, innocent eyes.

'I've made my decision, my bag is packed and I'm ready to buy my train ticket,' Sylvia insisted.

'But he's not taking your phone call?' Pearl ignored a beady-eyed gull that soared on a wind current above their heads and the constant lapping of waves against the iron legs of the pier some twenty feet below.

'No, and I want to know why not. And even if Mr Burns is not there in person, surely he has a secretary – an assistant of some sort.'

'You would think so.' Pearl glanced along the pier to see Bernie loping towards them, forelock curling on to his forehead, shirtsleeves rolled up and wearing his soft-soled brown suede shoes. Lord; she loved the man to bits! 'Try to be patient,' she advised Sylvia. 'I know – I'm a fine one to talk. But I don't see what else you can do other than keep on trying his number until you eventually get through.'

'Yes, sorry – you're right.' Sylvia reined in her frustration in time to greet Bernie with a brittle smile. 'I'll take your advice,' she promised Pearl. 'Bye for now.'

'What's up with her?' Bernie asked as Sylvia rushed off towards the prom. 'Never mind – guess why I'm late.'

'You slept in, you got waylaid, you lost your door key . . .'

'None of the above.' Evidently chuffed with himself, Bernie dipped his hand into his pocket. 'I popped into Hartley's on the way here and bought you this.'

She stared at the small blue box in the palm of his hand. 'You never!' Alfred Hartley owned one of the most expensive jeweller's shops in town.

'I did. A ruby and four diamonds, just like you asked for.' In Bernie's mind a grand gesture was needed and this was it.

'It must have cost a fortune!' Pearl took the box with trembling fingers. She opened it and saw a sparkling ring nestled in dark-blue velvet.

'I bought it on tick – half a crown a week. If it's the wrong size we can take it back to the shop and have it altered.'

'Oh!' For once in her life, Pearl was speechless. A rich red ruby set between four dear little sparkling diamonds; a dream come true.

'Try it on,' Bernie urged.

'I can't – my hands are shaking.'

So he took the ring from the box then slid it on to the third finger of her left hand. The jewels shone in the sun as the curious gull landed on a nearby rail and cocked its head to one side. The restless seawater swirled and stretched for ever, blue as the sky above.

On her way back to the telephone box Sylvia gathered the remaining threads of her worn-out patience. This time Mr Burns must answer the phone – this time!

Coins once more at the ready, she entered the glass box that stank of sweat and cigarette smoke then picked up the heavy black receiver. *This time!* A glance into the tiny mirror above a shelf for handbags showed the strain she was under – despite the weight gain, her face looked gaunt and there were dark circles under her wide-apart, heavily lashed eyes.

It took a long time for the operator – a different, more sympathetic one – to deal with her request then an age for the ringing tone to begin. Sylvia was on the point of replacing the receiver yet again when there was a click and a woman's voice spoke.

'Who is this, please?' Officious, curt, almost hostile.

At last! 'Oh, good morning. This is Miss Ellis, wishing to speak to Mr Burns.' Sylvia's voice was soft and breathless with apprehension.

'Miss who?'

'Miss Ellis – Sylvia Ellis. May I please speak to Mr Burns?'

'Sylvia Ellis, you say?' There was a long pause, then, 'I'm sorry – Mr Burns has recently spoken with Mr Seymour and now wishes to have no further communication with you. Please don't ring again.' There was another click before the line went dead.

Sylvia dropped the handset in utter confusion. She left it dangling on its cord as she leaned against the heavy door then stumbled out on to the pavement, almost bumping into a couple of elderly holiday-makers on their way to the beach.

'Watch where you're going.' The old man shook his walking stick at her.

'Youngsters these days . . .' his wife muttered.

Mr Burns has recently spoken with Mr Seymour. It was as if the secretary's words were branded on Sylvia's brain. Why? What had the two men cooked up between them? There was only one way to find out. Oblivious to her surroundings, Sylvia stumbled on up North View Parade, past Ibbotson's to the sign that read 'Learn to Dance with Cliff – Live in Your Dreams'. She hammered on the door with the side of her fist.

'Hold your horses.' Cliff seemed in no hurry to answer. He eventually opened the door to find Sylvia looking dazed and distraught. 'You'd better come in,' he said at once, ushering her into the empty studio, to the alcove containing his gramophone, where he made her sit down.

'What did you say to Mr Burns?' Sylvia managed to frame a few sentences out of the chaotic jumble of her thoughts. 'Did you tell him that I wasn't a good enough dancer to go to London? Don't lie to me – tell me the truth.'

'I told him no such thing.' Cliff played for time. 'What makes you even think that we've spoken about you?'

'Because the secretary in his office told me so.' Hot, angry tears stung her eyes.

'Mitch doesn't have an office or a secretary.' *Stretch it out, soften the blow.*

'So who was the woman I just spoke to?'

'Most likely Mitch's wife, Veronica. I don't suppose she was very obliging.'

'No, she wasn't. Why not?'

'Veronica Burns considers herself respectable. She doesn't like to be reminded of how her husband earns his money.' Sooner or later the penny must drop with Sylvia. 'She dislikes talking to his girls.'

His girls. Sylvia stared at Cliff. 'I don't understand.'

He pulled up a chair and sat facing her, forcing eye contact. That moment had arrived; he would have to spell it out in words of no more than two syllables. 'Don't you see – ballroom dancing is not what this is about?'

'What do you mean?' She held her breath and shot him a pitiful look that would have melted the hardest of hearts.

'Viennese waltz, tango, quickstep – it's all a sham. The clients are real enough, but what these men are really looking for is an exceptionally beautiful girl, the younger and more inexperienced the better, so long as she's . . . obliging.' There; he'd said it! 'The clients pay Mitch a fee and to my shame I've accepted a small share. I'm sorry, Sylvia; I really am.'

The image of castle walls crashing down, the sight of towers crumbling, of fairy-tale princesses buried beneath rubble filled Sylvia's head. 'Princess' had been Cliff's nickname for her from the start and now she knew why. What a fool; what a naive, ignorant idiot she'd been!

'You see?' Cliff asked gently. 'I tussled with my conscience and in the end I couldn't allow it to happen to you, so I telephoned Mitch and said I'd made a mistake, that you weren't suitable after all.'

'So Terry has moved out of Silver Street,' Joy informed Lucia as they put the finishing touches to the shimmering blue taffeta dress that she would wear on Saturday night to dance with Eddie. She'd explained the situation in full, taking care not to pass judgement on either Cliff or Terry. 'He's taken a room in Joe Taylor's house and it's good riddance to Mrs Grigg.'

The two women sat side by side in the living room above the ice-cream parlour with the wireless playing in the background. Benny Goodman, the King of Swing, played a tune that was as bright and light as the evening sun streaming in through the window.

'But you, poor girl, must stay in the house with this Mrs Grigg?' Lucia's needle was poised above the shiny fabric as she waited for an answer.

'Yes, for the time being,' Joy said with a sigh.

'*Scortese.*' Lucia shook her head then continued hemming the dress.

'What does that mean?'

'The woman is not kind, not good.'

'You're right there.' Joy sewed on a hook and eye to secure the neck fastening. 'Her son is just as bad. But let's not talk about them any more. The fact is that Terry hopes to make a fresh start.'

Needles flying, they sewed on in harmony until an urgent knock at the door took Lucia downstairs. She returned with Sylvia, who was in a pitiable state – her eyes were puffy and red from crying and her hair was in disarray.

The lively song on the wireless encouraged everyone to forget their troubles and chase their cares away. Shout hallelujah; the sun is shining . . . get happy, la-la-la.

Joy jumped up to turn off the wireless. 'Sylvia, whatever is the matter? Sit down. Can we get you a drink?'

Without waiting for a reply, Lucia hurried back downstairs to the kitchen.

'Please don't look at me!' Sylvia covered her face. 'I'm a fright. Sorry, I just couldn't bear it.'

'Bear what?' Joy drew her chair close.

'Being alone with no one to talk to. I thought if I stayed in my room a moment longer, I would go mad.'

'Tell me what's happened,' Joy said gently. 'Take your time.'

'It wasn't as I thought,' Sylvia confessed amid a fresh outburst of crying. 'Mr Burns didn't mean to help me become a professional dancer after all.'

'Slowly,' Joy recommended, her fears rising.

'I found out this morning – from Cliff. At the

eleventh hour he told me the truth. I've been a fool, Joy – a complete and utter fool.' Crushed all day under the debris of a shattered dream, hardly able to breathe, sobbing her heart out.

'And what is the truth?' Joy held Sylvia's hand tight, motioning at Lucia who had reappeared in the doorway with a tray of tea things. *Later*, she mouthed.

'I can't say the words!' They were too vulgar, too crushing, to speak out loud. Sylvia stood up suddenly then just as quickly flopped back down into the chair, overwhelmed by a burning sense of shame.

'What exactly did Cliff say?' Joy coaxed.

'The gentlemen at the Savoy – they don't want a dance partner. They want something else entirely. Cliff's job was to find the girls and forward their names to Mr Burns.'

Joy had heard of such things, perhaps read about them in the newspapers, so she was dimly aware that some men paid women to go to bed with them. But she'd assumed that it happened at the seedier edges of society, not in the heart of the nation's capital. Gradually the implications of what Sylvia was telling her crept into her consciousness.

'A lamb to the slaughter – that would have been me.' Sylvia laughed mirthlessly.

'Good heavens above!' Joy breathed.

'My mother was right. So was Eddie. Everyone had the wit to suspect the truth except me.'

'Not me – I didn't.'

'No; because you don't think ill of anyone. Pearl probably saw it for what it was – she'd have put me straight if I'd asked her. Only I wouldn't have listened, would I?'

327

Joy tried to calm her. 'It's good that Cliff came clean at last.'

Sylvia laughed the same dry, hollow laugh. 'Apparently he wrestled with his conscience. But really I ought to have worked it out for myself. When I met Mr Burns at Cliff's studio, he wasn't the least bit interested in whether or not I could dance.'

'Cliff was to blame, not you.' Joy was adamant.

'He only worked for Mr Burns because he was short of cash. But in the end he's done the right thing by me. Now he and Mr Burns have cut all ties.'

'Do you forgive him?'

Sylvia shook her head. 'Not yet, but I do have some understanding of why he did it. Cliff was determined to set up his studio by any means possible – just as I was driven to reach the top as a dancer even if it meant riding roughshod over Eddie and my mother's feelings. I didn't care about anyone or anything else.'

Joy took her point. 'We all love to dance – you, me and Pearl. Nothing equals those giddy times when the music takes hold of your body and your partner whirls you around the floor. For that moment it's the only thing that matters.'

'But you wouldn't trample on other people to succeed and neither would Pearl. That's the difference.'

Lucia reappeared in the doorway and this time Joy beckoned her in. 'Here comes the tea.'

Lucia put the tray down on one of the low tables then prepared to back out of the room. 'Do not cry,' she told Sylvia kindly. 'Smile – *sorridi* – beautiful girl.'

'Look at it this way,' Joy continued as Lucia tactfully withdrew once more. 'When one door closes, another is bound to open.'

Sylvia pushed her hair back from her wet cheeks. 'I don't think so,' she said with a vehement shake of her head. 'Not now that I've put on weight.'

Of all the odd, unexpected things to emerge from Sylvia's lips! Joy paused, teapot in hand.

'Two whole pounds through eating sweets and fish and chips,' Sylvia groaned. 'It's disgusting.'

'But your gaining weight is a good thing, I promise you. Pearl and I have been worried to death about how thin you were getting and how little energy you had.'

Sylvia brushed away Joy's concerns. 'And all for nothing, as it turns out.' At least she would now be able to throw away the latest bag of sweets stashed in her bedside cabinet.

'That's as may be.' Joy had the sense to back off. She poured the tea then handed a cup to Sylvia. 'But why not go and see Eddie – ask him if he wants to pick up your partnership again?'

The cup rattled so hard in the saucer that Sylvia was forced to put it down. 'I wouldn't dream of it – you're Eddie's partner now. You've entered Saturday's competition together.'

'Yes, but I'd be happy to step aside. Truth to tell, you'd be doing me a favour – my Tommy is the person I really want to dance with.' To waltz with the man she loved in Lucia's halter-neck gown with its big skirt and layers of net petticoat, drifting across the Tower floor, was Joy's dream.

'Too late for that,' Sylvia said sadly. There were so many regrets, so much that couldn't be altered. 'There's less than a week to go. And besides, you and Eddie are the odds-on favourites to win the quickstep section. It's your passport to a golden future. I wish you luck, Joy – if anyone deserves it, you do.'

'Engaged?' Pearl's news stopped Sylvia and Joy in their tracks.

It was Tuesday evening and the three girls had decided to pay a surprise visit to Terry, armed with items that would help him settle into his new life on King Street. Pearl had begged a spare tablecloth and some pillowcases from her mother, while Joy carried a box full of crockery and cutlery donated by Lucia. Sylvia's contribution would be two packets of cigarettes purchased at the last minute from her landlord's shop.

'You and Bernie are engaged?' Joy could hardly believe what she'd heard.

'Yes – look!' Pearl switched her parcel of linen from one arm to the other then flashed her ring at them. 'He asked me on Saturday night out of the blue and I said yes.'

'Of course you did.' Sylvia inspected the ring. 'Beautiful,' she breathed.

Pearl's eyes sparkled with excitement. 'There's no rush to get spliced. I want to do it properly: the dress, the church, the bridesmaids, the flowers . . .'

'Of course you do,' Sylvia repeated, her lips twitching with amusement. Pearl was like the cat that got the cream and Sylvia couldn't be more pleased for her. The news allowed her to put her own troubles to one side and revel in her friend's happiness.

'Mum was thrilled to bits when we told her,' Pearl babbled as they continued on their way. 'You know what my mother is like – never one to make a fuss.

But she burst into tears in front of the little ones and squeezed me half to death. I had to explain to Elsie that they were happy tears.'

'What about your dad?' Joy asked.

'He shook Bernie's hand and said, "About time too", then went off to the Black Horse to tell his pals that he'd got one daughter off his hands. The thing is, it would be plain sailing if Bernie hadn't been called up – we'd be able to set a date for the wedding and make all the arrangements. As it is, we'll have to hang fire.'

'Until when?' Sylvia lagged behind as they crossed the empty market square. Her energy still flagged in the evenings and the struggle to regain weight felt like a losing battle.

'We don't know yet. Perhaps until the war finishes, or sooner if Bernie applies for special leave from the army once he's finished his training.' A fleeting shadow passed over Pearl's face, like clouds in front of the sun. 'This wouldn't be happening if Bernie still had his job at Squires Gate,' she reminded them. 'It's not fair – Mick's in no danger of being conscripted, damn him, and he's the one who got Bernie the sack in the first place.'

'It's rotten when families fall out,' Joy remarked before casting an apologetic glance in Sylvia's direction. 'Sorry.'

'Don't be. Mother and I have had a heart-to-heart. We're friends again.'

'Hooray!' Pearl's smile returned. 'Good for you.'

'She'll be pleased that I'm not going to London after all, but I'm adamant that I won't be moving back in with her,' Sylvia told them.

'Adamant, eh?' Pearl repeated the Sylvia-word with a smile.

At the corner of King Street Joy set down the crockery on the pavement. 'This box is heavy.' She flexed her tired arms and wiggled her fingers. Fat drops of warm rain started to fall, splashing the dusty pavement and wetting the bare skin of their arms and legs; a warning of the storm to come. Lightning forked over the Tower, followed soon after by a clap of thunder that rumbled on as Sylvia attempted to pick up Joy's box.

'Here – let me,' she offered. 'Oof, you're right – it is heavy. Let's carry it between us.'

They arrived at Joe's door, already soaked by the rain and eager to gain shelter. Pearl knocked and waited. When there was no answer, she ducked down and hollered through the letter box. 'Yoo-hoo; anybody there?'

A second lightning fork split the bruise-blue sky and thunder rattled the panes of glass in Joe's front window.

'Just our luck – no one's home,' Joy decided. 'What do we do now?'

'Wait a sec.' Pearl peered through the letter box to see a pair of legs descending the stairs. 'Joe, is that you?'

'No, it's me.' There was another delay before Terry opened the door and braced one arm against the jamb. 'Yes?' he asked his three bedraggled visitors.

'Don't be like that.' Pearl pushed against the door and Terry relented. 'We come bearing gifts,' she announced as she stepped inside.

Unsure of their welcome, a dripping Sylvia and Joy followed her with less confidence.

'Do I want gifts?' Terry queried. The gash on his forehead was healing nicely and a surrounding bruise was fading from blue to yellow.

'You do,' Pearl assured him as she thrust her soggy parcel at him. 'No need to thank us; we're doing it out of the simple goodness of our hearts.'

'Sisters of mercy.' He shut out the rain then invited them to follow him upstairs. He was clean-shaven and smartly dressed in a stylish waistcoat and matching trousers; seemingly back to his confident self but quieter and without the exaggerated swagger of yore.

Pearl gave a thumbs-up to Joy and Sylvia. 'So, Terry, how do you like your new landlord?'

'Joe seems decent enough. Let me take that box,' he said to Joy.

'It's just a few basics from Tommy's mum,' she explained, looking around the room to see that the walls were freshly papered and the furniture was modern if sparse – a bed, a utility chest of drawers and a table with two chairs.

'And these are from me.' Sylvia handed over her meagre gift. 'Sorry; it's all I could think of.'

'I never say no to a packet of Player's.' His smile was intended to put her at her ease. 'How are the London plans progressing?'

'It's all off, thanks to Cliff.' She answered with a toss of her head, clamping her mouth shut and refusing to elaborate.

'I see.' Unsurprised by the revelation, Terry raised his eyebrows. 'I can't say I'm sorry, but what will you do instead?'

'I haven't the slightest idea.' Limbo stretched out

before her; she experienced an unanchored sense of drifting on currents beyond her control.

'Will Cliff invite you back to teach at his studio?'

'No, and I wouldn't go near the place even if he did,' Sylvia declared hotly.

'You and me both,' Terry mumbled through a clenched jaw as he opened one of the packets and took out a cigarette then lit it. 'Not that he did anything wrong as far as I was concerned.'

'You didn't argue?' Sylvia was curious to find out exactly what had taken place in the few days following the brawl outside Cliff's studio.

Terry inhaled deeply then blew smoke towards the ceiling. 'No. He looked after me well enough, but I came to the conclusion that there was no future for us now that our cover is blown. That gang of thugs will come after us again, whenever they get the chance. And that's the reason Cliff and I parted company.' He didn't tell the girls how long and hard Cliff had protested, how desperate he'd been for them to go on as before, how the decision had been Terry's alone.

'That's a shame.' Pearl stood at the window watching the downpour. The guttering on the houses opposite overflowed on to the pavement, drenching whoever was passing beneath. One stationary figure on the street corner caught her eye – a man in a belted raincoat whose face was hidden beneath a black umbrella. His stance seemed familiar. 'I don't blame you, though.'

'But not all people think that way,' Joy tried to argue. 'Take Joe, for instance—'

'It's the ones who do that matter, though,' Terry

334

cut her off. 'It would be dangerous for Cliff and me to stay together.'

The man on the corner was about to step off the pavement into the road when a car drove through a nearby puddle at high speed. He stepped back nimbly to avoid the splash, an agile, graceful movement that allowed a glimpse of his face and confirmed what Pearl had already suspected: that umbrella man was none other than Cliff Seymour. Opening her mouth to share what she'd witnessed, for once she thought better of it.

'But girls – I want you to know that I appreciate everything you've done.' Terry singled out Joy for special thanks. 'I was at my lowest ebb when you stepped in.'

'She's a saint,' Pearl assured him gaily. 'Sylvia and I can't hope to compete.'

'Some saint!' Joy blushed and smiled.

'Not with Tommy Rossi to lead you astray,' Sylvia teased. The visit had gone well but she was keen not to outstay their welcome. 'I don't know about Pearl and Joy, but I have places to go, people to see,' she fibbed as she headed for the door.

Joy took the hint. 'Come along, Pearl – we've pestered Terry for long enough.'

With a final glance out of the window to check that Cliff still stood on the corner, Pearl followed. 'Ta-ta for now, Terence. Don't do anything I wouldn't do.'

'We'll get soaked,' Sylvia predicted as she descended the stairs.

'We're already soaked.' Joy didn't care – Terry was back on track and she was satisfied.

'Don't look now,' Pearl said as they stepped out

into the rain and she glanced towards umbrella man, 'but I bet you ten bob that Terry is about to receive another unexpected visitor.'

'Who?' Joy and Sylvia ducked their heads and splashed through puddles towards the market square.

'Someone with the initials C. S.' Pearl toyed with them. 'I said, don't look!' Sylvia's and Joy's heads swung round as she herded them forward. 'Eyes straight ahead. Keep your fingers crossed that it works out for them both. Mick Greene and Sam Grigg, put that in your pipes and smoke it!'

CHAPTER TWENTY-ONE

Up in his room Terry stubbed out his cigarette then immediately took another from the packet. The girls meant well, but it would take more than a change of lodgings, a few cups and saucers, a couple of pillow-cases and some John Player's for him to get out of the hole he was in. How had it come to this – divorced and jobless, his reputation in tatters? In the end, all the work he'd put into fooling people – the bravura presentation of himself as a man about town – had come to nothing. It was a bloody mess.

He sat on the side of the bed, unlit cigarette hanging from the side of his mouth, head bowed and hands clasped. *A bloody, bloody mess.* Thank heavens he and his ex-wife had never had kids. He was glad to be without that complication at least. And Annie had let him vanish without trace from their home town of Blackburn, hadn't pursued him with angry recrimi-nations, which, looking back, she would have been within her rights to do because their marriage had been a sham from start to finish. When it came down to it, this was Terry's biggest regret.

He had no idea what had happened to Annie since the divorce. He hoped she'd found somebody who deserved her and could make her happy and give her the kids she'd always wanted. The look of horror on her face when she'd found out his true nature would remain with Terry for the rest of his life.

True nature. According to most people, there was nothing natural about it. Lighting the cigarette, he took a deep drag, breathing smoke into his lungs then exhaling through his nose. *It is as it is. If I'm unnatural, so be it.* Joy, in her innocence, had hit the nail on the head: the way to turn things around was to stick with his own sort and they were most likely to be found in the dance and theatre world. Perhaps not here in Blackpool, as she'd suggested; maybe back in London or Manchester or Birmingham, where it was easier to melt into the crowd.

After another drag on his fag and a glum glance around the simply furnished room there was a knock on the door. *What now?*

Cliff had waited in the rain until Sylvia and her pals had turned the corner before crossing the street. He hammered hard on Joe Taylor's door, waited again.

Terry stayed where he was. If he sat tight for long enough the latest visitor was bound to give up.

Cliff knew that Terry was at home. He'd seen him answer the door to Sylvia and crew. He would keep on trying.

'Bloody hell!' Using one of Joy's donated saucers as an ashtray, Terry ground out the stub of his cigarette with undue force then clomped down the stairs intending to give the unwelcome visitor a mouthful. He answered the knock.

'Hello, Terry.' Cliff took the precaution of wedging the door open with his foot.

'What the hell?' Terry shoved back hard but soon gave up.

'I'm getting drenched. Can I come in?'

Terry glanced up and down the thankfully deserted street. Rain bounced off the pavements and thunder rumbled in the distance. He stepped back and allowed Cliff to enter. 'Make it quick,' he muttered.

They stood face to face in the narrow corridor with Cliff's closed umbrella dripping on to the tiled floor. 'I'm sorry – I couldn't help myself; I had to find out how you were.'

'As you see,' Terry said with a dismissive shrug of his shoulders. God, Cliff looked even worse than Terry felt – his sharp features were pinched and he'd lost pride in his appearance, dressed as he was in an old mackintosh and without a hat. 'You'd better come up.'

So Cliff followed Terry upstairs to his room. 'Not too bad,' he commented as he put down his umbrella and looked around. 'I've certainly lived in worse.'

'What do you want?'

'Like I said, to check how you're doing. Obviously smoking too much,' he added as he sniffed the air then glanced at the improvised ashtray.

'I thought we'd agreed it was best not to meet.' Terry stood with his back to the door. 'Are you sure you weren't seen?'

'Positive. I've been thinking a lot about that agreement.'

'And?'

'I'd like you to reconsider.' Cliff had changed his mind a dozen times. Yes, it was sensible for him and Terry to part, but then, what did common sense have to do with it? It was how you felt that mattered. And he felt wretched alone in the flat above the studio, wretched even when he had the distraction of teaching civil service twerps and GI know-it-alls to do the cha-cha. The enforced separation lay in the pit of his stomach like a lump of lead, preventing him from eating, sleeping and going about his normal business. And now that he saw Terry's dear face again – the half-healed scar, his dark brows over brooding brown eyes, his perfectly symmetrical features – Cliff knew that they couldn't be apart.

'Reconsider – how?' Terry reached for another cigarette then changed his mind.

'I know I said we wouldn't.' Cliff sat down on the nearest chair.

'Because it was dangerous to go on as we were.' Terry felt his heartbeat quicken. He needed that cigarette after all.

'You know that I'd risk it if you would.' Best not to beat about the bush. 'The genie is out of the bottle. People will just have to get used to it.'

'Why, though? Why would we take that risk?' Terry spoke from behind a fresh screen of cigarette smoke.

'Because you mean more to me than any of the others.' More than the fellow MCs and cabaret dancers with whom Cliff had associated in Berlin, more than the men in Mitch Burns's shady circle. He was done with that occasional pimping lark, thank God; in their last phone conversation, Cliff had told Burns to get lost in no uncertain terms. 'Much more.'

Terry's heart thudded against his ribs. *God almighty!*

'I've waited a lifetime for what we have together. I thought I'd never find it because of the life I've led, but now I have: every second I spend with you. And I know you feel the same way.'

Terry didn't deny it. Instead, he thought of the obstacles ahead. 'The studio – how would you make it work? You'd need people to come back to your classes.'

'They will – eventually.' Cliff relied on the fact that he was good at what he did; the best in town at teaching Latin, without a doubt.

'And I suppose I could get a job in a chorus line – eventually.' Terry gave a self-conscious grin. *Perhaps, perhaps . . .*

Cliff felt hope flicker in his chest. 'I'd help with that.'

'There'd still be the Mick Greenes and Sam Griggs of this world to contend with.'

'To hell with them. We can choose not to live in fear of what lurks around every corner – we can lead our lives with our heads held high if we want it enough.'

'If only I could believe that.'

Cliff took Terry's hand. 'I'm not saying it won't be tough, because it will. But it'll be worth it.'

'Because?'

'Because I love you and you love me.' Loud and clear, not a shred of doubt.

'Well, then.' Terry took time to absorb what he'd heard. As his heart hammered away against his ribs, his trapped hopes escaped from the cage and soared skyward. 'You'd better take off your coat if you're stopping.' He helped Cliff to undo the buttons and kissed him softly. 'Easy does it, though. No running before we can walk. One small step at a time.'

*

Joy was back where she belonged: in Tommy's arms, waltzing under Lorna's watchful eye.

On the previous night she'd gone straight from Terry's house to the circus and found Tommy in the clowns' dressing room, waiting to re-enter the ring after the interval.

The ringmaster in curled moustache, top hat and tails had barred her way. 'Not now, girlie. Whatever it is, it'll have to wait.'

'I just want a quick word . . .'

'Later,' he'd insisted.

But Joy had refused to back down. 'It'll only take a minute,' she'd countered as she'd brushed past the imposing figure and opened the dressing-room door.

'Blimey, Joy!' Tommy had advanced, trumpet in hand, sequins glittering. 'What the heck are you doing here?'

Two other clowns had carried on as normal – checking their make-up and adjusting their wigs. The room had been the usual riot of colour. Brass instruments had glistened and the brightly lit mirror had reflected the clowns' exotic outfits in a dazzling rainbow of stripes, diamond patterns and swirls.

'I'm here to say one thing,' Joy had declared. 'I don't know what I was thinking – the truth is, I want you to be my dance partner this coming Saturday, not Eddie.'

'Shake a leg, gents; you're on in two minutes.' The ringmaster had poked his head around the door.

'Bloomin' heck!' Tommy had exhaled loudly. 'Does Mrs Ellis know?'

'Not yet. I'll tell her tomorrow. Will you come with me?'

342

'You bet,' he'd promised with undisguised delight. 'We'll face the music together.'

'I love you,' she'd murmured as the cramped, stuffy room had emptied. Unsure whether or not Tommy had heard and left alone with the smell of grease-paint and hot bodies in her nostrils, Joy had been certain she'd done the right thing.

'She loves you,' the ringmaster had repeated with a wry smile. 'You're a lucky chap, Tommy Rossi. Now get in that ring and do the job we pay you for.'

Joy had left the circus and hurried across town to Sylvia's lodgings, where she'd passed on her news. 'I went ahead and told Tommy that I wanted him, not Eddie, to partner me on Saturday. I thought you should know.'

It had taken a while for it to sink in with Sylvia. 'You ditched Eddie?'

'Yes, but I haven't told him or your mother yet. I'll do it tomorrow, before my lesson.' It had been late and without further ado Joy had rushed to catch the last tram home.

And now here she was, here *they* were: she and Tommy at the Lorna Ellis Dance Academy in ballroom hold. Mrs Ellis hadn't hidden her disappointment at Joy's decision but Eddie had been gracious as he'd agreed to step aside.

'On your own head be it.' Lorna had frowned at Joy's change of heart. 'I had high hopes for you and Eddie. I felt the sky was the limit.'

'Do what you feel is right for you,' Eddie had said. 'Tommy is a very good dancer – you have every chance of doing well together on Saturday.'

'Back to the basic waltz,' Lorna reminded the

dozen couples who took to the studio floor for their lesson. 'Thirty bars per minute, a smooth, diagonal, counter-clockwise progression around the dance floor, body swing on the first beat of each bar.'

'It's good to be back,' Tommy murmured in Joy's ear. 'You've no idea how much I've missed this.'

She beamed back at him. *Sway into the centre of the turn, smoothly rise on to toes and repeat; one-two-three, one-two-three.* Joy felt that she'd come home.

'Heads up,' Lorna instructed sharply. 'Look into your partner's eyes. Don't forget to smile.'

Past the unlit entrance to the Majestic Hotel, drab and dowdy behind its sandbag barrier and blackout blinds, Sylvia walked up the street that she'd known for as long as she could remember. Impossibly slim mannequins posed in shop windows. They were dressed in the height of wartime fashion: knee-length dresses with wide, padded shoulders and sweetheart necklines. Drinkers at the Queen's Arms spilled out on to the pavement. The colourful, cluttered window display in Dawson's Gift Emporium was unchanged.

The only difference was in Sylvia herself. Gone was the pampered, lonely princess who had hogged the limelight. In her place was a chastened young woman who had gained two firm friends in Pearl and Joy but who had lost the over-confident sheen of one who expected the world to fall at her feet. The close shave with Mitch Burns had truly humbled her. Now she returned to her mother's dance academy, unsure what her reception would be.

'Sylvia. What are you doing here?' After the lesson had finished, Joy emerged from the studio hand in hand with Tommy. Other pupils followed them so they waited for a quiet moment before Joy gave her friend's arm a sympathetic squeeze.

'I've come to give Mother the glad tidings about London,' Sylvia said with a sigh.

'She'll be relieved.' Joy crossed her fingers for her, then she and Tommy went on their way.

Sylvia was about to open the door into the studio when Angela came out carrying a brown leather case containing her sheet music. She almost bumped into Sylvia, who took a quick step to the side.

'Well, well; look who's back,' Angela said, as if Sylvia had just popped out to the shop, as if her whole life hadn't been turned upside down.

'Yes, it's me.' Colour rose in Sylvia's cheeks.

'Good to see you, love. Your mother's upstairs.' And Angela walked on with a satisfied nod.

Taking a deep breath, Sylvia ascended the stairs. She stopped on the landing next to a stained-glass window overlooking a yard at the back of the house. For two pins she would have turned around and fled. The door to the sitting room stood open and she could see her mother methodically pulling down the blinds in the main bay window. Next she would plump up the cushions on the sofa before pouring herself a small glass of sherry: her unvarying routine. Sylvia forced herself to go forward along the landing.

Midway across the room, Lorna heard footsteps. She glanced towards Sylvia then quickly turned her head away. She needed a moment to compose herself.

'It's all right – I'll leave.' Sick at heart at the apparent rejection, Sylvia turned around.

'No.' Lorna rushed out on to the landing. 'Darling girl, don't go!'

'You're tired; my coming here was a mistake.'

'No, no. I've been so miserable – I'd almost given up hope of seeing you again.' Lorna pulled Sylvia into the sitting room, where they stood awkwardly in the middle of the room.

'I thought you should hear this from the horse's mouth: I won't go to London after all.' Sylvia's voice was drained of emotion. 'The arrangement with Mr Burns didn't work out.'

'I see.' Lorna's hand shook as she raised it to stroke her daughter's cheek. There were tears in her eyes.

'Why are you crying? I thought you'd be pleased.'

'I am.' Lorna dabbed at her wet cheeks. 'You must be extremely disappointed.'

Sylvia nodded. Her lips trembled and she felt hot tears mirror those of her mother. 'It's probably for the best,' she managed to say.

'There will be other opportunities.' Lorna drew her close. 'Your talent will see you through.'

Lorna's arms were around her; all Sylvia could do was sob with relief and gratitude.

'Meanwhile, you can come back and teach here – as many hours as you like.' Lorna stroked her hair.

'Yes,' Sylvia sniffled. 'Please. But I'd like to keep my room on North View Parade.'

'As you wish.' *Dear, darling girl; my everything!* 'Now dry your eyes and make yourself presentable. Maurice is due here any moment. He and Edward are taking me to a piano recital at the Majestic.'

'I'd rather leave before they arrive.' Panicking, Sylvia blew into her handkerchief.

'Dear Edward's already here – he's tidying up in the studio,' Lorna explained. 'He stepped in as my assistant for my last lesson of the evening.'

Dear Edward. Eddie. It was one thing for her mother to make peace, but would he be prepared to follow suit? Feeling that she absolutely must find out, Sylvia rushed downstairs.

Eddie was switching off the studio lights. He felt dissatisfied and on edge. Who would be his dance partner now that Joy had chosen Tommy? And did he even care? Certainly he would carry on providing support for Lorna, no question, but even if they found a new partner for him among the dozen hopefuls who had attended this evening's class, there would be a long road ahead before they were ready to compete. He switched off the last light and stood in the gloom.

Sylvia found him there: a dejected figure lost in thought. He hadn't noticed her so she watched him sigh and shake his head before drifting towards the piano then sitting to play a few notes from a wistful popular song. Soon he was caught up in the music, his head bowed and fingers flowing over the keys. 'Every time it rains ... each cloud contains ... pennies from heaven . . .' The sentiments were familiar (a change in fortune had to be endured, one was to find blessings in storm clouds) and the sight of him sitting alone in the semi-darkness moved her. She didn't speak until he'd finished playing and had closed the piano lid.

'That was beautiful,' she murmured.

Eddie looked up as Sylvia approached. His mood lurched from quiet regret to sudden alarm. 'Is everything all right?'

She nodded. 'London is off.'

'Just like that?' he queried, his mind snatching at possible explanations.

'Yes. Mother is glad.'

Eddie stood up but kept his distance. 'There must be a reason for you not to go.'

'Let's say Cliff and Mr Burns pulled the wool over my eyes.' Sylvia's attempt to adopt a flippant tone crumbled. 'Oh, I was a fool!' she cried. 'In their eyes I was goods for sale to the highest bidder, nothing more. Do I have to say more?'

Anger flared in Eddie's eyes. *Damned pimps, the pair of them – the lowest of the low.*

'You don't seem surprised,' she stammered.

'I am, a little. I suspected something was afoot but I wasn't sure what. How did you find out?' He clenched his jaw in an effort to control his anger.

'In the end Cliff couldn't go through with it. He says he regrets the role he played and I believe him. Please don't think too badly of him.'

'How can I not,' Eddie demanded, 'when I remember how close you came to leaving? There's no excuse; none!'

'But it hasn't happened. And some good has come out of it: Mother and I are on a much better footing. I've learned a good deal about her early struggles and I know now that she truly loves me.'

'As do I,' Eddie said quietly but without much hope. 'You know I do.'

Sylvia remained silent. Her spirits didn't lift as they ought; there was no flutter of excitement, no reciprocal longing in her heart. *I'm sorry*, she thought. *For everything; not least for the fact that I don't love you back.*

Silence would have to be enough; for now, at least. Practicalities would see them through. 'Joy's back dancing with Tommy,' Eddie said.

'Yes – she told me.'

'Shall we be partners again?' He offered her his outstretched hand.

Sylvia's reply came readily. 'Yes, please; I'd like that.'

'Starting this Saturday at the Tower?' he suggested.

'Oh, but we're out of practice.' Nerves came back into play. Was she ready to face the attention that their reappearance in the competition would attract? Tongues would wag; there would be speculation, wild theories and unkind comments about her changed appearance if not her technique.

'Nonsense.' Eddie invited her into ballroom hold and swayed her into a slow turn. It was growing dark; there was no music. Sylvia leaned into the turn, supple as a sapling, rising on to the balls of her feet then dipping, following his lead.

'You see,' he commented. 'An elephant never forgets.'

'Me – an elephant!'

That old teasing tap on the shoulder, the wide-eyed stare. Eddie's smile covered his heartbreak and they danced on.

The old partnership performed another turn on the diagonal and then another in a silent waltz – as natural as drawing breath. 'Let's show the judges we can still do it,' she whispered at last. 'Who cares what people think?'

CHAPTER TWENTY-TWO

'Dad twisted Wilf's arm to help him run the new arcade tonight,' Pearl informed her mother, who was hard at work on her stall, chopping potatoes and filleting cod ahead of the next influx of customers. 'Yes, I know: it's child labour; but I can't complain cos it allows Bernie and me to have the night off.'

'Lucky for some,' Maria grumbled. 'I can't remember when I last had one of those.'

'Come off it, Ma,' Pearl protested. 'Since when was it a crime to want to spend time with your fiancé before he's shipped off by the army to God knows where?'

'Fair enough,' Maria conceded. 'Where is Bernie, by the way?'

'He's gone to collect my ring from Hartley's – they've made it smaller for me.' Pearl displayed her ringless finger. 'We were lined up for one last Latin lesson but when we got to Cliff's studio, we found a notice pinned on the door saying it's shut for the evening.'

'Why's that?' Maria was only half listening. Potatoes didn't peel themselves and batter didn't materialize out of nowhere.

'Cliff didn't give a reason.' Pearl spotted Bernie jogging along the prom with the precious ring in his pocket, spreading good humour as he hailed Tommy and Joy, who had emerged from the side entrance to the Tower. The four of them gathered outside Madam Rosie's fortune-telling booth.

'I'm parched,' Tommy announced. 'Anyone fancy a pint – on me?'

Bernie was quick to take up the offer. 'Not at the Black Horse, though. How about the Queen's Arms?'

It was agreed. 'I do like to stroll along the prom, prom, prom!' Pearl marched arm in arm with Bernie, warbling Reggie Dixon's theme tune.

They walked through shadows cast by the setting sun, soaking up its last rays, scarcely noticing the trickle of lobster-red holidaymakers who climbed the steps from the beach, abandoning their elaborate sandcastles to the incoming tide. One small wave and towers and turrets would collapse, whole empires would be washed away.

The small group arrived at their destination in high spirits. Drink was taken, tactics for Saturday's competition were discussed.

'We'll be up against Eddie and Sylvia,' Joy informed the others. 'Yes, they're back together – dance-wise, at least.'

'And more, maybe,' Pearl burbled. Cloud nine ought to be shared with friends, not hogged by her and Bernie.

'Don't worry; they'll be in a different section to you,' Tommy reminded her as he downed his second pint. 'Joy and I will have to go head to head with them, though.'

'Pearl and I needed to polish up our cha-cha,' Bernie confessed. 'Lord knows why Cliff shut up shop for the night.'

'What's the betting Terry is at the root of it?' Pearl's ruby ring sparkled as she displayed crossed fingers. 'Don't you two go pooh-poohing my idea,' she scolded a sceptical Tommy and Bernie. 'Tell them, Joy – we spotted Cliff hanging around outside Terry's new lodgings earlier this week.'

'In the middle of a thunderstorm, getting soaked to the skin,' Joy confirmed. 'Sylvia, Pearl and I predict that they'll find a way to sort out their differences.'

'So now you're giving Rosie here a run for her money,' Bernie teased his fiancée with a jerk of his thumb towards the fortune teller's sign.

'Good luck to them both,' Tommy concluded. End of subject; as long as Terry and Cliff were discreet like many of the men – and girls, for that matter – in the circus business, who the hell cared?

Pearl looked at her watch: almost nine o'clock. 'Time to head home?'

Back on the prom, they ambled towards Central Pier, where they would part company: Pearl and Bernie to his untidy room and single bed while Tommy would escort Joy to Silver Street before walking home alone. Daylight was fading but traffic on the wide road was still heavy; buses and trams trundled by every few seconds, interspersed with taxis and private cars, motorbikes and bicycles. Blackout regulations meant that headlights were reduced to narrow slits that scarcely allowed drivers to see six feet ahead.

'Watch your step.' Approaching the Tower and preparing to cross the road, Tommy alerted the others to a taxi that had pulled up at the kerb without signalling. A cyclist swerved to avoid it and almost careered into them. The unfortunate lad braked hard then toppled sideways on to the pavement. Bernie helped him set his bike upright and saw him safely on his way.

Meanwhile, two men got out of the taxi. Terry paid the driver while Cliff, dapper in a light jacket and stylish panama hat, wished the astonished group good evening. If he was nervous about the encounter, he didn't show it. 'I'm sorry you missed your lesson,' he told Pearl and Bernie. 'We could fit one in tomorrow night if you like.'

Terry joined them, more obviously ill at ease. The night was warm so he'd slung his jacket over one shoulder and loosened his tie. His shirtsleeves were rolled back to the elbow. 'We thought we'd risk a quiet twilight stroll along the prom,' he explained sheepishly.

' "We"?' Pearl asked.

'Yes – we've decided to give it another go.' Cliff made no attempt to conceal their reunion; in fact, he glowed with pride and pleasure.

'What did I tell you?' a gleeful Joy whispered to Tommy.

'We didn't expect it still to be this busy, though.' Terry glanced anxiously in both directions.

'Shoulders back, heads up and smile!' Pearl's decent impersonation of Lorna Ellis helped ease the tension.

'Pearl's right,' Cliff told Terry. 'If you and I are going to stick together we have to act as if we don't have a care in the world.'

Joy took Terry to one side. 'Whose idea was this?' she asked quietly.

'Blame Cliff – he talked me into it,' he confessed.

There were uneasy smiles all round as Cliff tipped the brim of his hat by way of a goodbye. Then he and Terry waited for an approaching tram to disgorge its passengers before venturing across the road.

Tommy was the first to spot Mick Greene holding on to the steel pole on the open platform at the back of the tram, ready to alight. He gave a sharp warning of 'Watch yourselves!' to Cliff and Terry.

Mick swung from the platform before the tram had fully stopped, closely followed by an inebriated Sam Grigg and two more members of their drinking crowd: Howard Reynolds and Fred Salter, who both worked at Squires Gate alongside Mick and Sam. Reynolds was a young, brash type with a penchant for loud ties; Salter was older and quieter, but with an air of glowering menace, especially when drunk.

'Bad timing.' Bernie pulled Pearl back from the kerb. His brother swayed and slurred his words, waving his arms and laughing at his pal's jokes. 'Make yourselves scarce before they see you,' he hissed at Terry and Cliff.

'Why should we?' In a sudden surge of defiance, Cliff stood his ground. 'We're not running from those idiots.'

A flat-bed army truck carrying a load of sandbags crawled by. Sam yelled at the driver for him to get a move on. 'Too slow to catch bloody cold!'

For no apparent reason Howard and Fred found this hilarious.

Glancing sideways, Mick caught sight of Bernie. He

issued a volley of vicious oaths then rushed towards him, hauling him backwards before shoving him against the side of the tram shelter and ramming his forearm against his throat. 'What the hell are you playing at, hanging around with that pair of perverts?'

Bernie managed to thrust him away but wasn't prepared for Mick to rush at him a second time. He felt a heavy punch to the side of his jaw that felled him and left him flat on his back, dazed and helpless.

There was instant, uncontrolled chaos. Tommy went to Bernie's aid but Mick, standing astride his brother, kept him at bay while Sam, Howard and Fred threatened Cliff and Terry with knives seemingly pulled from nowhere – long, thin kitchen blades sharpened to a deadly point. With a flash of steel, the brawl had changed gear. Now life and limb were at stake.

Ignoring the danger, Terry lunged and succeeded in swiping the knife from Sam's hand. It clattered to the ground. Terry swept it up then lashed out in a wide arc that forced Fred and Howard back into the shelter where Tommy and Cliff trapped them.

'Don't just stand there – fetch the police!' A distraught Joy begged a woman bystander to act. She saw that Tommy's forearm had been cut; there was a thin trail of blood soaking into his rolled-up shirtsleeve. The woman ran to do Joy's bidding.

Covering his head with both arms, Bernie managed to roll free of the frenzy of stamping, crunching, kicking boots. Back on his feet, he shoulder-charged Mick from behind, sending him crashing into Terry, who managed to pocket the knife then tackle Mick to the ground. Grunting and swearing, the two strong men wrestled their way back into the middle of the melee. Terry pulled free, only to find Sam coming at him from behind, intent on grabbing his knife back. But his slight physique hampered him – he was no match for his athletic opponent, who quickly overpowered him.

'I phoned 999. The police are on their way.' The breathless woman had returned. By now a crowd of twenty or so spectators had gathered, none willing to join the fray. Fists were one thing; knives were another.

Fred and Howard forced their way out of the shelter. Now Mick's gang were able to line up, shoulder to shoulder, heads thrust forward, knives at the ready. They advanced slowly towards Bernie, Tommy, Cliff and Terry; the two sides evenly matched in number engaged in a strangely choreographed, deadly finale. Terry took out Sam's knife once more but the handle seemed to burn into his flesh. Horrified by what he might be tempted to do with it, on impulse he flung it with all his might over the promenade railing on to the beach below.

Pearl and Joy gasped. Their boys were undefended against a brutal, drunken gang of bigots. Tommy's arm still bled and Bernie's shirt was ripped. Terry's and Cliff's faces were grim and pale.

'Now look what you've gone and done,' Mick sneered at Bernie. Crouching low, he flicked his knife towards him. 'This is where your fancy footwork gets you – you and your scum-of-the-earth pals!'

With an agile twist of his torso Bernie dodged his brother's blade. He, Tommy, Cliff and Terry continued to back away slowly until they reached the kerb.

Traffic trundled by. Another unlit tram offloaded its passengers then rumbled on along the tracks.

'You're a dirty, bloody disgrace; that's what you two are.' Mick spat contemptuously in the direction of Terry and Cliff. He, Reynolds and Salter jabbed their knives at their opponents, forcing them off the pavement into a raucous racket of honking horns, dim headlights and furious cries. In the darkness and confusion Pearl and Joy lost sight of Bernie and Tommy and in a blind panic they too stepped on to the road.

'There they are!' Pearl caught sight of their sweethearts on the far side of the road, outside the entrance to the Tower. She couldn't make out Cliff or Terry in the melee but she was aware that Mick and his hoodlums continued to cause confusion by weaving through the traffic in pursuit. A taxi driver gave loud, angry blasts on his horn as Reynolds lurched in front of his cab then landed spread-eagled on the bonnet. The driver jumped out of his cab but when he saw the knife in the thug's hand he quickly backed off.

'Cliff and Terry are there too!' Joy gasped as she saw them join Tommy and Bernie under the wide entrance, its plate-glass doors gleaming behind them. She and Pearl continued to ignore the car horns and pressed onwards.

'Stay back!' Tommy pleaded with Joy. His plan was to lose Mick and co. by darting down one of the alleys leading to the market square.

Dizzy with fear, Joy glanced up at the immense black silhouette of the Tower that seemed to tilt towards her in nightmare fashion. Afraid that she would scream out in terror, she grabbed Pearl's hand.

'Ready to make a run for it?' Tommy checked with

Cliff, Terry and Bernie above the blaring of horns, rumble of car engines and rattle of yet another approaching tram.

They nodded. 'Stick together or split up?' Cliff checked.

'Stick together,' Bernie answered in a flash.

'Don't let 'em get away, damn it!' Mick's fury reached boiling point as he stepped into the road and was forced to sidestep a van and then a motorbike. There was more yelling and honking of horns.

'Ah, to hell with it.' Unarmed, Sam suddenly lost interest in the pursuit. 'I'm off back to the beach to find my knife.'

'Over my dead body.' Mick launched himself at his accomplice while Reynolds and Salter seized their own chance to retreat to the safety of the pavement where the fight had begun.

The crowd of nervous onlookers parted to let them through. The woman who had called the police station shouted to a couple of thick-set ARP men who had appeared on the scene. She gave a rapid explanation and the wardens moved in on the two nearest culprits.

Marooned in the middle of the road, Mick sent Sam reeling. Then he swiftly stooped to haul him upright. 'Those perverts need a good thrashing,' he spat. 'We'll be a laughing stock if we give up now.'

'I don't give a monkey's.' Sam wriggled and writhed. 'Let go of me, damn you!'

By this time Pearl and Joy had reached the far pavement to find that Tommy, Bernie, Cliff and Terry were poised for flight. But something had caught Bernie's attention and he pointed frantically towards the unequal tussle between Mick and Sam. As the girls turned, they heard the driver of an approaching tram give a long blast on his horn followed by the skid of wheels on steel tracks and horrified gasps from the crowd. Joy and Pearl shrank from a shower of bright orange sparks that flew from the end of the metal pole connecting the tram to its overhead cables.

Governed by uncontrollable fury, Mick kept tight hold of Sam, almost throttling him as he dragged him on across the road, straight into the path of the oncoming, open-topped tram. In a split second of horrified realization, he released his unwilling accomplice and leaped clear. Sagging like a ripped sandbag, Sam disappeared from view.

The cacophony of horns died away. There was a stunned silence amid infinite blackness of night sky. The Tower loomed over the scene and ceaseless waves broke on the dark shore, washing away children's sandcastles and all that remained of the day.

'Not one person screamed when Sam went under that tram.' Next morning Pearl woke beside Bernie in his room on Market Street. 'There was deathly silence.'

'It was the shock.' A close call like that hollowed you out. There were no words to describe how you felt. Bernie had been awake for most of the night, staring up at the ceiling, trying to make sense of what had taken place.

Sam Grigg had fallen between the steel wheels of the tram and by some miracle he'd survived with nothing worse than broken ribs and a smashed foot. No one had attempted to pull him clear until the medical people arrived. Sam had been conscious all the way through – moaning and crying out in agony as the ambulance men had stretchered him away.

'I honestly thought he was a goner.' Pearl shuddered as she remembered the sequence of events; how the tram driver had calmly ordered everyone to stand back before squatting down to comfort the trapped victim. He'd advised Sam not to move; an ambulance would come and carry him off to hospital. They would fix him up and he would live to tell the tale. All true, as it turned out.

The two air raid wardens had arrested Reynolds and Salter then carted them away, while Mick had been intent on making a getaway. Damn everyone to hell; who cared whether Sam Grigg was dead or alive, as long as he, Mick Greene, managed to save his own skin?

It was onlookers who had prevented him: two stout, wheezing, middle-aged men who happened to believe in fair play, who had blocked Mick's path with a stubborn 'Oh no you don't!' and pushed him to the ground then, egged on by the crowd, had sat on his chest until the coppers had arrived.

'That's right, Granddad – give the bastard what-for!'

'Knock him flat, our Raymond – the lousy so-and-so deserves everything he gets.'

So Mick had ended up a laughing stock after all. He'd been arrested and taken off to the police station, where he would be charged with GBH and causing an affray.

'He'll lose his job, his home – everything,' Bernie said with a sigh as he turned on to his side to face Pearl. 'If a jury finds him guilty, they'll lock him up for God knows how many years.'

'Hand on heart, I can't say I'm sorry.' Pearl couldn't disguise her satisfaction at the prospect of seeing justice done. 'I know he's your brother, but . . .' She stroked Bernie's forehead as if caressing his cares away.

'I'll go and see him later today – I owe him that much.'

'Would you like me to come with you?'

'No – best not.' Face to face with his brother, Bernie would try to convince Mick that he hadn't come to gloat, that blood would always be thicker than water. He would remind him of family life before their parents' accident when, despite their differences, they'd all rubbed along together in their little terraced house on Empire Street – Mick the surly son with a permanent chip on his shoulder, Bernie the breezy, happy-go-lucky one. But after a night in the cells would a hungover Mick accept the olive branch or would he lash out at Bernie with another foul-mouthed rant? It remained to be seen.

'I lay awake half the night thinking.' With her heart beginning to race, Pearl swung her legs over the side of the bed and sat up so that her back was to Bernie. This had to be handled carefully, not with a rush.

It was time for them to get up and face the day but he was reluctant to move. 'Uh-oh; thinking, eh?'

'I'm serious. After what's happened to Mick, the managers at Squires Gate will need a new foreman.'

'Huh?' Bernie made a noise, half grunt, half question.

She turned her head to judge his reaction. 'They'll need a man who knows the ropes.'

'So?' He could see her face in profile: her small,

turned-up nose, her short, dark hair pushed back behind her ears. He knew what was coming without her having to spell it out.

'So you could be that man,' she whispered.

'Come again?' He stood up from the bed and went to the window. The damned blind was still sticking – he gave up tugging at it then reluctantly turned to face her.

'You've worked on building those Bellmans. Why not apply?' During the long, sleepless hours Pearl had convinced herself that this was the most practical, sensible plan in the world. With his knowledge, skills and enthusiasm, Bernie was the ideal candidate. He would be welcomed with open arms and step straight back into a reserved occupation: building RAF hangars and maintaining runways. He wouldn't have to join the army after all; simple as that.

'You know why not.' *If only!* For a few moments Bernie let his imagination run wild. He was back at Squires Gate operating a crane, lifting girders and swinging them into position as Spitfires, Mosquitoes and Hawker Hurricanes flew in and out. He would lead a skilled engineering crew that was vital to the war effort. *If only.*

'But don't you see? You'd be involved in important work and you'd be doing it a darned sight better than Mick did. The powers that be would see that . . .'

'No, they wouldn't – they sacked me,' he reminded her gently.

'Because Mick held a grudge and he lied to them. You can tell them the truth; they'll believe you. And you know that once they've finished erecting the

Bellmans the Ministry will need to build more accommodation blocks for the Yanks out at Warton Aerodrome – they're already calling it Little America. There'll be no end of work for you to do; it could last right through to the end of the war. See? It makes perfect sense for you to apply.' Pearl only paused because she'd run out of breath.

Extending runways, laying strips of bitumen on what had until recently been a golf course, building more anti-aircraft pillboxes among the sand dunes in order to protect Manchester and Liverpool – it was true that the list of jobs was endless. Bernie could see himself as a part of all that. 'So what do you suggest I do – burn my call-up papers?' He crash-landed into reality; abandoned his dreams of staying in Blackpool with the girl he loved and of walking her down the aisle.

Pearl grew desperate. 'Explain to them,' she pleaded. 'Tell them that there's been an injustice, that it wasn't fair to sack you in the first place, that it was all Mick's fault.'

'Let's face it, it won't make any difference.' He sat beside her, head hanging and hands clasped in front of him, waiting for her to see sense.

'But won't you at least try?' she pleaded. It felt as though there was an iron vice clamped around her heart, squeezing it to death. 'Do it for me,' she added in a faint whisper.

Bernie reached for her hand. 'Don't say that.'

'You're right; it wasn't fair – I take it back. But do it for yourself; forget about visiting your brother and take the tram out to Squires Gate instead. Knock on the manager's door and convince him to give you the job. Don't take no for an answer.'

'I can't.' His brief, toneless reply came after what felt like a lifetime.

The vice squeezed her heart tighter until she felt faint. 'Why not?'

'Because it wouldn't be right. Think about the thousands of men and women who get their papers through the post and report for duty. How could I hold my head up, knowing I was the one who wangled my way out of fighting on the front line?'

Pearl had stopped breathing. Tears scalded her eyes.

'It's not that I'm not tempted – I am.'

'I don't want to lose you.' Hope ebbed and tears flowed freely. She would give anything – *anything* – for Bernie to have said yes to her plan. 'I don't think I could bear it.'

'You won't have to,' he promised. 'Even if I go away to fight and don't come back, there'll still be these memories between us.' Raising her hand to his lips, he kissed it softly.

'You're a good man, Bernie Greene.' She breathed again and wiped her eyes as acceptance flooded in. 'Better than I deserve.'

'Wear my ring. Write me those letters.'

'Every day.'

'And tomorrow we have our swansong,' Bernie reminded her as he put his arm around her waist and whirled her round. 'Get your glad rags on, Miss Scott, and prepare to dazzle the judges. Stand by, Blackpool – here we come!'

Sylvia found Cliff and Terry in the North View Parade studio, working on a tap-dance routine. It was the morning after the big fight outside the Tower building and, as usual, news of it had travelled fast. Mr Ibbotson's young shop assistant – a scrawny lad with buck teeth and savagely cropped brown hair – had run upstairs to Sylvia's room to pass on the main gist – Sam Grigg had been pushed under a tram and got carted off to hospital. Three men, including Mick Greene, were currently under arrest. And guess what: the dance teacher next door had been seen out and about with his fancy man! The two of them had been strolling along the prom together, large as life, and that's why the brawl had started in the first place.

Now Sylvia opened the door into Cliff's studio without bothering to knock. Sun flooded the room and a record was playing with the volume turned up high. Cliff's and Terry's backs were turned. Cliff was demonstrating a sequence of steps while Terry paid close attention. Neither heard Sylvia enter.

She watched for a while. Terry attempted the complicated steps and was corrected by Cliff, who laid a patient hand on his arm before repeating the demonstration. This time Terry copied him perfectly and Cliff praised him. 'Again!' he instructed, before standing back to watch Terry rehearse. The metal toes and heels of Terry's tap shoes clicked rhythmically across the floor. 'Timing!' Cliff reminded him. 'Use your arms to help you balance. Shoulders back. Don't look down; look up!'

As the record finished, Sylvia approached Cliff with a nervous smile. 'Can you teach me to do that?'

'Seriously?' Overcoming his surprise, he treated her to a long, questioning look while Terry picked up a towel to mop his brow.

'Yes; I'd like to learn.'

'Add a tap-dancing string to your bow, eh? But that's not the real reason you came.'

'No,' she confessed. 'I heard what happened last night.'

Cliff narrowed his eyes. 'And?'

'And I wanted to know if there was anything I could do.' Sylvia looked awkwardly from Cliff to Terry then back again.

'No – as you see, we're fine. It turns out we had the crowd behind us – they cheered when the police drove Mick Greene away in their Black Maria. Not to mention the helping hand we had from Bernie and Tommy – without them we might not have got off so lightly.'

Slowly Sylvia absorbed the details. 'That's very good to hear,' she breathed.

'So no more hiding.' Terry stood with the needle poised over a new record. 'We're out in the open and not ashamed to be seen together – are we, love?'

'No,' Cliff confirmed. 'Blow Mick Greene and his like – we don't give a jot.'

'Quite right.' Sylvia was genuinely glad.

'And?' Cliff prompted again, this time with a hint of impatience.

'And I think there is a way for me to help – two ways, to be precise.' Glancing around the studio and taking in the smart, contemporary decor, she summoned the courage to continue. 'I can send new pupils over from the Lorna Ellis Dance Academy for a start. I'll persuade Mother that it won't harm her business if people come to you to learn Latin because the two styles are chalk and cheese. Blackpool is a big town and ballroom dancing has never been so popular, which means that there's plenty of room for two dance schools to succeed. Office girls from town and RAF men from Squires Gate are falling over themselves to learn.'

'Not to mention the Yanks.' Cliff took her point.

Now she came to the crunch. 'Secondly, I could carry on helping you with the teaching, if you'll have me?'

Cliff gave the signal for Terry to lower the needle on to Astaire's famous number, 'Top Hat, White Tie And Tails'. He darted into the alcove to pick up two canes – one for him and one for Terry – then began a series of nonchalant hitch steps and walks in time to the music. He motioned for Terry to join him. 'I'll think about it,' he told Sylvia, pretending to use the cane as a rifle and aiming it in her direction. Then he and Terry performed tap shuffles on the spot before launching into rapid steps into the centre of the floor followed by perfectly synchronized heel jabs.

Sylvia waited on tenterhooks. Would they – *could* they – forgive her for her carelessness in giving away their secret?

'On one condition,' Cliff told her as the tempo increased. Inviting Terry to copy his movements, he tapped his cane on the window ledge as he flew around the room then made a series of carefree *grands jetés* – ballet leaps that brought him close to Sylvia. Their faces were six inches apart and he stared directly into her eyes. 'You can come back and teach here as long as you give up the slimming nonsense.'

'I don't understand,' she murmured.

'Let me spell it out. As your employer I'm saying categorically: no more starving yourself and falling down in a faint and no more staring at your reflection and finding fault with every little detail. Agreed?'

'Easier said than done,' Terry commiserated with Sylvia as the record finished and he switched off the gramophone. 'But at least tell him you'll try.'

Sylvia took a deep breath to compose herself and gather sufficient resolve to agree to Cliff's latest condition. 'I'll do my best,' she promised. 'No guarantees . . .'

'Then welcome back, princess.' Cliff threw down his cane and embraced her. 'If you stick to our new agreement for three months and you get yourself back to a healthy weight, we'll alter the sign above the door – Learn to Dance with Cliff and Sylvia. Live in Your Dreams!'

Iris Grigg stood in her kitchen doorway with her arms folded, watching Tommy carry Joy's suitcase down the stairs. She'd just been to see Sam in hospital and had returned to find Joy packing her belongings and preparing to leave.

'You need to give me more notice,' she said with a defiant stare. 'You can't just walk out without a by-your-leave.'

'Fair enough; I'll send you a postal order for two weeks' rent once I'm settled,' Joy promised in the midst of a whirlwind of activity following Tommy's arrival early that morning.

'Come and stay with us!' he'd declared. 'Pack your things; now, this instant!'

'But what will people think of us living under the

same roof?' Caught off guard, Joy hadn't said yes straight away.

'They can think what they like. It was my mother's idea. Neither of us wants you to stay in this miserable dump a moment longer than necessary.'

Lucia and Tommy's offer had flooded her heart with happiness. To be welcomed, included, loved – it was everything she desired. So she'd thrown her clothes into her case then finally slipped her precious family photo into her handbag and they'd been halfway down the stairs when her landlady had materialized, gaunt and severe in her grey coat and hat.

'How's Sam?' Joy asked Iris as Tommy went on ahead, telling her he would wait for her outside.

'Why should you care?' The dour landlady kept up a sullen appearance to hide her shock at almost losing her only son.

'But I do care,' Joy insisted. 'I was there – I saw everything.'

'The doctors can't save his foot. They'll have to amputate later today, as soon as they can find a surgeon to do the operation.' Iris had understood the risks: Sam was weak from loss of blood – there was a chance that he might not pull through. Nevertheless, she'd arranged to go back to the hospital later that evening with his pyjamas and a washbag. *Be practical; keep the terror at bay.*

'I'm sorry.' It was Mick Greene's fault; it had been obvious to everyone that Sam had been backing away from the fight as the tram had approached. 'Really, I am.'

'What's done is done.' Iris had instructed Sam to bear his suffering like a man. 'I've promised to have

369

him back here after his operation. I can move into Liddle's room and Sam can take my bedroom on the ground floor.' Make arrangements and get on with the cards that life dealt you – this had always been Iris Grigg's way. 'He'll have to find an office job eventually; I can't afford to go on looking after him long-term.'

'You'll manage.' Recognizing that any show of sympathy would bounce off Mrs Grigg's impenetrable shell, Joy prepared to leave.

'Aye – I always do.' Iris was eager for Joy to be gone. 'Two weeks' rent – in the post,' she reminded her.

'Well done,' Tommy told Joy as she stepped out on to the pavement. 'Don't feel guilty; you're better off out of there.'

The sun was peeping through white clouds and there was a fresh breeze as they walked the short distance between Silver Street and the ice-cream parlour. A smiling Lucia waited for them under the green-and-white-striped awning. Tables and chairs were already set out, ready for the day to begin.

'*Benvenuta!*' Lucia welcomed Joy with open arms. She hugged her then led her to a spare room on the first floor overlooking the sea. '*La tua stanza, mia cara.* Is good?'

'The room is lovely.' Better than anything she could have wished for, with its pale-blue embroidered bedspread, starched net curtain and a homely vase of cornflowers on the bedside cabinet.

Tommy hovered in the background as Lucia fussed.

'Here, Tommaso; give me the case. I put it here on the bed. Joy, you stay with us long time. Many weeks, months – *casa mia è casa tua.*'

My home is your home. Joy's Italian was improving in leaps and bounds. She unpacked hastily then went downstairs to greet the café's first customers. There was a busy day ahead and afterwards the event that they'd all been working towards for weeks: tonight's competition at the centre of their magical world of dance.

CHAPTER TWENTY-THREE

Sparkling chandeliers and gilded cherubs adorned the wonderland that was the Tower Ballroom. It was a fine, warm night and the roof was open to the stars. Entranced by the rich mixture of crimson and gold, of frescoes, ornate pillars, intricate latticework and tiered balconies, Joy, Sylvia and Pearl knew that no matter how often they stepped out on to this floor they would never tire of its glory.

They joined a throng of dancers for the number before the interval: a smooth foxtrot enjoyed by beginners and ballroom veterans alike. All was movement and colour – the men expertly steering their partners across the crowded floor, the girls swaying and smiling at their friends as they whirled by.

Hello to Ruby with her striking auburn hair swept up and her shoulders bare. Hello to Mavis in the pink dress that Joy had borrowed at the start of her dance career. Hello to market-trader Joe, grinning broadly as he swept by with Ida in his arms, and to Doris and Thora who, sick of waiting to be asked to dance, had taken to the floor together.

Lorna sat alone in the front row of the lower balcony, gazing down on the scene. She followed her daughter's every move: Sylvia in a beautiful pink chiffon gown that Lorna herself had once worn, its skirt hanging in permanent pleats, its hem trimmed with ostrich feathers, with an elegant train trailing from one shoulder. Perfection. Eddie, too – tall, dignified and solicitous. *If only!* Lorna dismissed the notion with a small, impatient shake of her head.

'Good evening, Lorna.' Cliff leaned forward from the row behind, where he sat with Terry. Here was the ideal opportunity to call a truce between the rival establishments, but would Lorna Ellis feel the same?

Bold as you like; the two of them together! Lorna raised an eyebrow as she glanced over her shoulder. But then she experienced a sudden change of heart; after the stresses and strains of recent events, why on earth not? What's more, she had reason to be grateful – but for Cliff's revelation of the truth about Mitch Burns, Sylvia would have boarded the London train and been lost for ever. So Lorna softened as she turned in her seat. 'Good evening, Cliff. Good evening, Terry.'

'My money is on Sylvia and Eddie to do well tonight.' Encouraged by her polite response, Cliff ventured his professional opinion. 'It's grand to see them back together.'

'It is,' she agreed.

Satisfied, Cliff sat back in his seat. One small step at a time, as Terry had said.

The interval was soon over. Tension rose as musicians returned to the stage and the MC invited competition dancers on to the floor. 'We begin with the English-style section,' he announced, backed by a low drum roll to attract attention. 'This is for the more traditional ladies and gentlemen; please take your partners for the quickstep.'

'That's us.' Tommy took Joy's hand, proud as could be, as they prepared to take their place alongside Sylvia and Eddie.

'Wish us luck,' Joy whispered to Pearl and Bernie, who stayed by the bar. Their turn would come later, in the Latin section.

Smile. Be bold. Joy's taffeta dress rustled as she walked with Tommy. She and Lucia had sewn every last sequin in place. *Bellissima!* With an excited clap of her hands, Tommy's mother had sent them on their way. Now here Joy was, beneath the chandeliers, knees shaking and desperately repeating to herself Lorna's instructions for the fast-moving dance – heel lead, two forward steps followed by lock step and repeat. Tricky, light, upbeat – lots of low kicks and flicks.

'Nervous?' Tommy murmured.

'Petrified,' she confessed.

'Don't be. You'll knock the socks off the rest of them; you always do.'

His bright confidence encouraged her as they chose their spot in front of the judges close to Eddie and Sylvia. The two couples exchanged warm glances. The up-tempo music began and they stepped out – bold promenade steps, hops and chassés increasing in speed, swift turns that allowed no thinking time, long skirts swinging, spines gracefully bending and faces smiling, always smiling. Joy's nerves fled. Her head was tilted slightly back and she felt the warmth of Tommy's hand on her back. Slow-quick-quick-slow – they whirled past Eddie and Sylvia, the hems of the girls' gowns touching as one by one other couples were eliminated.

Sylvia smiled up at Eddie, their bodies in close contact as they reached the corner of the floor closest to the stage then executed a natural pivot turn; smooth and balanced, easy as you like. Organ music filled the vast space. It lifted Sylvia's spirits in a way that nothing else did, made her heart soar as though it had wings; here, dancing the quickstep with Eddie, back where she belonged.

Without a doubt they had the technique to outdance everyone here. Fast, snappy as you like, back to her old self; the prize was theirs for the taking. But no; unbeknown to Eddie, Sylvia had other ideas. In fact, it was hardly a conscious thought. As the tempo increased yet again, still 4/4 time, demanding more tricky steps and complicated figures that Sylvia could have executed in her sleep, she made a basic mistake – quick on the first beat of the bar when she should have been slow, out of step with Eddie, whose forehead creased in a puzzled frown.

Eliminated! The judges pounced and Sylvia and Eddie left the floor. She walked away from the prize with her head held high, smiling at Joy and Tommy and softly wishing them luck.

'Well, I never!' Cliff remarked from the balcony.

Yes indeed! Lorna turned her head to silently acknowledge what they had just witnessed – for the first time in her life, Sylvia had relinquished first prize.

Only five couples remained. Joy's feet skipped across the floor, turning, locking, easing from heel to toe then back again. Under the chandeliers her dress sparkled like the Mediterranean Sea. It was beautiful. *She* was beautiful.

The music stopped and the judges conferred. After a short discussion, the MC declared Joy and Tommy the winners. Ripples of applause filled the ballroom as they stepped on to the stage to receive their reward, Joy in a daze, Tommy holding her hand as they mounted the wide steps, the MC congratulating them. Then down on to the floor to be slapped on the back and offered drinks, smiles all round from pals Ruby, Ida, Doris and Thora, lapping up the congratulations – she, Joy Hebden, basking in the limelight, holding hands with the man she loved.

Now for the Latin section and the jitterbug; take your partners, please! The evening reached its energetic climax.

Pearl and Bernie ran to take up position in the centre of the ballroom floor. They were up against uniformed GIs and RAF men partnered with dressed-to-kill local entrants, the girls' faces alive with anticipation, silk flowers in their hair, their gaudy, daringly short dresses demanding attention.

Pearl was aware of none of this; only of Bernie, her handsome Bernie, whose dark eyes were willing her to forget about the uncertain tomorrows, to concentrate on this precious moment when they would dance their favourite dance.

He wore his brown suede shoes; all the better for the madness that was about to begin. She wore her diamond-and-ruby engagement ring. *I'm yours and you're mine!*

'Do you come here often?' Bernie quipped.

The music started and couples sprang into action, holding hands and swinging wide, breaking all the rules of decorum in a wild explosion of kicking, finger clicking and hip shaking – the more frenetic the better. Freedom!

Bernie swung Pearl out then drew her in. He stood on the spot as he raised one arm and whirled her round, clockwise then anti-clockwise, then drew her close and rocked her back and forth – oh, the thrill of making that warm contact, of smiling at each other and swinging out again, back and out, shuffling and clicking, hunching forward and facing each other to shake their shoulders, click, click, click. Miss the beat and you were out.

Eliminated couples left the floor – all the more space for Bernie and Pearl to leapfrog, slide and glide, to spin and kick, gyrate and swivel; to dance like there was no tomorrow. Perspiration trickled down their cheeks and still they smiled and jitter-bugged with four remaining couples until at last the music faded and the judges gathered in a huddle to decide on the victors.

Bernie breathed hard, standing with his arm around Pearl's shoulders. She crossed her fingers.

A slip of paper was handed to the MC, who made the announcement. Mr Bernie Greene and Miss Pearl Scott! Amid raucous applause Sylvia and Joy ran to congratulate Pearl. Worthy winners and so very special tonight of all nights. Don't think of what was to come. Enjoy this moment. Hurrah!

A cloud of confetti showered down from the ceiling as Pearl and Bernie received their prize. Golden cherubs smiled down on them – all was glitter and happiness. The lights dimmed for the last waltz, soft and slow.

Sylvia and Eddie, Joy and Tommy, Pearl and Bernie stepped on to the floor. Flakes of confetti drifted down and landed in their hair. One-two-three, one-two-three, the couples danced smoothly on, past midnight into a brand-new day.

ACKNOWLEDGEMENTS

A big thank-you to Holly Hulme and the press office team at Blackpool Tower for an enthusiastic, information-packed guided tour. Much appreciated.

If you enjoyed stepping on to the dance floor with *The Ballroom Girls*, you'll be swept off your feet by the second book in this sparkling series:

The Ballroom Girls: Christmas Dreams

Read on for an opening extract
Available in print and ebook from autumn 2023

CHAPTER ONE

Bernie Greene's train approached its destination. Lost in thought and leaning back against his cushioned headrest, he scarcely registered his fellow passengers or the condensation trickling down the windows of the crowded carriage. Daylight was fading, wheels rattled rhythmically over steel rails – *nearly there, nearly there, nearly there.*

'No high jinks for Guy Fawkes last night, worse luck,' the woman in the seat opposite remarked to no one in particular. 'Mr Hitler has put paid to that.'

'Remember, remember the fifth of November.' A man in a trilby hat and belted raincoat, in charge of two boisterous lads, took up the theme. 'In the good old days, we had bonfires all along the coast, as far as the eye could see. Catherine wheels, jumping jacks, skyrockets – the lot. Gunpowder, treason and Lord knows what.'

'Not during this rotten blackout,' the woman said with a sigh. 'Show one chink of light after dark and the blessed wardens will nab you, sure as anything.'

A weary Bernie closed his eyes. *Nearly there.* A canvas kitbag containing his shaving kit and pinstriped suit perched in the luggage rack above his head. Pearl had told him not to bother bringing a change of clothes; she'd rather he showed up at the church in his army uniform, but he'd brought the suit in case she changed her mind. Forty-eight hours' home leave before an imminent posting to Egypt – that was all he had.

One of the lads jumped up from his seat and stamped on Bernie's polished boots as he lunged towards the window to wipe away the condensation with the sleeve of his school mackintosh. 'I can see the Tower!' he crowed.

'Can't!' the second boy argued for argument's sake.

'Can!'

'Can't!'

Bernie opened his eyes. Sure enough, they were within sight of his home town's most famous landmark. The near-miraculous construction of steel girders soared skywards, a giant metal finger standing out against a background of heavy grey clouds, signifying that his long journey from the west coast of Scotland had reached its end. He stood up and took down his kitbag, keen to be first to leave the compartment, to be out in the corridor waiting for the train to grind to a halt, to fling open the door and step down on to the platform where, fingers crossed, Joe Taylor would be waiting. Bernie slid down the window and leaned out. The air smelled of smoke, steam belched from the engine up ahead and brakes screeched as his train entered the glass cathedral of Blackpool's North Station.

Not far away, in a room above Ibbotson's tobacconist's shop on North View Parade, Pearl Scott watched

Sylvia Ellis put the finishing touches to the dress Pearl would wear for the most important day of her life.

'I don't know what's wrong with me,' she'd grumbled as she'd handed her needle and thread to Sylvia. 'I'm all fingers and thumbs.'

'You've got the wedding jitters; that's what's wrong.' Sylvia made tiny, neat stitches in the delicate fabric of the cream silk gown – one inherited from her dance instructor mother, passed on to Sylvia and now to Pearl. It had a narrow waist and a full skirt, a scooped neckline and long sleeves: ideal for petite, dark-haired Pearl's bridal outfit.

'What if Bernie changes his mind?' Pearl voiced her worst fear. *Where is he now, right this second? Is he as nervous as I am? Oh Lord, why ever did I say yes?*

'Don't be silly. I've never seen a man more head over heels in love than Bernie is with you.'

'What if his leave is cancelled?'

'It won't be.' Sylvia had almost finished hemming the shortened skirt. Pearl was a good three inches shorter than her; hence the adjustment.

The nervous bride-to-be refused to be comforted. 'But the way things stand in North Africa, his regiment could be sent there at the drop of a hat.'

'Unlikely.' Sylvia prided herself on keeping up to date with the news. 'Monty's got Rommel on the run from El Alamein. It's been heading that way since the end of October.'

'All right, Miss Clever Clogs.' Pearl went to the window then peeked around the side of the blind to frown down on the busy shopping street below. A tram stopped and several passengers disembarked. 'Here comes Joy with the bouquets!' she reported to

Sylvia before dashing downstairs to greet their friend. 'Quick, come in before you catch your death. Close the door behind you. Sylvia's upstairs.'

'Is the dress finished?' Joy had rushed straight from the florist's with three bouquets of pink roses. 'Have you tried it on?'

'Not yet.' Pearl led the way upstairs then stopped on the landing outside Sylvia's room. 'I still can't believe it's really happening. I'm thinking of all the things that could go wrong – from Bernie's train breaking down in somewhere like Carlisle to him getting cold feet.'

'Stop!' Joy swept ahead of her then carefully deposited the armful of flowers on the nearest flat surface – a green baize card table standing in the bay window. The room was small, with a bed in one corner, a wardrobe in an alcove and armchairs to either side of the cast-iron fireplace. Ornaments and lamps enlivened the otherwise utilitarian effect, as did red velvet curtains (one of many donations by Sylvia's mother).

Bright posters advertised past productions at the Grand Theatre; Sadler's Wells had performed there with Margot Fonteyn and Frederick Ashton, as had the Old Vic Company with Jean Forbes-Robertson as Portia in *The Merchant of Venice.*

Sylvia looked up from her sewing with a knowing smile. Her fair hair glinted gold in the firelight and her wide-apart blue eyes sparkled with amusement. 'Don't tell me – Pearl's been regaling you with more imaginary catastrophes. Lovely flowers, by the way.'

Pearl had no idea what the word 'regaling' meant but she got the gist. 'Maybe we should have waited.' A new train of thought steamed into view as she hovered pale-faced in the doorway. 'People might wonder why we're rushing to get married. They'll say it's a shotgun affair: my dad is marching Bernie to church to make a respectable woman of me.'

'But you're not expecting,' Sylvia pointed out as she approached Pearl and held the dress up against her. 'Are you?'

'No!' Pearl was adamant. 'But the gossip doesn't end there. You know what they say even if there's no baby in the picture: "She's only getting hitched so she can claim the soldier's separation allowance or the widow's pension if the worst were to happen."'

Handing the finished gown to Joy, Sylvia used her fingertips to gently wipe away the tears that had begun to trickle down Pearl's cheeks. 'There, there,' she murmured. 'This isn't like you. You're the fun one of our little trio, the live wire who jitterbugs and sambas your way through life with a smile.'

'Oh!' Pearl sobbed helplessly. 'Oh, oh, oh!'

'Here; blow your nose.' Joy handed her a handkerchief. 'It's only natural to be nervous but there's no need. Everything's in hand.'

'Flowers.' Sylvia gestured towards the bouquets.

'The special licence is in order, thanks to your mother charming the socks off the vicar at All Saints,' Joy continued. 'Joe has the ring and he's organized a car to take you from Empire Street to the church. Your father has borrowed a camera for the photographs. We've all begged and borrowed enough food coupons to feed an army in the church hall afterwards. A leg of lamb, cured ham, tinned meat, pickled eggs, butter, bread, jam . . . It'll be a feast, I promise you.'

'And gramophone records,' Sylvia continued. 'Victor Silvester, naturally. Joe Loss, Jack Parnell; you name it and Mother has loaned it to us.'

'Yes.' Pearl blew noisily into the handkerchief and made an effort to pull herself together. 'Sorry, I don't know what on earth's got into me.'

'That's better.' Joy smiled at Sylvia. 'Now for this gorgeous wedding dress. Are you ready to try it on?'

Yes, she was. Pearl took a deep breath. *So silly.* She couldn't thank Sylvia and Joy enough. Off with her cardigan, blouse and slacks, on with the cream silk dream of a dress, zipped up by Joy, creases smoothed out by Sylvia while Pearl covered her eyes and allowed herself to be led to the wardrobe mirror.

'Open your eyes,' Joy breathed.

A magical transformation had taken place: from hard-working live wire who ran Great Scott's North Shore Amusements at the end of North Pier practically single-handed to shimmering, glowing, dainty princess. Pearl gasped and stared. She turned this way and that. The fabric swished and swayed.

'What do you think – will Bernie like it?' she whispered.

'Like it? He'll love it!' Sylvia sang out in sheer delight at the result of their handiwork.

'If not, he's an idiot.' Joy beamed. 'Tomorrow will be perfect – just you wait and see.'

Pre-order now to read the rest of the story as soon as it's available!

After *The Ballroom Girls* and *The Ballroom Girls: Christmas Dreams,* comes the dazzling third book in the series by Jenny Holmes:

The Ballroom Girls Hit the Big Time

Book 3 in *The Ballroom Girls* series

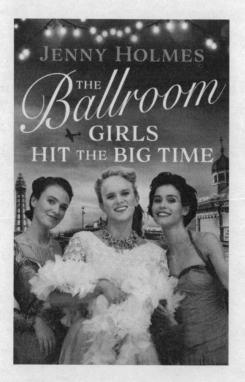

Available in 2024

Have you read the other wartime trilogies by Jenny Holmes? They are *The Air Raid Girls, The Spitfire Girls* and *The Land Girls,* out now in print and ebook.

The Air Raid Girls

Book 1 in *The Air Raid Girls* series

May, 1941

Connie's life has taken an unexpected turn since her husband died – she's living at home and working in the family bakery – but night shifts as an ARP Warden give her a firm sense of purpose.

Her younger sister **Lizzie** is eager to play her part too, perhaps as an ambulance driver. Her fiancé refuses to support her decision . . . but does he really know what's best for her?

Twenty-year-old **Pamela** has led a sheltered life, but when her family's home is destroyed in a raid she must learn to stand on her own two feet – helped by new friends.

As bombs fall and fires rage, the young women face the destruction of everything they've ever known. Can their fighting spirit prevail?

Available now

The Spitfire Girls

Book 1 in *The Spitfire Girls* series

'Anything to Anywhere!'

That's the motto of the Air Transport Auxiliary, the brave team of female pilots who fly fighter planes between bases at the height of the Second World War.

Mary is a driver for the ATA and although she yearns to fly a Spitfire, she fears her humble background will hold her back. After all, glamorous **Angela** is set to be the next 'Atta Girl' on recruitment posters. **Bobbie** learned to fly in her father's private plane and **Jean** was taught the Queen's English at grammar school before joining the squad. Dedicated and resilient, the three girls rule the skies: weathering storms and dodging enemy fire. Mary can only dream of joining them – until she gets the push she needs to overcome her self-doubt.

Thrown together, the girls form a tight bond as they face the perils of their job. But they soon find that affairs of the heart can be just as dangerous as attacks from the skies.

With all the fear and uncertainty ahead – can their friendship see them through the tests of war?

Available now

The Land Girls at Christmas

Book 1 in *The Land Girls* series

'Calling All Women!'

It's 1941 and as the Second
World War rages on, girls
from all over the country are
signing up to the Women's
Land Army. Renowned for
their camaraderie and spirit,
it is these brave women who
step in to take on the
gruelling farm work from the
men conscripted into the
armed forces.

When Yorkshire mill girl **Una** joins the cause, she
wonders how she'll adapt to country life. Luckily she's
quickly befriended by more experienced Land Girls
Brenda and **Grace**. But as Christmas draws ever near,
the girls' resolve is tested as scandals and secrets are
revealed, lovers risk being torn apart, and even patriotic
loyalties are called into question . . .

**With only a week to go until the festivities, can the
strain of wartime still allow for the magic of Christmas?**

Available now

SIGN UP TO OUR NEW SAGA NEWSLETTER

Penny Street

The home of heart-warming reads

Welcome to **Penny Street**, your number **one stop for emotional and heartfelt historical reads**. Meet casts of characters you'll never forget, memories you'll treasure as your own, and places that will forever stay with you long after the last page.

Join our online **community** bringing you the latest book deals, competitions and new saga series releases.

You can also find extra content, talk to your favourite authors and share your discoveries with other saga fans on Facebook.

Join today by visiting
www.penguin.co.uk/pennystreet

Follow us on Facebook
www.facebook.com/welcometopennystreet/